HOLLYWOOD
PLAYS
FOR KEEPS

Also by *Dale E. Manolakas*

Veronica Kennicott Series:
Hollywood Plays for Keeps
Death Sets Sail

Sophia Christopoulos Series:
Lethal Lawyers
The Gun Trial

DaleManolakas.com
Excerpts of books, Ray Bradbury
reminiscences, free poetry, and other free reads.

HOLLYWOOD PLAYS FOR KEEPS

DALE E. MANOLAKAS

Hollywood Plays for Keeps

This book is a work of fiction. Names, characters, businesses, organizations, places, events, and incidents either are a product of the author's imagination or are used fictitiously. Any resemblance to actual persons, living or dead, events or locales is entirely coincidental. All characters appearing in this work are fictitious. Any resemblance to real persons, living or dead, is purely coincidental.

FIRST EDITION

Library of Congress Control Number: 2013923036

eISBN 978-1-62805-000-4 (e-publication)
ISBN 978-1-62805-001-1 (Paperback)
ISBN 978-1-62805-002-8 (Audio)

DEDICATION

WITH DEEP APPRECIATION TO THE
LATE **RAY BRADBURY** WHO
ENCOURAGED MY WRITING, LOVED
THE THEATRE, AND WROTE AND
PRODUCED BRILLIANT PLAYS THAT,
TO MY JOY, I HAD THE PRIVILEGE OF
PERFORMING FOR HIM PERSONALLY.

ACKNOWLEDGEMENTS

I would like to thank my family for their support, encouragement, suggestions, and editing: my husband Roy L. Shults; our daughters Heather J. Manolakas, Anne C. Manolakas, and Kathleen E. Manolakas; Bob Cornez who formatted formidably; and James Garrison who covered the covers.

Thank you also to my wonderful parents from the Greatest Generation: Betty Jane Heise Manolakas, the first published author in our family, and George S. Manolakas, M.D., a World War II veteran who served with General George S. Patton's Seventh and Third Armies, a University of Michigan football half-back with Tom Harmon, and a dedicated surgeon from the old school who always put his patients first.

I also would like to remember: (1) John Blankenchip, now deceased Professor Emeritus at the University of Southern California School of Theatre, who in 1966 founded the Festival Theatre USC-USA—the first American troupe in the Fringe of the Edinburgh International Festival in Scotland—and returned until 2005 [this author had the privilege of being a member of the Troupe in five of those years]; (2) Alan Hubbs, also now deceased, who was second in command of the Edinburgh Troupe and the director of our friend Ray Bradbury's plays at the Fremont Center Theatre in South Pasadena; (3) Anne Paul who is a treasured personal friend of mine and the wonderful woman who opened her home and heart to our Troupe every summer; and (4) all of my dear friends who have answered, and continue to answer, the call to the Edinburgh Festival, as well as to varied positions in film, television, and theatre.

"All the world's a stage,
And all the men and women merely players.
They have their exits and their entrances . . ."

-*As You Like It*, Act 2, Scene 7
William Shakespeare, English Dramatist,
(Born April 26, 1564, England)

PROLOGUE

On a cold fall Saturday morning at 2:00 a.m., Charlie
Valentine hurried down Hollywood Boulevard in east
Hollywood's seedy low rent district. He was California
coatless and getting chilled. Charlie had dined and then
closed the bar at the local shabby-chic French
restaurant. He was alone, without his usual Hollywood
"D-list" parasitic friends.

Charlie's appetite for food and drink satiated, he
headed back to the small Valentine Theatre he had
owned for years. On the way, he did business with his
regular street dealer to satisfy yet another appetite.

"My usual," Charlie slurred.

Vicodin in hand he hurried down the street.

Charlie entered the Valentine through the wood
framed glass double doors. They were as weathered,
cracked, and beat up as Charlie and his theatre from
years of hard use and neglect.

In the empty theatre, Charlie rushed to his dimly lit, small office emboweled at the back. He shut the door and burrowed through the clutter: old set furniture from past plays; boxes of props and costumes; dust-encrusted memorabilia; and paraphernalia from his indulgent life.

Charlie plopped into his dirty gray tweed chair. He shoved aside the litter on his battered oak desk and grabbed his paper cup of stale morning coffee. With the last gulp, he downed four of the Vicodins he had scored.

Then Charlie sat and waited. He waited for the familiar head-float to start and complete his alcohol initiated escape from his life. A life he had not chosen. A life dictated by his mother Olivia Valentine and the dilapidated theatre he inherited from her—along with a modest Hollywood Hills bungalow and too little cash.

Through his welcomed, mind-numbing haze, Charlie spotted a rat crouched near the door. He smiled at his company and held up his plastic baggie of pills.

"Here, boy," Charlie beckoned. "Come here. I'll share."

The rat ducked behind the stacked cardboard boxes. Charlie's smile faded.

Charlie turned to the morass of papers on his desk. He rummaged through the old show programs, opened envelopes, unpaid bills, and scribbled notes. After knocking half onto the floor, he found his prize, the Crenshaw Theatre Acting Troupe's business card. The troupe needed a new theatre. It had offered to lease the Valentine for real money, unlike the occasional limited cash intake from Graham Alford's the current resident acting troupe.

Charlie wanted the money. Charlie needed it. He had squandered mother's nest egg on drugs, his "D-list" friends, and parties in the now mortgaged bungalow.

Charlie stood unsteadily. He stuffed the card in his pants pocket for a call tomorrow at home.

He tottered and then fell forward, catching himself on the desk. Charlie felt weak when he should have been feeling euphoric and relaxed. He suddenly needed to get home very badly.

He braced himself on the desk and focused on the door to try to leave. It was not to be. With his first step he stumbled, grabbing the tall glass cabinet that housed the Valentine family's legacy—65 years of acting memorabilia. The cabinet, the legacy, and stacks of boxes toppled with him.

From the floor, Charlie peered up at the dusty, three-armed chandelier. It had two burnt out bulbs and the third glared too brightly down at him. He saw the broken curio cabinet laying across his chest, but he didn't feel it. He didn't feel anything now.

Charlie stared over at the door. He thought if he could just get home everything would be all right.

He reached out for the brilliant hall light streaming in from under the door. Then he saw the rat crouched again behind a crushed box. It stared at him. Charlie stared back.

"Help." Charlie pushed the word out with an inaudible breath.

He tried to move, but his body refused. He fought for every shallow breath. A tear snailed down his temple into his graying sandy hair.

Charlie wished he hadn't left rehab eight months ago. He wished his mother hadn't left him alone. He wished he wasn't staring at a rat and the rat wasn't staring back at him.

Charlie squinted to focus.

Through the spiraling haze of alcohol and Vicodins, he saw the rat was not staring back. The rat's eyes were lifeless. It's body crushed.

Charlie looked away, back into the single, lit bulb above.

It grew dim.

He was alone and afraid.

At 4:00 a.m. Saturday, Charlie Valentine was dead.

⌘

CHAPTER 1

"We have seen better days."
-Shakespeare, *Timon of Athens*, Act 4, Scene 2

At 4:00 a.m. Saturday, I, Veronica Kennicott, woke before dawn as I always did—every day. And, as usual, nature's pre-dawn darkness was tempered with the fluctuating light from my old box television.

"Good morning," I mumbled as I pushed the remote's off button.

Every night, all night with the volume low, I play the commercial-free classic movie channel. It has been the human presence in my bedroom for the three years since my husband, who lived an over-full life, left for the hereafter. The television is present enough and human enough to connect me with a serviceable sleep. This serviceable sleep, however, ended always with an unwelcome, lonely day-before-dawn.

Time. Time—that during those three years slowly evolved.

The first several months of my post-husband, pre-dawn insomnia I drank my decaf tea with non-fat milk and honey while I channel-surfed. I flipped between the shopping network, news, documentaries, series re-runs, and movies. Finally, the shopping network's disingenuous friendships became too expensive, the news and documentaries inbred, the series and movies too repetitive, and the channel surfing an eye strain. The programming was becoming a training ground for brain atrophy. The network shows were a transparent pabulum-fill for commercials. The "news," and I use the term charitably, was an indoctrination seeking to make me care about anyone's life but my own.

After months of this ever-present pre-day, I finally turned to crime. Not committing it, but creating it.

I became the mystery writer and the person I am today. I am the author of three books with a fourth in progress. Admittedly, they are as yet unpublished. This is simply because, although my books are excellent, I have never properly edited them or, truth be told, submitted them to an agent or publisher.

But still, all-in-all, I am known amongst my friends and neighbors now as a professional writer. To them what else could I be, having written so many books? And to be honest, I feel every bit the consummate professional that they believe me to be.

I have a life that excites and interests me and everyone else. I am knowledgeable and respected. I am sought after professionally—or more accurately quasi-professionally—as a writer and crime aficionado and consultant. I created a new life, a new profession, a new persona, and my own fascinating pre-dawn companions.

As a crime consultant my neighbor entreated me to solve the mystery of her missing front porch wicker furniture. Of course, any one could have solved it if they were rattling around their house at four in the morning and witnessed the crime. But, I naturally didn't disclose that fact. I also solved the mystery of the death of my friend's ever-barking dog. Poison over the gate. Again, I never mentioned that she could have easily prevented the poisoning with a modicum of neighborly regard.

As a writer and local mini-celeb, I have more social invitations than I can manage. I attend parties, dinners, and luncheons where I am now center-pieced, not as Mr. Kennicott's widow, but as an author and part-time sleuth.

I use these criminal forays and social functions as my personal excuse to avoid editing my books, submitting them to anyone, or learning to self publish. And, frankly, I see no point in undertaking such arduous tasks. Why should I?

My mysteries are praised and already sought after. I do readings from my books at local senior citizen homes and libraries. Each time, I receive great praise with commitments to buy my mysteries when they hit the bookstores or the internet. I am also complimented and fondly admired every week by my creative writing teacher and my classmates. I have been for years.

Furthermore, I have all the accouterments of a published author, including a mystery writer's website designed exactly like my favorite author's. It teases all comers with several pages of my books, which I did carefully select and polish. They are terrific. The website is terrific. And my life is terrific.

I want to clarify, in case you think I am a liar by nature—I am not. I have been honest and straight-forward to a fault my whole life. However, when it comes to my mystery writing, it seems I do nothing but lie—quite believably and naturally, of course—but I lie. After all, as you can see, I have a reputation to maintain.

However, this foggy Friday damp morning in my north Santa Monica costal enclave I was alone and in trouble.

* * *

I sat in my study at my laptop in my usual jeans and baggy beige cashmere sweater. But instead of communing with criminals and my fictional friends, all I did was sip my tea. I watched the overcast dawn arrive through the bay window overlooking my pool—unable to write. I tried desperately to connect with the protagonist in my fourth book. But instead, I found myself studying the dead, brown leaves in the pool. Some were floating, some sinking, and some already decomposed on the bottom waiting to be rescued by my "pool man"—me.

Finally, I looked back at my draft. I had told everyone what great progress I was making. Unfortunately, however, the truth was that I wrote the first chapter seven months ago and not one word since. I had writer's block; the curse and dread of every author.

"Where are you?" I snapped at my heroine.

I didn't expect an answer, but I expected something. Usually, my mystery characters spoke to me. They told me what to write. But this heroine, this very professional woman lawyer, who first screamed at me to be alive on paper, abruptly quit me and my mystery. Her proposed destiny was to solve two murders at her law firm and save a life—her own. However, she simply up and walked out of my book, my mind, and my heart months ago. I couldn't get her back. I not only couldn't get her back, but I also couldn't think of any character to take her place.

And don't get me wrong. I would have loved to kill her and the book off, but what difference would it have made? My muse had gone. It had deserted me for the first time.

I was in trouble not because my fans would ask about book number four. Indeed, I would eventually simply shamelessly announce it was done. To me that was a minor half-truth since technically it was done, unfortunately and evidently, when it was begun. Rather, I was worried because I had no muse-induced cohorts alive and murdering to occupy me in the wee hours of the morning. I was truly alone, again.

As the morning wore away, my writer's block did not.

Then just before noon, I was rescued. My suffocating inertia was interrupted by the ring of my cell phone.

I recognized the number. I was elated. It was Graham Alford, a fellow theatre arts major and friend from college. We had reconnected some years ago at the Valentine Theatre where he now ran the resident acting troupe.

I leaned back in my chair and put my feet on the desk next to my fallow laptop. I flashed back to college and the play productions Graham and I acted in together—the good, the bad, and some even ugly.

"Hello," I gushed, welcoming his intrusion into the nothing that was my morning.

"Veronica, its Graham. I am desperate. I need your help."

⌘

CHAPTER 2

"The play's the thing . . ."
-Shakespeare, *Hamlet*, Act 2, Scene 2

"Graham, I was just thinking of you."

I nudged a little white lie to the tip of my tongue. I wanted to please the old friend who recently had drawn me back into the theatre world with occasional acting gigs.

"Really?" Graham was charmed.

After our college graduation, Graham took off for the Big Apple's theatre world. I stayed in Los Angeles and married my college love. I had Googled Graham's not un-noteworthy acting career in New York for a while, but stopped. I was envious. Then, twenty years later, but before my husband died, I discovered Graham had returned to Hollywood and the once famous, or infamous, old Valentine Theatre. I attended a production and had a late supper with Graham whose girth reflected too many late suppers. But, aside from that, we were friends and fellow thespians again for a heartbeat that night. I jumped at a small part in his next play. It led to six others.

"I read about your world premier next week at the Valentine. Exciting!"

"Oh, yes. A new play," Graham replied with no humor and less enthusiasm. "But you know how that goes. Remember the last original and the rewrites?"

"Do I? Of course, my role ended up cut to 12 lines. I could have killed the playwright."

"I remember, but you know, there are . . ."

"'There are no small parts only small actors.' I know," I snickered. "Don't worry. I had a ball with my twelve lines."

"You should have, you scene stealer. You quadrupled your stage time with all your dramatic pauses during you lines and, my God, the business you created."

"I milked it mercilessly." I chuckled at the little busy things, called stage business, I had done to lengthen my role. "Am I forgiven?"

"You were forgiven on opening night." Graham gushed with his theatrical vocal affectation that smacked of a British accent. "You were wonderful."

"I was, wasn't I?"

"The audience adored you."

"I know."

"But the lead didn't. Upstaging him like that night after night wasn't nice," Graham chuckled. "You can do more with the business of carrying a vase across stage than any actor I know."

"Thank you." I enjoyed the repartee that came naturally with my fellow thespian.

Then Graham stopped the levity.

"I don't think you're going to thank me for this call, though. I need help and you have the perfect talents."

"Of course, anything."

I readied myself to accept an offer of a last minute role in Graham's play.

* * *

With an original, many an actor gets angry as their part shrinks. But I would take up the gauntlet. After all, I loved the theatre, adored Graham, but most of all needed an escape from the insubordinate protagonist. Besides, I knew Graham was not beneath putting a microphone in my ear if I couldn't learn the lines. I was not beneath it either.

Furthermore, it's true, what they say. The roar of the crowd and the smell of the grease paint never leaves you. I was an acting junkie. An acting junkie who had actually used the grease paint of "olden times" instead of pancake makeup. An acting junkie who not only loved performing but loved it all: musty old theatres, crowded smelly dressing rooms, waiting in the wings for an entrance, ticket taking, curtain pulling, running follow-spot, tech runs, opening night, and closing nights. While I loved it all, I didn't love all the people. But I did love that they loved the theatre. It was a calling for most of us.

"I knew I could depend on you." All the tension fell from Graham's voice.

"Of course you can. Always. Who left the play? Someone I know?" I was ecstatic at the prospect of not suffering with my fourth mystery and my recalcitrant muse any longer.

In an industry town like Hollywood, too often actors in non-paying, 99-seat theatre productions like Graham's would quit without notice, even without having their lines cut by a newbie playwright and even though understudies for their parts were rare. Small theatres had become the actor's training ground after the death of the studio system. But actors didn't give a second thought to deserting a small theatre production for a paying gig or just trading up.

To be clear, while not acceptable, it was the way of things now. Little was said, except amongst intimate friends. After all, if the deserting actor did make it big, everyone wanted to be on good terms. This town was based on friendships or, more accurately, on what passed as friendships. This culture of trading up is why Graham rarely cast his plays from open calls with unknown and untested commodities. Open calls too often left him open to trouble. At least with friends, he knew what kind of trouble he'd get.

"No. No, dear. No one left the play."

"But I thought . . ."

"I need your writing expertise. I need you to rewrite the play."

"Rewrite the play!"

I was shocked. It never occurred to me that my impostor-author status was now extended to playwriting. Though, I had to admit a small part of me was titillated at this new aspect to my authorial reputation.

"Yes. This original play is more like an original mess. The running time is too long by at least an hour."

"An hour?" This was unheard of, especially so close to opening night.

"Maybe more."

"And the author? What does the author say?"

"He has decided his play is not the problem. It's the actors who are causing the over time."

"Are they?" I knew all to well that hammy actors, like me, sometimes were the problem.

"No. They're fine. The play's repetitive."

"Can't he cut it down?"

"No. I need a real writer to do drastic cuts and make this author see the light."

"Oh?"

My heart sank. Of course, Graham believed I was a "real writer." I guess I had made sure of that?

Apparently, I had bragged once too often to Graham about my busy authorial life when in reality, I lied. I did it to escape Graham making me his resident backstage mother for ingénue's and their wardrobe changes. To me, no self-respecting woman my age, even with no real life, would spend three nights a week plus a Sunday matinee wet-nursing young actresses.

"You know theatre and writing. You're the perfect person. You have to help," Graham pleaded. "There's no one else."

"But I'm in the middle of my fourth book, you know." I lied by omission because I had been in the middle for months.

"Please, Veronica."

"I don't know . . ."

Oddly, my authorial self wanted to charge into the fray and save the day, but my impostor meter blared a warning at me to back off. Not only was I an unpublished writer, but certainly no playwright.

"I need you."

Graham used a tone I had heard before. It meant do it or you'll be on my "don't call" list forever.

Graham, who lives and breathes theatre, catalogues everyone's assets so he can use them for his productions. He had re-catalogued me now, not as an old friend to be used for menial labor and mostly bit parts, but as a successful writer who could save his production.

Of course, he had no idea I had never published anything, let alone authored a play. Well, actually, that wasn't true. I did author a silly, self-indulgent one act for a class with Graham back in college, *Orange Crates and Kisses*. It earned a C minus but deserved a D. Obviously, Graham had forgotten my grade or he was desperate enough to rewrite history and connect the widely scattered dots to conclude I could help him.

"Okay. I'll take a look."

I was reluctant, but I also was not ready to make the leap to Graham's *persona non grata* list. Graham was a friend. He was a friend who had helped me earn my precious, and hard to obtain, Equity card into the stage actor's union.

"Great! I am so relieved."

I realized, of course, that he wouldn't be if he knew about my authorial secrets and my debilitating case of writer's block. If he had any inkling, I would definitely be *persona non grata* now.

"Graham, remember I am just taking a look."

I was being rail-roaded in impeccable Graham style. I knew the price of jumping off the train and wondered if I could rely on my editing skills learned in my many novel writing courses.

"This won't take long and then you can get back to your book." Graham intentionally disregarded my reservations. "Besides, you know most of the cast. They won't grumble about the line cuts if they're from you and the others will follow suit."

"Very calculating." I recognized Graham's underlying motive. "Who's in the cast?"

"You'll see. Rehearsal's at seven-thirty, so we'll meet at five. Come with your quill and your muse. We'll talk."

"Five? Tonight? But I have plans. I . . ."

"Cancel them, dear."

I always made Saturday night plans as a single person, just as I had as a couple. Tonight was my neighbor's 40th Over-the-Hill birthday party for her husband in the "biz." They gave great parties, but I didn't need to go. My invitation was an obligatory neighborhood invitation to head off noise complaints. I decided my extremely pointed Over-the-Hill gift about balding, although funny, was probably better off not given and I was probably better off not going.

"All right. I'll cancel for you." I milked the favor aspect of my decision.

"Wonderful."

"But what about the playwright?" In case I did commit, I wanted assurances that the dramatist's muse was still intact because I knew that mine was a daily no show. "Is he on board because . . ."

"You're my only hope. See you tonight."

Graham ignored my inquiry and hung up quickly, as was his habit when he sensed a hesitation not to his benefit.

"But . . ."

I objected to an empty phone.

⌘

CHAPTER 3

"Rich gifts wax poor when givers prove unkind."
-Shakespeare, *Hamlet*, Act 3, Scene 1

Five short hours later on Saturday evening, I arrived at the Valentine Theatre, the home of my only acting gigs since college. I was excited to be back at the theatre. At the moment, it didn't matter that I was about to be exposed as an authorial fraud.

The Valentine was well-known as the oldest continuously running small theatre in Hollywood proper. It had always been family owned and operated, first by Olivia Valentine and then her son Charlie. Its dubious artistic reputation had improved since Graham established his resident acting troupe there. He produced more than a few well-reviewed, but still sparsely attended, productions.

Although it was just past dusk, I could see the old Spanish-style courtyard building was still dilapidated, even more so than the last time I had visited. A piece of the clay tile roof had even fallen into the corner dirt planter next to the drought-resistant Oleanders and weeds.

The theatre sat mid-block. It had a pot-holed, unlit, and narrow parking lot squashed between it and a 1960's box-like two-story office building.

As usual, I parked on the street and fed the meter until the 6:00 p.m. free time. No one used the parking lot or adjacent stage door unless absolutely necessary. The parking lot is a depository for cigarette butts, used syringes, and empty dime bags. It served as a refuge for the homeless, petty criminals, and the disenfranchised.

I tried the wood trimmed glass double doors. They were unlocked.

* * *

When I entered the theatre's narrow, long lobby, it was dimly lit and cold. It was as cold inside as outside. Mismatched salvaged chairs ran along three walls and a long glass concession stand, filled with goodies Graham sold at intermission. At the end of the lobby was a lit gas fireplace and a narrow stairway which led to the balcony that had housed an organ used in the old funeral services. Now it housed Graham's stage lighting, sound effects, and old props.

I heard the balcony floor boards above creak with the weight of someone walking.

"Graham?" I called.

The creaking abruptly stopped.

The Valentine Theatre was a converted funeral home with a long history of supposed hauntings, apparitions, creakings, and other unexplained phenomena. Decades ago the lobby was used as a mourners' viewing room for bodies prepared and displayed in caskets.

"Graham, is that you?"

In the silence that answered, I headed toward the stairway.

"Bryce?" I called, thinking it might be Graham's regular light man.

No answer. I stopped and warmed my hands at the gas log fireplace near the stairway. It felt good.

The old funeral home was closed and boarded up in the 1950's when the owner was arrested for the improperly disposing of bodies. By the time it went on the market, it was not saleable. It was decayed, rat infested, and reputedly haunted by the ghosts of those outraged bodies.

As I leaned closer to the fire, I looked up over the mantel at the one dimensional, amateur oil painting of Olivia Valentine. She was a middle-aged woman who loved acting and inherited just enough money to indulge herself. She bought the dilapidated funeral home for almost nothing. Then, on a shoe-string budget, she turned it into the Valentine Theatre--to showcase her long fallow, unappreciated, and unpolished acting skills.

In her day, Mrs. Valentine had nourished and embellished the funeral home's popular ghost stories. During play performances, she staged hauntings to get publicity. The audiences came to the Valentine more to see her staged apparitions than her plays, but she didn't care. She produced plays with roles she wanted to perform whether or not she was too old for them, had the emotional range, or looked ridiculous. She only cared that her thespian career, once thwarted by the burden of marriage and raising her son Charlie, was renewed.

I admired her and wished my husband had left me enough money to dabble like she had. Then, Graham would be coming to me to direct plays in my theatre and I would, naturally, play the leads.

Cash poor, like Graham, Olivia traded on using the free labor of hungry Hollywood hangers-on, wannabes, and has-beens—a cavalcade of actors, directors, lighting and set designers, and stage managers.

Later, when Mrs. Valentine died, her profligate son Charlie began sucking the rents from the aging Valentine and used none for repairs. He needed to maintain his decadent lifestyle in his inherited Hollywood Hills home.

Warmed by the fireplace, I lifted my bottled water from my purse and took a drink.

As I recapped the bottle, I heard three more quick creaks from above and again silence. Although I didn't believe in the still popular ghost stories, I felt a chill that had nothing to do with the weather.

* * *

I put my water back in my purse and went to peer up the steps.

"Who's there? Graham?"

Suddenly, behind me the large oak lobby door which led to the theatre and stage burst open.

I jumped.

I turned to see Graham holding an unusually thick script in his customary black director's binder.

"Veronica!" Graham barreled towards me with a smile stretching across his big round face horizontally.

Graham was over six feet tall and a big man and a little bigger every year. Despite his girth, he had boundless energy and a full head of graying hair. He was light on his feet and, even recently, had danced and sung in productions of *South Pacific* and *Oliver.* After all, grease paint roared through his veins too.

"There you are. I thought I heard you up in the balcony." I left the warmth of the fireplace behind.

"No, I was checking the set."

"It must be Bryce then." I glanced back toward the balcony stairs.

"Is that a joke? Bryce this early?"

"Are you sure?"

"I'm sure."

Graham reached out with both arms, script in hand. He pulled me into his rounded stomach which blocked his attempt at a full-body hug. The onerously large script pressed into my back.

"I'm so glad you're here."

"Me too."

I was glad I was there too. I was just not comfortable being there as an author instead of a player.

"Forget the balcony." Graham released me and his smile dropped as he flailed his arms airborne in agitation. "And don't start on the hauntings. You're too level-headed for that. Besides, we have real problems."

"Problems?" I said, noting the word "we" and the plural of the word "problem."

For almost a decade now, Charlie had rented the theatre to Graham for very little. Graham had slowly established the Valentine's low budget, but occasionally well-reviewed, resident theatre troupe. Like Mrs. Valentine, Graham was a purveyor of hope. He used the free labor and efforts of the same hungry Hollywood hopefuls.

Problems came with the territory; the foremost being barely able to pay the rent with an habitually small box office take. Even small donations from old friends like me didn't put Graham in the black most months.

"Yes, come with me and I'll get you a fresh script to edit."

Graham led me toward the oak door leading into the theatre.

"I'll see what I can do."

I didn't add the words "if anything" at the end. Now, I was more concerned about Graham's expectations than about who or what was creaking in the balcony.

"I need this play to be a hit and bring in real money."

"Real money?"

I had never known Graham to be interested in making any money, other than to get by, let alone real money.

"Charlie's doubling my rent," Graham announced.

"Can he do that?"

"Apparently. And even worse, the Crenshaw Theatre Acting Troupe is willing to pay it if I don't."

"The Crenshaw Troupe? Why?"

"Their theatre was sold last month for retail space. They're desperate and they have the money. They have patrons. High rollers."

"I know."

"And don't forget the actors monthly dues."

"Yeah, they pay for the privilege of auditioning and never get a role." I knew about the avaricious director there and a couple of other places. "Ninety percent of them don't even get a walk-on. There aren't enough roles to go around."

"I don't know how he gets them all to pay?" Graham mumbled.

"It's a lottery ticket. He's charging them for nothing. It's not fair."

I knew even Graham had tried it several years ago, but didn't have the draw to get actors to pay. In my own self interest, I didn't want him to try again.

"Not to worry."

Graham gave my shoulders a small pat and then turned and opened the large door to the small theatre.

* * *

In the theatre, the stage was sparsely lit with work lights, but I still saw a beautiful Victorian living room set displayed in front of me.

"That is really gorgeous."

"Thank you, dear. But let's get you that script."

It was rare when Graham didn't have time to be praised, but he didn't.

"I left a few in the women's dressing room. We'll grab one and then we'll talk."

Graham was back to his single-minded objective.

We hurried down the center aisle leading down to the raised stage. It had a gentle slope with its intermittent sets of steps and old maroon carpet. On each side there were rows of worn cherry red velvet seats. The theatre walls were painted matte black and topped by an impressive dark walnut ceiling with cob webs scattered on its large cross beams.

We went up the black access stairs onto the stage to get to the wings and the backstage dressing room.

As we did, I admitted to myself that despite Graham's problems, I was still grateful for this reprieve from my thwarted fourth book. My muse and protagonist had abandoned it and now, hopefully, I could too.

As we crossed the stage, a loud boom echoed through the empty theatre.

"What was that?" I whispered.

⌘

CHAPTER 4

"Oh hell, what have we here?"
-Shakespeare, *The Merchant of Venice*, Act 2, Scene 7

Graham stopped and walked to center stage. His eyes scanned the dark balcony and then the entire theatre. He was analyzing what the noise was, as only a person who intimately knows his theatre could.

"Ah, the parking lot door in the hall. That's it," Graham announced as he flung his arms in the air. "Charlie uses the door to that damn dark parking lot when he wants to score. And he never remembers to lock it. I'll have to check."

"So Charlie's using again. That's why the rent hike?" I asked.

I was unable to ignore the soft spot in my heart for the aged teenage star. He was always friendly and charming to me in his strung-out way.

"Yes."

"So evidently nothing came of the treatment program I found for him last year."

"That lasted two months. It's been downhill since."

"And his big talk about refurbishing the theatre I see was just that; big talk."

"Obviously, Veronica."

"Too bad for the theatre and for him."

I was genuinely sad because I had always liked Charlie. He was very thoughtful three years ago after my husband died, actually much more so than Graham.

"Too bad for me!" Graham said angrily. "Now he's using with his old gang. All his rents and residuals from his television days are just going up their noses, again. And, I'm going to pay for all the partying with a rent hike. That is if I can scrape the money together."

"Can you?"

"I don't know. I need good reviews and a hit play. Instead, I committed to this ridiculous original script."

"I'll talk to Charlie about another rehab program."

Charlie's attempts at rehab had never worked. His problem was too well-rooted. As a child Charlie began helping his mother with the theatre and doing small roles. As a teenager, he started using at the cast parties and eventually ferreted out other parties to get high. At sixteen, he landed a television series, but quickly partied his way into oblivion. Afterward, Charlie had made a bare living doing extra work until Mrs. Valentine passed and left him the theatre and her house. Now, he still parties in the Hollywood Hills, while he sucks every meager dime out of the aging theatre, leaving it to decay

"He's always liked you. He might listen. At least you could stall the rent increase. We need a chance to up the box office draw. I've tapped out all my friends, including you?"

"Unfortunately, yes." I had donated a little in the past but this shortfall was too big for my pocketbook. "I'll talk to him tomorrow."

"That might help." Graham led us through back through the wings.

* * *

Backstage, Graham knocked on the women's dressing room door.

"Anna?" Graham called.

There was no answer. We entered. Graham flipped on the bright makeup lights above the mirror-lined walls over rows of narrow dressing tables.

"Who's Anna?" I wondered if she had been in the balcony.

"She's the lead. She waitresses up near Vine Street and she usually comes here early to study her lines."

The small dressing room was cluttered with boxes, old set pieces, and props like most of the Valentine's backstage areas. In the far corner. there was an ancient wall heater and an old, flimsy accordion-style changing screen made of black framed white rice paper.

Below the bright lights, in black marker on white cardboard, were hand printed signs with the names of actresses in the play: Nicole, Renee, and Anna. The signs denoted the traditionally sacred territory of each actor in communal dressing rooms.

"I see Renee's in the play." I recognized the woman I had acted with several times. "Renee's a pro. You were lucky to get her."

I wished I had been asked instead of her. I could have aged myself twenty years for the part and then escaped my dreadful writing rut.

"She's gotten old, dotty, and nutty." Graham searched for the scripts. "Between you and me all my patience is eaten up by Renee and Nicole."

"Too bad." I rummaged for the scripts, too.

"I need help with the infighting to get this play up and running. I need to turn a profit. Frankly, I need you. You know the drill. Be positive . . . upbeat. There's only one seasoned professional still behaving like one, Kevin. You know him."

"Kevin Locke?"

"Yes."

"Of course I know him," I said excitedly.

I recalled the undeniable chemistry Kevin and I had together when we played a romantic duo eight years ago.

"You didn't mention he was in the play."

"I didn't?"

"His girlfriend was beautiful. Are they still together?"

"Who knows and who cares?" Graham was annoyed that I wasn't focused on his problems. "Where are the scripts?"

"I don't see them anywhere."

Graham dramatically slapped his hand to his forehead. "Oh, I must have put them in Charlie's office. You know how actors walk away with things. Look through my copy here. I'll get you another one after I check the parking lot door."

"I'll come with you."

I knew from experience that two were always better than one when dealing with the parking lot and the back entrance. The Hollywood underbelly had slipped in before, sleeping on the sets, stealing costume coats to keep warm, and taking anything valuable to trade for their Hollywood cocktails of assorted illegal substances.

"No, you need to start on the script. I'll go."

Graham thrust his script into my hands.

"Graham, I . . ."

"I'll be back."

Before I could clarify that I had not committed to the rewrite, Graham rushed out the opposite dressing room door to the long back hall. It accessed the parking lot door, Charlie's office, storage rooms, a snack kitchen, and restrooms.

I was left standing with Graham's script in hand. And of course I turned to the title page to see the author's name.

"Melvin Yates," I mumbled.

The name struck a bell but I couldn't place it.

I flipped through the rest of the script. It was many, many pages. Too many pages. And every page had its share of long wordy speeches and even longer monologues.

I panicked.

* * *

I looked around for a place to sit and read. Anna's dressing table was the neatest and frankly the most inviting with organized little boxes and a line of cranberry herbal iced teas. They looked good, but you never touched a fellow actor's things. Nicole's was a cluttered mess, Renee was the senior diva, and the vacant tables had props and random detritus.

I sat down, put my purse on Anna's dressing table and opened the monstrous script. I scanned the first act, ignoring Graham's blocking notations along the margins. The dialogue was nothing but dense, stilted, wordy, and repetitive. The monologues were worse. Graham was right. I could tell it was not the actors who were making the play run too long.

As I read, I started to get a headache. I assumed it was from the hackneyed recurring dialogue I was plodding through, not to mention the monotonous monologues.

I reached for the water in my purse and dug around for my aspirin.

Suddenly I heard Graham yelling from down the hall.

"Veronica. Help. Help." "Graham?"

I hurried to the hallway lined with set furniture from shows long past.

"Graham?"

"Come here," Graham shouted from Charlie's office. "Quick."

"Coming."

I ran down the hall to Charlie's office. At the doorway, I stopped. I saw Charlie lying on the floor.

"Oh, my God," I cried out.

"Call 911."

⌘

CHAPTER 5

"Confusion now hath made his masterpiece."
-Shakespeare, *Macbeth*, Act 2, Scene 3

I stood frozen in the doorway staring at Charlie lying on his back. He was motionless. His untrimmed graying hair was egg-beatered around his face. His skin was a strange, unnatural pink color. His lips were open and reddish. Charlie's dark eyes stared vacantly at the ceiling.

"What happened?" I gasped.

"He OD'd"

"Oh, my God." I thought of the hours I had spent trying to get him sober.

Charlie's cabinet lay across his chest. Glass shards, old Valentine Theatre programs, and photos of his mother were everywhere. Next to his head lay Charlie's Emmy from his long-gone acting career eroded by his Hollywood Hills parties with women, booze, and assorted Hollywood "drugs of choice."

"For God's sake, don't just stand there. Call 911," Graham yelled again as he moved the cabinet off Charlie's chest.

I was jarred into action, but there was no office phone to be had in the mess.

"I'll get my cell."

"Hurry. Get the paramedics."

I ran back to the dressing room, grabbed my cell phone from my purse, and got 911. As I responded to the 911 operator's questions, my headache became unbearable. I rummaged through my purse for my small aspirin bottle to no avail.

Finally, I took my purse and ran back to the hallway to update Graham. My cell reception dropped and so did the 911 operator.

"They're coming," I called down the hall. "I'm going to the lobby to meet the paramedics."

"Veronica," Graham called.

I looked back and saw Graham emerge from Charlie's office. He staggered toward me and then leaned on the wall, unable to go any further.

"Help me."

I ran to Graham and guided him to a nearby sixties love seat to sit. Its thin legs and old springs creaked under his weight. I sat nearby in an even more rickety wood chair, afraid the love seat would collapse with both our weights.

"Are you all right?" I asked absurdly, because obviously he wasn't.

"Dizzy." Graham shook his head and leaning forward with his face in his hands. "Charlie's dead."

"Dead? Are you sure?" I hoped against hope Graham had seen some sign of life in Charlie's still body.

"I'm no doctor, but . . ." Graham suddenly stopped talking.

"What's wrong?"

"Give me a minute. My head."

Graham leaned back and took deep breaths. We sat quietly. Graham slowly began breathing normally again. He finally looked at me.

"Wow." Graham shook his head and sat upright again.

"Do you feel better?"

"Yes, I don't know what happened. I just . . . I . . ."

"There!" The paramedics hurried towards us.

* * *

The paramedics stopped at Graham and flung their equipment around him.

"How do you feel?" the first paramedic asked Graham.

"Not me," Graham waved them away and pointed to Charlie's office. "He's in there."

The paramedics grabbed their things and hurried into Charlie's office. Three firemen came an instant later and Graham directed them down the hall also.

We waited.

"Charlie's partying finally caught up with him," Graham said, taking a few more deep breaths.

I was overwhelmed as I sat there and listened to the paramedics working on Charlie down in his office.

"Poor man."

"Poor man?" Graham retorted. "He hasn't worked a day in his life. He partied away his inheritance, his residuals, and every cent of rent from those charlatans he rents this place to in the daytime. They take money from starving actors who they know will never make it in the business."

"That's true," I agreed, because I knew about the bottom feeders who peddled stardom to wannabes who had no chance in hell.

"And now he wants . . . wanted . . . to raise my rent to party with."

"When you're right you're right."

Charlie had made passive profits from the dilapidated theatre. During the day, the profit is not generated by tickets sold, but from rent paid--cash up front--by the Hollywood hungry who cannibalize on each other: actors, who never "made it," teaching prepaid acting classes with no refunds or make ups to those who never will "make it;" singers with failed careers teaching voice, breathing, and relaxation for cold hard cash; and dancers whose short-lived span of employability has expired, teaching movement and posture. They all recommend each other.

Unfortunately, bottom feeders abounded in Hollywood, preying on hope and desperation. They multiplied and then divided "necessary acting skills" into microscopic absurdity to suck money from the starving hopefuls. Qualified or not they taught dialects, accent reduction, fencing, stage combat, acting preparation exercises, vocal preparation exercises, stage audition techniques, film audition techniques, masks, pantomime, memorization techniques, cold readings, Shakespearian acting, Method acting, the Meisner Method, the Stanislavsky Method, and the "Method Method."

While it was true that the Valentine Theatre housed a day-time den of thieves, at night it offered a respectable, although sparsely attended, theatrical experience thanks to Graham's dedication and his magical ability to bring free talent together.

"He should have just raised the daytime rents, but he said they couldn't pay. I can't stand those blood suckers taking money for nothing."

"I hate them too. But there's nothing we can do. You're not part of Charlie's daytime den of thieves."

I admired Graham's respected, although not profitable, theatrical experience. Graham put it together with his dedication and magical ability to bring free talent together as had Charlie's mother.

"I like to think of myself as a broker of opportunity and hope," Graham said, riding the gray line between fraud and investment.

I smiled and patted his hand. Graham used people, but we all got what we wanted out of it.

After a few minutes, two young uniformed cops, a female and a male, strolled in from the lobby. The male was inappropriately laughing, until he saw us.

He then approached with the female trailing and interviewed us. He jotted down the facts, the bare facts, in his notebook.

Evidently, it was the end of their shift and they were not happy with the call.

The laughing cop sauntered down into Charlie's office. He took his inappropriate laughter with him and we heard it coming from Charlie's office.

The female continued to quiz us.

* * *

Soon, the paramedics rolled Charlie's covered body out from his office on a gurney. Laughing cop, one of the paramedics, and the firemen hovered in the hallway over the body. They filled out paperwork and conferred quietly. There was no joviality—no urgency—no hope.

Reality hit me hard when I saw Charlie's body being rolled out of his office.

Our cop, done with her sparse questions, which appeared to me to be in keeping with her sparse knowledge, joined them.

"He is dead," I whispered to Graham.

"We've got to keep this quiet if we can. I don't want tonight's rehearsal ruined. Opening night is next Friday. Preview's Thursday, but I could cancel it."

"I understand. All we can do is try."

"If they'd get the body out of here before everyone shows, we could," Graham thought for a minute. "I wish he hadn't chosen to OD before we opened."

"That's cold. Don't let anyone hear you talk like that."

"Come on, Veronica. You know the cast will use it as an excuse. They'll latch on to any excuse to justify a bad performance in a mess like this that's already going south," Graham grumbled, looking quietly at Charlie's body down the hall. "Plus I'll have to deal with a new owner, probably Charlie's cousin. And don't forget the Crenshaw Troupe licking at my heels."

I didn't respond. I thought Graham should at least pretend to be sorry Charlie died, if only for a moment.

Suddenly, two more men in blue jumpsuits with work gear darted down the hall past us to the gathering of Charlie's body-contemplators.

I read the back of their jumpsuits as they passed.

"The gas company?"

"Who's next? Homeland Security?"

Graham threw his hands up.

⌘

CHAPTER 6

"That it should come to this!"
-Shakespeare, *As You Like It*, Act 2, Scene 7

Graham and I watched the talking, debating, conferencing, and arguing over Charlie's body. The two recently arrived blue jumpsuited men opened their bags and took out masks, gas masks. They popped in and out of the office and women's dressing room. They returned, took off their masks, and deliberated again with the assorted uniforms in the hall. Then they disappeared out the parking lot door where the gas meter was. In five minutes they returned.

"I told you there was no danger," the lead fireman pronounced. "We know what we're doing. It's off."

There was more debate and conferring. The gas company workers went to investigate the main theatre and the rest of the building.

The paramedic doing the paper work came over. After we answered repetitive particulars, he told us Charlie had died of carbon monoxide poisoning.

"Carbon monoxide?" Graham was shocked. "We thought it was drugs."

"No. Carbon monoxide poisoning from the wall heater."

"You're not closing the theatre?" Graham challenged.

"No. It's fine," the paramedic answered. "They're making sure now. It was the vent for that double sided wall heater between the office and that room next door with all the lights and mirrors."

"The women's dressing room?" I asked.

"I guess," the paramedic replied. "The vent was detached up at the top from the office side. With all that junk, it was an accident waiting to happen I think."

"What do you mean?" Graham demanded.

"It was knocked apart. The gas leaked into both rooms. It's gone now, dissipated. Carbon monoxide is odorless so the guy didn't know what hit him. We think he grabbed the cabinet to get his balance. It fell on him, but he died from the carbon monoxide."

"How horrible," I said.

"Lucky no one else was around. Except we did find a rat."

"A rat?"

"Yeah. Smashed, but we bagged it too."

Graham and I looked at each other. We didn't say a word, but we knew we had been in both rooms and dodged a bullet. The paramedic droned on reassuringly about how good the gas company procedures were now, turning off the wall heater gas feed, and looking over the building. I knew how lucky I was to get out of that dressing room and Graham out of Charlie's office.

Graham didn't mention Charlie's drug habit since Charlie hadn't OD'd, nor did he volunteer anything about the unlocked door and past break-ins. What difference did it make how the vent fell apart? Charlie's death was a terrible accident.

I followed suit. But my mystery writer's mind was running wild. I remembered the noises in the balcony and the alley door. I thought an intruder could have knocked the vent loose burglarizing Charlie's office or attacking him.

My thoughts were derailed when a young woman raced into the hall from the dressing room. She didn't see us sitting there and ran directly to the uniforms gathered in front of the gurney.

* * *

"What happened?" the young woman cried out.

"Hold on," the male cop ordered.

He was only too glad to enforce that order by grabbing the stunning young woman at the waist. He held her tightly to his body as she struggled to reach Charlie's covered body.

She struggled just enough to demonstrate resistance, but not enough to get away. Her long, straight blonde hair pendulumed across her back. She had on low-riding black jeans and a tight white sweater that showcased her pale, flat stomach as it rode further up with every move. A small, dark skull and crossbones tattoo bounced just above her jeans on her back right hip as she tried to push free.

"Let me go." The cop did, reluctantly.

She pushed away, her chest heaving from the struggle.

"Look I . . ." the young woman stopped arguing with the cop when she saw us.

Her face registered unmistakable surprise, but she immediately recovered. She hurried toward us, the cop's eyes consuming the entire length of her body as she walked away from him.

"Is she dead?" the woman squealed, her ice blue eyes sizing me up.

"She? Who are you talking about?" Graham barked with no patience for her and her drama. "It's Charlie. Charlie Valentine's dead."

"Oh?" The blonde sat down in a straight-backed chair near Graham and looked intently at the covered body.

"What are you doing here early?" Graham asked, seeing his cover up thwarted.

"Nothing . . . I . . . I was on this side of town," the young woman stammered.

Graham explained what happened. The young woman listened quietly and with no visible reaction. When she caught me studying her coldness, she immediately emoted. She hid her face in her hands, shook her head, and uttered little sobs.

"How awful," she cried loud enough to draw the attention of every male down the hall.

"Nicole, settle down," Graham ordered, annoyed at her little show whether sincere or not.

Nicole waited an appropriate length of time, took her hands down from her dry-eyed and composed face, and pleasantly introduced herself to me.

"I'm Nicole Jensen. I'm in the play."

"Veronica Kennicott, a friend of Graham's," I said, reaching out and shaking Nicole's hand, which returned a limp disinterested non-grip.

"Of course," Nicole said.

It was clear she had heard of me and I presumed my possible task in this troupe of actors. How? I didn't know. I didn't care at the moment. I was more curious about her presumption the body was female.

"Who did you think was on the gurney?" I asked.

"What?" Nicole was taken off guard and her ice blue eyes darted at me.

"Who did you think died? You said 'she.'"

"I was so afraid it was Anna."

"Why?" I probed.

"It's just . . ." Nicole avoided my gaze, looked down the hall at Charlie's body. "It's just that she's usually here early."

"We can all be thankful she wasn't." Graham then put on his directorial hat. "And listen, Nicole. We have a rehearsal tonight and it has to go forward. I want you to keep this quiet."

Nicole continued to stare down the hall at the body.

"Did you hear me?" Graham asked.

"What?" Nicole's emotionless blue eyes turned to Graham.

"Let's not upset the rest of the cast with this. That is, if they find out. Play it down. Not up. It was just a tragic accident that Charlie brought on himself. He never maintained anything here."

"Sure." Nicole stood abruptly with her youthful firm exposed belly at our eye level. "I got it."

She walked toward the main lobby down the hall.

Every red-blooded male emergency worker followed her exit with hungry eyes, except the female cop who followed it with envious eyes.

* * *

Graham and I watched the circus of the emergency responders crescendo. And then it abruptly ended. The building was deemed safe and they all left. We were again alone in the empty, quiet hallway.

"I guess we both dodged a bullet," Graham broke the silence. "Anna too."

Graham spoke in an unsteady, quiet voice that I had never heard before.

"I know." I felt hollow and tired, but my headache was better.

"We can't go over the script now. Look over my copy. I'll find another. I'd better call Charlie's cousin before the rehearsal," Graham sighed. "Nicole has a big mouth. We're in damage control mode."

I hated to admit it to myself, but I knew he was not sighing over Charlie's death. He was instead contemplating my lost time on the script revisions and whether Nicole was going to be the hysterical town crier.

"I'll go sit in the theatre and look over your script." I wished I hadn't told Graham I would even consider editing the play. "We'll talk later."

I went to the now safe dressing room to get Graham's script. I looked at Nicole's name over her dressing table and then scrutinized myself in the mirror below.

I was not young, but I had my own assets. I had often admired my high cheek bones and my own blue eyes, though they were darker than Nicole's. I ran my fingers through my shoulder length dark hair. My face was pale and I pinched some color in my cheeks. As I cleaned a smear of mascara from under my eyes, Charlie's vacant stare flashed back at me. I remembered his strange doll-like pink face and reddish lips. I looked away and went out and through the wings to the stage.

I stopped at the edge of the stage and couldn't resist walking out onto the Victorian set. I wished Graham had called me for a role instead of a rewrite. I stood center stage under the lights and leaned with one hand on a paint stained wood-work ladder that had been left there. I looked out into the empty audience and reveled in my memories under the spotlights, acting.

When I felt the weight of the script in my hand, I stopped my reminiscences and took a seat in the back of the theatre to read.

I had to see if I could even help out.

* * *

The cool theatre air cleared my headache and I felt more energized. I opened the play and did admit to myself that it might be therapeutic for me to take out my authorial frustrations on someone else's writing.

As I skimmed through the scenes of the first and second acts, I wondered why Graham had chosen it. It was an unauthentic Victorian copycat with cardboard characters who repeated and rephrased the same ideas in every scene. The plot was derivative and age old. A father forcing a financially advantageous marriage on his daughter. It would never draw a big audience and make enough money to cover anything, especially the increased rent that was looming.

I had read enough. Unfortunately, if I cut all the repetition, the play would be one act instead of three. I had to tell Graham I thought the play was unsalvageable before rehearsal started.

I was going to opt out of Graham's demand to edit this mess, even though it might mean opting out of our friendship as well.

⌘

CHAPTER 7

"The very substance of the ambitious
is merely the shadow of a dream."
-Shakespeare, *Hamlet,* Act 2, Scene 2

As I leafed quickly through the third act, I heard people in the lobby. I was excited to see which of my old friends were here for rehearsal. I wondered if Kevin was. I slipped the play script in my purse and went out to the lobby.

Outside through the glass theatre doors, I saw a silhouetted group of animated actor types, back lit by the street lamps. They were smoking, eating, and sipping coffee. I couldn't make them out.

But inside the lobby at the foot of the balcony stairs, I saw Bryce McConnell, Graham's lighting man, and Alastair Trondheim, Graham's resident stage manager. They were both my buddies from other performances. They were bantering with a third older man whom I did not recognize.

"Veronica," Alastair rushed over to me with his signature swagger and gave me his always brief, barely there hug.

Alastair was a slight, charming gay man with the body and walk of a dancer. In his prime, he stage-managed off and on Broadway where Graham had met him. There, Alastair had gleaned endless stories, true or not, about Broadway's biggest names that he now shared with us, the Broadway uninitiated. Alastair left his fantastic New York career several years ago so his long-time partner could "act" in Hollywood. Once here, his partner dropped him for a Hollywood hottie. Graham found Alastair wallowing in depression as an assistant in a small film distribution company. As usual, Graham got this great talent to stage-manage for free at the Valentine for him.

"Hello." I initiated our normal Hollywood air kiss.

"Graham called and told me you would be joining us again. Delightful!"

"We'll see," I hedged, feeling Graham's net pulling me into a hopeless situation.

Alastair ignored my equivocation because it suited him.

"Did you bring your cookies?"

"No time." I wished I never had started bringing cookies because now it was expected; still appreciated, but expected. "How are you?"

"Burning the candle at both ends like always and loving every minute of it." Alastair swept his hand back through his salt and pepper hair, straightened his fuchsia cashmere suit coat, and then whispered, "I saw Graham in the office. He said you both found Charlie?"

"Yes, an unlucky accident." I downplayed Charlie's death as Graham instructed.

"Don't worry, I'm on board. We play it down, if it gets out tonight," Alastair whispered. "But you two were lucky."

"I know."

"If Charlie had ever put money back into this rat trap, instead of partying with it, he'd still be alive, too."

"Bite your tongue."

I believed Alastair was right, but he had a bad habit of being too frank too often.

"At least Anna wasn't here working on her lines," Alastair noted. "With no lead we'd have no opening next week. And with no opening, no money. We'd be done here for sure."

"Yeah, Graham told me about Charlie's plans to get the Crenshaw Troup in."

"Well maybe now we'll get a new owner with a heart." Alastair then shifted gears. "So tell me, how's the writing?"

"Great. On my fourth."

I answered without fear of the usual inevitable publication dance. I knew Alastair was never interested in an in-depth conversation about anything or anyone, including himself.

"Wonderful. Well, we all hope you can help us with his monstrosity of a play, and don't quote me."

"That may be impossible from what I've read so far, but don't quote me either."

"I have hope. With some edits and great acting many a borderline play has opened and had a good run," Alastair replied, heading back to the stairs. "Come on over."

I didn't know how many of the troupe thought I was going to be their savior, but I did know Graham was doing his damndest to suck me in.

* * *

At the foot of the stairs Bryce, Graham's superlative lighting designer, greeted me with his always close-lipped smile, a habit developed to hide his crooked and smoke-stained teeth. Bryce always had the musty, dirty smell of cigarette smoke in his hair and clothes, which battled with the sweet, pungent smell of the weed he invariably had in his pocket. His deep, soft, raspy voice was earned by years of abusing his throat with his choice of escapes.

"Veronica, we've missed you. I've had no beauty to put the spot light on,"

I laughed and enjoyed his light blue eyes which always radiated friendship to me. He was a very old fifty. His prematurely aged face was framed by his long, curly smoke-saturated gray hair. He usually kept to himself up in the balcony, unless he was arguing lighting with Graham or outside smoking, both cigarettes and marijuana.

"Come now," I teased. "I hear you have been two-timing me by illuminating several beauties."

"Not true," Bryce objected a little too seriously. "I would trade any of them in to get you back under the lights. You appreciate my lighting and always move into the hottest spots."

"Some actors call that upstaging," Alastair smirked, and jiggled the coins in his pocket as was his habit, even unfortunately backstage during performances.

"No. No," Bryce said with a wink and a grin. "It's skill and appreciation of my art form. Without it, by the way, actors would be on a dark stage. It's respect."

Bryce was a has-been in theatre lighting before he was thirty. His career ended years ago in Dallas. At a large Equity theatre premier, he left the actors performing on a pitch black stage. They found him in the lighting booth asleep. The room reeked of marijuana. He was fired on the spot, but he didn't leave until he urinated on the lighting board and fried it. Now,

Bryce watches old movies by day and ekes out a bare living designing and doing lighting in non-equity Hollywood theatres. He still gets high and makes mistakes. Graham and others continue to use him partly because Bryce can still create masterful visual stage environments, but mostly because Bryce is all they can afford.

"Did you just get here?" I asked Bryce, thinking of the noises in the balcony earlier.

"Not long ago. Why?"

"Oh, nothing." I was flexing my detecting muscles.

My suspicious nature and desire to attribute fault had become more active, and some might say overactive, since my mystery writing and crime solving career began. I could not leave my now noteworthy—and in local circles highly respected—semi-professional detecting skills at the theatre door.

I instinctively decided Charlie's death from the vent displacement could use a look-see. After all, this would be my first investigation into a real death instead of a fictional one. I relished it. And, even though it was probably just an untimely and accidental demise, it did fall squarely into my lap and my jurisdiction as a mystery solver extraordinaire.

I put my sleuthing instincts aside for the moment and introduced myself to the third man in the group who was tall, thin and stooped with age.

"I'm Veronica Kennicott."

"Geoff Millard," Geoff said with a British accent as he took my hand and with great flourish raised it to his thin lips and gave it a non-contact stage kiss. "I am so happy to meet the person who is going to bring the playwright to his senses and dispel the ghostly beings who have possessed not only the Valentine, but the playwright's judgment."

I was startled by Geoff's eloquence, British accent, and the fact that ghostly possession was being blamed for the playwright's problems. However, I was not startled that another person assumed I was, in fact, going to edit this play. It was part of the Graham tactical strategy. And it was effective.

"Gotcha." Geoff flashed a mischievous smile.

Alastair laughed and all the men followed suit.

"You did." I took back my hand and laughed too.

Geoff was a charming, frail looking man whom I wanted to get to know.

"Geoff is old RADA," Alastair said. "He takes nothing seriously but his acting."

"Not that old." Geoff objected with a glint in his dark eyes and a wink.

Geoff had a beautiful head of wavy white hair and an attractive but well-worn face belied his objection.

"I can see that," I said, buying into his vanity.

I was curious why this graduate of the Royal Academy of Dramatic Arts in London was in our little production. RADA. After all, it was the ultimate training ground for actors and had produced many of the greats like John Gielgud, Anthony Hopkins, Vivien Leigh, Diana Rigg, Kenneth Branagh, Glenda Jackson, Ralph Finnes, Alan Rickman, and endless more. I decided I would peek at his biography in the program. I knew how to glean truth from fiction in the habitually overstated program bio's of actors. Graham, the master, had helped me enhance my own when I reentered the milieu. I barely recognized myself in it.

"Geoff is playing the good doctor and friend." Alastair looked at his watch. "Oops, I've got to wrangle the troops. Good luck with the rewrite."

"Thanks." My heart sank. Declining Graham's request was becoming ever more difficult.

I noticed Alastair had honored Graham's order to keep Charlie's death under wraps because neither Geoff nor Bryce had mentioned it.

"About the rewrite," Geoff said. "I can always use more lines. And if . . ."

Geoff was cut short when Graham blasted through the large oak door from the theatre.

⌘

CHAPTER 8

"Nature teaches beasts to know their friends."
-Shakespeare, *Coriolanus*, Act 2, Scene 1

I stifled a laugh when I turned to see Graham in the middle of the lobby, flailing his arms, and pacing like a caged lion.

"Places," Graham roared, zeroing in on the gathering outside the glass doors. "Places! We're late."

The actors outside on the sidewalk looked in at the spectacle that was Graham through their cloud of secondhand smoke. They did not move. I surmised that they were chuckling as well.

"Alastair," Graham snapped without ceremony. "What are those people doing out there? Get them in their places. And get the stragglers in the men's dressing room. We're late. Top of the third act."

Alastair as usual remained cool under Graham's outbursts. That was part of his talent.

Although Graham was brilliant and knew something about everything and everything about theatre, at the Valentine directing plays he was always agitated by something or someone, justifiable or not. Directing was people control and it had worn away his charm over the years. Everything was either a crisis or ignored.

As Alastair went to get the group outside, Graham barked, "And get Scott's ladder off the stage. He can build sets but he can't clean up after himself."

Scott Tram was the young man who always constructed Graham's elaborate sets in the scene dock at the back of the theatre. He was creative, skilled, and a hard worker, but childlike in his sloppiness and disorganization.

"Later," Bryce whispered, scurrying away up the narrow stairs to the balcony and his lighting.

Geoff gave me a quick bow from the waist.

"Nice to have met you."

I sat on the stairs, got the script out of my purse, and buried my head in it waiting for Graham's storm to subside. I had learned from experience it would go as quickly as it came. He was the epitome of compartmentalization. He moved from one task to another, with equilibrium or not, but rarely carried the baggage from one to the other with him.

Alastair herded everyone quickly through the lobby and down into the theatre.

* * *

Graham and I were left alone. It was quiet. Graham walked over to me and smiled, a pleasing I-am-going-to-tool-you smile.

"Now," Graham said hopefully. "What did you think of the play, dear?"

"Truthfully?"

"Yes."

"It has cardboard characters who repeat everything twenty different ways and seems never to go anywhere."

Graham's face fell. I recognized I had been too honest. I need to soften the truth with the requisite upbeat enthusiastic lies of the theatre world. I chose my words carefully. After all, I was a skilled writer—a crafter of words.

"But some edits and great acting could bring it to life." I mirrored Alastair's optimism.

"Well, sadly we don't have great acting bringing anything to life," Graham blurted. "So I need great writing. Please, I need your help. Can you edit it?"

Graham looked at me so desperately and I knew I had nothing to go home to but writer's frustration. I was weakening. Besides, after reading what I had of the play I was confident that I couldn't make it any worse. And more importantly and obviously, Graham had already committed me openly to my friends, his tactical *coup de gras*. And truth be told, I was excited about working with Kevin again.

I smiled. "Sure."

This was the moment of my official acquiescence. Although, unofficially and deep down, I knew from the minute Graham called that this was inevitable given the Graham machine, my theatre addiction, and the writer's block that I could not shake. I told myself that it would turn out all right in the end.

"Good. I knew I could depend on you."

Of course, he knew I would do it. We all kowtowed to Graham or were blacklisted by him. For most of us, Graham was the only thin thread we had connecting us to our drug of choice, the theatre.

"Let me get you one of the fresh scripts. Turns out I put them under lock and key here in the concession stand."

Graham got a script, a cast contact list, and program from the locked ticket cupboard under the glass concession stand.

"Here. You'll need the program too. Read the bio's of the new people. Cut the lines of the real amateurs and don't forget all the bio's are inflated. Take them with a grain of salt."

I will," I chuckled. "Just like I do mine."

I handed Graham back his director's script. I took my fresh script and slipped my contact list and program in it

"Come watch," Graham led the way into the theatre. "You'll get the idea. We're running the third act through. No breaks. No scripts. Off-book."

Graham had sealed the deal.

* * *

We went into the theatre and down the center aisle.

"Who's this Melvin Yates?" I wanted to know how Graham had decided to produce this awful play. "The name is familiar for some reason."

"What?" Graham said, distracted by rowdy actors talking backstage and a woman giggling loudly.

"The author?"

Graham ignored my question and bellowed, "Quiet, people."

Graham and I sat in the front row of the worn sagging velvet seats. As he settled in, his seat groaned under his bulk, and mine even complained with my slight weight.

The house lights were low and the stage had working lights up. For the first time, I really focused on Graham's impressive authentic, condensed Victorian set. It was picture perfect. The living room filled every inch of the very small space, similar to a detailed oil painting consuming the last particle of a canvas. Graham had learned theatre from the best and never wavered from perfection. To him the new young directors, who used bare black stages with a chair or two, were lazy amateurs. From experience, I knew once Bryce's lighting design was up it would dramatically enhance the set's mood for the audience and the actors.

I leaned over to Graham and whispered, "You have outdone yourself. It's breathtaking."

"Thank you, dear. Too bad it's wasted on this group." Graham reached over and patted my knee.

"And the Victorian staircase is the *piece de resistance*," I gushed, sincerely.

Upstage center was an ornate Victorian wood staircase that was a work of art. It led up and off stage just right of center and funneled the exiting actors into the narrow backstage crossover.

The crossover was used for these backstage exits, set changes, and to get to the opposite side of the stage. In the crossover, I knew behind the staircase the actors had to exit down steep ladder-type stairs. After all, I had exited that way in a prior play, but from a more modest staircase. I also knew they had to work their way through through a mountain of clutter once down.

Unfortunately, Graham condensed reality in his sets with great skill, but with little regard for actor safety. He also used every square inch of space for storage, just like Charlie, including the crossover. In the crossover, he stacked set furniture, props, and rolling platforms with complete collapsible rooms for quick scene changes. These were modeled on the efficient settings used in London's cramped centuries-old stages. But they were not condensed enough or efficient enough for the tiny Valentine Theatre.

Graham jarred me from my thoughts by bellowing, "Alastair, five minutes. Get these people in their places."

"Did you tell anyone but Alastair about Charlie?" I thought an announcement nipping rumors in the bud might be prudent.

"No, " Graham glowered at me. "And you don't either. I need this rehearsal to go smoothly."

"Just asking."

"It's probably all academic anyway. Nicole keeping her mouth shut may be an impossibility. But we'll see."

We heard Alastair herding the actors backstage.

"I need to get this mess up next Thursday," Graham said.

"You'll pull it together. You always do." I reassured Graham, despite knowing his track record, unhappily, was not good with original plays.

"Not without your cuts. I'm so glad you're here."

Graham patted my knee again. I knew he was nervous.

"As a last resort, we could draw an audience in with publicized stage hauntings like old lady Valentine used to do," I chuckled.

"Not funny. That's all I need. Half the cast is superstitious and seeing apparitions already. Besides, the playwright would hit the roof. He thinks the play is wonderful."

"How'd you meet this his guy?"

"Melvin Yates?"

"Yes, and why is that name ringing a bell? Is he in the industry?"

"Hardly," Graham scoffed. "Two years ago he got that multi-million settlement for his clients against the city for the police brutality. It happened during the protest after the elections. Remember?"

"Ah, I do remember. What a big fee that must been. And we taxpayers footed the bill."

"Shh. How do you think he's paying for this show?"

"Oh."

"Don't say another word, Veronica. Judge not lest ye be judged."

I understood now why Graham was producing this play. It was Melvin's vanity play. He was the angel fronting all the money.

"Will he be here tonight?" I asked.

"Are you kidding? He wouldn't miss a rehearsal. I'm sure he already slipped in backstage," Graham grumbled. "And, like always, he's giving the actors line readings with specific word inflections."

"Are you serious? What a pain. Is everyone ready to kill him?"

"They can't. And I can't. We'll lose our financing. And this time I'm getting paid too. Everyone is getting something for each rehearsal and performance."

"In this 99-seater?"

I was surprised money was changing hands because the Equity union that controlled remuneration was not involved in any 99-seat theatre productions unless there was a long run.

"Now I get why you got stuck with this play."

"Why else? Melvin's paying to chase his college dream: theatre . . . films . . . youth . . . women," Graham whispered. "He's divorced and looking for action."

"I see. I hope only one little actress at a time."

I knew multiple romances in a production never went well.

"Who cares? He can have anything he wants. Mel thinks our theatre company fits his vision. And who am I to argue. I just want a good long long run on his money, hopefully not with one of his plays after this one."

"That would be better. Have you told him about the rent hike?"

"No. And neither should you."

"I won't. But don't you think Mel should be editing his own play instead of directing the actors backstage?"

"Thank you, Veronica." Graham's words were engorged with sarcasm. "Everyone is ready to kill him."

"Better to direct the plays of dead authors."

"I may be soon, if they kill him." Graham laughed at his dark humor.

"You can blame it on ghosts."

"Seriously, the play will be fine if you cut it by a quarter." Graham stopped laughing.

"Too bad the author is the angel paying for everything."

"More like the devil," Graham said. "The only reason he let me call you now is that he's too busy directing my actors by night and doing his film project by day. He . . ."

A woman's shrill scream from backstage interrupted Graham and penetrated the entire theatre.

Two men catapulted in combat from the wings stage left. They landed center stage rolling and flailing at each other.

They were too closely entwined to land a blow and instead landed one epithet after another.

⌘

CHAPTER 9

"Double, double toil and trouble . . ."
-Shakespeare, *Macbeth*, Act 4, Scene 1

I watched as the two men wrestled center stage. The younger man with sandy hair was buff and agile. He gained the advantage by rolling to the top position. The older man, now on the bottom, was tall and wiry with brown hair thinning at the crown and receding at the hair line. That was Mel. I recognized him from his seven seconds of fame representing his now rich "victims."

"I guess he gave one too many line readings to the wrong actor," I chuckled.

"Not funny," Graham snapped.

Unexpectedly, a young, well-endowed, dark haired woman ran on stage. She worked past the fight to the apron at the edge of the stage. She leaned over precariously.

"Graham. Graham. Do something."

"Just keep away from them, Anna. Get away."

Graham freed himself from the armrests that captured his broad hips and headed up the side stage access steps.

"Stop them, Graham," Anna cried. "Joel's going to get hurt."

Anna stood her ground at the apron. The stage lights washed over her long mahogany hair. Her delicate, beautiful face absorbed her worry and was still gorgeous.

"No one's going to get hurt," Graham snapped, hurrying his great weight up the steps.

"Please," Anna screamed.

She ran across the stage to Graham. Her tight low-riding designer-knock-off blue jeans and breast-hugging cropped sweater displayed a thin, tanned, toned stomach.

I stood. I felt like I should answer the pleas of this helpless young woman too. But, in reality, I knew I wasn't going to get anywhere near this testosterone-charged wrestling match.

Geoff looked in from the wings and shook his head, obviously disgusted by the free-for-all on stage. Bryce blazed a follow spot down on the intertwined men. Knowing Bryce he did it, not to stop the fight, but to get a better view. Alastair came in stage right and stood exasperated with his hands on his hips. Some cast members ran in, huddled up stage, and became the perfect spellbound "involved" audience.

I watched the "author," with whom I was going to work, rolling around fighting like a 4th grade boy on the playground. Too bad he was an adult male fighting on a black painted dusty wood stage with Bryce's spotlight on his red face and thinning hair.

Then Nicole ran in from the wings stage left. She claimed a possessory interest in Mel by running around the tumbling men shrieking.

"Stop. Stop. Joel, get off. You're hurting Mel."

"Get back, Nicole," Kevin Lock yelled, running past Alastair onto the stage.

Nicole moved upstage with the cast and watched the men, her ice blue eyes wide and worried.

Kevin grabbed Joel off Mel who was on the bottom yet again.

"What the hell are you doing, Joel?" Kevin yelled holding Joel by the shirt.

I watched Kevin. He hadn't changed in five years. I couldn't take my eyes off him. He was still knock-down gorgeous with just a little more gray in his sandy hair and a few more wrinkles around his deep green eyes. As Kevin stood, dragging Joel with him, I saw he was still his six foot fit, lean, and camera-worthy self. Although he had never broken into the big time, I admired that he had supported himself over a lifetime acting in minor movie parts and television spots.

"I'm tired of this guy hounding me," Joel screamed, struggling in Kevin's grasp, but unable to break away—perhaps by choice. "I'm getting into character and he's thumping on my shoulder telling me how to say my lines."

"You don't know how to get into the character, you arrogant punk," Mel yelled back at Joel as he got up with a speed commensurate with his extra years.

"You don't know how to write a character, you hack."

"Settle down." Kevin kept hold of the handsome, hot-headed lead. "It's over."

"And you'd better keep your hands off Anna, too," Joel said, jerked lose from Kevin's hold.

When Joel lurched forward Mel stood his ground, tall and imposing.

Graham got between the two and said loudly but calmly, "Let's everyone settle down. Joel, go out into the lobby and cool down."

"Like hell. I . . ." Joel started to argue.

"Go . . . go," Graham ordered with a commanding volume and a simple turn of his huge body in Joel's direction.

Joel obeyed. He jumped off the stage and defiantly stomped up the center aisle out into the lobby. Anna went down the front stage access stairs and followed him. Her tiny blue and red butterfly tattoo peeked out on the small of her back between her low riding jeans and her sweater as she took the steps up the center aisle.

"He's out of here," Mel spit with venom leaning into Graham's face at the same level as his. "I want another actor."

"Are you all right?" Graham said, ignoring Mel's unrealistic demand a few days before opening and trying to redirect Mel's anger. "The most important thing is that you're not hurt."

"I'm fine," Mel said as he brushed off his well-pressed gray slacks and straightened his black sweater. "I'm fine."

"Mel," Nicole cried running up again and helping Mel brush off his shirt. "I can't believe Joel jumped you, baby."

"Don't, Nicole," Mel barked, brushing aside the young, striking blonde actress.

"We'll take a dinner break," Graham called out. "One hour. Then a run-through of the third act off-book. Look at your scripts. You people should know your lines. We open next week.

"I don't need a break," Mel snapped.

Mel glared at everyone still gawking at him.

"I'm fine."

The cast retreated to the dressing rooms where they deposited their jackets and bags during rehearsals.

"Look at your hand, it's scraped. I'll put a bandage on it."

Nicole reached for Mel's hand.

"Go eat." Mel grabbed his hand back and glared at Nicole. "I'll take care of myself."

"Sure," Nicole said.

She turned and sashayed off stage left, displaying her skull and crossbones tattoo undulating on her backside.

"Turn that spot off," Graham yelled up at Bryce.

The spot light went off immediately.

Graham guided down to the edge of the stage.

"Kevin," Graham whispered. "I want you to go out and get Joel and Anna and take them up to the coffee shop. Joel has to apologize to Mel and remind Anna where our bread is buttered."

"Okay," Kevin agreed.

"I'm taking Mel and Veronica to dinner at the Chinese place. Don't show up there. We don't want another scene."

"What? Veronica's here?" Kevin beamed looking around. "Where?"

"Over there," Graham said, nodding his head in my direction and then calling out to me. "Veronica, you wait. We'll have a working dinner with Mel."

Graham trotted over to Alastair across the stage and had a quick animated interchange with him. Graham gestured emphatically and Alastair jingled his coins. Alastair then followed the actors to the dressing rooms, obviously with marching orders.

Graham headed for the little kitchen where Mel had gone to clean his wound.

* * *

Kevin spotted me and jumped down from the stage and walked towards me with his arms out.

"Veronica. It's been too long."

"I know."

I took a step toward Kevin and held out my arms.

Suddenly, our bodies met in more than a hug. It was an embrace; a long full-body embrace that lasted and lasted. I finally became self-conscious and hoped that I had not been the one who unilaterally and unduly prolonged the greeting. But as I released my hold, Kevin did not. He was glad to see me. Finally, he stood back and held me by the shoulders.

"You look great." Kevin gave a gentlemanly glance to the full length of my slender and fit body. "How have you been?"

"Wonderful," I answered with too broad a smile.

"I was so sorry to hear about your husband," Kevin said releasing me.

I became appropriately subdued and thanked him.

"Let's have dinner soon and catch up," Kevin suggested.

"Love to." I enjoyed looking into Kevin's deep green eyes too much.

"Soon." Kevin started up the center aisle. "I have to go talk some sense into Joel and Anna now, before the production collapses."

I watched Kevin jump back onto the stage like an agile twenty year old. I smiled ear to ear and my heart giggled like a school girl's. Thank God no one saw me.

As he disappeared through the wings, I remembered how much I liked him; how much fun we had always had on stage. I wondered if I was just feeling my character's tender emotions as I had felt them in our play. I didn't know. But one thing I did know was that I was single now and looking for companionship.

I was glad Kevin had suggested dinner. Perhaps he didn't have that girlfriend any longer.

* * *

I got my purse with the script and went out to the lobby and sat in a chair to wait for Graham and Mel for dinner. I dreaded talking about the play, if you could call it that.

The large oak door from the theatre opened.

"Come on, people. One hour. Eat. Look at your third act. You heard Graham. You people should know your lines," Alastair parroted Graham's orders; that was was his job—enforcement.

Alastair marshaled the chattering actors out of the theatre, including Kevin who was obviously lecturing Joel. No one noticed me, at least no one but Nicole.

I heard her telling Geoff about Charlie's death. When our eyes met she smiled, but her ice blue eyes were not friendly. She continued talking about Charlie's death, defying Graham's direct orders.

Since she was Mel's, I now understood how Nicole recognized who I was before. I also understood that her smile was a shot over the bow. She was Mel's current flavor and despite the little tiff on stage, I understood the pecking order. I would not be cutting any of her lines from the play if I could help it.

I gave her a friendly smile back.

Trailing behind the group were Howard Baumgard, a small older man, and Renee Richter, an elegant silvery haired very senior actress.

I had been in several plays with them and liked them both. Renee was, as usual, chatting away. Howard, who was a quiet man by nature, listened attentively with a sparkle in his eyes that I had never seen before. It was obvious he was in love. I didn't know if it was requited love, but I was happy for him.

I chose not too insert myself into their moment by saying hello. They were absorbed in each other.

I noted they went to dinner in the opposite direction of the large group.

I thought of Graham's troupe and the sacrifices they make. To actors rehearsals and performances replace all normal weekend and family life. I rethought my envy of Graham and his New York adventure. I would have missed so much.

While I waited in the empty lobby, I opened the script to act one, scene one. I edited two long speeches down to one sentence and kept going.

⌘

CHAPTER 10

"There's daggers in men's smiles."
-Shakespeare, *Macbeth*, Act 2, Scene 3

At dinner, Graham displayed his masterful manipulation of, and groveling to, Mel. I was hungry and focused on my cashew chicken, steamed brown rice, and green tea.

Mel was all ego, and obviously subsisted on incessant stroking. After I took the edge off my hunger, I decided I should relieve Graham. While Mel finished his second Tsingtao beer and picked at his lobster in oyster sauce with black straw mushrooms, I continued the sucking up at our small corner table. I took my cues from Graham.

"I love the characters," I lied easily for the good of the order. "They are so real they spoke to me immediately."

My lies were born of necessity, much like they were with my writing. I was so gratified when I saw Mel's deep brown eyes sparkle with pleasure that I decided to stretch the truth even more.

"I wish Graham had called me to do a part for you."

"I do too." Mel grinned, baring the virgin white teeth of a teenager—obviously his own, but grossly over bleached. "Next time."

Mel dangled his empty beer bottle at the waiter to signal for another.

"Yes, next time." Graham was transparently pleased that Mel referred to a next time. "Veronica's an excellent actress. An Equity actress."

"I'm impressed." Mel clearly knew that gaining entry into the stage actor's union was hard to achieve, especially here in Los Angeles with all the 99-seat non-union houses.

"She has written five books, too," Graham said, not knowing he was skating onto dangerously thin ice.

"Not really. I'm on my fourth."

I quickly corrected Graham because I believed some truth must be the cornerstone of all lies, especially ones as elaborate as my writing career.

"I know. I found Veronica's internet site," Mel said plainly ready to start the usual competitive writer's interrogation mano-a-mano. "Have you . . ."

"I'm considering several agents as we speak." I arrested Mel's inquiry with bravado and graceful avoidance of all questions containing any variation of the word publish, which I knew was on the tip of Mel's tongue. "But I set everything aside to help Graham out."

"Well, if you need another name I have a few," Mel puffed and poured his third bottle of Tsingtao into his glass. "Beer?"

"Oh. No. No, thank you," I smiled and wondered if he ever huffed and puffed enough to blow his own house down.

Graham interrupted the love-fest.

"We need to talk about the running time of the play."

"So let's talk." Mel sat back and shoved his barely touched plate away. "The lobster's tough."

"Oh?" Graham said. "Too bad."

Mel turned his attention to me, and his beer. "I think every one of my scenes push the plot forward, don't you?"

"I agree from what I've read," I let untruths flow from my mouth unashamedly.

I now understood Graham's uphill battle with this man's vanity and ignorance. I decided to use the audience as a scapegoat to shorten the play.

"And I'm sure the actors don't want any of their lines cut too" I said. "But you know how short an audience's attention span is, Mel."

"Humph," Mel glowered, chugged most of his beer, and ordered a fourth.

"Even if every scene is a gem, we have to do something."

I had transformed into the ultimate suck up, not only for my friend Graham, but also for me. I was an acting junkie and not above taking up Mel on his offer of a part in his next play, whether it was good or bad.

"What do you think, Graham?" I engaged Graham.

"We've pushed the actors as much as we can. There's no give there. Any ideas?" Graham punted the ball back to me while he finished off his steamed rice with sweet and sour pork.

I needed to find a chink in Mel's armor and a way for him to save face. I changed my focus from the audience's attention span to the actors as scapegoats.

"If the actors aren't good enough to speed up the run, we have to cut something or, better yet, condense."

There was little distinction between cutting and condensing, but the latter sounded better.

"Too late to recast," Mel said with resignation drinking his fourth beer. "Too bad too. Because that college kid Tim Matsuda, who plays Joel's friend, says his lines really fast and good."

"I can hardly wait to see him, but we are at the eleventh hour," I countered, definitively rejecting any cast changes.

I was barely able to keep from laughing out loud in the face of Mel's arrogant obtuseness and ridiculousness at equating good acting to speed.

"You know," I added, thinking if Mel did not care about the audience or the actors, he would definitely care about the reviewers. "We don't want the reviewers walking out because it's too long."

"I hadn't considered that."

Mel took a thoughtful pause and then took a long drink of beer.

Graham looked at me, pleased with my tactics and handling of Mel. His happiness, however, was interrupted when Mel slammed his hand down on the table with the abandon of a man who was drinking his dinner.

"All right. We'll cut the worst actors' lines. Anna and Joel," Mel declared loudly, getting more pompous and judgmental with his fourth beer disappearing. "And Howard, the father, cut his. He's terrible."

I was getting angry at this arrogant and malicious man. But I had to cover my anger for Graham's sake. Mel was transparent in his desire for revenge against both Joel and Anna. He was also just as transparent in his disposable attitude toward Howard who was a lonely man living with his mother and dedicated to the theatre.

"It might not be good for the story line to do cuts with that agenda," I cautioned.

"Don't worry. I won't sacrifice my story line. But I want Renee Richter, the mother, cut too. She can't remember her lines and I'm tired of her constant mumbo-jumbo about spirits and ghosts. Nicole told me she was backstage claiming the ghosts got Charlie."

I recognized Nicole was not trustworthy and had indeed selectively "let the cat out of the bag." I also knew that Graham should have explained Charlie's death to the entire troupe.

I glared at Graham to be rescued. I was just a breath away from condemning Nicole's big mouth and then slamming Mel for his devaluation of Renee. Poor Renee had nothing left in life but a studio apartment near the theatre and trying to maintain her dignity by trading on her past. Although I personally doubted ghosts inhabited the theatre, I hoped there was a spiritual justice on earth to get Mel.

"I'll talk to Renee." Graham gave me a cautionary glance as Mel signaled for a fifth beer. "But can you try to keep Nicole under control, Mel?"

"She's fine. It's Renee and that fool Bryce with their ghost stories. Nicole's a smart kid." Mel was defensive and getting more critical and less abandoned as he sipped his fifth beer on his empty stomach. "Ironic. Nicole even complained to me that the girls' dressing room was freezing. Charlie should have gotten a new heater when I told him. He'd be alive."

"It was the vent, not the heater." Graham was agitated that Mel would not cooperate by talking to Nicole.

"So what?" Mel retorted pompously, taking his prerogative and having the last word. "What's the difference? Bottom line his own heater killed him."

I stepped in and changed the subject before Graham butted heads with his deep-pocketed angel.

"Back to the play," I said. "Just give me a day to redline some things."

"Redline?" Mel zeroed in on me.

"I can use another color." I chuckled.

Graham laughed heartily and, after a pause, Mel broke into laughter too.

I stared at Mel's face. It was not able to consummate his laughter because it was over-botoxed and over-stretched to smooth out his labial folds and jowls. In profile, I also saw his nose was over-reduced by some well-paid but knife happy plastic surgeon. This was a man in his forties who aspired to be twenty again. But the only thing youthful I saw was a pimple on his chin and his snow-white teeth.

"Look, Veronica," Mel said, leaning over the table to me and shoving his plate further until it hit Graham's. "I'm no fool. We can't fire anyone with opening night Friday and a possible Preview Thursday. But I want Joel, Anna's, Renee's, and Howard's lines hacked first."

"I'm on board."

I smiled while I internally condemned Graham for bringing me into this festering hornet's nest. I knew in a pinch the Preview could be cancelled. It was for special guests and reviewers who couldn't make opening night.

"I should have taken Howard's role and done it myself. I still could . . . Naw. I'm too busy. I'm pitching a pilot project next week and I'm trying to fund a movie I wrote." Mel postured and embellished his own beer-enhanced importance.

"Impressive." I sucked up even more because I recognized how dispensable we all were to Mel.

"Sure. And, oh yeah, see if you can beef up Nicole's part. She's good," Mel smiled at Graham and winked.

Graham pasted a smile across his chubby face.

"Right." I did too, knowing his favoritism had nothing to do with her acting ability.

Graham reached over and touched my knee under the table to make sure I didn't make any comments about Mel's extra-curricular activities with Nicole. I forced my smile to stay in place.

Mel signaled for the check and put his credit card on the table.

"Good meeting. I'll get this one."

"If we are having more meetings, maybe we should stay Dutch," I said reaching for my purse.

"You can get the next one." Mel finished every drop of his beer.

"All right."

I had to back down, but I preferred to pay my own way, especially when I ate out with men. Men had big expensive appetites that dwarfed mine and this one really enjoyed drinking.

"So, Graham, you think with that cheap-skate Charlie gone someone may actually spend some money fixing up the theatre?" Mel smirked.

"It'd be nice. But you don't want to pay more rent for this production."

"I won't."

Graham had tested the waters to see if Mel was amenable to a a rent increase and he wasn't. Graham knew he had to make some cash at the box office.

"Gentlemen, a man is dead," I chastised these men's ill-timed condemnation of Charlie. "And it's late. We'd better go."

"Here's my card." Mel handed me his business card with a B.A. and J.D. after his name followed by a panoply of the various hats to which he aspired or claimed to wear, including producer-writer-director. "Give me yours and I'll email you the script. Use tracking so I can accept or reject the changes when you email it back."

"Sounds efficient."

Now that I had met Mel, I was ecstatic he had no expectation that we would sit together and discuss each change to be made. It would all be done by email.

I took out my carefully designed business card with a B.A. after my name followed by the word "Mysterian." This was a label I had carefully picked and the sole hat that I comfortably wore. It avoided all authorial and publication issues because it was specific and witty, yet vague. Simply put it avoided the issue of setting myself forth as a published author.

Graham smiled. "I knew you two would hit it off."

I bit my lip to keep from laughing out loud.

⌘

CHAPTER 11

"Now is the winter of our discontent."
-Shakespeare, *King Richard III*, Act 1, Scene 1

Back at the theatre, I sat with Mel in the third row, my script open and pencil poised to redline the third act. The entire cast was assembled on stage.

Before the rehearsal started Graham stood in the center aisle and gave a stirring oration on cooperation. He announced Charlie's tragic accident, but only because Nicole had forced his hand. There was no reaction by the cast because, during the dinner break, Nicole had made it old news to everyone. After Graham's assurances that the theatre was safe, he closed with the old show business cliché "the show must go on."

Unfortunately, Joel and Mel just glared at each other the whole time.

Defeated by the evening, Graham turned to me and introduced me with unexpected and overdone accolades. I was evidently tantamount to the Second

Coming of Christ—an adrenaline shot injected through Graham's eloquence into a dying body of performers.

I saw hope on the younger actors' faces who actually believed Graham.

The old war horses, however, simply smiled politely.

From the stage Renee put her hand up to block the lights. Her dark, almost black eyes landed on me. She gave me a charming wave.

I loved Renee's silver hair that sparkled under the lights. In her youth, Renee was a Broadway ingénue with a short and not well-reviewed career. When she immigrated to Hollywood, she spent years doing bit parts in studio films and non-paying independent films. Finally, she turned to waitressing by day. By night she traded on a touched up headshot and her Broadway vetting to get parts at 99-seat non-equity houses. It filled her otherwise empty life.

Howard stood next to Renee. He bent his portly body and bowed to me.

Howard's display of respect exposed his bald spot that he always plastered over, inadequately, with long dark dyed hairs. Howard was an unattractive man with a large nose who worshipped the theatre and now evidently worshipped Renee. He made a bare living doing theatrical publicity and happily took every small role Graham gave him just to be part of the process.

The large role of the father in Mel's play was a real plum for him.

* * *

The house lights went down, the stage lights went up, and the third act began. I read along with difficulty in the dark and noted "bring flashlight" on the first page of the script.

Although this was an off-book rehearsal, Alastair had to feed everyone lines--everyone but Geoff and Kevin. They were professionals, the only consummate ones in the cast. I was intrigued watching Kevin play his evil character. He was very good at it.

During the run, I caught Mel salaciously riveted on Anna's tanned stomach topped by her bulging red sweater. Mel ignored Nicole despite her upstaging the leads by crossing on their lines. I knew enough about Nicole to know she was doing it on purpose. Crossing on another actor's line is never done unless there is an important reason on a rare occasion. It draws attention away from the actor speaking.

I smiled. Nicole was certainly making the most of her minuscule maid's part. She was ad-libbing more lines as she spoke, creating endless business, and standing in the hot spots.

I laughed to myself. She reminded me of me.

* * *

All of a sudden the laborious but forward moving rehearsal came to a grinding halt. Renee forgot her long monologue. She put her hand over her eyes breaking character and the fourth wall to speak to Graham in the front row.

"I need to use my script," Renee demanded. "I can't remember anything."

"I don't believe this," Mel said, turning to me, far too loudly and obviously still animated by his liquid dinner. "I should get rid of her."

"Don't worry. I'll cut her lines down. At least, this monologue," I whispered in a low voice to calm him. "Let me focus now on rehearsal."

Mel was angry. He got up and went to stand at the back of the theatre.

"Renee, you're doing fine." Graham reassured her from the first row. "Let's keep going. We've got to get through this act tonight. Geoff, give Renee her cue."

"'Come with me . . ,'" Geoff repeated, cueing Renee with his line right before her monologue.

Renee stood silently in her spot, left of center stage. She looked down at the stage and didn't move or speak.

"Line," Renee called as she raised her chin indignantly, exposing her drooping jowls.

The stage lights cast a shadow accentuating her deep bags and wrinkled face.

From the wings Alastair prompted Renee with her line slowly. "'I . . . just . . . don't . . . know . . . if . . . we . . . should . . . force . . .'"

"I just don't know if we should force her to . . . ," Renee parroted and then stomped her foot breaking character again. "Graham, I can't concentrate with Charlie passing to the other side . . . all this fighting . . . the negative energies . . . the incorporeal beings . . . and apparitions watching . . . I've played Broadway and never . . ."

"Get off your high horse, lady." Nicole laughed crossing center stage over to Renee. "Admit it. You just don't know your lines."

"Don't worry, Renee. Just take a minute," Anna said from her Victorian chair upstage.

Just then a low abrupt rumble came from the narrow crossover behind the black velour upstage traveler, the bi-parting curtain used at the back of the stage to hide scenery or the cyclorama.

"What was that?" Renee said backing away from the sound and bumping into Nicole. "Who's back there?"

"Watch out." Nicole pushed Renee away and then taunted her. "Oooooo . . . Charlie's ghost is coming for you."

"Leave her alone, Nicole." Anna got up from her chair and crossed to Renee. "Don't worry, Renee, it just the junk shifting back there."

Graham's precarious stockpile of props and set furniture from old plays sometimes shifted rousing cockroaches and rats from their backstage homes.

"Get back to your chair." Nicole shoved Anna.

"Nicole, stop. We don't need any of that going on. Please." Graham was red-faced and angry but he moderated his tone because she was still Mel's flavor-of-the-month with a special status. "And, Anna, get back to your chair. Renee, Scott is probably working in the scene dock and making noise. It's nothing. Everyone get back to your places."

"Yeah, Anna," Nicole said viciously.

Suddenly, above Renee's head, up in the lighting trusses, there was a metallic scrape and rattle.

"What is . . ." Renee asked looking up.

"Watch out! The lights!" Howard yelled.

He jumped forward with his little barrel body propelled by his spindly legs. He pushed Renee out of the way into Kevin.

Renee screamed as Kevin caught her slight body catapulting into him.

Howard landed face down with his head at Renee's feet.

"Are you nuts?" Renee shrieked getting her balance and pulling herself out of Kevin's hold. "You could kill some one."

"It's only a light up there creaking." Tim studied the lighting above.

Joel burst out laughing at Howard and everyone joined in; everyone but Tim who was embarrassed for Howard, Kevin who never acted unprofessionally under the lights and Geoff who was RADA.

I hate to admit that I did smile. I couldn't help it. Howard's rescue of Renee would have been heroic if a heavy light had actually fallen and snapped its safety cord. But with no light plummeting to the stage, it was simply comedic in its monumental disproportionality.

"I can't believe this," Mel grimaced, seething as he sat back down in his seat next to me. "We open in a few days."

"I can't either," I muttered.

I knew now what Graham was up against. I had never seen such unprofessional conduct and such open hostility between two actresses as between Anna and Nicole.

On stage Nicole walked over, stood over Howard still spread out face down on the black painted floor boards, and taunted him with her hand on her hip.

"Howard the hero."

"All right. All right, people. Enough. Get back to your places," Graham ordered.

"I can't. Howard's lying in mine," Nicole rejoined, howling at her own joke and taking all the prerogatives of a woman who was in a relationship with the author and backer of the play.

"Stop, Nicole," Anna yelled, tired of Nicole taking advantage of her status.

"Oh, shut-up. You laughed too." Nicole lashed, squaring up face-to-face with Anna. "Don't you belong in your chair?"

Anna stood her ground.

* * *

"Cat fight." Mel turned to me and grinned with heavy stale beer breath. "It would be more interesting than Renee's acting. You had better slash her part, Veronica."

"I will," I answered, glancing into his angry dark eyes and then turning back to the stage to avoid his intensity and bad breath.

Graham yelled. "All of you just stop."

Nicole and Anna's stand-off ended with a whimper.

Anna went back to the Victorian chair where she spent a good part of the third act.

There was silence. Kevin helped Howard get up.

Howard did not look at anyone, least of all Renee. He walked back to his position stage left and brushed off his clothes. He timidly reached up and checked that his lacquered down hair had not moved to reveal more of his bald spot. Satisfied that it hadn't, he put his hand by his side.

"We'll pick up at Renee's speech," Graham called out. "Give her the cue, Geoff."

As Renee struggled through her long speech, Mel shifted impatiently in his seat.

I watched Howard. He was embarrassed and dejected. He looked at Renee with a hurt and sadness that was very personal. It had nothing to do with his character. The happiness and love for Renee I had seen in Howard's eyes earlier was gone.

Graham had finally had enough. "It's late. You people go home and learn your lines. We're done. Act one tomorrow."

As Bryce started to close down the stage lights, every one left quickly, including Mel paired with Nicole

Graham and I trailed slowly up the center aisle together without saying a word. At the lobby door, Graham turned to me with a weary look.

"I'm so glad you're here, dear," he said giving me a squeeze.

Suddenly, we heard a loud crash from the stage. Graham let me go and we both looked back at the stage which was still lit with general lighting. A heavy Fresnel light had fallen on the Victorian chair where

Anna had been sitting. The disconnected safety cable swung above.

"Bryce," Graham bellowed.

⌘

CHAPTER 12

"We know what we are, but know not what we may be."
-Shakespeare, *Hamlet*, Act 4, Scene 5

Sunday morning I got up as usual at four in the morning to darkness. That hour was my nemesis. I lingered for a moment and thought of the tranquil Sunday mornings with my husband reading the paper then going to brunch or very infrequently his local Catholic church. The activities were interchangeable to us because we were members but not religious.

But then those days were gone. I got up now to the days that were solely mine.

"Good morning," I greeted my overnight companion, the classic movie channel.

It was a "good" morning compared to the last seven months. At least, I wouldn't need my recalcitrant muse because I was editing another author's play. I pushed the TV off button, threw on my usual jeans and beige cashmere sweater, and headed for the kitchen and my morning tea.

On my way down the hall, I glanced at the carbon monoxide detector my husband had installed in the hall near our heater. I decided to get a plug-in one for the women's dressing room at the theatre. Mel's self-aggrandizing vanity production seemed to be ill-fated. Not only had Charlie been gassed, but I had never seen, or for that matter heard of, a Fresnel light falling without its safety chain in place to stop its descent to the stage.

In my study with my tea, I was uneasy. I was now a sought-after editor of plays. This burgeoning aspect of my authorial life into playwright, or at least play editor, status was not comfortable like my well-honed mystery writer status. But I had to pull this charade off for Graham, my theatre friends, and myself.

Graham and the Valentine Theatre were my last outlets for my acting addiction. At my age and self-admitted mid, if not low, range acting talents I was dead-ended at the Valentine with his troupe. After so many years away from the theatre, when I had first met with Graham at the Valentine, my long fallow acting juices flowed. I shamelessly promoted myself that night until Graham put me in front of the proverbial "footlights." As a matter of practicality, for good or ill I would never go on the audition circuit again.

I thought back to the very bad plays I had read or performed in. Then, I recollected the excellent ones like the much-worshipped "Scottish Play," namely

Shakespeare's *Macbeth* as non-theatre people would say. I hoped I could edit Mel's mess.

"There's no time like the present," I announced to myself—my rusty archaic playwright self.

I muted my cell phone to dig into my work, not that I'd get any calls at this hour anyway.

I opened Mel's email with his play attachment. The email read, "Waiting to review suggestions." His use of the word "suggestions" was a not-so-subtle reminder that he was in control. After meeting him, however, I didn't need a reminder.

The email was sent at two-thirty this morning.

I surmised Nicole had occupied him until then.

* * *

As the overcast fall day emerged, I rearranged, condensed, and slashed repetitive chunks of dialogue and monologues. To please our angel, Mel, I also added lines for Tim and Nicole, repetitive or not.

As it turned out, it was a relief to focus on someone else's writing instead of being tortured by my own.

I was happily divorced from the recalcitrant protagonist in my fourth book. This delightful female lawyer who had activated my muse and then turned from a delight into a shrew. She killed my muse and mocked me with her silence. She had quickly and abruptly quit me, my mystery, and her proposed destiny. Now, I no longer needed her.

I was content editing Mel's play.

* * *

Mid-morning, I unmuted my cell and checked my messages. Friends had called, but not Kevin. I knew he still had my number, however. All theatre people kept their phone lists from past productions. They were invaluable for industry contacts.

By eleven, I had edited my edits for the first two acts and eaten a turkey sandwich.

I took a break and sent an email to my long-time writing teacher Mavis Osborne. I now had a perfect excuse not to attend her classes. I stretched the truth and used my new gig as "play editor" to bow out. I left my return date open ended. For months I had been embarrassed with my writer's block and being devoid of any manuscript pages. Besides, I conveniently rationalized that Graham would need editing help even after opening night, and also an assistant wrangler for this unusually rowdy cast.

Even if Graham didn't need any further help with the script, I would be his audience or even sink to helping the baby actresses backstage with wardrobe changes. I simply didn't want to return to class. Writer's block was normal for most writers but not for me. I had the reputation of being prolific while simultaneously searching out just the right agent. After all, I was on the verge of being published.

I knew if my muse did not return, I needed to hide even longer than this play editing gig might last. I could hide from my muse and my classes, after the holidays, at a writers conference. There amongst strangers, with a clean slate, I would present my exaggerated persona anew. Or, with luck, I might disappear into Graham's next production if there was a role for me.

I hated to give up my regular class and Mavis, who I thought of as a friend, but I couldn't go back empty-handed with no new manuscript pages.

After I finished Mavis's email, I called Graham to update him on the edits and, yes, to suck up.

"My savior, how's it going?" Graham asked optimistically.

"Good. Actually."

I had surprised myself that morning, but didn't reveal that.

"I'm so pleased. I knew you were the answer."

"Did you get Charlie's cousin?"

"Yes. She's taking the body up north to bury."

"No memorial here?"

"I don't know. They'll do what they want." Graham changed the subject. "Where are you in the play?"

I had experienced many deaths, aside from my husband's, but I had never seen less note taken of someone's passing. Graham was like a machine and only focused on his impending opening. Charlie was a forgotten irritation.

"I'm getting there. It isn't as bad as I thought."

"Are you kidding?"

"Not the play," I corrected myself. "The editing. Editing is much easier than writing. And the play is salvageable."

"Thank you, dear. I owe you."

"I'll think of something." I knew Graham had a short memory for his indebtedness so repay was doubtful.

"Are you almost done?"

"Well, you can always keep editing."

I was thinking of my books and painfully aware how that was true only if you actually started the editing process.

"Don't be coy, dear."

"I'm done with the first two acts."

"Unbelievable," Graham said with genuine surprise.

"I'm still worried about Mel accepting the changes. He's a wild card."

"He's too lazy to do his own editing. You've handled him marvelously so far. If he accepts half your cuts, we'll be fine."

"Glad to help. Just look for a part for me in the next production. I've missed you."

I didn't disclose that I needed a prolonged escape from my authorial life.

"I will." Graham quickly moved on to his present agenda. "Did you cut Joel's and Anna's lines?"

"Some, but they are major characters. Mel's going to have to accept that fact or write a different play."

"We can only hope he'll be more rational today."

"On the upside, I did give more lines to Tim and Nicole. But truthfully, Nicole's whole maid part could be cut out completely."

"Don't even think that."

"I know. I know. But I did take care of Renee and Howard. I got rid of three of their tete-a-tete's and cut their long monologues. Most of Renee's lines are one word responses now."

"Good. Secretly she will be grateful. I won't cast her again in a major role."

"Next time call me. I can play older characters." I was not shy at all about foraging to satisfy my addiction to the stage and escape my authorial life. "Renee may be old Broadway but I can remember lines."

"She seemed so right paired with Howard. Like you and Kevin in that play you did. But poor Howard would still have his lines if I had cast you."

"I know. I hated cutting the biggest part Howard ever had."

Graham sat silently for a moment, but only a moment.

"Forget it. Mel's the angel who financed this. Just get something back to him by two and you'll be my savior."

"Graham, you're giving me too much credit."

I discreetly failed to mention, too much pressure, too.

"Oh, I almost forgot. We're meeting Mel at five at the French restaurant up the block from the theatre. We've eaten there a few times. Remember?"

"Right."

I knew the restaurant was pricey and anticipated being stuck with the bill.

"I'll announce the cuts before the rehearsal and hand out new scripts tonight. Now I have to go and find a Victorian gramophone for the second act. Playwrights shouldn't write in such hard-to-find props," Graham grumbled, with the irritation of a director under the gun. "You don't happen to have one do you?"

I laughed.

"No, I don't. You are going to kill yourself trying to be authentic someday," I remarked and then had an epiphany. "I'm editing the play! I'll get rid of it. Mel won't notice and if he does I'll handle him."

My easy solution hadn't occurred to Graham. He was always obsessed with authenticity, but I had observed the older he got and, quite frankly, the heavier, the more he was willing to compromise. I was happy to give him a remedy and license to do it.

"You're brilliant. Why don't I think of these things? Thank you, dear. See you at five."

"Wait. Have you talked to Bryce about that light last night?"

"I called him, but he just started in on that ghost business."

"That's ridiculous. He's got to be more careful. C-clamps can't give way and Fresnels don't just fall."

"I told him I'd fire him if he got high again."

"Sure." I snickered because I knew Bryce wouldn't stop getting high and Graham could never afford anyone else.

"I told Bryce to double check all the lighting this afternoon before rehearsal. He's getting Scott and Nicole to help him, but not telling them why. I guess they helped him put up the lights," Graham added quickly. "But I told him to keep his mouth shut about the falling Fresnel. You too. I don't need more trouble with Renee. She's so skittish."

"Well, you know Scott has a megaphone mouth."

I knew that Scott had no discretion and indiscriminately talked to make himself look important. Once, he even gave investment advice to a stock broker in the lobby after the show, referring erroneously to bank certificates of deposits as stocks.

"Don't borrow trouble, Veronica. We need the man power. I'll see you at five."

Graham hung up abruptly.

I was not offended. His nerves would only get worse as opening night approached. I would be surprised if he didn't have a heart attack.

* * *

I edited the third act quickly. I deleted the lines I had already marked at last night's rehearsal before Renee's melt-down. I didn't edit Mel's climax. It was unexpectedly tight and hard-hitting.

When I finished, I emailed the edited play back to Mel. The ball was in his court now.

I took a break. I snacked on tea, water crackers, and cheddar cheese, as I perused read the play program.

Tim Matsuda had graduated recently from a local college where he did major roles outside his ethnicity, which was a trend in theatre. Anna and Joel were graduates of Yale's renowned School of Drama. Nicole had no training, minor roles in 99-seat theatres, and some movie extra experience. She was below Graham's standards, but up to Mel's. Geoff, since RADA, had collected impressive London theatre and British television credits. I didn't understand what he was doing at the haunted, dilapidated Valentine Theatre in Hollywood's small theatre milieu.

I tried to rest for an hour, but Mel's characters tormented me as much as my own. I would never ghost-edit again. I decided I preferred my own creative hell , which I would have to expand to editing. I would have to join the writers who actually edited and submitted to agents and publishers or on their own published independently on the internet and were known as "indy" authors

Either way, to be a published writer, "indy" or traditional, was to be a self-editor or have the money to hire editors: copy editors for grammar, spelling, and the like; technical editors for coding digital publications; line editors for the flow of ideas and rearranging content; structural editors for your narrative arc, point of view, voice, character development, and the like; development or story editors to work to flesh out your book ideas, plot, and characters; and perhaps a writing coach for the obvious.

I personally knew I couldn't afford any of these people. Therefore, sooner than later I alone would have to not only self-edit, but probably put myself on the line with the thousands of other "indy" writers and self publish. With the advent of electronic books that miraculously uploaded to electronic readers, more and more authors, including some of the prolific and even some of the greats were publishing independently. The world of the traditional publishing houses and literary agents was going the way of typewriters, snail mail, and dinosaurs.

Enough! All these thoughts were onerous and overwhelming.

I hated this introspection spawned by Mel and got up to ready myself for rehearsal.

I had experience on how to dress for the Valentine Theatre. It was cold in the winter and hot in the summer thanks to poor Charlie's lack of maintenance and care.

I put on black jeans and a heavy green sweater. I packed my old black canvas theatre bag with a hat and gloves, jacket, flashlight, waters, can of peanuts for energy, my driver's license, and a well-worn black leather change purse with a few dollars and one credit card. I had learned the hard way not to leave my purse lying around with any real money in it.

I was ready early.

With the extra time, on the way I stopped and bought the carbon monoxide detector. Then, I decided get cookies at Cookies, Inc. near the Beverly Center. They made great gooey, soft cookies, among them Howard's favorite oatmeal raisin.

I felt good about myself as I parked near the Valentine Theatre. It was Sunday and there was no parking limit or meter feeds.

I grabbed my theatre bag and walked to the little French restaurant not far up the street.

⌘

CHAPTER 13

"He hath eaten me out of house and home."
-Shakespeare, *King Henry IV, Part II*, Act 2, Scene 1

Even with a stop at the hardware store and Cookies, Inc., I got to the French restaurant at twenty to five.

"Welcome." The hostess interrupted her paperwork and greeted me more harried than friendly. "How many?"

"Three. And we are having a dinner meeting so can we please have a larger table?"

"Sure."

She took me to a larger back corner table. There was a wide choice since the entire place was pre-dinner empty and there was no one at the little bar in the front.

The restaurant had charm, but a careful look showed that its try for "shabby chic" ended with "shabby." The thin, white non-linen table cloths did not sufficiently mask the old tottering round wood tables. The mismatched small chairs also failed to achieve the rustic, quaint ambiance intended. They were simply junk and too rickety for most people of girth.

I switched chairs from other tables to get three larger ones and arranged the largest for Graham to sit in. I put my theatre bag on the floor at my feet.

There were only two other patrons. An older couple, sitting at the front window. They were enjoying themselves as couples do. As I had for many fond years before my husband died. I mused that my husband would have laughed at my preposterous posing as an author. But I also believed he would have been proud of my tenacious reformulation of my life; a life which might someday be validated with my publication of at least one book.

I studied the expensive menu, printed in French with parenthetical English explanations following. I wouldn't have predicted that this hole in the wall would have survived charging the high prices it did.

I shifted my chair several times to stop it from rocking, but finally gave up.

* * *

Graham arrived before five. He breathlessly ran the gauntlet of narrow aisles. His large body rubbed several of the permanent press table cloths out of position.

"Hello, dear. You're early." Graham approached.

"So are you."

I stood and, with the requisite animated enthusiasm of the theatre world, accepted Graham's usual bear hug.

"I'm surprised I even got here." Graham sat in the chair I had chosen for him—a chair which, despite my care, still loudly complained about his weight. "It's been a horrible afternoon."

"Oh, no. What now?"

"I was at the theatre and the gas company showed up again. This time with some city inspector. They asked me questions, you know, about the leak."

"Well, someone did die you know."

"I told them I was just a renter and didn't know anything."

"That's fair," I reassured Graham. "Speaking of the leak, I dropped by and got a carbon monoxide detector for that heater."

"Thank you, dear. You know so much about so many things."

Graham smiled and then was quiet.

"What's wrong?"

"I was just thinking of fate. Evidently, the vent wasn't knocked apart by the boxes. The gas man said someone took out the screws and didn't put them back. The vent slipped or was never properly put back in place."

"You're kidding?"

"No I'm not. I told him I didn't know any thing about any repairs."

"Poor Charlie," I sighed. "He cut too many corners with cut rate repairs."

I applauded myself that my instincts last night told me that Charlie's death could use a look-see. My investigative nature had been justifiably piqued. Although I hadn't followed through, the officials had. It was enough for me that I superb detecting radar and had noted the suspicious nature of this nonfictional, real death.

"Or was Charlie playing repair man himself? Who knows?" Graham said. "The gas guy was an officious, pompous idiot and the city inspector was no better."

"So a carelessly wielded screw driver caused Charlie's demise and not the toppling boxes?"

"Looks like."

"Too bad," I said, still delighted with my talents.

"I know, but life goes on. And so must our show. Remember, mum's the word."

"My lips are sealed," I agreed, knowing my lips being sealed was irrelevant to the information grapevine at the Valentine.

I had more questions about the vent, but they had to wait. It was safe for now and my carbon monoxide detector would be the back up. That had to suffice.

"Now, tell me," Graham said. "Were you able to cut enough from the third act?"

"Of course. I cut and slashed. The third act was almost nothing but repetition."

"I'm so glad you became an author." Graham patted my hand resting on the table and picked up his menu. "I knew you were the right person for the job."

"Thanks." I beamed at the accolades for my authorial status.

"You should write an original now. Mel seems to like you. Who knows? He could be your angel for it." Graham did not take his eyes off the menu.

"Not today." I mused in the back of my mind that maybe playwriting was my calling.

"What and who did you cut in the third act?"

"Don't worry. I catered to Mel's vindictiveness."

"Good. You had no choice. And no one can say much." Graham glanced up from the menu. "In the end Renee will be grateful for the cuts, but only after she publicly protests, and even if Howard's upset, he won't complain. He never does."

"Sadly, I know."

"Did you add more lines for Nicole and Tim in the third act?"

"Yes."

"Excellent. That will please Mel."

"Speak of the devil."

I smiled and waved at Mel coming at us in caffeinated double-time, carrying a box.

* * *

"Good evening." Mel grabbed the last seat and put the box on the floor between Graham and him. "The final scripts."

"Final?" Graham smiled. "Wonderful."

"I emailed it back to you, Veronica. Did you get it?"

"I must have left." I wondered if he had accepted my edits.

"Apparently. Am I late or did you two set up an early secret meeting to talk about me?"

Mel proceeded to eyeball his silverware and then rubbed one fork with his napkin. He put the napkin back on the table and not on his lap.

"That might have been fun, but we just arrived too." I recoiled at his egocentrism and poor table manners.

Although everyone in Hollywood was to some extent an egocentric, Mel was such an unaccomplished, extreme one it was particularly annoying.

"I like this lady. Good sense of humor." Mel signaled the one visible waiter lurking near the kitchen door. "We'll have the Chateau Gruaud Larose St. Julien 1983. Three glasses."

"Not for me." Graham put his menu down.

Graham rarely if ever imbibed and never when he was working. And tonight he would be working hard.

"Come on . . . a toast with my favorite cabernet to the writer who cut what I could not," Mel insisted with over-caffeinated intensity.

"Sure." I planned on just a sip because I was going to have to make sure the revised play worked.

"Bring three glasses, garçon," Mel commanded.

"Then you liked the changes?" I put my white linen napkin on my lap.

"I pushed the accept button on most of them . . . some I fine tuned . . . not many."

"That's wonderful." Graham was relieved. "Thanks for getting. . ."

"Hold on," Mel interrupted, pulling his cell phone out of his pants pocket. He looked at it annoyed and then answered it in a low voice. "I'm in a meeting. We'll talk later."

Graham finished his sentence. "Thanks for getting them printed out."

"No problem," Mel said, turning his attention to the waiter who came with the wine.

The waiter poured Mel a taste. Mel ceremoniously swirled it in his glass and smelled it. He then took a sip, held it in his mouth, and swished it around with his cheeks rhythmically bulging.

I watched him and laughed inside. My husband appreciated and drank wines. He taught me that when you order in a restaurant you are supposed to taste to make sure the wine remained properly corked. This taste takes one second and does not involve the facial gymnastics Mel just went through. Those machinations are for comparative wine tastings only, like the lovely wine tasting parties we used to go to officiated by a wine sommelier.

As he swallowed, Mel nodded for the waiter to pour. Graham turned his glass over and took none. I signaled for a little.

"When you write something you love, it is impossible to cut with such brutality." Mel raised his eyebrows at Veronica.

"We had no choice." I wondered if eventually I would have to do the same to my books.

"Besides, I didn't have the time. I may have funding for my movie."

"That's exciting,"

I pasted a forced smile on my face. I hated this man. I hated him even more now. He sounded like me. He made faux excuses for not editing his play just like I did with my books. But the difference was that he had gotten my free help to edit his. I couldn't get that nor could I afford to pay someone to edit my books. It would not only put a crimp in my budget, but I admitted to myself it would also sap the joy out of my free and fun author persona.

"She's wonderful. So many talents," Graham said. "There's no one more multi-talented."

"I'll second that. To Veronica." Mel raised his glass and took a long drink of wine like a marathon runner drinking water after a race. "If I need help on my other projects I may call you."

"Yes." Graham raised his water glass, took a sip, and then picked up the menu again to indulge his own addiction.

"Thank you."

I took a very small sip of my wine with no intention of drinking the rest or helping him edit anything else.

"Let's order," Mel said, filling his glass again and not gesturing, let alone offering, to refill anyone else's.

I ordered first and got the onion soup and the smoked salmon and dill crepes. Graham chose the country pâté with black truffles to start and for dinner a roast pork loin with red wine truffle sauce, white bean ragout, and frisée salad. Mel ordered the mesclun salad with champagne vinaigrette and prosciutto, fontina cheese, and truffle stuffed fillet mignon in a red wine truffle sauce.

By the time we were through with our starters and the plates cleared, Graham had eaten the entire basket of French bread, Mel had slurped down half the bottle of wine, and I had learned more about Mel than I ever wanted to know.

* * *

When Mel and I got our entrees, I waited for Graham to be served and sadly watched my wonderful crepes cooling down. Mel, however, just dug into his steaming filet the minute the waiter set it down. When Graham was served, I began. Graham grabbed the salt and shook it vigorously over his entire dinner before he even tasted it.

"We'll start from the top tonight and do a complete run-through with the new scripts in hand . . . no breaks," Graham said, taking his first bite of pork loin. "Hmmm, this is magnificent"

"You know the cast will need a break," I said.

"Forget it. Who cares what the talent wants. We need a timed run," Mel said while gnawing open-mouthed on his mouth-full of filet and truffle sauce. "How's your crepes?"

"Wonderful." I lied. They were lukewarm and needed to be hot.

I avoided looking directly at Mel's mastication, born of wine-relaxed table training which was questionable to begin with.

"Thanks for getting rid of Renee's big monologues and her drawn out boring scenes with Howard. She's over the hill and he can't act his way out of a paper bag." Mel was getting louder and more rude and judgmental with each gulp of wine. Observing him minute by minute made me feel more and more like downing my short glass of wine and then chugalugging the rest of the bottle.

"The monologues were just unnecessary to the story," I said diplomatically.

I was repulsed by Mel's license to degrade Renee just because he was able to finance his play with his windfall fee from the city settlement. I refrained from telling him that long monologues were usually written by amateur authors without skills or craft enough to write dialogue. The amateurs do character studies and then put them in plays as monologues just because they "wrote" them and didn't have the heart to discard them.

"You should have cut more of Joel and Anna." Mel finished his dinner and pushed his plate away. "But good job on Tim's new lines and Nicole's."

"Thanks."

I stuck to monosyllabic responses while Mel continued his character assassination of anyone not in his good graces. After all, money did make him the king of the converted funeral home known as the Valentine Theatre.

By the time we finished dinner, Mel had killed the bottle of cabernet and Graham another half basket of bread slathered with butter. I couldn't finish my crepes and keep Mel happy too. Not only was Mel's demand for ego stroking intensified with his libation, but Graham withdrew from the conversation entirely, engrossed in his meal.

"Three espressos and the check." Mel looked at his cell phone time. "And a Drambuie. Anyone else for an after dinner libation?"

I shook my head no, but inside screamed for a double.

Graham checked his watch.

"It's late. Nothing for me. I've got to open the theatre. See you there."

Graham bent over precariously in the wobbly chair and grabbed the box of scripts off the floor. He made an abrupt exit without another word or a mention of the dinner check.

He ambled out carefully through the tables, now populated with a few more diners. He made it almost to the door and the end of the gauntlet without brushing against the tables. Then, he bumped the last two empty tables almost dragging the tablecloths with him and nearly sending the place settings to the floor.

* * *

I turned my attention back to Mel. I racked my mind for something to talk about besides him.

"I am so full," I said. "I wish I had room for dessert. I saw that couple's and . . ."

"Excuse me."

Mel's cell phone signaled a text message and he read it

"Sure." I was glad to be ignored as Mel read his text.

Our waiter brought two espressos, Mel's Drambuie, and set the small black leather folder with the check inside in the middle of the table. Mel went for the Drambuie the minute the waiter set it down, ignoring the check that he had run up with booze. I ignored the check and justifiably so.

I sipped my espresso. I would have preferred decaf tea but needed the jolt. I was already drained and the night had yet to begin.

Neither of us touched the check. It was a standoff.

"Good little restaurant." Mel put his phone on the table and leaned back in his chair, wine-relaxed and happy with himself. "Now, tell me, do you think . . . ?"

Mel's cell phone now rang, interrupting his question. He looked at the incoming number and, animated by his consumption of alcohol, blurted, "Damn. Let me take care of this."

Mel took another drink of his Drambuie and then answered his phone. "What! I got your text."

Then he listened impatiently.

I heard Nicole yelling on Mel's cell from across the table. Mel turned down the volume.

"Stop bitching at me, Nicole. I said I got all your texts this afternoon too. It's too close to the opening night."

I smiled nicely. I decided I'd leave if he didn't. Lover's spats were not my forte, unless they were mine.

"I've got to deal with this. Your turn." Mel slid the leather encased check into my espresso cup and saucer. "See you at the theatre."

Mel finished his Drambuie and then stood and started his exit through the tables.

"I'll meet you there, Nicole," Mel spoke loudly into his cell phone as he stood by his chair with imbibed unsteadiness. "But I can't get rid of Anna now. You got more lines so what are you complaining about? Nicole . . . Wait . . . Damn it. I . . ."

As Mel wound through the restaurant tables, he got more agitated. The other diners glared at him.

I understood now exactly what that beautiful blonde wanted from Mel—Anna's lead role.

I opened the black leather folder and read the check. It was five times the amount of the Chinese dinner the day before. Most of it was Mel's wine, Graham's truffle dishes, and Mel's Drambuie.

No more dinners with them, I decided as I got my credit card out of the change purse in my theatre bag. I slid my credit card into the leather case with the check.

I stayed and finished my espresso. I looked at Mel's untouched espresso I had paid for.

I saw the older couple at the window leave

holding hands. I yearned to find that again and decided to ask Kevin about our dinner.

⌘

CHAPTER 14

"What 's done is done."
-Shakespeare, *Macbeth*, Act 3, Scene 3

I started back to the theatre well ahead of call time, thanks to Nicole's cell-phone attack on Mel.

I relished in the thought that Mel was being tormented by Nicole. He deserved it, he had made promises he never kept. Now, even if he wanted to, it was too close to opening night for any novice actor like her to learn a lead. I had seen a very experienced, very intelligent actor do it once, but with the help of a skilled prompter in the wings. That was not the Nicole I had observed.

I got my cookies and other things from the my car and hurried to the Valentine.

As I approached, I saw the proverbial theatre smoking klatch was on the steps: Bryce, Alastair, and Geoff. I smelled tobacco intertwined with pot. It was a smell I had fondly associated with my love of theatre since college.

So much for Graham's warning to Bryce to stay off the pot. I just hoped there'd be no more lights raining down from the trusses.

"Veronica," Alastair called flicking his cigarette butt into the bushes. "Graham handed out your new scripts."

"Oh, what do you guys think?" I asked putting down my things on the steps.

"I'm good," Geoff said in his British accent as he took a long drag on his cigarette.

"Well, I'm not good," Bryce said, flicking the minute stub of his joint into the bushes. "I have to change half the lighting cues before Friday's opening."

"I'm sorry. Just following orders." I smiled and handed him his small box of cookies. "Here."

"You're bribing me with cookies?" Bryce exclaimed, taking his box of cookies with his close-lipped smile. "It works. Change anything you want."

From a long history, I knew when Bryce emerged from his hallowed lighting booth in the balcony, he rarely interacted with anyone except his smoking buddies. I was the exception.

I had befriended Bryce years ago with special cookies and jokes about my desire to be in his "spotlight." I acutely appreciated that from up there on high, he created visual support for whom and for what he chose. Lighting and creative illumination could make or break an actor on stage. Besides, I liked

Bryce's rugged independence, falling lights and all. He had created a niche for himself and looked out for his own life, as I recently had learned to do with mine.

"I'm happy with it," Alastair volunteered taking out another cigarette and lighting it. "Renee's got less to forget which means fewer cues for me to give her. I hate prompting that old bitch."

"We'll all be there someday." Geoff was obviously sensitive to the aging process. "She's just old and forgetful."

"Old and superstitious," Alastair sneered. "She thinks Charlie's death was an evil omen."

"Who knows? I for one believe the supernatural does exist," Bryce said. "I see things from the booth, especially when the gels wash different colors."

"You have a pot-enhanced imagination," Alastair snorted, putting his left hand in his pocket and jingling his coins.

"Don't knock the existence of incorporeal beings," Geoff said seriously. "I've seen amazing things at séances. And, Renee and I have both felt chills sweep through us backstage."

"Ooooooo," Alastair mocked, throwing a second cigarette into the bushes. "I'll explain that. It's called bad heating or, more exactly, why Charlie really died."

"Maybe," Bryce muttered.

I thought of the gas company and the city inspector's conclusions about the exhaust vent, but followed Graham's marching orders and didn't say a word.

"We believers will convince you." Geoff smiled and winked.

I smiled back. "If nothing else, ghosts would bring in a larger audience. Old Mrs. Valentine had a good marketing brain."

"Let's go in and break out the cookies, Veronica." Alastair grabbed the box with child-like enthusiasm. "What kind did you get?"

"A lot of chocolate."

"Oh, goody."

Alastair and I went into the lobby, leaving Bryce and Geoff to their ghost stories. It was warmed from the gas log fireplace, at least at the far end. Alastair tested a cookie or two and then started setting them out for the troupe.

I warmed my hands for a minute and then took my things to the women's dressing room.

* * *

In the dressing room, I plugged in the carbon monoxide detector in an outlet near the heater.

Then my compulsive sleuthing spirit got the better of me. I headed for Charlie's office. After Graham's encounter with the gas company and city inspector, my curious nature was piqued. I went to check out the vent myself and look for clues to see who unscrewed it.

Besides, I thought, working on this real death might jar my creativity and dislodge my writer's block. In all the history of mankind, back to the cavemen who were inspired to do primitive drawings, no one has yet discovered the catalyst for man's creative muse.

In Charlie's office, I confirmed that the old metal vent and straps were tightly secured back on the wall with new shiny screws. A sad legacy for Charlie, especially if he'd forgotten to re-screw it himself. When I reached up to jiggle the vent it was solid. It also had no marks, scratches, or dents from being knocked apart by tumbling clutter or mythical ghosts. Perhaps a careless repair man or Charlie had not put the vent back in place.

I searched the desk and then the detritus strewn across the floor for repair receipts or a screw driver. Nothing. But then there were screwdrivers in the scene dock to build sets and Charlie often bartered services for pot or an invitation to one of his parties.

With unsatisfied curiosity, I returned to the women's dressing room and found Graham going through the Victorian dresses on the wardrobe rack.

"I'm glad you're here, I said, shutting the dressing room door.

"Trouble with the script?" Graham said, continuing his wardrobe check.

"No, nothing new with the script. But I looked at the vent," I whispered. "The gas company is right. It was definitely unscrewed and it wasn't knocked apart."

"But it's fixed now?" Graham whirled around annoyed.

"Yes, it's solid now with new screws, but . . ."

"Then forget it." Graham turned back to the costumes. "I need to get this done. I have an opening night staring me in the face with a rewritten script. There's no mystery here. Charlie was cheap. He always used fly-by-night repair men or, worse, himself. What's your point? An accident's an accident."

"I . . ."

I stopped short. I felt silly letting my self-created, mystery-solving persona go to my head. I had no standing here to investigate anything, let alone Charlie's unfortunate end. Graham wasn't interested and my appetite to investigate a real death was trumped by the play and out impending Premier night. More importantly, I wanted to please Graham and be a part of this production since I had no writing to go back to.

"You're right. I got carried away." I knew my only role here was to support and edit.

Graham turned his back to me and flipped impatiently through the Victorian dresses.

I went back to the lobby.

⌘

CHAPTER 15

"The empty vessel makes the loudest sound."
-Shakespeare, *Henry V*, Act 4, Scene 4

Back in the lobby, Alastair had set up the cookies on the top of the locked glass concession counter. Its cabinets housed the intermission treats: discount candies, chips, and sodas. Graham sold them at five times their cost. He didn't miss a trick to make money.

"I'll get everyone." Alastair grabbed a chocolate walnut cookie. "And thanks, Veronica, for coming here and helping Graham. He really didn't know what to do until I thought of calling you."

"You mean I have you to blame?" I was only half joking for obvious reasons.

Alastair had a habit of taking underserved credit for ideas, but only after they panned out.

"Well, maybe it was Graham's idea." When he heard the word "blame," Alastair back peddled. "Who really knows?"

Alastair went to gather the troupe.

I closed the book on Charlie's death in my mind and thought of ways to mend fences with Graham. He was under a lot of pressure.

I wanted to stay part of the scene here at the Valentine. Even though I spent most of my busy adult life outside the theatre, I never lost my special love for it, perhaps because I never had to make a living in it, unlike Renee and Geoff.

In the last few years, since I reunited with Graham, I always jumped when he called. I in my way was as bad as Charlie. I was a junkie who would do almost anything if it meant I could get my next theatre-fix.

* * *

In a few minutes people began trailing in for cookies, everyone except Mel and Nicole. I suspected they were someplace still arguing about Anna's part. It crossed my mind that if the Fresnel light had dropped on Anna's chair last night with her in it, Nicole wouldn't be fighting for the lead. She'd have it.

Bryce and Geoff came in the double glass front doors, still talking about ghosts and séances. Bryce grabbed three cookies and then hurried up the balcony stairs with his own box. Geoff took a chocolate chip and stood near me quietly enjoying it.

Scott, always up for food, ran in from the theatre door like a child on Christmas morning. His dark hair was sprinkled with sawdust from working in the scene dock. He was short, handsome, energetic, and his dark brown eyes always appeared to be twinkling.

"Veronica, I heard you brought your cookies." Scott walked past me, grabbed a couple of cookies, stood near Geoff, and downed one cookie in four huge bites. "Glad you're back. Welcome aboard."

Scott was dedicated to the theatre and acting. He could build anything, design special effects, hang velours, set lights, and repair everything. Scott had given up on television and film work because he was too short to be a romantic lead and too good-looking to be a character actor. He had a photographic memory, which his fellow actors resented, especially Renee. He earned a living doing not-so-skilled woodwork and mooching off his consecutive girlfriends.

Kevin and Tim wandered in conversing intently and didn't come over for a cookie. They joined Geoff and Scott. Renee ignored the cookies and the group. She sat at the far end of the lobby and reviewed her lines near the new cappuccino and chai tea machine Charlie had installed to bring in more money. Howard slipped in at the other end of the lobby and was studying his lines. He was obviously still on the outs with Renee. I was sad.

I, naturally, made a beeline over to Kevin's group.

"Cookies, guys?"

"Later." Kevin looked down at me with his deep green eyes. "Nice to have you here."

"Yes," Geoff said. "And these cookies are good for the spirits, but not for the waist line."

"Don't you Brits call them biscuits?" Scott razzed Geoff.

"First off, when in America do as the Americans do," Geoff said, laughing. "But, believe it or not, in Britain hard plain type cookies are biscuits and the soft gooey ones are called cookies, like here in the colonies."

"The colonies?" Scott mocked. "Come on."

"Cookies or biscuits. I don't care," Tim laughed too. "I came straight from work and they're my dinner. You always feed us, Veronica."

I looked around. Everyone was smiling. It was a unifying moment. A single box of cookies made morale soar. With my gooey sugar fix, the stress of opening night was forgotten and so were my onerous edits. I compared this moment to grade school when the birthday-kid's mom brought cupcakes for everyone in class. These actors were like the grade-schoolers, puerile idiots made happy by free sugar when really nothing had changed at all.

"I have to look at my lines." Tim went, grabbed two chocolate chip cookies, and sat alone on the balcony steps near the fireplace with his script.

"Where's Nicole?" Scott looked around.

"I haven't seen her." I knew full well she was somewhere with Mel trying to get him to fire Anna.

Scott popped the last bite of his second cookie in his mouth and chewed as he talked.

"Graham said you've saved the day and cut the play?"

"I just did what I was told. Actually, Graham and Mel made the hard decisions about the editing," I said, disclaiming responsibility for the major cuts because Scott had a megaphone mouth.

Anna and Joel came in from the theatre together, grabbed cookies, and munched them in the middle of the room

"Excuse me," Kevin said. "I'll catch you guys later."

I watched Kevin head over to Anna and Joel. I had wanted Kevin to mention dinner, but perhaps it wasn't the time.

"I didn't know you were a writer," Scott blurted into my thoughts. "That's amazing. You never talk about it. What do you write?"

I turned back to Scott and answered casually "mystery novels."

I was not worried about any deep inquiry into my publication status by Scott. He basically only liked to hear himself talk and ultimately answered his own questions with great authority.

"A writer," Geoff said enthusiastically. "What do you write about?"

Scott, on his usual caffeine high, interjected before I could answer Geoff. Scott explained how he was actually a frustrated writer. He enumerated every essay and story that he wrote in his college freshman writing class. Geoff listened politely and I watched Kevin out of the corner of my eye talking urgently and quietly to Joel. Joel did not smile and shook his head from side to side. Kevin was clearly still working on Joel's requisite and obviously not forthcoming apology to Mel.

Scott was still prattling. He had switched his monologue from his writing to an explanation of how difficult it was going to be to reassign actors to move the set pieces and props between scenes because of my changes.

"Earth to Veronica," Scott called out, irritated because I wasn't giving him my full attention. "Did you think of me and my set changes while you slashed the play?"

"Of course." I turned back to Scott and barbed him playfully. "You, your set changes, your props, and your special effects were my prime concern."

Geoff laughed. "Why do I not believe you?"

Tired of my inattention, Scott departed to get another cookie and another, more attentive audience for his monologues; monologues that should be cut down or at least edited out of my life.

⌘

CHAPTER 16

"Love is a smoke made with the fume of sighs."
-Shakespeare, *Romeo and Juliet*, Act 1, Scene 1

Geoff and I, deserted by all, stood in the middle of the cookie party. We silently surveyed the gathering of the assorted people essential to a theatrical production; the nuts and chews, the sweet and bitter, the hard and soft, the used up and spit out.

"Theatre is a strange art form, isn't it?" Geoff whispered.

"What do you mean?"

"To succeed it requires the complete cooperation of strange bedfellows."

"Just my thoughts exactly."

"Unfortunately most of them are competitive and egotistical, and completely narcissistic."

"And artistic in every good and bad sense of the word," I added, wondering what this very well-trained, knowledgeable actor was doing with our little troupe. "How did you get introduced to the group?"

"Graham recruited me from a summer production of *Mourning Becomes Electra* at the Crenshaw Theatre. I met him on one of his missions to poach disgruntled actors. He talked me into this original play," Geoff answered with a cheery British accent.

"Ah, I see."

"Yes, I was infinitely poachable," Geoff snickered. "And I thought getting paid for a change would hit the spot. Besides, I wanted a 'world premier,'"

"Money is always a draw, but originals are so unpredictable!"

"I know." Geoff chuckling and leaned over to my ear. "But between you and me, I had nothing else on my plate. I'll let you in on another secret, too."

"I like secrets."

"If the play has a decent run and gets published then my name will be printed in the script as an original cast member." Geoff smiled and shrugged his shoulders. "I just can't resist another chance to see my name memorialized forever, even if it's only in a flash-in-the-pan play like this."

"Very shrewd. You're right, I do always read the original casts. I've found some of the greats in small first roles and actors who became famous producers or directors."

"Yes. And I am sometimes amazed to find me," Geoff said proudly.

"I'll watch for you now, too."

I was enjoying myself with Geoff.

"Brilliant," Geoff said. "Excuse me. It is time for my last cigarette before the firing squad, so to speak."

As I watched Geoff go outside, I suspected he had more reasons for being here at the Valentine than he disclosed. Through the glass doors, I observed Geoff lighting his cigarette. I realized my curious, investigative nature had reared its ugly head yet again. I quickly slapped it down. It was, indeed, none of my business.

* * *

"Thank you for the snack." Howard came over and stood next to me with three oatmeal raisin cookies in hand. "You remembered my oatmeal raisin."

"Of course."

I was pleased Howard was brave enough to mingle with everyone after yesterday's humiliation. I also knew I had to clear the air about reducing his role so much.

"Did you get the revised script?"

"Yes." Howard shrugged his shoulders and looked down.

"I'm sorry."

"You don't have to apologize. Mel doesn't like me." Howard took a small bite of his cookie. "It's not like I don't know that."

"That's not true. The play had to be shorter. And between you and me, Mel didn't think Renee could memorize her lines by opening night. You were just part of that fallout."

I tried desperately to make Howard feel better by blaming it on Renee, even though I knew he was right. And so did he.

"She a professional. She would have learned them." Howard was still obviously in love with Renee. "Renee's a great actress."

"She is and you're a trooper." I didn't call him a professional because he wasn't.

We stood silently. Howard watched Renee despairingly. Renee caught Howard's gaze. She gave him a cold hard glare and then went back to studying her script. Howard's face was swept with pain.

"You did the right thing, you know? Last night, I mean."

"I don't know." Howard's eyes were fixed on Renee.

I wished I could tell him about the Fresnel that fell, but I owed my allegiance to Graham. Besides, I believed Howard was the only one smitten in this relationship. Renee was not.

In my view, the relationship was destined to end before it really began, like my fourth book. Except, unlike my book dying in silence in the wee hours of the morning, their relationship ended publicly, too publicly.

Howard observed Renee studying her lines. "I couldn't get her the publicity she wanted anyway."

"What publicity?" I didn't understand what Howard meant.

"Nothing," Howard whispered sadly. "Forget it."

"Do you want me to talk to Renee for you?"

"No. But thanks."

Howard got out his wallet and abruptly went over to buy a drink from the cappuccino machine near Renee. He fumbled with his wallet and the machine as he glanced hopefully and repeatedly over at Renee.

Renee looked up at Howard and then moved three chairs further away.

Howard's eye's transformed from hope to despair and then to anger. I had never seen a look like that coming from Howard before, even on stage.

Howard threw his full, hot cappuccino in the trash can and stomped by me into the theatre.

⌘

CHAPTER 17

"False face must hide what the false heart doth know."
-Shakespeare, *Macbeth*, Act 1, Scene 7

As I watched a very hurt and very angry Howard disappear into the theatre, I was startled by a gentle touch on my shoulder from behind. I turned to see Anna.

"Hello. I'm Anna Delarosa. Thanks for the cookies."

Anna shook my hand with an energy and joy that was in stark contrast to Howard.

"My pleasure. I'm Veronica Kennicott."

I noted Anna's stomach was not peeking between her jeans and sweater. Instead, a hip length white, very low-cut tight t-shirt revealed two rounds of tanned cleavage.

"I know." Anna shook my hand so vigorously that her cleavage oscillated. "Nicole said you discovered the theatre owner's body."

"Yes, a terrible accident." I adhered to the party line.

"My boyfriend, Joel, told me I was lucky not to be here early after work."

"You would have gotten a headache for sure."

As per Graham's orders I down-played the leak, but knew with prolonged exposure she could have ended up like Charlie. I thought of the light falling last night too. This poor girl seemed to be "saved by the bell" when it came to being in the wrong place at the wrong time. I changed the subject.

"I'm sorry you and Joel lost so many lines in the rewrite."

"We expected it after yesterday. "Anna lowered her voice. "Mel's a jerk and a backstage groper. But nothing will make us give up the leads."

"Good." I saw backbone in this young woman.

Anna smiled. "This lead got Joel his agent who's sending him out a lot. Movie auditions too. SAG movies."

"I'm glad." I knew getting an agent or manager in this town wasn't that hard, but getting one that actually worked for you was a real triumph.

"I noticed in your bio's that you both studied at Yale."

"Yes, together. Then we did the New York theatre scene for awhile, but Joel wanted Hollywood and the movies."

"And you?" I probed to determine if she was more serious about Joel or acting.

"I love New York theatre, but Joel loves film. He finished his training in Meisner and we came to Hollywood," Anna said proudly, obviously invested more in Joel than herself. "Do you know the Meisner Method?"

"Of course."

I was not insulted, but amused with her youthful assumption that Meisner was something just discovered by her younger and cleverer generation. His method was generations old. I remembered my own Meisner courses with endless repetition, rigid structure, and practice with impediments.

"Wow, I didn't know it was that old," Anna said with her big dark eyes popping out of her smooth delicate face.

"I guess it is." I—the apparent pre-historic dinosaur—chided Anna.

"I'm sorry." Anna's face blushed. "I just meant . . ."

"Forget it," I laughed. "I know what you meant."

Unfortunately, I did know what she meant but my laugh sparkled and my smile engaged my anger. The little princess believed she was absolved. Just for a moment, however, I wanted to tear her apart with my evidently "aged" sharp tongue.

"Thanks," Anna said disarmingly, searching for a neutral conversation to neutralize her mistake.

I searched for a new topic, as any "mature" person would, to fill the awkward silence that followed. "Mature" was all I was to most of these baby actors. They really did treat me like a dinosaur, or worse than that, like a mother. They needed to pigeonhole older actors to separate themselves from their probable shared eventual fate of less-than-star status. The label "mother" was expeditious for them because it affirmed their distinction from elder actors, convinced them their future was not the same, and allowed them to rise above. I was repelled the few times I was actually hugged and called "mother." It negated me as an actual person. It also made me their functionary for menial tasks, which I performed when it was easier than not.

Anna, finally and naturally, continued on the Joel topic. "Joel hasn't done much but he says it's harder that stage acting."

"He's right about that."

Then, to rehabilitate my worth to myself, I played the acting pro much like I daily play the writing pro.

"In a close shot, which most of them are now, the camera is so close and there always seem to be multiple takes. You have to hit the emotional mark and then often do it again and again until the director is satisfied with lighting, sound and everything else.

"I never thought of it like that. It would be hard to do everything again and again."

"And it's not like creating a role in the nice, safe cocoon on stage with a nice set and lighting to obscure the audience. On a film set there is always activity and crew and just plain people around you. If you're on location there is heat, freezing cold, insects, snakes. It can be rough."

"That's what Joel says. He says people don't realize how hard it is." Anna lowered her voice. "I'll tell you a secret. Joel has an audition with Stephie Sevas coming up for a lead. I can't believe it. I mean she's huge."

I was impressed. "That's a great opportunity."

"Don't tell these people. They don't respect movie acting."

"Sure." I looked at Anna's dark expressive eyes. "I wish him luck, Anna."

I realized Anna had no idea that every one of these actors would jump at a big budget movie audition with a big name, but they couldn't get them. In fact, most of them have never had or couldn't get an agent or a manager. They all feign dedication to the theatre because they were washed up or wannabes who didn't have the "it" factor for film and earning big money.

Joel waved at us from the front doors.

"Nice meeting you," Anna said. "I have to go. Joel needs food before we start."

Anna left with Joel and her uneaten chocolate chip cookie. I suspected she would toss it without taking a bite. She was a disciplined young actress who knew she had to pay attention to her body because everyone else in the business would. Mel had been obviously charmed by her display of cleavage, and this evening it looked like Scott and Kevin were too. Even Joel was probably with her, in part, because of that charming cleavage.

I liked Anna, despite her shortcomings born only of youth. I was glad she had not been hurt by the carbon monoxide leak or the falling Fresnel.

Anna hurried away with the steady walk of a ballerina in her tight black skinny-leg jeans tucked into her spiked calf high boots.

As I observed her, I embarrassed myself with a flash of primal jealousy. It was aimed at Anna's magnetic, youthful, and fertile attraction, which was long exhausted at my age. But I liked her nonetheless. She was Nicole's competitor, not mine. She had attached herself to a young man she thought was a shining star and was happy with her life.

Anna and Joel disappeared.

* * *

I turned my attention back to the gathering and felt the collective good mood.

I noticed Graham slip in, grab four sugar cookies and stand across from me happily chomping them down. His large frame was silhouetted by the warm light emanating from the fireplace.

Tim, who was now finished skimming through the script, joined Graham. Tim was animated and smiling. I presumed because he knew now I had enlarged his part.

I saw Renee, still sitting alone at the far end of the lobby, thumbing through the new script with her own lines slashed to "nothing."

I decided to get myself a chai tea and Renee a cappuccino. I needed to clear the air about cutting her lines and find out exactly what Howard meant about not getting Renee the publicity she wanted. I suspected Renee had been getting close to Howard to use poor Howard for publicity spots. That would be par for this industry. If it were true then he could never resurrect their friendship, let alone have any hope for something more.

I took a deep breath and fortified myself.

* * *

As I approached the cappuccino machine, Mel burst into the lobby through the outside glass doors. He was still obviously worked up from his Nicole encounter and inebriated from the French restaurant.

Everyone in the lobby watched him.

I was glad Joel had left because I had learned Mel was a malicious loose cannon when he was imbibed.

Mel was what is commonly known as a heavy presence when sober and that presence, at the moment, was made heavier by his dinner libations.

Mel surveyed the gathered troupe with disdain and then walked falteringly to the cappuccino machine. Everyone there, dependent on his play and money, slowly went back to their conversations, but more subdued. There was a pall on the party. It was clear Mel's drinking was not new to the group and they had learned to be on guard.

Oblivious to his path, Mel cut me off at the cappuccino machine and inserted two dollar bills from his wallet. The machine rumbled loudly as Mel's cappuccino dropped into a paper cup.

"Mel, is everything okay?" I asked over the rumble of the machine.

It was an innocuous question on its face, but I knew everything was not okay and fully intended to needle the self-absorbed, pathetic jackass publicly.

"Sure," Mel snarled, grabbing his cappuccino. "Why wouldn't it be?"

Mel drank his steaming and too hot cappuccino. He burnt his lips.

"Damn."

"Be careful. These come out too hot."

Mel glared at me. I delighted in stating the obvious to irritate him more.

"That bitch. She's good enough for a lay and she thinks that makes her good enough for the lead," Mel muttered shaking his head. "I'm through."

"What?" I pretended I didn't hear.

I wanted his outburst to be repeated even louder and heard by the troupe. He was just such a stereotype.

"Nothing," Mel said dismissively.

Just then, Nicole charged into the lobby from the street and marched straight through to the theatre ignoring everyone and the cookies. Kevin greeted her and she ignored even him.

"Nothing I can't handle." Mel watched Nicole disappear through the oak theatre door.

If that was an entree into an intimate conversation about Nicole, I wasn't interested. I knew all I needed to know about the two.

My needling to expose Nicole's plot to get the lead didn't work. The moment had passed. I refused to have a tete-a-tete with Mel about his Nicole problems.

I busied myself getting my tea and Renee's cappuccino.

The noise and inattention annoyed Mel. He went away and sat. He blew on his hot cappuccino.

I held my drinks carefully. I went over to Renee.

* * *

I sat in the seat next to Renee. She looked up at me and did not look friendly.

"Here. I got you a cappuccino. We can all use a pick-me-up." I gauged how upset Renee was with me for hacking her role down.

"Thank you, dear." The smile came.

Renee took the cappuccino. She blew on it and took a sip.

"And how have you been, Veronica? It's been a couple of years since we've worked here. I hear you're a great writer now."

"Not really. You know Graham and his hype. But I enjoy it." I did not sit down to do the authorial-dance and changed the subject quickly. "How are you?"

"Wonderful. I love this play and all the people here," Renee said, with a dullness in her dark eyes that belied her enthusiastic intonations and word choice.

Renee had been in the film and theatre world her whole life. She was well schooled in the habitual and sometimes actually authentic, positive "industry" enthusiasm for everyone and everything and every project. From Graham I understood that, that was how she had survived since her salad years on Broadway; being a cheerleader and being liked by everyone. She would even mend fences with Howard again eventually, I was sure.

It was a requisite in the industry and the theatre world, to be liked and always enthused, delighted, and ecstatic. A requisite, of course, unless you happened to be rich, a money-making marketable talent, an icon like Stephie Sevas, or just sleeping with the right people. Renee was none of the aforementioned and, thus, traded on the words "wonderful" and "love" to get what she wanted from whom she needed to use.

"Good." I did not want to crack her delicate façade. "I came over because I was worried. I know some of your speeches were cut, but we had to shorten the run. I hope you are not too upset."

"I'm not upset at all. I have several auditions to prepare for and I can use the extra time to do that," Renee replied and then skillfully changed the focus of the conversation back to me. She needed to avoid my probing her obvious lie about several pending auditions. "Graham told me you have written some books. Mystery books. I'd like to read one,"

"Wonderful." I parroted Renee's enthusiastic intonations and word choice. "I have a site on the internet."

"Can I pick up one at a store?" Renee looked at me with her ebony eyes that were uncomfortably perceptive and revealed a high social IQ.

"Not yet. I haven't decided on a literary agent."

"I see. I'll wait then." Renee scanned the gathering with a Cheshire cat smile. "I'm going to get one of your delightful cookies. Thank you for the coffee. You are so thoughtful. And don't worry about the cuts."

I had skillfully tossed the ball into Renee's court and she had volleyed it back again to me. It appeared we were cut from the same cloth and she knew it. A cloth somewhat South of honesty.

I watched her take a sugar cookie and join Graham's entourage.

Renee glanced over at me with a sparkle in her dark eyes. She gave me a smile and took a small bite of her cookie. Then, she looked back at Graham in time to laugh on cue at one of his either boring or off-color stories.

I knew then that our secrets and untruths were safe with each other. After all, what would be the point in exposing each other?

We were two con artists appreciating each other's creative facades.

⌘

CHAPTER 18

"Delays have dangerous ends."
-Shakespeare, *Henry VI, Part I*, Act 3, Scene 2

Alastair ended the cookie fest by herding us all into the theatre for a pre-rehearsal meeting.

Alastair and Bryce sat at the back of the house as usual, Mel and I midway, and the cast down near the stage, chatting and laughing

The cookie party had made everyone happy, everyone but Nicole. Nicole came from the dressing room, down the stage stairs, and planted herself alone on the aisle. She stared at her script, not acknowledging anyone. Mel was seething and glared at the back of her head.

As soon as Graham took center stage everyone came to order. He explained the sole reason for the script cuts and rewrite was the running time. That was true as far as it went. But he, Mel, and I knew the choice of the edits was vindictive. Graham said nothing that would invite questions and there were none.

"The play's the thing," Graham concluded, giving himself blanket absolution, with this Shakespeare quote.

I knew the silent-and-cookied troupe accepted that the play was "the thing." But they also knew Mel was the driving force behind the play and certain of the cuts were obvious payback.

I caught Howard glancing back at Mel with unmistakable anger. Mel was the thief who stole two things precious to him: the largest part in his career and Renee's self-respect.

Mel was oblivious.

"You can hold your scripts tonight. We'll adjust the blocking as we go. Be off book tomorrow. It shouldn't be difficult. For some of you who were having trouble with your lines, life will be easier." Graham put a positive spin on everything. "We'll work in the set and prop changes and Bryce will be doing the new light cues. Scott, see if you can get the special effects timed in."

"Yes, sir," Scott said, standing at attention and saluting Graham.

"Can it, Scott," Alastair ordered from the back of the room.

Scott sat and "canned it," but not without attitude.

"Now, let's start from where we left off in act three. Howard and Renee's fight scene," Graham continued. "It's complicated. We're all fresh. Bryce and

Scott have to get the special effects right tonight before the full tech run. Then we'll do the first and second acts."

"But you said act one." Nicole leaped up angrily, her ice blue eyes riveted on Graham.

"Sit down, Nicole," Mel yelled.

Everyone saw there was trouble in paradise.

Nicole turned and looked at Mel defiantly. She put her hand on her hip which today was covered with a blue sweater topped with her firm pale cleavage popped by a push up bra. I was sure that Nicole's and Anna's coordinated choice of breast exposure tonight must be either subliminal competitiveness or ordained by a cosmic synchronization of this theatre generation's fertility rituals.

Nicole thought for a minute. Then she flopped back into her seat causing a spring to pop loudly and her breasts to bounce boldly enough to catch Kevin and Tim's admiration. She crossed her legs and swung her spiked, booted foot up and down in the aisle. The heel was not quite as tall as Anna's and was tattered at the bottom.

"We'll go into act one when we finish this," Graham said, dismissing Nicole with as much Mel-based deference as he could. "Mel and Veronica will be watching for continuity, but we anticipate no modifications from here on. Places, people."

Alastair walked forward down the center aisle with his left hand in his pocket jiggling his coins and the new script in his other hand.

"Places everyone. Now!" Alastair shouted and then zeroed in on Scott defiantly not moving a muscle in his seat. "Scott, get back there, check the props, and get ready for the storm special effects."

Scott saw no benefit in not obeying. His fellow actors were getting in their places on stage and for entrances now. He had no captive audience.

"I need to go potty," Nicole announced.

She grabbed her script and marched down the center aisle to get to the restroom backstage.

Mel glared at her as she trounced down the aisle toward the stage stairs in her tight jeans with a rhinestone heart on the back pocket. The heart was noticeably missing rhinestones at the tip.

"Nicole," Alastair called out with no deference. "Get on stage. We need you in this scene."

"Start without me," Nicole said going up the stage access stairs. "Nature calls."

"Nicole," Graham stepped in her path on the stage. "You're in this scene. Take your potty break later."

"Alastair can read my lines," Nicole huffed, stepping around Graham's large body.

Before Nicole reached the wings Mel stood up.

"Nicole, get back here or you're out of the show," Mel commanded.

He was enraged by Nicole and their fight over the lead. But he was also emboldened by too much wine. The harlot, or I should say starlet, had driven him too far.

She stopped and slowly turned around.

"Sure, hon," Nicole said cheerily. "If that's the way you want it."

She looked at Mel for a long minute. Then she walked stage right with script in hand and stood quietly with her fellow actors in the scene.

* * *

On stage, Renee and Howard were ready for their big fight scene about their daughter's impending marriage. Nicole, Geoff, Kevin, and Tim are in the scene and have their own comments about the arranged marriage. Finally, Renee runs up the staircase and Howard follows while a raging storm is beating at the house.

In the scene, I cut Renee's lines down to a few words each to speed the action. I had also given Nicole more lines to please Mel.

"Get those house lights down," Graham called. "Stage up. Let's start people."

The house lights came down and the stage lights up. Alastair pulled the bi-parting red grand drape, or main traveler, shut it smoothly and then reopened it. When the grand drape opened for the first time I saw Bryce's lighting design washing over the set. It was magical.

The problem was that the scene was not magical. It went so much faster with the line cuts that it was technically more difficult. Bryce's lighting changes went faster. And Scott's special effects needed to come up just as quickly. The lightning, rain, a broken window, and wind needed to be almost simultaneous. Mistakes were made. We needed a tech run.

Mel leaned over to me and whispered approvingly with sour wine breath, "Look how fast it is running without Renee's monologues."

"Yes," I agreed, turning away from Mel's foul smell as much as I could without actually turning the back of my head to him. "Let me listen to the flow of the dialogue."

"Oh . . . sure," Mel said focusing on the stage and leaning forward. "Nicole looks good up there. She's a pistol."

I didn't answer. I was poised with my version of the script, a flashlight, and a pencil to fine tune if necessary.

"I'm going back to the restaurant to get another Drambuie. Let me know how it goes," Mel slurred, standing and leaving up the side aisle.

I hoped he stayed away. The Mel and Nicole drama was annoying and Mel's lack of focus was irritating me. Our tech run and final dress rehearsal were upon us and we had just done major script changes. This was not the time to be getting drunk, it was the time to work hard.

* * *

Onstage, Renee and Howard shouted their lines at each other. Bryce flickered the stage lights and made lightning flash. Scott sounded the thunder and made the storm rage outside the Victorian house.

Renee and Howard built the fight to its crescendo before Howard chased Renee up the Victorian staircase.

At the foot of the staircase, Renee screamed her lines at Howard with so much hatred and venom that it actually scared me.

Then, Scott increased the sound level of the rainstorm with rain, thunder, and wind howls. It was so loud it drowned out Renee's and Howard's dialogue.

"Cut that noise down, Scott," Graham yelled over the cacophony. "I can't hear a damned thing."

Scott reduced the storm sounds as Bryce put lightning flashes across the stage. Then Scott increased the thunder rolling, too loudly again.

"Come on Scott. Pay attention," Graham bellowed. "Cut that thunder down and get the rain sound a little higher."

Suddenly, the stage went black. The bright lightning flashes strobed repeatedly and uncontrollably across the stage.

"What the hell are you doing, Bryce? You're going to blind us. Get the general lighting back up. Cut the strobes. That's too much lightning," Graham ordered. "Renee, keep going. Don't stop. We're never going to get through this."

In the flashing light, Renee went up three steps holding the rail and then turned back to Howard and shouted, "How dare you do that to your daughter?"

"You come back here," Howard commanded from the foot of the staircase as the lightening flashed.

"Fix those lights," Graham bellowed.

Renee turned back to Howard again and shrieked, "I'll never forgive you."

Howard chased Renee up the stairs in the flashing lights holding onto the rail tightly.

"Come back here."

"Get away from me," Renee screamed.

She made her way up the carved wood staircase as Howard chased after her. The special effect of a window breaking in the storm sounded.

"That's too loud too, Scott. Do you want to make us deaf?" Alastair boomed at Scott backstage. "Bryce, get the general light up. Those flashing lights are killing my eyes."

As Renee ascended to the top of the stairs, Scott repeated the window breaking sound, first too low and then too loud again.

Alastair shouted, "Bryce stop that damn lightning. I'm going blind."

"I'm trying." Bryce answered. "It's out of control."

"No, you are," Graham retorted.

Scott repeated the glass breaking sound and then turned on the high-powered fan for the burst of wind that hits Renee at he top of the stairs through the broken window.

In the flickering lights I saw Renee's hair flying wildly in the wind and her fighting to get it out of her face.

Howard reached the top of the stairs and grabbed Renee's arm. She jerked it away and opened the black velour upstage traveler to exit. As Renee went through the curtain, the lightning flashes stopped and the stage went black. A wave of blue light streaked across the top of the stairs. It lit Howard, gripping the rail at the head of the staircase. Alone.

The stage faded to black. The thunder and lightning stopped.

In the blackout and silence, a shrill scream sounded from backstage.

* * *

"Renee," Howard cried out in the dark. "Renee."

"Light that stage, Bryce," Graham yelled.

All we heard was the faint sound of the fan blowing from backstage.

"Light that stage," Graham yelled again. "And stop the fan, Scott."

Alastair called from the wings, "Bring up the general lighting. Get the backstage lights up. We can't see a thing,"

"Renee," Geoff called from his position near the foot of the staircase.

"Nobody move until the lights are up," Alastair yelled. "Nobody move. Bryce, get the damn lights up. Scott, where are you? Get that damn fan off.

I stood up and called out, "I have a flashlight."

I heard heels clicking across the stage and actors shuffling.

"Stay where you are, people, until the lights are up," Graham said. "Damn it, Bryce, get something up."

All movement stopped. The house lights finally came up in the audience seating, but instead of the general stage lights the lightning started flashing again across the black stage.

"Stop that strobe," Graham yelled. "Get those stage lights up."

"Renee. Renee," Howard called.

Howard was visible moving in the strobe lights across the top of the staircase to the backstage traveler. He opened the black velours and peered into the crossover behind.

"I'll go, Howard," Geoff said running in the flickering lights, stage right, to the wings and crossover.

"Renee? Renee?" Howard called at the top of the stairs.

In the flickering light, I saw Kevin's strobe-lit body follow Geoff. The strobe light effect turned the actors' movements into the macabre.

The stage lights finally came up and the flickering stopped. Howard and Tim were the only persons left on stage. Nicole was gone too.

Graham struggled out of his chair and headed for the stage steps.

"Call 911," Nicole yelled coming out from the wings. "Hurry. Renee's unconscious."

Nicole went back into the wings with Tim trailing.

⌘

CHAPTER 19

"What is past is prologue."
-Shakespeare, *The Tempest*, Act 2, Scene 1

I grabbed my flashlight and followed Graham up onto the stage. Graham's set had no throughways in his set upstage where the crossover was, so I followed him to the wings. Graham tossed the heavy vertical velours, known as the legs, apart as if they were silk. The heavy drapes clapped silently together behind us, throwing the smell of ancient dust into the air.

I stayed at Graham's heels, winding through the dark backstage. The walls were painted black to obscure backstage activity from the audience.

We went quickly past the open dressing room door and overtook Tim and Nicole.

"Step aside," Graham ordered as he bounced Tim and Nicole out of his way with his stomach.

"Hey, watch out," Nicole snapped as Graham squeezed his large body between her and the wall.

"You two should go sit in the theatre. The paramedics will need room," I said as I passed them, too.

"Let's go Nicole," Tim said quietly.

"You go. I'm staying."

Nicole exercised her prerogative as Mel's current favorite whether they were fighting at the moment or not.

"Whatever."

Tim left by himself, unwilling to tread on Mel's territory.

I glanced back and saw Tim return to the theatre, but Nicole followed us.

We zigzagged through the dark backstage maze.

We rounded the end of the velour upstage traveler to the dimly lit crossover behind the stage. That is where Renee had exited from the Victorian staircase.

We inched along between the black velour separating the stage from the crossover and brick wall painted the proverbial backstage black. The crossover was narrowed by wood and musty-smelling upholstered furniture, boxes, and props piled precariously high against the brick wall. It was salvaged to use as is or be transformed with Scott's skillful hands.

This stockpile from old plays left scarce room for actors to crisscross for entrances or costume changes on the opposite side of the stage. Sometimes a careless actor caused a stack to tumble, with no real harm so far.

We, who crossed at our own peril, also often shared the crossover with scurrying cockroaches or rats. On more than one occasion, I had barely been able to suppress a shriek when undesirable co-inhabitants surprised me.

* * *

As we approached the exit ladder, I saw Howard above. He was kneeling on the small black platform which bridged the Victorian staircase to the ladder before us.

"Kevin," Howard called out. "How is she?"

"I don't know."

Howard stood up and started down the ladder.

"Stay where you are, Howard," Graham bellowed. "We don't need anyone else back here."

"I'll let you know," I called to Howard who obeyed Graham's order and stopped his descent.

I thought Graham was cruel. I knew Howard did not view himself as "anyone else" even if he and Renee had experienced a falling out.

"Move. Move, people. Let me by," Graham shouted impatiently. "For God's sake, people. Move."

I followed behind Graham, who cleared the way with his commanding voice and unchallengeable size.

Anna and Joel backed into a nook near an old stove and Geoff squeezed into a niche formed by boxes married to a curved ottoman. Scott hopped up on the stove near Anna and Joel.

"Did someone call 911?" I asked Geoff as I squeezed by him.

"Alastair did," Geoff said, speaking in his British accent with calm efficiency.

Graham and I side-stepped until we reached Kevin kneeling over Renee. His back was pressed into the upstage black velour and his head was inches from a tower of straight-backed oak chairs.

"It's Renee." Kevin turned to us.

When Kevin moved, I saw Renee lying on the floor. She was twisted around the foot of the exit ladder which dropped into the crossover from the high platform behind the Victorian staircase. Under the stairs, I noticed Renee's revised script with her drastically cut role that had diminished her worth as an actress. Regret overwhelmed me.

"How is she?" Graham asked.

Graham kneeled over Renee. His large body did not fit in the tight space and collided with the stack of oak chairs.

"Careful," Alastair said as he studied the column of chairs.

"She's not moving. It's bad," Kevin whispered.

His assessment was intended only for Graham's ears but reached mine and everyone else's around as well.

"Help her," Anna screamed.

Anna burst out crying and buried her head into Joel's chest, her long dark hair draping down.

"Why don't you take Anna back into the theatre, Joel," I suggested, as the young man snuggled Anna's body, blatantly combining consolation with tactile pleasure.

"Okay."

Joel looked at me. His blue eyes with specks of emerald green were magnetic. I understood how he had gotten his agent and auditions, especially if his talent matched his looks. I knew his eyes would electrify audiences on the big screen if he could Meisner-up at the auditions.

For just a moment, I watched Joel and Anna walk away intertwined in the dimly lit crossover. I remembered those days of emotional highs and lows. I recalled the feel of my husband's chest against my cheek as I sobbed and he snuggled me into calm. Joel put his hand on Anna's head and stroked her hair.

As Anna and Joel squeezed past Nicole, Nicole did not give an inch. I concluded that she never did.

"Veronica," Graham called out, shattering my reminiscences. "We need you."

* * *

I immediately knelt next to Kevin by the velour. Renee was lying very still.

"How bad is it?" I asked Kevin.

"I'm sorry," Kevin looked over at me sadly. "She's gone."

"No," I stammered as tears streamed from my eyes.

I cried as much for how I had treated her as I did for Renee. Kevin reached over and touched my knee sympathetically. I was embarrassed and surprised when desire stirred at his touch and not consolation. I immediately looked away at Renee because I knew my attraction would be transparent.

Kevin then reached over and hugged my shoulder. I liked that too, far too much. But I did not like the fact I was not thinking of Renee and I was not crying any longer.

"Veronica, you don't have to be here," Kevin leaned his head nearer and whispered softly.

I smelled his musky aftershave and felt his breath through my hair on my ear.

"Yes, she does. She knows about these things," Graham blurted out, jarring me back to the reality at hand. "Is she dead, Veronica?"

The look on Graham's desperate, hopeful eyes squelched my desire for Kevin.

I was proud and pleased that Graham thought I knew about "these things," meaning deaths. It meant that Graham viewed me not only as a writer, but also as a criminalist, an authority qualified to declare Renee dead.

I pulled gently away from Kevin, reprimanding myself for turning a death into an intimate moment.

"Give me a minute," I insisted, always rising to an occasion that needed my "expertise."

I took charge at once, much as I had when my neighbor's front porch wicker furniture went missing.

* * *

In point of fact, this was only my second "live," or should I say "in-person," dead body, Charlie being the first. That, of course, excludes dead bodies at family and friend's funerals.

With a glimpse I was, however, confident that Kevin was right. Renee was dead. Her ebony eyes were motionless and mirrored the lifelessness that had emanated from Charlie's eyes. Graham nonetheless wanted my pronouncement, my authority as a mysterian and criminalist, to declare it so. And I would—but only after I did what any self-respecting mystery writer would do: examine and assess.

I would like to say that the impact of two dead bodies in two days devastated me, but to my embarrassment it didn't. The numerosity simply piqued my mysterian curiosity.

As I began my examination of Renee, all romantic thoughts of Kevin disappeared.

Renee's black wool sweater was bunched, exposing her loose white skin, sphincter'ed by the elastic waistband of her black polyester skirt. As I would have liked, I pulled her sweater down to meet her pants. I looked into her dark eyes. Even in the dim light, it was easy to see they were lifeless, just as Charlie's had been.

My investigative instincts took over. These instincts, although not practiced, were in point of fact well-honed. In my third book, my character had discovered and examined seven bodies with her analytical, knowledgeable eyes. Thus, I put myself in detecting mode, followed my character's lead, and began.

I reached out to test Renee's pulse. I felt Graham and Kevin's eyes on me. I hesitated midair, but took a deep breath and then carefully picked up her hand and turned it over. I did exactly what my character did to the seven bodies she found in my mystery book. Through simple research I learned my character should place my two fingers on her wrist, not the thumb, and feel for a pulse. There was none.

I was delighted with my ease at following the investigative procedures from my book.

"Can you hold this for me?" I asked Kevin, handing him my flashlight. "Just follow my hands with it."

"Sure," Kevin said. "What are you going to do?"

"The usual," I said with a confidence born of total book-learned ignorance.

As Kevin and Graham watched me, I then carefully examined Renee's head. It was twisted and dropped down to her chest. I saw an open gash above her ear and the blood from it had turned a patch of her silver hair red.

"More light, please."

"Where?"

"Right here."

"All right," Kevin said inching the light into position. "Oh, my God."

The gash was large, but blood had stopped oozing. From my forensic studies, I knew that meant. She was indeed dead because there was no longer blood flowing through her body.

I shocked myself because I was actually enjoying this process. I was no longer timid touching this authentic dead body. I wished I had examined Charlie's body at the time. I was starting to feel ghoulish, but kept on. I noted her battered arms and legs. But the bruising and blood was minimal, confirming to me that she was indeed dead with no blood flow.

To be thorough, I carefully, but unnecessarily, swept my arm dramatically across the body and leaned over to test Renee's neck as well for a pulse on the jugular vein.

"Slow down," Kevin said, following me with the flashlight.

I caught Kevin's green eyes in the soft light. He was anxious and upset. I wanted to take his face gently into my hands and tell him it would be all right. But I didn't.

Instead, I announced, "She's dead."

"Not so loud," Graham said throwing his hand in the air.

"She's dead. She's dead," Nicole screamed from behind me, bursting into a loud theatrical crying jag.

I was certain Nicole calculated this demonstration of hysteria to be louder and more hysterical than Anna's had been.

"She's dead?" Howard asked in disbelief from the platform above.

"Yes," Nicole screamed up at Howard covering her eyes so she could dry-sob without being transparently phony.

Howard started to come down the ladder but slipped and caught himself before plummeting down on Renee's body.

"Don't, Howard," Nicole shouted. "The rail is loose."

"The rail is not loose," Scott barked at Nicole.

Howard stepped back up on the platform and said, "I'll come around."

"No. Get off the stairs and get back into the theatre, Howard," Graham said, as he struggled to his feet again knocking the chairs and boxes of props. "You can't do anything here but be in the way."

Kevin stood also and helped me up in the narrow space.

"Graham, they were friends," I nudged Graham's huge arm. Then, I called gently up to Howard. "Howard, there's nothing to do for now."

Howard hesitated and then without saying a word went back through the upstage traveler and returned to the stage. I heard him go down the Victorian staircase on the stage. Then there was a clatter of indistinct conversation in the theatre as the troupe digested the fact we had lost a member.

"Thanks," I said taking my flashlight from Kevin.

I illuminated the ladder with my flashlight. It was painted black like everything else backstage. The steps were intact and covered with dusty footprints. I ran the flashlight up the length of the handrail and up and down its posts. I noticed some shallow gouges through the black paint around the base of the top outside post and a few screw holes without screws on top of three posts. I pushed on the rail near me at the bottom.

"It looks good to me," Kevin observed.

"Do you think it could be loose up there?" I asked Kevin.

"Of course not," Graham answered. "Stop that. Put your flashlight down. Let's get everyone out of here."

"The rail's loose?" Nicole shouted, looking up and abruptly stopping her tearless staged sobbing. "That's why she fell."

"No, Nicole it's not." Graham retorted, not testing or touching the rail himself. "Scott, get her out of here. Now."

"Sorry." I turned my flashlight off and put it in my pocket.

"You can't order me around," Nicole reacted, glaring at Graham. "I know the rail's loose."

"Shut up, Nicole. That rail's fine," Scott said, hopping down off the range and seizing her arm. "Come on."

"Don't touch me," Nicole protested, grabbing her arm back. "This is your fault. You did the rails."

"You're nuts." Scott went over to the rail and grabbed as hard as he could. He pushed it and it didn't move.

Scott went back to Nicole.

"Let's go or I'll drag you out of here."

"I have to pee anyway," Nicole said, transforming her exit into a voluntary act.

Scott escorted her out through the narrow passage without ceremony.

Nicole's back pocket rhinestone heart sparkled and bounced defiantly in the dim light.

* * *

"I called the ambulance," Alastair announced. "What else do you want me to do?"

"Get everyone in the theatre. Tell them to look at their damn lines. Then go outside and wait for the paramedics. Bring them through the parking lot and the backstage door," Graham ordered. "Kevin, go with Alastair. Veronica, you stay here with me until the paramedics come."

Graham was ever the director, calculating how this death, like Charlie's, would least disrupt his production. He had to make opening night still happen.

"Are you all right, Veronica," Kevin asked touching my shoulder.

"I will be. Go on."

I lowered my eyes and relished his touch. I was fine but I didn't want Kevin to know that. He hesitated and then followed Alastair out through the passage.

Alastair and Kevin collided with Mel running in through the crossover.

Mel shoved past them.

"What the hell happened?" Mel shouted at Graham out of breath. "There's an ambulance outside. "Where's Nicole?"

"Nicole's fine," I said.

"It's Renee." Graham stepped aside to show Mel Renee's body.

"Renee?" Mel took a close look at Renee lying on the black painted floor. "What happened?"

"We don't know what happened," I answered.

"How is she?" Mel asked.

"She's gone," Graham said somberly.

"Gone?" Mel questioned as he leaned on the rail, which seemed solid under his weight. "You mean dead?"

"Yes," Graham said.

"Like Charlie?" Mel exclaimed. "What is this, an epidemic?"

Mel was shoved aside by a tall male paramedic and his female partner.

"Make way. Get out of the way."

These were not the same paramedics who had come to the scene of Charlie's demise. But trailing behind them were the same young cops; laughing cop and the female copette.

We all cleared the way by squeezing into whatever space we could find.

As laughing cop passed he did a double take, recognizing Graham and then me.

"Start with those two," he ordered his partner. "They were here with the last body. Remember?"

"Yeah." Then his partner took out her notebook and pen to take everyone's statements.

There were few facts to record because Renee, like Charlie, had died alone. Her job was pro forma. He closed her notebook quickly.

We stood quietly and watched the paramedics try to revive Renee.

They couldn't.

But they did take Renee, with all the proper tubes extruding from her, out the rarely used backstage door to the hospital.

⌘

CHAPTER 20

"This above all: to thine own self be true.'"
-Shakespeare, *Hamlet*, Act 1, Scene 3

After the paramedics took Renee's body out, Mel pushed past me to Graham. He was angry. He shoved his face into Graham's in good cockfighting mode.

"We have to talk. Now."

Graham and Mel marched away through the passage. Mel led the way and his thin wiry body was eclipsed from behind by Graham's substantial girth. I heard the women's dressing room door slam.

* * *

Alone, I sat on the ottoman in the crossover's dim light. I listened to the faint creaks of the stacked furniture and boxes that had been disrupted by the business of death. I suddenly shuddered, unexpectedly and uncontrollably. Two bodies in two days. I hoped that bad things did not come in threes as superstition dictated.

I ran my flashlight over the ladder. There was no white reflector tape on the steps. I wondered if it would have spared Renee this fate. I saw Renee's script under the ladder. As I picked it up, I regretted making her last role a public humiliation by slashing it down to nothing.

To calm myself I took a few deep breaths. I leafed through Renee's revised script. She had already highlighted her lines in yellow and transferred her blocking, in pencil. Howard was right. Renee was a dedicated actor and she would have been ready for opening night. She always had been in my experience.

I closed the script and set it on the ladder. I didn't mind helping Graham salvage his play, but I was ashamed that I had been the instrument for Mel's vindictiveness.

I started through the crossover to get back to the stage. I stopped. Then, I whipped around and zeroed in on Renee's script on the ladder.

"Why not?" I whispered to my self.

I hurried back for Renee's script. I felt like a ghoul. But someone had to do Renee's role. I grabbed her script from under the ladder.

"Who could do it better?"

"No one," I answered myself.

I decided, however, that I would not volunteer too quickly or publicly. I would secretly start memorizing Renee's lines and blocking tonight. I tucked the script under my arm.

As I walked back thought the crossover, I felt like a vulture feeding on Renee's misfortune. Then with each new step, I convinced myself someone had to step in and I was the logical choice. I already knew the play. I was so excited about the prospect of being on stage with Kevin again, especially in the tender scene between Kevin and Renee, which fortunately I had not cut.

I went to deposit Renee's script in the dressing room for later, but stopped outside the closed door. I heard arguing.

* * *

"What the hell do you mean you didn't get the insurance?" Mel yelled. "I gave you the money."

"But we had to have the set finished," Graham explained and justified.

I, of course, knew Graham's reality did not include any thought of insurance, let alone budgeting for it. So, I wasn't surprised at his answer. It wouldn't be the first time Graham used money he shouldn't have for his set. I understood now why Graham hid the incident with the Fresnel falling the other night. It was not only for everyone's morale, but also because he knew the subject of insurance would come up with Mel.

I crept by the door with the script and decided to deposit it near Graham's usual seat in the theatre.

I slipped through the wings and crossed to the stage access stairs. As I went down to the seats, I glanced up at the balcony and saw Bryce standing there. He caught my eye and scurried back to his lighting board. I knew Bryce had entertained himself at Renee's expense with his lighting tricks feeding on her fears of ghostly machinations. I suspected he intentionally created the uncontrolled flickers and the blue light sweeping across the stage in the black out just before Renee fell.

Although I didn't know if Bryce had actually caused Renee's fall, I did know I didn't want to see him right now. And he obviously didn't want to see anyone either.

I took a nearby seat in the front row and set Renee's script near Graham's. Nicole, who was sitting up a couple of rows on the other side of the center aisle between Geoff and Kevin, stared at me.

Tim, Scott, Anna, and Joel sat silently in the front row below Nicole. Anna rested her head on Joel's shoulder. Howard was up behind me and over several seats, sitting by himself. His elbows rested on his knees and he leaned forward with his face buried in his hands. Alastair stood at the back of the theatre leaning on the door jam that led to the lobby. I heard him playing with the coins in his pocket.

No one spoke.

I glanced over at Renee's script and felt sheepish about my plan to start memorizing her lines tonight. I remembered Kevin's touch and smell backstage and the many stage kisses we had shared years ago. I began to feel guilty because I knew I was planning to take advantage of the tender scene I would have with Kevin onstage as Renee's character.

Then, I looked at the beautiful Victorian set and all my guilt washed away. I wanted that part. I wanted to act on that stage with Kevin. I also needed that part to legitimately desert my writing class and my authorial career for the run of the play, however short it was.

I reached for Renee's script just as Nicole planted herself in the seat next to me.

"Renee's script?" Nicole asked.

"Yes," I said, drawing my hand back. "I brought it out for Graham."

Nicole grinned. I felt as if she had been reading my mind.

"Renee's dead because of Scott's rail," Nicole said in a stage whisper to me that carried throughout the theatre.

"We don't know that."

I thought it odd that she was so invested in blaming the rail and Scott.

"I heard you, Nicole," Scott called over. "That rail was solid."

"I don't think so," Nicole hissed, venomously glaring at Scott with her pale blue eyes.

"You don't think at all, bimbo." Scott stood and stared with no deference to Mel's proprietary interest in Nicole. "That's bull. My rails are solid as a rock. Tell Bryce to stop jerking off in the lighting booth."

"Hold on, Scott." Joel pulled Scott back into his seat. "For all any of us know, if the rail is loose, she knocked it when she fell."

"It's not loose," Scott insisted. "And, Nicole, you shut your big mouth about it."

"I think we should all settle down. The rail was fine," I interceded, not defending Scott but thinking of Graham's insurance status, or lack thereof.

"Right," Joel agreed. "She was old. I mean she probably had a heart attack."

"It was me," Howard said looking up and straight ahead into the void. "I pulled too hard on her arm and then let loose too fast. I know it. I was mad."

"There you have it," Scott said. "It was Howard's fault."

"Back off, Scott," Kevin responded and then looked up at Howard. "Renee was holding her script, Howard, she just didn't have a good hold in the dark. I think she . . ."

"The blue light," Geoff interrupted with urgency. "The blue light . . ."

Just then Mel marched onto the stage with Graham following and the bickering stopped in its tracks.

* * *

"Don't start on the blue light and ghosts," Mel boomed. "You and Bryce have had all the fun you're going to have. Did any of you idiots think that maybe she just took a header?"

Drunk and unsteady, Mel leaned on a Victorian set chair down stage. Graham sat opposite.

All eyes were on Graham as he sat uncharacteristically quiet. When he looked up and out into the audience he held his hand over his eyes to block the bright light.

"Turn that spot off, Bryce," Graham barked at Bryce in the balcony.

The spot disappeared and Graham then addressed the cast assembled in the theatre.

"I want . . . No. I am telling you all to stop this. Renee fell. It's tragic, but accidents happen in the theatre."

"Yeah," Scott agreed. "Like Charlie. Just bad luck."

"Scott, quiet." Graham went on. "We all know that Renee wouldn't want us to jeopardize this production. For now, we need to cooperate. The sooner we finish the rehearsal, the sooner I can go and take care of arrangements for Renee's body."

"Renee's body . . ." Anna started to sob.

"Can it, you drama queen," Nicole yelled. "This isn't about you."

"Please everyone," Graham dug deep and asserted his best leadership skills. "One of our cast members and a dear friend of mine is dead. Let's all take a moment."

Graham arrested the cat-fight with a reverent tone, whether sincere or merely feigned with his not unaccomplished acting skills. I knew Renee was no "dear friend" of his. I was one of the only people here who would come close to claiming that dubious title and I couldn't claim it. Graham's "friends" were actually merely necessary functionaries. That is not to say he didn't like some people more than others, but I believed he was missing the deep warm and fuzzy friendship button.

Graham bowed his head for a long moment of silence and then addressed the subdued group.

"I understand we are all upset," Graham said. "But we have to finish our rehearsal here. I have to notify Renee's relatives afterward. Renee spent her life in the theatre and she knows we have responsibilities beyond sorrow."

Graham had remediated his perfunctory attitude toward Renee's death.

"How can I rehearse now?" Nicole cried out. "How can any of us?"

"Settle down, Nicole," Mel commanded from the stage and sat in the chair that had been holding him up.

Nicole followed Mel's order for now.

"She's right. I need to take Anna home. She's upset. Can't you rehearse around her?" Joel asked. "I'll be right back."

The baby actors were not going to rehearse whether Graham wanted them to or not. We more seasoned, or merely more callous, members of the troupe knew, and accepted, that a play opening trumped even death.

More importantly, I knew how Graham's mind worked. At the moment, Graham viewed Renee's death only as an obstacle to be overcome to get this play open and running. He would be sad later. But not sad for her. Instead, sad because he knew her death reflected exactly how his own demise would someday be handled with an unceremonious functionary analysis.

I had been through actors' accidents, injuries, and illnesses with Graham before. His only concern was always the effect on the show. He wasn't heartless, but he was the captain of the ship and always first considered the good-of-the-order. And even more so tonight, because without the show up and running and earning money, he would lose the theatre to the Crenshaw Troupe.

Even with this burden, however, I saw he was behaving unreasonably. I had to intervene.

"Graham, if you call the rehearsal tonight and start earlier tomorrow, you can release everyone to study their lines," I suggested from the front row quietly. "We can work around anyone who has to be late."

"Good idea, Veronica," Mel validated.

Graham looked at Mel and then me.

"Right," he agreed, but reluctantly. "Fine. But I need to talk to you before you leave, Veronica."

"Okay." I hoped I hadn't overstepped my bounds.

"Alastair, get down here," Graham called.

* * *

Alastair came down the center aisle and conferred with Graham.

Alastair strutted back up the center aisle to do his job. "Can everyone make it an hour and a half early tomorrow?"

There was a clamor of "yeses" and nods.

"I'll call in sick at work," Scott volunteered, trying to put himself above the fray.

"I have an audition for a film, but I think I'll be done," Joel also called out, letting the whole cast know that he was a busy actor on the way up in the fast track.

Alastair looked up at Graham, and Graham nodded a go ahead.

"Just get here as soon as you can." Alastair was pleased there were no bigger problems with the change in schedule. "Everyone is released. Come prepared and study your changes. I don't want to be standing in the wings feeding you lines tomorrow."

"Wait. We don't have a Renee replacement," Mel shouted, leaning forward in his chair. "I dumped a fortune into this production and no one is leaving until I know what's up."

"Yeah, Mel," Nicole chimed in. "Are we going to open or not?"

"We're opening, honey. And no one is leaving here until we straighten this out," Mel ordered, smiling at Nicole and running his eyes down to her sweater and below.

"Right."

Nicole grinned and leaned back, arching her body so that her breasts popped under her sweater, rounded and soft. She bathed in Mel's gaze. She knew she still had what it took to control him, at least tonight.

"Yes, we're going to open. And we have who we need right here to make it happen," Graham announced, looking straight at me. "I was going to ask Veronica to help us out after everyone left but now is as good a time as any."

All eyes turned to me in the front row. I was ecstatic. I didn't even have to hint for the role and it had fallen into my lap.

"I don't know if I can do it, Graham," I said, feigning resistance. "That's a lot to learn by the Preview Thursday."

"Less than yesterday, thanks to your cuts," Mel chimed in. "And you have a head start over anyone else we would try."

The reality hit me that I had the role tonight if I just acquiesced. I hesitated for show, but also because this reality triggered self-doubt about memorizing lines.

Memorizing verbatim was harder for me with age. I was not as bad as Renee, of course, but still it was hard. I had to use tricks, acronyms, sense memory, and the physical blocking to make it my own before I could put the lines solidly in my head. I worried that I couldn't do the work.

"You'd be perfect," Kevin joined in. "And you're a great actress."

I looked over at Kevin's hopeful eyes and that was all I needed; that and the thought of a wonderful extended reason not to "resume writing" my fourth almost non-existent book. Being in this play would be a very valid and public excuse for not writing. I could invite everyone, including my teacher Mavis and my fellow students, to see me acting in the play; a play that, with any luck and my help, might have a good run and absolve me from writing for months.

"Help us out," Anna urged with her sweet voice and pleading black eyes. "It'll be fun."

"I can get an ear microphone to feed you lines if you need," Alastair said. "We've done it before. Remember, Graham?"

Graham ignored Alastair and waited for me to answer.

I looked at the script near me on the theatre seat and then up at Graham on the stage.

"I'll do my best." I accepted.

"Wonderful," Graham exclaimed, leading the entire troupe in a short applause.

Graham immediately turned director again with his organizational dictates.

"I am cancelling the Preview Thursday, if that's all right with Mel. It'll help Veronica and the rest of us too."

"I don't see any choice," Mel agreed.

"Good. It's settled. We'll do the tech run Wednesday and the final dress Thursday. Open Friday," Graham announced. "We're done tonight. See you all an hour and a half early tomorrow, except Joel. Joel, for God's sake try to get here on time. We have a lot to do. And make your auditions earlier from now on. Films can't trump our production."

"Yes, sir," Joel responded.

We all knew that films would trump any 99-seat theatre production in this star driven town. Hollywood was, after all, Hollywood and we all knew why the young and beautiful came here.

"We'll start at the top of act one tomorrow and run straight through. Off book." Graham added.

"Act one tomorrow. Straight run-through," Alastair announced, in true stage manager form. "You're released."

* * *

As everyone started to leave. I didn't stir. I felt guilty about being happy. But, I had been in the right place at the right time and poor Renee had been in the wrong place at the wrong time. A great character and wonderful role, reduced but still wonderful, was handed to me on a silver platter. A late silver platter with a lot of time pressures, but a silver platter nonetheless.

I smiled as every one said good night and welcomed me on board. When I reached over for Renee's script, Nicole stood up.

"Lucky you salvaged her script," Nicole taunted.

I looked up at her and shrunk in my chair. I knew that she knew when I carried the script out that I had planned on asking for the part. She knew because she would have too. I hated the fact I had behaved like Nicole, but not enough to give up the role. Nicole walked up the center aisle to leave without another word.

"It'll be nice working together again," Howard said to me as he followed the others out.

"Thanks. I'm so sorry about Renee."

"At least you're here to help out."

I watched him go. He was overcome by Renee's death. I needed to console him. I had his cell and home phone on the company list.

"Thanks, Veronica," Mel said as he hopped down from the stage.

Mel lost his balance. I thought we were going to have a second fall tonight, but he caught himself on the theatre seat next to me. Mel laughed and so did Nicole, who was waiting for him up the center aisle.

"Let's get out of here," Mel said to Nicole, staggering up the center aisle toward her.

"Sure, baby."

Nicole grabbed Mel around the waist and took him up the center aisle. His eager hand grabbed her ass and covered the rhinestone heart on her jean pocket.

"You have your work cut out for you," Kevin said, walking over. "Let me know if you need extra rehearsal."

"Thanks. I will."

"See you tomorrow," Kevin smiled.

I watched him take the center aisle steps two at a time and out of the theatre. I thought of his offer of dinner and now an offer of help to learn my part. I smiled. I looked forward to both.

I headed up the center aisle to the lobby myself.

"Veronica?" Graham called out. "Wait up."

"Thanks," Graham said, coming up and giving me a big hug.

We walked through the lobby together.

"We'll see if you thank me opening night," I said, wishing it was Kevin who had given me the hug.

"You're a trooper," Graham said.

As I opened the wood-framed glass door out to the street, I heard Alastair shouting at Bryce to get the lights off so he could lock up.

"Poor Renee," I said to Graham.

"Yes, poor Renee," Graham echoed with an unexpected reverence.

"What do you think happened?" I asked with a twinge of guilt.

"I don't know. I don't want to know."

We left, Graham to the hospital and me for home.

⌘

CHAPTER 21

"Sweet are the uses of adversity."
-Shakespeare, *As You Like It*, Act 2, Scene 1

On the drive home Renee's lifeless eyes wouldn't leave my mind. I called Howard on my cell to console him. With each ring, though, I felt I had less to say to Howard because he had admitted to jerking Renee's arm on the stairs.

The phone went to message. I didn't speak.

I got home after midnight, tired.

I went to bed, but couldn't sleep. I was enthralled and surprised at my ease in examining Renee's body. I was proud of myself, a homicide virgin, who had essentially exercised the postmortem acumen of my fictional protagonists and those of Sir Arthur Conan Doyle or Agatha Christie. I also couldn't get Kevin out of my mind. He was so caring tonight and his touch so intoxicating.

I watched a 1939 black and white big production musical on my old movie channel as a sleeping pill. It didn't work. My mind replayed Charlie's death and then Renee's. I couldn't reconcile two deaths in two days.

* * *

Unable to sleep, I got up and went to my computer. I knew my muse was gone, but I thought of editing one of my books. After all, I had edited Mel's play well and quickly. I felt that all I needed was motivation, a real deadline like with the play. I decided a query letter to a literary agent would give me just that.

I updated a query letter I had drafted for my third book years ago. I chose a first rate New York agent who specialized in mysteries. I printed out the query letter. I was pleased with myself and set the query letter on my desk in a stack of to dos. If the agent wanted a draft, it would motivate me to edit it.

I went to bed, again.

As I studied my lines for the first act in Renee's old script, I suppressed any analysis and suspicions as to how Renee fell. I had other fish to fry. But, as I memorized lines, the touch of Renee's script reminded me that I had coveted her role too soon. I decided in the morning I would print my own, fresh script untouched by Renee. I also realized that I would not have time for dinner with Kevin until these lines were memorized. But, since we were going to be cast-mates again, there was plenty of time for that.

After a short time, I did drift off to sleep with my lines running in my head. My overactive mind was occupied, as it always had to be.

* * *

Monday morning I got up late for me, at seven-thirty. I sat in my study with a cup of high-octane ginger peach tea. I needed the caffeine. I watched my printer spit out a fresh copy of the final script Mel had emailed back to me. Then, I began studying my lines without the ghost of Renee bothering me.

Surprisingly, after a short time I did know of the lines in act one. I attributed that to unadulterated fear and also the fact that I had cut most of the lines down to one word or sentence. I was glad with the Thursday Preview cancelled I had until Friday's opening night. I knew it killed Graham to cancel anything.

I started memorizing act two and coveting Renee's monologues I had cut. Even though they were repetitive, I might ask to add them back after we opened. After all, I loved the spotlight as much as any actor.

At nine the phone rang.

"Veronica, you awake? It's Mel."

"Good morning." I steeled myself against meeting him for dinner after being stuck with the outrageous dinner tab last time. "How are you doing?"

"Fine," Mel said dismissively, not bothering to inquire about my state after such a horrendous evening.

"What's up?" I asked, incredulous that I heard a woman, obviously Nicole, giggling in the background.

"Are you comfortable with taking over Renee's part? I mean, frankly, can you act?"

There it was. Sobriety, in the clear light of morning, had raised doubts about handing me Renee's role. Sobriety, and, I was sure, a little nudge from the lovely Nicole, who was a proven pot-stirrer and trouble maker, even in the very short time I had known her.

"I suppose that answer would depend on who you asked, wouldn't it?"

I chose to answer his question with a question to passively torment this egocentric 99-seat theatre playboy.

"That's funny," Mel chuckled with an edge. "Graham says you're okay. Kevin likes being on stage with you. But this morning I found some marginal, well, let's be honest here, a few bad reviews on the Internet from a couple of your old performances."

I was annoyed that my whole life was on the Internet without my permission and I was more annoyed that Mel was an Internet snoop.

"Look, Mel, I have a lot to do. I'm editing a book and completing another." I puffed self-importance easily to this habitual puffer and, furthermore, didn't consider it dishonest at all.

"I . . . wait a . . ." Mel stammered, undoubtedly slowed by his hangover.

"If you don't want me to step in, I'm fine with it. But I have to be honest with you, too. I don't think you can find another Equity actress who can drop everything and be ready to open in a few days. I'm happy to do it for Graham and I think it'll be fun, but you really have to make up your mind because I'm memorizing this stuff and it's no picnic."

I purposely checkmated him with the exigent circumstances because, in point of fact, I did want the part. But I was not going to beg.

I added, "Quite frankly, I'm concerned about stepping into Renee's shoes anyway before we find out what happened last night."

"What do you mean? She probably had a heart attack or something."

"Precisely. But it's the 'or something' that would concern any actress."

I was using reverse psychology and playing on Mel's desperation. I wanted back on stage more than anything, especially with Kevin. And, of course, I did need the escape from my non-writing authorial life.

"Even if she did trip it was her fault. Do you know if she has any family?"

"I don't think so," I said, appalled at Mel's transparent concern about being sued.

I heard more of Nicole in the background. This time she was moaning. I was being subjected to their sexual foreplay. I'd had enough.

"Look, Mel. Graham is my friend and I'll help out. If you want someone else you . . . ."

"No. Fine. Look. It's fine. I don't see how Graham's going to pull this together. But it's fine."

Mel backed away from his attack on my acting and artfully deflected to a focus on Graham's ability as a director. I was sure Nicole's more urgent moaning in the background had something to do with Mel's loss of interest in my acting capabilities.

"Believe me, Graham will get it done," I said. "I've seen him open a play to great reviews with no full dress rehearsal and nothing more than a tech run."

I did not add that Graham was working with a great play then, not Mel's piece of hackneyed fluff.

"Really? Are you . . ." Mel stopped talking abruptly. "Nicole, stop."

I heard Nicole in the background telling Mel to get off the phone and whining that she was hungry now.

"Don't let Graham's nervousness fool you," I said, wanting to extricate myself from Mel's morning playtime with Nicole. "He knows what he's doing. I gotta go."

"Fine," Mel said, unsatisfied but hanging up.

The part was mine whether it was by default or not. I knew Mel had admitted to himself he couldn't get anyone in at this late date and open on time to start bringing in box office receipts. I was victorious and excited.

* * *

After studying more lines, I checked both my email addresses. The one for my family and friends was empty. The one I had set up long ago to be an author, however, was full. It had become a catch all for acting and purchases.

Because I was in the "biz" again, I skipped to my "actor" emails; my actor's unions and theatrical announcements. Actor's Equity posted a free audition class and a career development panel discussion next month. SAG-AFTRA sent news about its upcoming elections which I would vote in this time, an actors Conservatory for a mere $25, and several classes on actors' film contracts. Theatrecrazy, the site for local theatre news, productions, and discount tickets, sent me the weekly email about current shows. I saw the opening date of our production and it gave me butterflies.

I wanted to get the audiences and money into the Valentine for Graham. I sent emails to my friends and book fans. I linked them into Theatrecrazy for tickets and the Valentine Theatre with its history and ghost lore. I knew the senior citizen's homes, where I did my readings, had bus outings for Sunday theatre matinees. I would get them to our production.

L.A. had an incestuous small cottage theatre industry of actors watching actors. Usually, actors populated performances with their own roving groups of fellow thespians. I, however, was bringing in "real" audiences.

I was so enthused about my rejuvenated acting endeavor that I re-subscribed to the Upstage Today site. It had entertainment news, but more importantly casting notices for union and non-union theatre, student and graduate films, independent films, and union waiver films. I remembered the hard copy version I subscribed to in college. As I skimmed through, I found three independent film parts I was right for.

Who knows, I thought? If my muse and my query letters fail me I might decide to audition after all.

I glanced over at my query letter for my book and decided it could wait. I went back to memorizing my lines.

The trick for my memorization was to learn the lines rapid-fire in a continuous monologue with no cues or other actor's lines in between. I typed them up that way and carried the page around as I did my household chores. Memorizing while you did physical things made mishaps on stage less likely to throw you.

* * *

At three in the afternoon, I called Graham while I watered my potted plants on the back patio.

"So how did it go at the hospital?"

"Not well," Graham said. "There was no heart attack or stroke. She broke her neck when she fell and she didn't die instantly. Evidently, she was conscious for a few moments."

"Oh, my God." I had to sit on my nearby weathered redwood bench. "This is . . . it's just horrible."

"I'll get on Bryce about playing with the lighting and Scott about timing the special effects. And I told Mel to have Nicole stop talking about loose railings."

"But you should check the screws missing at the top," I urged. "I saw some holes."

"Veronica, the rails are firm. And don't repeat that," Graham harped. "There are unpainted old screw holes all over sets from changes. You know sets never fit the first time, especially ones like that tight staircase."

"You're right," I said, trying to calm Graham down.

"And never mention that damn Fresnel falling light to anyone. Anyone at all. I hope Bryce hasn't. That would be a disaster on top of Charlie and Renee." Graham became uncontrolled. "I can't believe the bad luck."

"Graham, settle down. You're going to have a coronary. Nothing else will go wrong."

"Let's hope not."

"It won't."

"I want to give you some blocking before we start tonight. Can you be there at four-thirty?"

"Sure, but before you hang up, you should know that Mel called."

"I know. He called me after you with Nicole egging him on in background. Just ignore him. Who does he think we're going to get at this late date?"

"Hey, I'm not chopped liver."

"I know, dear. Not to worry. I told him you were great," Graham said dismissively. "How are the lines going?"

"Good."

I chalked Graham's lack of coddling up to his belief that those who are closest to him need the least stroking.

"See you at four-thirty then."

Graham hung up.

* * *

If I was going to make a four-thrity call in Monday afternoon rush hour traffic, I had to get in high gear.

I got my black canvas theatre bag. I used it for rehearsals and performances so I wouldn't forget anything, like the time I forgot my skirt and had to perform in a black slip. The audience didn't notice but I sure did. Interestingly, the added tension I felt heightened my performance. That is often true in acting.

I packed it with a fresh peanut butter and honey sandwich on whole wheat for dinner, mints for close scenes, and tissues. I threw Renee's old script in it to give back to Graham. I didn't feel right putting it in my trash bin.

I dressed in black jeans and a green cable knit wool sweater. I was excited. Harnessing adrenaline was what acting was all about. I applied my make-up carefully for the scrutiny of close encounters under bright lights, all in hopes that Kevin and I would eventually have a closer encounter under less light.

As I looked in the full-length mirror in my bedroom, I compared my mating dance of a more mature woman with that of Anna's and Nicole's more urgent and overt display of plump young wares.

The sad, observable difference in the marketing came down to me covering up what wasn't there any more. The end-game, though, was identical.

⌘

CHAPTER 22

"The better part of valor is discretion."
-Shakespeare, *Henry IV, Part I*, Act 5, Scene 4

When I arrived at the Valentine, Graham was in the lobby jabbering excitedly to two men in unkempt suits. His arms were waving around. Graham saw me and pointed in my direction.

"There she is," Graham announced, disappearing through the lobby door into the theatre.

Both men marched on me displaying their detective badges.

"Veronica Kennicott?" The older, heavier detective asked with an inquisitional tone.

I froze. The scene in my last book where the protagonist was arrested and jailed replayed in my mind. My heart beat overtime. What had I done?

"Yes."

"You got Renee Richter's part in this play?"

I spent the next few minutes explaining to both of them that I was a writer here to edit the play and I took over Renee's part as a favor to Graham. Then, I made the mistake of asking a question; that one-too-many question we have all heard about.

"Is there something I don't know about Renee's fall?"

"Just routine inquiry in an accident like this," the young detective said.

"Like this?"

First, I knew from mystery movies and reading and my mystery writing that nothing was "just routine" with detectives. Second, I knew instinctively from my foray into my limited crime solving endeavors that these men knew something critical that I did not.

"And what department are you from?" I asked.

"Homicide," the young detective answered.

"Homicide!" My heart sank and my mind raced and I tried to think of an exit strategy. None came to mind so I stoically stood my ground.

The older detective said, "So you're an author and actress?"

"An author," I corrected, wishing I had mailed that query letter.

"Your director says you write crime novels?" The young detective asked the question with a friendly, almost collegial smile as he flipped through his little notebook.

"Mysteries. Suspense. Yes."

I avoided the label crime novel, under the circumstances, as I steeled myself against the dreaded "no-agent-yet" dance I expected.

"Then you're not an actress?" the older detective queried yet again, appearing not to understand people can do more than one thing.

"Right." I didn't like their questions

Accuracy was of the essence in a situation like this. Many a convicted criminal wished they had been more accurate from the onset. I needed at this moment to be simple and clear and set myself forth as an unadulterated professional writer who did not covet Renee's role.

"I'm a writer. I have a web site you can look at, three books and a fourth on the way. That's my life. Ask anyone."

"But you can do this role?" The older detective questioned looking around at the lobby.

"I used to act." I tried to explain everything simply to his meat-and-potato brain, but had little hope of getting through to it. "I just stepped in yesterday to help Graham out."

"I see. Trying to break into the business again." The older detective said, narrowing his eyes and thinking.

"No."

All the acting parts and union activities I had coveted at this morning lost their attraction to me. I didn't like either detective's innuendoes and reverted to repeating, in many different ways, that I knew nothing. I emphasized that I had been called by Graham to edit the play, not to act in it; that I was a writer, not an actress; and that I did not want to "break" into the biz again.

"Have you talked to Howard?" I asked, desperate to get the older detective off his single-minded thought process focused on me and my lust for a part.

"Howard?" The young detective flipped back in his notebook to the names he had written down. "That's the boyfriend."

"Yes." I was ashamed of myself for using Howard as an exit strategy, but felt justified because Graham had no qualms using me as one in this game of hot potato. "He was on the staircase with her in their fight scene."

"Howard," the older detective said with interest. "The boyfriend?"

"Yeah," his partner confirmed. "That's the guy who fights with her on the platform."

"Hmmm." The older detective eyeballed me. "You know this Howard?"

"Yes." I announced in good "traitor-like" form.

I was now a stool pigeon, a squealer, a rat, as well as an author turned actress. It appeared I had many talents but no fiber. I was "yellow."

"He'll be here tonight?"

"Yes," I answered, feeling even guiltier. "I really have to go now."

"Go," the older detective released me. "But not too far."

As I went through the lobby door and down the theatre center aisle, I heard them talking about Howard. I had a twinge of regret, but it was overridden by my feeling of relief.

I needed to find Graham. I needed to give him a piece of my mind for pointing the finger at me. I also needed to ferret out what the detectives had told him.

⌘

CHAPTER 23

"More sinned against than sinning."
-Shakespeare, *King Lear*, Act 3, Scene 2

There was no one in the theatre. I went up the stage to the women's dressing room. Still no Graham.

I dropped my bag at the dressing table where Renee's name already had been replaced with mine.

Anna's dressing table was to my right. She had not arrived yet, but there were several bottles of a cranberry herbal tea lined up against the mirror.

Nicole's table across the room had a big black gym bag with a red stripe along the top zipper. Her script was thrown on it. She was here already. Somewhere. I got Renee's old script out of my bag and headed through the crossover in search of Graham.

In the crossover, I heard rats scurry through the stacked set furniture near me. I stomped my feet to forewarn them to stay in their own territory.

I passed the spot where Renee had fallen. It was already freshened up with a new coat of matte black paint. I went up the ladder and tested the rail. It was solid. I considered why the detectives were so aggressive. I noticed the posts were freshly touched up, including to the mars at the bottom. But there were dried drips of black paint everywhere. That wasn't like Scott. He was not a sloppy painter. As I got down, I decided he must have been in a real hurry.

I scrutinized the empty screw holes. Graham was right. They were just from set changes.

* * *

On the other side of the crossover, I found Graham. He was quarrelling about set changes with Scott in the men's dressing room.

The men's dressing room was larger and as brightly lit as the women's with the same tables and mirrors. There was one overriding difference. It was a cluttered, unkempt mess. Even the cupboards at the far end were hanging open and stuffed full with clothes, costumes, and props.

"Hey, you threw me to the wolves," I shouted at Graham as I threw Renee's script in his hands.

Scott stepped out of the line of fire and gawked at me with his innocent face. "Don't include me. I didn't do anything."

"I know," I said turning my attention to Graham. "What did you tell them about me? Those detectives as much as said they thought I killed Renee to get her part."

"Hell, that's nothing," Scott interrupted amused. "They asked Graham how badly he wanted to get rid of Renee because she couldn't learn her lines."

"Scott," Graham reprimanded, irritated at his levity.

"At least, I'll have company in prison." I sat down and looked at Graham seriously. "They're homicide detectives. What's going on, Graham?"

"There were marks on the front of Renee's ankles," Scott blurted out, relishing being the know-it-all, as always. "I heard them talking in the lobby when they got here. Renee didn't fall. She was tripped."

"I can't believe that? Why would someone trip that old sweet woman?" I paused. "Or not so sweet old woman?"

I thought about my backstage assessment of Renee's body. I guess I wasn't as sophisticated as I believed. I wished I had paid more attention to the cuts and bruises on her arms and legs. I just assumed they were from the fall. But then I was no Sherlock Holmes, not yet.

"I don't know," Graham said getting more irritated with Scott. "I don't even know if it's true. The detectives could just be looking for a cushy assignment and are making a mountain out of a mole hill. But they said they believed someone tripped her on the stairway."

"What do you mean?" I asked. "Who?"

"'Therein lies the rub,' as Shakespeare would say." Graham shook his head and threw Renee's script unceremoniously into the trash nearby. "Who would do this?"

I watched it sink into the trash can along with my confidence. Evidently, my investigative skills in finding and evaluating clues on dead bodies needed some work. In the future, if I wasn't in prison for Renee's murder, I would never forget to scrutinize the feet again and, naturally, neither would my mystery characters.

"It's a mystery," Scott said with a big smile. "Go for it, Veronica."

"Don't be silly, Scott. But, how was she tripped? With what? By whom? I didn't see anything," I said, knowing any answer that was obviously beyond these two.

"With whatever," Scott answered sequentially like a game of "Clue." "But my vote is Howard for the 'whom' . . . because she broke up with him . . . for revenge."

"Scott, go do something. Anything," Graham ordered. "And keep your big mouth shut for once. Stop making a game out of Renee's death."

"Revenge? Don't be silly, Scott," I ignored Graham. "Did you leave anything on the steps?"

"No."

Scott got defensive and was not having quite as much fun.

"No, he didn't. I can't believe this." Graham yelled, the protective reflex for his show reared its head. "The detectives are crazy if they think anyone would put something on the ladder to trip Renee."

"You mean this was planned? Intentional?" I said, slowly letting the grim reality sink in.

"No, it was unfortunate," Graham corrected me.

Ever the bloodhound, I ignored his mincing word choice and asked, "You mean she was murdered?"

"Don't use that word, Veronica," Graham ordered getting more upset.

"Murdered?," Scott chimed in. "But why? She was just a . . . an old . . ."

"An old what," I interrupted.

"Has-been," Scott responded with a casualness born of youth and a callousness born of pop-culture's indoctrinated disregard for the elderly.

"Woman is a better word choice." I was offended by his limited view of life.

"Sure. Woman. I don't care. Either way, she was murdered," Scott retorted and then went over to Graham. "Give me the money for the new brush . . . brushes. I'll buy two. And more black paint."

"Keep the brushes put away. We don't want any more missing. It's a waste of money," Graham said, handing Scott forty dollars from his small worn canvas wallet. "And get two gallons of paint. We'll need it to touch up the stage floor before opening night and who knows what else."

"It looks fine," Scott objected.

"No it doesn't," Graham argued angrily. "And I'm telling you, Scott, don't use that word 'murder' again."

"Yes, sir." Scott stood at attention and mock saluted Graham. "I bet Howard murdered her."

Scott relished taunting Graham with the word "murder."

"Damn it, Scott." Graham jumped at the bait. "I don't want any one using that word around here. We don't need more trouble. You hear me?"

"Yeah. Yeah." Scott sauntered out of the dressing room door and then shouted back, "But my money's still on Howard."

"He's an idiot," Graham mumbled and then turned to me. "We have to focus on the show, Veronica. Get it up and running. We can't do that with all this murder business. So, let's be discreet with the 'M' word around here. I don't want my show shut down over this."

"Sure. It can't be true anyway," I said, putting my hand on Graham's large stooped shoulder. "The detectives are barking up the wrong tree. It was an accident. A terrible mistake. It was dark. It was a misstep. It had to be. If they knew what made the marks then they'd be satisfied."

"Well, they don't know and they took thorough pictures of everything today. They didn't like the fresh paint," Graham said, shaking his head. "And they wanted to know why I didn't call the police and report it."

"Report it? Report what?" I remarked taking a seat nearby. "Why would anyone call the police for someone falling?"

"Because you wanted her part," Graham answered, standing up and waving his arms up and down. "There I said it. That's what they said."

"I can't believe this." I was just glad I hadn't volunteered for Renee's role. "You drafted me to take the part. You begged me."

"I know that."

"And so did everyone last night."

"True. I told them that."

I thought back to the detectives' questions and saw exactly where they were going.

"That's preposterous," I shrieked. "No one would kill for a part."

"In Hollywood? Come on, Veronica, everyone would."

"I suppose that's true. But I wouldn't," I objected. "I mean, let's be honest, it's not much of a part after my edits. And, it's not much of a play for all that matters."

"It may be salvageable," Graham said defensively.

"Precisely. Might be," I argued. "And remember why I'm here. You asked me to salvage the play because I'm a writer. I hope you told the detectives that at least."

I was suddenly glad I had printed out the query letter for my third book, but I wished I had mailed it. I opined that it would go easier for me at my murder trial if I actually had a book in print.

"Of course, I told them," Graham said, with too little conviction for my comfort level. "Don't worry. This will all clear up."

"Not without my help," I muttered.

"What?"

"Nothing." I was convinced Graham was the reason the detectives had focused on me. "I should bow out of the play, Graham."

If I had known Renee was tripped I wouldn't have taken her role at all. I kicked myself.

"No, I need you to play the mother or we won't be able to open. I need to keep the Crenshaw Troupe from weaseling their way in here," Graham said. "Anyway, the damage is done."

I thought for a minute. I knew Graham had betrayed me, but not maliciously so. He was just a coward who wanted his play to open on time. I was sure he had minimized his betrayal and rationalized it as being for the good of the play. I supposed as a writer my job was done and any good actress could play Renee's pared down part now. But the damage was done.

"That's true," I agreed, thinking that dead bodies seemed to be following me around. "You can't un-ring a bell. Besides, it might look worse if I quit now."

I calculated that the best way to defend myself from the detectives' folly was to stay here and find the true killer if there was one.

"Precisely. Now, come on. I have to get this show up and running," Graham said heading out of the dressing room. "Let's go over your blocking before everyone else gets here."

"Okay." I followed Graham. "Did they know about Charlie and the gas leak?"

"No, and don't you tell them. Just keep your mouth shut."

I only wished he knew how to keep his mouth shut.

* * *

Graham and I went over the blocking for all three acts quickly on stage. It didn't take long. Basically, the mother sat in her favorite chair and called Nicole as the maid to do everything. My only real movement was periodically going to her bedroom up the staircase, at one point exiting the house, and the fight scene with Howard.

Bryce arrived early and watched from the balcony, synchronizing some of the lighting cues. He didn't say a word to anyone. It was all business.

Alastair came in and sat in the front row of the theatre eating a small carton of beef and broccoli from the Chinese restaurant across the way. He knew that food was only allowed in the dressing room or lobby, but he was the enforcer and wasn't enforcing himself.

After Graham and I finished on stage, he applauded loudly and vigorously.

"Bravo," Alastair called. "You are going to be wonderful. Much better than Renee. She was too old for the part anyway."

"Alastair, bite your tongue," I responded hoping the detectives wouldn't hear talk like that.

⌘

CHAPTER 24

"Age cannot wither her, nor custom stale her infinite
variety."
-Shakespeare, *Antony and Cleopatra*, Act 2,
Scene 2

After my encounter with the detectives and Graham's blocking session, I needed a caffeine boost before rehearsal. In my dressing room, I dug my change purse out of my bag. I went to get a caffeinated Earl Gray tea at Coffee and Conversation, a neighborhood institution up the block. It was a dimly lit, cozy coffee house; a local gathering place.

When I opened the glass door, the small familiar bell hanging on the inside handle jingled as usual. Not much had changed in the last several years.

There was the same array of old couches, easy chairs, and eclectic wood tables with assorted chairs. Perhaps there were a few more table and floor reading lamps. And at the back there was a long new computer bar with at least four caffeine-hyped college types banging on their keys.

Five years ago a retired Hollywood high school teacher bought the failing Thai restaurant here. He remodeled it and opened his own coffee house. As he tells all his customers, whether they have heard it before or not, his retirement dream was having this place for the neighborhood to congregate in and enjoy. That was why he named it Coffee and Conversation. He brags that his wife gets up before dawn every day to bake her pastry creations and unique muffins for him. They are wonderful, homemade, and sell like "hotcakes," so to speak.

I don't like to be judgmental, but I personally would rather be by myself creating fictional characters in the wee hours of the morning than slaving in a kitchen for a husband who sold my precious baking while blabbering all day about himself in self-absorbed, repetitive "monologues."

At noon, his wife also drops off less wonderful sandwiches. I like to think after dawn every day she saw see him more clearly and also her status as a functionary appendage. I eat the sandwiches infrequently during all day rehearsals and can attest to their mediocrity.

By evening, only a few leftovers are typically available, usually dried out pound cake or the broken cookies. Also, by this time the owner was usually tired of talking. He simply greeted you with a smile and took your order. I personally was always just as happy for that.

* * *

As I stood in the short line to order, I looked at the last piece of frosted lemon pound cake and then thought better of the sugar.

"Large Earl Gray, please," I ordered at the register and handed him my ones.

"Sure," the owner said. "Any thing else?"

"No, thank you." I dropped a dollar tip in the jar.

As I waited for my tea, I looked around and gave the owner credit. It was busy every time I came in.

Tonight, there was a high school group with backpacks at their feet and text books open on the table. They were ostensibly doing homework, but talking too much. They all had blue tooths at their ears. They were talking to a cyber interloper, listening to what passed for music these days, or wearing out their thumbs texting.

There were also two middle-aged couples at tables; one quiet but intense and one peaceful and happy. And, in the corner couches were two older couples validating their unions to spouses long changed and, unfortunately, still alive. Two young women, who wore contrasting navy and gray power suits, sat at an adjacent small table.

The two men ahead of me took their lattes and left. I got my tea, added the honey and half-and-half at the self-serve bar and sat down on the old maroon velvet couch in an unpopulated area.

I glanced at one of the middle-aged couples who had definitely started arguing. Then I observed the other middle-aged couple who sat quietly with their shoes intertwined under the table and happily laughed intermittently. I liked watching couples. I had liked being part of one.

I sipped my tea. I opened my script and stared at the first page of the first act. I planned on reviewing my blocking cues, but I woodenly turned page after page. I couldn't read, not a single word. I just stared and thought about taking Renee's role. I decided Graham was right. Quitting now would be worse than staying.

My thoughts were interrupted by the bell jingling as the glass door opened.

* * *

Kevin entered, tall and striking in his washed jeans, brown leather jacket, and black T-shirt. He had an animal magnetism that never turned off. He was also a man who loved being a magnet.

The two young women in power suits coveted him. When he smiled at them they each beamed back. Then, as he passed by their table, like mirrored duplicates, they crossed their unstockinged legs. He did glance down.

The middle-aged woman, arguing with her man, gazed at Kevin too long. The slighted man raised his voice.

The high schoolers remained in their own bubble, the happy couple didn't look over, and the computer bangers continued to bang.

I heard Kevin order a double latte non-fat, no-foam. My thoughts went from murder to the more important fact that my lipstick was on my paper tea cup and not my lips. I calculated whether I could reapply it before Kevin saw me. I couldn't risk being caught. I bit my lips and wet them to give them color and shine.

Just then, Kevin turned from the counter with his latte and noticed me. I had made the right decision. I would have been caught mid-lipsticking.

"Veronica, weren't you going to say 'hello'?" Kevin chided with his easy smile and his eyes crinkling in the corners.

"Of course." I glanced at the bobble-headed power suits still hopeful of a connection. "Have a seat."

Kevin leaned down and gave me a theatre cheek kiss. I returned it.

The power suits stopped beaming at Kevin and throwing off their pheromones.

"Sure." Kevin peeked at his watch. "I guess we have a minute. How are the lines going?"

I closed my script as Kevin sat in the low leather easy chair across from me. I was pleased he sat with me. I was anointed—selected—chosen by a man they had, in their own way, competed for. They still watched for another entre, perhaps on the way out.

"My lines are as solid as twenty-four hours will allow, given I don't have a photographic memory like Scott." I laughed an unnecessarily loud laugh declaring victory and possession.

"Yeah, not many of us do," Kevin chuckled and drank his latte.

"I was here early and did most of the blocking with Graham."

"It's a lot of pressure."

"Yes." I surmised that death and my new role had trumped any mention of dinner and logically they would.

"Too bad about Renee," Kevin said. "But a nice break for you."

"Oh, I don't know, I had to put a lot of things aside." In view of the detectives' focus, I didn't want anyone, even the handsome Kevin, to characterize my landing the part as a prize. "But I'm happy to help out. I love being on stage, especially with friends."

"Well, you are with friends." Kevin reached over and patted my knee.

It was a vigorous, asexual staccatoed thump that either lamentably defined our relationship or, I hoped, was simply a public gesture.

The power-suited women noted the pat. I was damned if I was going to let them discount my victory because of a neutral pat on the knee. I knew they couldn't hear our conversation, so I leaned over to Kevin to create a more intimate picture. Acting had taught me something after all. It was called staging and illusion.

I threw caution to the wind. I knew how to elicit a visible emotional reaction from Kevin to impress my competitors and seal my victory. I decided to use for forbidden "M" word.

"I just talked to two detectives at the theatre. Homicide detectives. They think Renee was murdered."

Kevin was shocked. He scooted forward, put his face closer to mine, and whispered, "What? Renee murdered. Why? How?"

I glanced at the professional women. I had achieved my end through my ruse. In the face of such apparent intimacy, the women returned to their conversation in defeat. I was done and would now keep my mouth shut as Graham had ordered.

"I don't know much else. But this is not for general consumption. So keep it quiet." I stood with my tea in hand. "It's time for rehearsal though."

Kevin and I stood. I saw the professional women eyeing me now, the victorious but aged competitor.

I had taken their prize with a staged ploy and, without remorse, used Renee's murder to seal the deal. I knew my exit with Kevin would be the frosting on the cake.

And it was.

⌘

CHAPTER 25

"Boldness be my friend!"
-Shakespeare, *Cymbeline*, Act 1, Scene 6

W hen Kevin and I arrived at the Valentine, everyone was already assembled in the theatre for the cast meeting; that is, all but Joel, who had not arrived from his audition.

Kevin wanted us to slip in at the back near Bryce. But I took us forward to the front row. I was not through branding him as mine. With the Coffee and Conversation cups in our hands and walking in together, I documented our out-of-the-theatre friendship.

We sat together in front beside Mel and Nicole. Everyone else was scattered closely behind us.

"Hey," Mel leaned over to me. "Graham called me about the situation and told me to get down here. Where did you go? We needed you."

"We had coffee," I said looking at Kevin.

"It's unbelievable about Renee," Kevin said to Mel.

I was thankful Kevin did not use the word "murder" because I knew I should have followed Graham's orders.

"Yeah," Mel said, dismissing Kevin.

In the theatre, and the industry, there was a demarcation line between the talent and the suits behind the scenes who made the project happen. Since I was Graham's confidante after and came in as a writer, Mel thought of me as a suit even though I had become talent by taking over Renee's part.

"Graham's backstage," Mel whispered, glancing at Kevin as an outsider. "Come with me."

* * *

I followed Mel to the crossover. Graham was sitting hunched over on the ottoman near the bottom of the ladder where Renee fell.

"Where were you?" Graham demanded, standing not without a struggle.

"I went to get tea." I was amazed that I was so missed by these two men. "What's wrong?"

"Besides the obvious," Mel replied sarcastically.

"Sorry." I realized I had to put my brainy-hat on.

"Look." Graham shook his head back and forth, shaking his white jello-like jowls under his chin. "The detectives said they are coming back tonight to interview every one. I think they want . . ."

"Stop pussy-footing around," Mel blurted. "In a nutshell, Veronica, we're afraid they're going to shut down the show."

"Tonight?" I observed these two men's desperate faces.

"Maybe," Graham answered.

"Can they?" I looked at Mel who, after all, was a lawyer.

"With a killer running loose?" Mel snapped. "Yes."

"Are we sure?" Graham asked hoping for another answer.

"Come on, Graham," Mel sneered. "They believe Renee was murdered. They can do what they want, when they want. Use your head. Especially if they find out about Charlie and make hay out of that gas leak. It looks like they're dropping like flies around here."

"Do they know yet?" I asked.

"Not yet," Graham replied.

"They will." Mel got louder. "And after the time we take to go to court to fight the shut down, we'll be under water financially. I'm not a bottomless pit and I have other projects."

"Hold on you two," I said sternly. "We need a game plan."

Graham turned to me. "How can we stop them?"

Graham was looking to me for answers that I didn't have. I solve my neighbor's problems, not murders. Truth be known, I had only proved the wicker furniture theft by actually seeing it happen in the wee hours of the morning.

"We need ideas." I stalled.

"I'm all out," Graham capitulated.

His unusual silence proved he was. I also didn't hear any from Mel either.

Then in a slow calculated thoughtful manner I filled the silence with the obvious just as the protagonists in my books do.

"We have to hand over the killer to the detectives," I declared.

"How?" Graham asked.

"Yes. How?" Mel probed.

I was amazed that these two men were both willing and ready to run with my simple and patently absurd idea. But then the drowning will grasp at anything to save themselves. And these men were drowning. They were both financially and emotionally totally invested in this production, which was on the brink of disaster.

I searched my brain for the "how"; the "how" for them and, more importantly, the "how" for me because the detectives had focused on me as a scapegoat.

Triumphantly, I announced, "We do our own parallel investigation."

I quoted my protagonist in my first mystery book. It seemed an elementary response, but it was all I had.

"That's easy for you to say," Mel snapped. "You're into this crime stuff."

"Yeah," Graham agreed. "We're not."

"Don't worry," I said thinking of another line from my first mystery. "The murderer will do our work for us if we are observant."

At this point, I bit my tongue. What was I doing? I wasn't anything but an unpublished mystery writer. Sure, I had helped solve some small mishaps around the neighborhood, but this was murder.

"Will it work?" Graham asked, looking at me with hope returning to his eyes.

"Sure. It has worked before," I said, unable to withdraw from the heroic path I had impulsively verbalized.

Graham was apprehensive, and looked at me for more assurances. Mel gazed down, thinking.

Emboldened, I quoted yet again from the first protagonist I had created years ago in the wee hours of the morning.

"Murderers always make mistakes. They always leave a trail. And they inevitably talk too much. We just have to do our due diligence."

Mel scrutinized me, his mind obviously churning behind his determined eyes.

"Besides, what choice do we have?" The platitude in all its banality slipped out.

"She's right. She knows the people and the inroads. No one we would hire could get up to speed quickly enough," Mel said with considered thought. "What choice is there? It might work. It's our best shot."

"Right," I confirmed.

Why shouldn't it work at the end of the day? It worked in my mystery books and for all the great mystery writers.

"Let us know if you need help." Graham headed out to the theatre. "I have to start rehearsal."

Mel stared at me, opened his mouth to speak, but didn't. He turned and followed Graham without another word.

I wanted to run after them and back out of my folly. But my feet wouldn't move.

* * *

I stood like a statue alone in the dimly lit, cluttered crossover as the two men disappeared around the corner.

I looked at the stacked furniture and props.

"Oh, God," I whispered. "I wish you could talk."

I studied the fresh matte black paint on the floorboards where Renee took her last breath. I brushed some adjacent rat droppings on the floor away with my shoe.

I wished there were real Valentine Theater ghosts to tell the story. But then, I wasn't actually a believer. Or was I?

I glanced around and then softly called out, "Renee? Renee?"

Of course, there was no answer. I felt like kicking myself. Even the greatest of mystery detectives did not have actual conversations with ghosts.

"What have I gotten myself into?" I mumbled as I left the crossover.

⌘

CHAPTER 26

"The miserable have no other medicine. But only
hope."
-Shakespeare, *Measure for Measure*, Act 3,
Scene 1

Back in the theatre, I returned to my seat between
Kevin and Mel. Graham had remained on stage for his
pre-rehearsal pep talk. He had two stacks of papers on a
Victorian side table.

Kevin smiled at me. I smiled at him.

"Graham's about to start," Kevin whispered
urgently, as if being late for Graham's repetitive words
of wisdom, pep talks, and Shakespearean references
was crucial to anything on the face of the earth, except
Graham's own ego.

For a moment—only a moment—I was
disenchanted with Kevin. He was behaving like the
grade school teacher suck-up we all hated. Then, I lost
myself in his green eyes again. Giving Kevin the
benefit of the doubt, I re-interpreted his words as
concern for me missing the meeting.

"Yes," I said, turning my attention to the stage, but not to Graham.

I studied the Victorian staircase, the vehicle for Renee's death. I planned to trace systematically everyone's whereabouts last night. That was my first step.

I had a lot at stake, my long friendship with Graham, my Valentine Theatre avenue into the acting world, and even my carefully honed reputation as a criminalist and mystery writer extraordinaire. But foremost at stake was my freedom. If the detectives were as mentally limited as they appeared, they would arrest their first and obvious choice—me.

It crossed my mind that the ridiculous, outspoken Scott might be right. In point of fact, Howard was a viable suspect. I certainly knew I was not the murderer.

Without ceremony or comment, Graham passed out the updated rehearsal schedule and the new contact list, which included my information in place of Renee's.

As I took one and passed the stack on to Kevin, I didn't use the potent opportunity to flirt with the man I had ruthlessly competed for earlier at Coffee and Conversation. Instead, I studied the list to see who else besides Howard could have strung something across the steps. Something that would to an effective certainty lead to Renee's death because of her age.

I listened with only half an ear to Graham's cheerleading speech, an animal I had heard too many times before. I surveyed the troupe and concluded it was falling on other deaf ears. The production and the troupe were in jeopardy. Everything Graham was saying, as always, boiled down to "the show must go on," obviously now even in the face of murder.

It crossed my mind again that perhaps Charlie's death wasn't an accident either, but I didn't see any connection to Renee's.

I ticked down the names on the new contact list sitting on my lap. Almost everyone had a reason to want Renee out of the show: Alastair was tired of prompting her from the wings; Howard was humiliated by her; Mel thought she was ruining his play; and Graham himself regretted casting her. Then there were Bruce and Geoff who liked her in the show but mainly to torture her with apparitions. Perhaps a practical joke gone wrong? Scott and Nicole just disliked the old lady.

But, all-in-all, I couldn't see anyone with a viable motive to murder Renee other than me.

Graham was right. In Hollywood lore, whether a correct perception or not, actors would kill for a part.

I decided I would talk to Howard first. Since he got flustered easily, whatever he had observed, or did, I could easily find out.

At that point, my critical analysis was jarred from my thoughts when Joel burst through the oak lobby door from his audition.

* * *

"Sorry I'm late," Joel interrupted Graham excitedly.

"Take a seat," Graham said. "As I was say . . ."

Joel did not do as ordered and instead blathered on.

"I had to stay for a bunch of test shots. They kept filming me."

"Really?" Anna said getting up and giving Joel a big hug on the steps of the center aisle. "They loved you."

"Yes. Yes, especially Stephie Sevas." Joel was on a high that could not be squelched. "She said she had looked long enough and I was perfect."

Joel had dropped the name of the biggest female film box office draw in the business, a woman at the top of the A-list. There was silence. All heads turned to Joel, except Nicole's. I saw her jaw clench as she glared down at her script.

"Did you get it?" Scott called across the theatre.

"Yes," Joel announced, kissing Anna.

"Great. Good show," Geoff said with his British reserve breaking the momentary silence.

Anna and Joel reveled with kisses and squeals in the center aisle.

I studied the troupe. Nicole stabbed her script with three short strokes of her pen ripping a hole in her pages. Beyond her, Scott could not conceal the envy on his face and looked down when I met his eyes. Kevin smiled a smile that I could tell was forced and coupled with a curios flash of sadness in his eyes. Tim grinned broadly and genuinely. Howard smiled with true joy for the first time since Renee's death. Bryce at the back of the theatre graced Joel with his tightlipped smile.

"Wonderful," Alastair stood in the second row and clapping for Joel.

"Congratulations, Joel." Graham called out and applauded.

He wanted to be liked by Joel now. And I knew why. Graham planned to suck as much publicity and money as he could from Joel and have the Valentine ride Joel's rising star until it burst or fell from favor.

"Bravo, Joel," Mel bellowed.

Mel followed suit because he knew the industry ran on contacts and Joel had them now, apparently bigger than Mel's.

Mel added, "We'll have to give you top billing."

Joel got a standing ovation from everyone, everyone but Nicole. She gave him a stand but no ovation.

All the baby actors were hopeful about their own careers again. It was the shot in the arm the cast needed, a unifying moment. It didn't matter what people's underlying motives or emotions were. We were ready to give the production our all.

⌘

CHAPTER 27

"Light, seeking light, doth light of light beguile."
-Shakespeare, *Love's Labors Lost*, Act 1, Scene 1

When everyone sat down again, instead of continuing with his pre-rehearsal pep talk, Graham gave an official congratulatory speech.

Graham was animated and happy. He bragged about other successful actors who had passed through the Valentine Theatre under his tutelage—a tutelage which, according to him, was their platform to stardom. He emphasized that each of them had come back and attended performances, contributed money to the productions, and that some had even acted in productions. All were B or C-list names, not A-list, but recognizable just the same.

Graham was never subtle in asking for support for his productions. In fact, he was shamefully overt. That, and Charlie's under-market rent, years-old, is why the company had maintained its longevity. Graham sucked money out of everyone he could, including me when my husband was alive. Graham's failure in charging actors monthly dues like the Crenshaw Troupe, I believed, was directly related to his abusive directorial style and evidently had sealed his insolvency.

Sadly and objectively, I knew Joel could not bring in money fast enough to save us this time even if he wanted to.

"Five minutes and then we start at the top of act one," Graham announced going down the stage stairs.

"Five minutes," Alastair echoed.

"Wait, people," Graham called out from the bottom of the stage stairs. "I should mention that the police will be here tonight to tie up Renee's unfortunate accident. Not to worry. This is all routine. There's really nothing to add to what Alastair and I told them. Our set is safe and essentially meets Equity standards. Keep your eyes on opening night. And, people, Charlie's mishap is not on their radar. We don't need unnecessary trouble. Be careful."

I noted the Graham's use of the word "essentially." We all knew it didn't meet any standard but Graham's aesthetic.

"Be careful?" Howard questioned standing up. "What does that mean?"

"It means keep your mouth shut about Charlie, stupid," Scott blurted out.

"Scott, shut up," Alastair said taking over as stage manager. "Howard, it means we don't want to borrow trouble. We're all sorry about Renee, but there is no need to make anything out of it other than what it was. A terrible fall. We have to focus on opening night now."

"Yeah, Howard," Scott said matter-of-factly. "Relax. She had already dumped you anyway."

Scott jumped up on the stage and disappeared through the wings. Howard sat with no response. I saw the pain in his face, but something else too that I couldn't decipher.

I hated Scott's usual and expected thoughtlessness. But I did believe that Graham should have headed off trouble and shared the truth with the cast; that the detectives believed Renee was murdered. Graham was banking too much on the detectives playing hide-the-ball during their interviews and his inner circle playing things close to the vest. I worried that Scott was a wild card and Nicole would get the truth from Mel during their nightly post-theatre activities--the truth that the detectives believed Renee was murdered.

"Five minutes and then places. Act one," Alastair called out jingling his coins in his pocket loudly to my annoyance. "Bryce, you up there?"

"No," Bryce called from the lobby door. "But I'm going."

Everyone scattered for a last smoke or a restroom visit. Graham took his director's seat down front.

"Coming?" Kevin said to me with his bright smile, offering me his arm to escort me up the front stage steps. "We will be under the lights together yet again."

I smiled and took Kevin's arm in a place where I could feel his round hard bicep flex under my hand. We walked by Graham toward the steps.

I was looking forward to being on stage again. Acting was like a child's structured play time, but with the intellect and emotions of an adult. To me, acting was akin to living your life again, but with the gift of hindsight. It was what most people always wanted; to relive their life knowing what they know today. And what I knew was to live through the moment you're in. That was the gift an actor gave to his audience. A very personal, deep gift.

"Veronica," Graham called after Kevin and I. "I need to see you."

For another second I clung to Kevin's arm, which to me was not an arm but instead a door to thoughts I had not had in years.

Then I uncoupled. I turned and walked back to Graham.

I sat one seat away as usual.

* * *

"Nearer," Graham said pulling me to the seat next to him.

Sitting next to Graham I felt his oversized, soft arm against mine on the arm rest. The touch was an abrupt and disappointing override to my sensual sense-memory of Kevin's strong hard lean arm. I scooted forward quickly, ending Graham's contact. It was too late. The feel of Kevin was relegated to intellectual recall now, like the stage kisses we had experienced years ago.

"Veronica, I don't want you even to intimate the word murder to anyone during your investigation," Graham whispered, giving me a very direct and very uneasy look.

"I hate to disillusion you, but I think everyone will find out anyway when the detectives question the troupe."

"You give too much credit to these people's thought processes," Graham said. "They're actors."

"Okay."

I ignored Graham's blatant disrespect of actors. I ignored a lot of things Graham said without editing himself.

"Veronica, you know I didn't mean your thought processes. I really meant the young ones," Graham said, trying to rehabilitate his comment.

"The young ones?" I said, goading him just a little.

"Of course, my dear, not to worry. You're a writer who acts anyway," Graham said with a smile and chuckle. "Forgiven?"

"Always."

I smiled at Graham thinking he was right that most actors were not that bright or they would have picked a profession that would feed them and put a roof over their heads.

"No one will get the idea of 'murder' from me," I assured Graham, knowing that I had already used the "M" word to Kevin, but had calculated it was well worth it—to me. "Frankly, since I appear to be the prime suspect, the less said the better."

I knew Graham did not think of me as a real actor. What he didn't know was that he shouldn't think of me as a real writer either.

I was a faux writer with an absent muse, an aversion to editing, and an inability to get even one query letter out of my to-do box at home. I was simply a person with nothing to do in the wee hours of the morning, who preferred writing fiction rather than reading it or watching television. But now, in escaping myself—or more accurately—my fictional world, I had become a murder suspect here at the Valentine Theatre.

"All I want to do is open and get the money in," Graham said, looking at me with decisive eyes. "Until then, Mel and I don't want this whole thing to Ouija Board out of control. I think if the detectives knew about Charlie's death and the Fresnel falling, we could be closed down, at least for safety reasons."

"I see your point," I said, coming back from my own concerns.

"Those detectives don't care about our show. Their job is to make an arrest no matter what. You have to do their job before they do, before they ruin us," Graham said taking my hand in his and patting it.

"I'll do my best," I said, finding Graham's plea in my self-interest anyway because I didn't want everyone to think I was a suspect. "But do you think the Fresnel or Charlie's death had anything to do with Renee's fall?"

"Come on, Veronica. Don't complicate things. Just remember we can't be shut down. We have to open and have a good run to bring in the money. Mel's no fool. If he loses his investment we'll lose him and if we lose him this theatre will go to the Crenshaw Troupe. I have no other angel in the wings And Joel is still pie-in-the sky until that movie is in the can and distributed."

"Graham," I said. "I don't . . ."

"Veronica, stick to the plan. The detectives obviously know things we don't, but you can beat them at their own game for me because we know things they don't, too. Now get up on stage. The show . . ."

"I know. I know." I stood.

I hurried up the access steps to the stage. I dropped my my script and pencil backstage to study and take notes between scenes. I dropped my other things in the dressing room.

As I went back to the stage, I decided I had to find the killer or to confuse the hell out of the cops. First, I had to find out what the detectives knew that we didn't.

I took my place on stage and waved at Bryce up in the balcony as I always had before Renee's death. He was still the man who would light me on stage. I didn't wave with any playfulness in my heart, though. I believed that, despite everything, Bryce's ghostly lighting games had contributed to Renee's fall.

I hoped Bryce didn't play with the lights when I exited down the steps backstage.

⌘

CHAPTER 28

"To climb steep hills requires slow pace at first."
-Shakespeare, *Henry VIII*, Act 1, Scene 1

Rehearsal began at the top of act one. I was in the first scene with Anna who is excited and happy when Howard tells her about her arranged marriage. It went quickly with the cuts and pacing. I said my lines on the heels of Howard's and Anna's last words which helped even more. It sounded natural and it is a way experienced actors shorten the running time.

At the end of the scene, Howard and I stood center stage and watched Anna. Her character runs singing up the Victorian staircase. She twirls at the top and then exits through the black velour upstage traveler on to the platform behind and down the fateful ladder steps.

Howard and I held our breaths as we watched her. All went well and we exited into the wings in a blackout.

* * *

I had a long break until my next entrance so I went to the crossover with my flashlight to look for missed clues. I went up the ladder. I searched it and the platform as the rehearsal continued on stage just the other side of the rear velour.

"Hey, what are you doing?" Scott approached carrying a lamp for the set change.

"Checking out my exit." I lied.

"That rail is solid, if that's what you're looking at," Scott whispered.

"I see, but your painting is getting sloppy."

"I didn't do that mess."

"Who did?"

"Who cares, but they left the brush full of paint and ruined it," Scott put his lamp down and jumped up, hanging off the top rail like a monkey. "See, it's solid."

I thought that posture suited him and smiled. "Do you know if Renee exited facing in or out on the ladder?"

"She used it like stairs. Facing forward." Scott dropped to the floor with a thud.

"Quiet in the crossover," Alastair shouted.

"Let me show you," Scott knocked me as he climbed up the ladder.

"Careful."

"Here." Scott retraced Renee's steps going down facing front. "Like this."

"Were you back here before she fell?"

"No, but usually I am. I move that table to the wings." Scott pointed to a small side table. "But someone already did it that night."

"Who did it?"

"I don't know. People help out. But I was nowhere around here, so don't try to finger me."

"I'm not," I said, thinking that wasn't a bad idea.

"Good. My money's still on Howard even though the detectives think it's you."

"Bite your tongue."

"Oops. My set change is coming up."

Scott grabbed his lamp and left me on the steps.

He never cared to remember anything that wasn't important to him.

I took out my cell phone and snapped pictures of the platform and steps.

Then I saw Kevin coming through for his entrance on the other side in act one.

"Veronica?" Kevin whispered. "Need help?"

"No."

I lied. I did want Kevin's help. I wanted to confide everything in him and bounce ideas around, but stopped. Not only was I sworn to secrecy, but what I needed was evidence, not conjecture or conversation.

"I was just deciding whether to go down front first or backwards."

"Backwards always. These are not really stairs. They are more like a ladder with wide steps. You'll have more control. Try facing front. I'll show you." Kevin offered me his hand to come down the stairs.

"You're right," I said tottering. "Hey, I was just talking to Scott. Did you move the table for him the night Renee fell?"

"Not that night, but I've helped out. We all do. Why?"

"Nothing." I slowed my descent because I was immensely enjoying Kevin's help.

"See," Kevin said, still holding onto my hand. "You have to face in."

"Thank you," I said, forgetting about who moved the table.

When I reached the bottom, I looked into Kevin's deep green eyes in the dim light. We stood facing each other. He didn't let go of my hand. I didn't let go of his either. I thought I would rather have had dinner with him than learning Renee's role.

We were interrupted by Tim running into the crossover.

"Coming through. Entrance on the other side."

Tim charged toward us.

"Oops," I said, stepping back quickly.

"Careful," Kevin said, as he was knocked against the stacked oak chairs on the opposite side. "You all right, Veronica?"

"Yes."

"Quiet in the crossover," Graham boomed.

"I have an entrance too," Kevin whispered and then followed Tim's path.

I wondered what would have happened if Tim had not interrupted.

I gazed at Kevin disappearing down the crossover.

⌘

CHAPTER 29

"How oft the sight of means to do ill deeds makes
deeds ill done!"
-Shakespeare, *King John*, Act 4, Scene 2

I went back to the wings. Alastair was there with a script to prompt actors who went up on their lines.

In my script I reviewed my next entrance, placed my pencil between the pages to mark it, and then set the script on the floor. I waited near Alastair, Tim, and Kevin for my entrance. As I did, I leaned on the black painted brick wall. It was lit with filtered vertical beams of stage light coming between the velour legs that create the wing areas on each side of the stage.

Anna and Howard were on stage. And thanks to Joel's exciting news, the rehearsal had an engaging energy.

We were almost to scene three. In that scene Anna's character tragically discovers her father arranged her marriage to an old wealthy factory owner who drinks and gambles with her father. In fact, the only difference between her father and Anna's aged betrothed is that her betrothed wins at gambling instead of losing like her father. In point of fact, her betrothed won her in just such a poker game.

As I waited for my entrance, I ran my lines in my head for the next scene.

Suddenly, Tim who was next to my ear shouted his off-stage line "from the garden" to Howard and Anna on stage. I was startled and lost my lines. I drew a blank. I reached down and got my script from the floor. I had set it in a pile of half eaten, crumbled square green cakes of rat poison and rat droppings. I shook it hard, slapping the pages together and dropping the pencil out on the black floorboards.

"Shh." Alastair popped his head from behind a velour leg.

"Sorry."

I re-claimed my pencil and reviewed a few pages of my next scene. My lines came back to me until Anna bounced in from the direction of the dressing room and chatted me up. She was drinking a bottle of her cranberry herbal iced tea I had seen on her dressing table.

"You did great in your first scene," Anna said.

"Thanks," I whispered. "It's wonderful about Joel."

"Yes, we are so excited. And Stephie Sevas really wants him to be her lover."

"Yes." I noticed the smile drop off Anna's face in the dim light.

"In her new movie, of course,"

Anna's energy and enthusiasm came back up. She beamed again with the pride of a young woman in love.

"Well, he must have impressed her."

I hoped Joel did not impress Stephie too much, because her appetite for her young male costars was common knowledge and tabloid fare. She apparently thrived on the sex and salacious publicity that helped her movies make money.

"Keep it down." Alastair popped his head from around the leg nearer the stage.

"Okay." Anna lowered her voice.

Joel came from the crossover.

"Hey, babe. Give me your tea." He grabbed Anna's tea, and gulped half the bottle.

Alastair popped his head out again, but did not tell Stephie Sevas's anointed young actor to keep it down. Alastair disappeared back behind the leg to prompt the actors on stage.

"Congratulations," I whispered to Joel as he drank more of Anna's tea.

"Thanks. Meisner paid off. " Joel took another gulp.

"Yes." I thought that both Meisner and his electric eyes—made for the camera—had paid off.

"I have an entrance on the other side. Can I take this?" Joel held the tea up.

"Sure," Anna chirped.

"Gotta go." Joel kissed Anna on the cheek and disappeared to cross backstage for his entrance.

Anna gazed after Joel as the darkness engulfed him in his path away from her to the crossover. Her smile dropped from her young and beautiful face. She knew, as did everyone, that Stephie Sevas made a career, not only of acting, but also of destroying relationships and marriages during her movie shoots.

Alastair leaned from the upper velour side leg into our space again and whispered, "The detectives are here. Geoff and Scott are done with them. Anna, you go out to the lobby and talk to them. I'll read your lines in the next scene."

"But I don't know anything and I need the rehearsal," Anna protested.

Nicole peered from behind the third side leg and sneered, "Anna's right. She does need the rehearsal. I'll go now. You read my lines, Alastair."

"Fine," Alastair agreed.

"Besides . . . I have a lot to tell them." Nicole glared at me and then left.

She was trouble.

* * *

Nicole strutted out on stage, interrupting the rehearsal and Kevin's long emotional monologue. She crossed center and put her prop tray with a cup of coffee on the side table. Kevin fought to maintain his concentration.

"Too early, Nicole. Your entrance isn't for two pages," Graham yelled from out front.

"I know. I'm not stupid."

Nicole went downstage and jumped off the edge defiantly. Then she started up the center aisle.

"I have to talk to the cops about who murdered Renee."

"Murdered? Anna turned to me with wide eyes lit by a beam of stage light coming into the wings. "What is Nicole talking about?"

"I don't really know."

I lied with a straight face. I'd had plenty of practice in the last few years.

Alastair came and stood next to me. "Neither do I and I'm the stage manager. I'm supposed to know everything."

On stage Howard, Kevin, and Tim stood, speechless. The rehearsal stopped. Everyone was still and silent. The stage, which was a place of energy and dynamic condensed life, became a void.

Scott stepped onto the stage from the opposite wings, even though the murder was no surprise to him. He loved chaos and I knew he was waiting to fan the flames. Geoff, bewildered, followed Scott onto the stage.

"Murder. What is she talking about?" Howard sat down in a Victorian chair on stage, looking paler than he usually did.

Geoff walked to Howard, put his hand on Howard's shoulder. "Steady, man."

"All right, people," Graham bellowed from his theatre seat in a voice that would be heard everywhere, including the dressing rooms. "Let's have everyone on stage."

We all walked out onto the stage, everyone except Bryce, who remained in his balcony.

I squinted and peered out into the house under the bright stage lights.

I saw Mel and Graham go up the center aisle. They went toward the back of the theatre arguing. The only audible word from that distance was Nicole, which was said repeatedly. Graham flailed his arms and his face turned red.

I knew why Graham was angry. Mel had confided in his little playmate about the detectives' investigation for murder. Unbelievably, he did it even before their pillow talk after rehearsal. I now, of course, understood the look Nicole gave me backstage as she went to talk to the detectives. This loose cannon knew I was the prime suspect and I now knew I had very little time to find out who had tampered with Renee's exit.

I expected the detectives to come in from the lobby and stop the fight. Then I realized Mel's and Graham's yelling sounded no different than the play to an untrained ear. Besides, no cop-type male would walk away from their interview with a Nicole-type female, unless there was a 9.9 earthquake to shake them lose.

* * *

"Enough," Mel hollered, going back down the aisle to his seat in the middle of the theatre.

Graham followed, but went up on the stage.

"Bryce, house up full and get out here," Graham called.

"Yes, Sir," Bryce called back, as the house came up.

Graham glared up at Bryce who stood at the edge of the balcony drinking coffee from a Coffee and Conversation paper cup.

"All present, Alastair?" Graham turned his attention to the rehearsal.

Alastair did his stage manager job and answered, "All present but Nicole, She's out with the detectives."

"Yeah, I know," Graham muttered.

"Murder? What's this about?" Joel asked, taking on his new-found position of leadership after his recent stature boost.

"Yes." Anna walked over and putting her arm around Joel as his anointed.

"It's 'much ado about nothing' as Shakespeare would say." Graham calculated how to make light of the detective's anticipated path to glory in their homicide department.

No one laughed or even chuckled. Reading his audience as he always did, Graham continued in a more serious tone geared to the moment.

"Look, everyone, the detectives were miffed that no one called the police when Renee fell because, I guess, they thought we should have. And now they're going to teach us a lesson with an investigation," Graham said matter-of-factly. "It's nothing really. We all know no one would want to hurt Renee, let alone murder her. I mean, isn't that silly? Howard, isn't it?"

"Yes, it is," Howard said, looking around at all of us. "Renee was a lovely person. Gentle and fragile."

"Fragile," Graham responded, picking up on a theme for Renee's death. "Fragile and delicate and a superb actress. We are going to dedicate opening night to her memory"

"That's a kind thought." Geoff began a slow clap.

"That's wonderful," the ever-positive Kevin added, joining in Geoff's clap.

Slowly everyone joined into a subdued applause. I clapped loudly, too.

Everyone needed this communal recognition of Renee's passing. I admired Graham who knew human nature and had dodged a bullet momentarily by changing the focus from murder to remembrance. He was a very bright guy, but I didn't believe bright enough to erase completely the word "murder" from their minds.

I surveyed the group. When I came to Joel, I was startled. Blood was dripping from his nose onto his plaid shirt.

I leaned over to Alastair and whispered, "Look at Joel's nose."

"What's next? Slip out and get some tissues from the dressing room. Were Mel and Joel at it again?"

"No, I don't think so."

I left to get the box of tissues.

⌘

CHAPTER 30

"Some rise by sin, and some by virtue fall."
-Shakespeare, *Measure for Measure*, Act 2,
Scene 1

When I returned with the tissues, Alastair had Joel seated with his head back. Everyone participated in the new crisis.

Anna was dabbing the blood off Joel's upper lip with one of the three lace prop napkins. She broke the bright-line rule of never using a prop for anything other than its intended purpose in the play.

Alastair grabbed the box of tissues from me and handed them to Anna. "Here are tissues. You can't use my props."

"I'm sorry. I'll get another napkin. I had to save his audition shirt." Anna tolled the napkin up and put it on the table nearby.

"Next time don't," Alastair snapped.

Alastair reached in his pocket and jingled his coins like worry beads.

"What happened, buddy," Tim laughed. "Did you pick it?"

"Joel doesn't do that."

Anna defended her man as she held the tissues against Joel's nostrils to stop the blood.

"You and Mel didn't . . ." Graham whispered to Joel.

"No, we didn't fight. I keep away from him," Joel answered quietly.

"Good."

"This has never happened before," Anna said, taking more tissues from the box, wetting them with the last of the cranberry herbal iced tea, and cleaning Joel's upper lip

"You have a little blood under your nose too," I cautioned Anna.

"Oh." She wiped it off with a tissue. "Weird."

"It's gone."

"Let's go people," Graham bellowed. "Joel's fine. Clear the stage. Anna, get Joel to his dressing room."

"Sure." Anna helped Joel off stage.

"Places," Alastair called, grabbed the rolled up napkin and headed to the wings. "Two minutes."

* * *

The cast took their places for the next scene, but not without grumblings. I followed Alastair to the wings near the women's dressing room for my entrance.

The impact of the word "murder" had definitely been diluted by the announcement of the memorial opening night for Renee, Graham's self-serving explanation for the detectives' questioning, and Joel's nose bleed.

I focused on and finished act one off script and with only two dropped lines. Alastair prompted me with a few starter words from the wings. I picked up the lines quickly.

Graham announced an hour dinner break before we did the second and third acts.

As most of the company went up the center aisle to get food, the detectives came down it to meet with Graham and Mel.

Nicole leaned on the lobby doorjamb, surveying the scene with a look of satisfaction.

I walked with my fellow actors, who were leaving for dinner, up the center aisle. I was headed to get a chai tea from the lobby machine and then have my sandwich in the dressing room while I reviewed my lines.

As I slipped past the detectives, the older one saw me.

"You talk to her again," he ordered his younger partner as he nodded towards me. "I'll check in with these guys."

"Right."

The young detective turned and followed me up the aisle.

I pretended I didn't hear and kept walking. I decided I would go with the group to dinner to avoid the detective if he didn't catch up with me.

Nicole called down the center aisle.

"Hey, Mel. Let's go get something.

"In a minute," Mel grumbled.

As Nicole passed me to join Mel, she looked over and gave me a big smile.

That always meant trouble.

* * *

In the lobby, the young detective caught up with me. My fellow actors left without me and went across the street to the Chinese restaurant. Howard separated from the group and turned right toward Coffee and Conversation.

Howard was alone again, as I had seen him for all the years before Renee.

The young detective had me take a seat right there near the lobby glass doors.

"So I hear you just pretend to be a writer. You don't have any books to buy," he began his questioning.

"I'm looking for an agent."

"Then you do want to get back into acting?"

"No," I responded to his assumption that I was seeking an acting agent. "I'm looking for a literary agent for my books."

"For acting too?"

"No. They are two different kinds of agents."

I tried to be patient. However, I was hungry and drained from the off-stage dramas of the evening.

"But you do want to get back into acting?"

"Who told you that?" I was surprised.

"I'll ask the questions and you can answer them here or back at the station."

"I like to act, but it's just a hobby."

I adjusted my attitude to comport with his threat and answered. I regretted my morning foray into the actors' casting notices this morning.

"Did you cut Renee's part down to get rid of her?"

"No . . . I mean it's true I cut her part down, but she was having trouble with her lines and everyone thought she'd be happier with a smaller part."

"Everyone?"

"Graham and Mel."

"Are you going to add that stuff back in now that you have the part?" The young detective probed.

"Who said . . ?"

"Are you?"

"No. I mean," I said, deciding at once that I would never add those long monologues back in. "I do whatever the writer and director want. But I don't . . ."

"We talked to Renee's boyfriend and he said you were jealous of Renee."

"That's impossible," I said, suspecting Scott may have been right about Howard after all. "You have to have misunderstood what . . ."

"Were you?"

"Was I what?"

"Jealous of Renee."

"Hardly?"

"And what does that mean?"

The young man had gotten to me exactly like my detectives do to the innocent and no-so-innocent characters in my books. I couldn't think of another response. They had made up their minds, but didn't have enough to arrest me yet. I had to play my cards close to the vest.

"Is there a reason you didn't tell us about Charlie Valentine's death?"

My heart dropped. "I . . ."

"You found his body?"

"No. I mean yes, but with Graham and . . ."

"And the light that almost fell on Renee? Were you there?"

"It didn't fall near Renee." I stammer taken by surprise because the Fresnel falling was not general knowledge.

"I understand Howard had to . . ."

We were interrupted by Nicole and Mel who burst through the theatre door into the lobby laughing. She was holding onto Mel's arm so tightly they melted into one.

"Good job tonight." Nicole praised me as her and Mel headed out to dinner. "Really professional."

"Yeah," Mel said looking over at the detective and me. "You're going to make the mother more alive than Renee ever did. Nicole thinks this could be your big chance."

As they disappeared through the front doors, my heart sank. Nicole was putting more nails in my coffin. I avoided looking at the detective who was writing his notes.

Before the questioning could continue, Graham and the older detective came into the lobby from the theatre.

"Let's go," he called to my interrogator.

"Yes, sir."

The older detective then turned back to Graham. "We'll know more when the autopsy is done and the forensics are in."

I sat stunned as the detectives left.

Graham turned to me with a defeated look in his eyes.

"They'll be back," Graham said.

"There isn't much time is there?"

"No. There isn't. We may not open."

Graham headed back through the theatre doors.

"That's the least of my worries," I muttered.

"What?" Graham snapped.

"Nothing."

Graham disappeared.

I got up to get my chai tea.

"Nothing. Yet," I mumbled to myself.

I was ready to go down fighting, or, better yet—sleuthing.

⌘

CHAPTER 31

"Thou art all ice. Thy kindness freezes."
-Shakespeare, *Richard III*, Act 4, Scene 1

W hen the troupe returned, we finished the second act and then got a ten-minute break. I hurried to the women's dressing room to grab the other half of my sandwich.

The door was shut and when I walked in, Nicole was leaning over Anna's dressing table. In the ricocheted reflection of the room's mirrors, I saw her startled face.

"Veronica," Nicole exclaimed.

She quickly retreated to her own dressing table where she nervously touched up her heavy red lipstick.

"I was just getting this stuff off all the dressing tables."

"What stuff?" I asked, sitting at my dressing table.

"The cakes of rat poison they set around."

"Good idea."

Nicole carefully widened her lips with a lip liner for a fuller appearance. Then she finished by slathering lip gloss on and closed her make-up bag. She blotted her lipstick and threw white imprinted tissue on her dressing table in the pile of others.

I was angry and decided to rattle Nicole's cage.

"Did you give the detectives the idea that I came here to get Renee's part?"

"That's nuts. Why would you want Renee's part? You're a writer," Nicole said with artificial animation and then a smug smile formed with her perfectly retouched lips. "Besides, what about you memorizing all the lines so fast? Isn't that hard at your age?"

I wanted to wipe that red neon smile off her face with a good come-back, but I didn't. Or, rather, I couldn't, because I drew a blank. It had been a long day for me. Maybe she was right. I was getting slow.

Nicole didn't bat an eye and walked out the door. She was cool, or more like frozen. I didn't know her, but I knew her type. She was the center of the universe and everyone was her functionary.

When I picked up my half sandwich, I saw scattered crumblings from the green cakes of rat poison nearby and near Anna's cranberry iced teas. I cleaned them up carefully with a tissue and threw them in the trash. There were no rat droppings, but Nicole was right about one thing, no one should put this poison on the dressing tables. I didn't know who to complain to since Charlie was gone.

I threw my half sandwich in the trash and took two dollars out of my change purse to get a cappuccino in the lobby for energy. Evidently at my age I required the boost.

* * *

In the lobby, Mel was sipping a cappuccino near the machine. I needed caffeine more than I needed to avoid Mel.

"Careful," I said. "It's always too hot."

"Veronica!" Mel stepped aside for me.

I put my two dollars in and pushed the cappuccino button. The machine groaned loudly as it worked up the frothy milk and brewed the coffee.

"This thing is loud. Graham better put a sign on it so no one uses it during the performances," Mel said, blowing on his cappuccino.

"Nothing to be done about it."

I took my cappuccino after the machine stopped rumbling.

"I could unplug it."

I chuckled and started back to the theatre.

"Hey, wait. Can you sit down a minute? We need to talk."

"We're starting the third act."

"I need a word," Mel called. "Have a seat."

"Sure."

I returned and sat. I regretted coming out to the lobby for a cappuccino because, not only didn't I like this man, but he was Nicole's source.

"What's up?" I asked.

"Do you have a problem with my relationship with Nicole?" Mel challenged me with no smile, no grace and no equivocation.

"No," I said, so genuinely shocked that my mouth dropped. "Where would you get that idea?"

Mel studied my reaction and then sipped his cappuccino.

"Never mind."

"I'm sorry if I gave you that impression. I'm happy for anyone who finds someone special."

"I believe you are."

I didn't like either Mel or Nicole and I certainly did not enjoy their relationship, but their love duo was none of my business. More than that, I certainly didn't want to be drawn into their little romantic drama. As far as the information leak to Nicole, that would have to be dealt with another way.

We sat in silence for a minute and then Mel left for the theatre without another word.

One thing was clear. Nicole was undermining me in every way she could.

* * *

During act three Anna felt sick. We took a break while she threw up in the women's rest room.

After rehearsal the troupe met in the theatre for notes.

Graham announced that Anna had the flu and no one was to share bottles of water or food with her. Graham made most of the cast notes upbeat for the sake of morale, but he did hammer in that we had to be quiet in the crossover. I slid down in my chair like a school girl getting reprimanded.

Graham did not note many of the obvious errors, which most of us knew anyway, especially the most seasoned of us. An experienced actor's third eye is always observing rehearsals. Improvement is impossible without it.

When Graham finished my two notes, I flew in the face of decorum and raised my hand to be excused. I wanted to look through Howard's things in the men's dressing room while everyone else remained assembled. Maybe Scott was right about him.

"What, Veronica?" Graham growled, irritated at the interruption during his notes. "What is it?"

"Sorry," I said. "I have to find missing hats for the dress rehearsal. Can I do it now."

I knew the box of hats was in the women's dressing room at the back of the cupboard, but it was a sufficient and time urgent ruse.

"Yes. Go. Go. Do it now if you need to. But no one else even think of being excused. Opening is upon us and tomorrow is the run-through. No stops for any reason."

As Graham continued the notes, I hurried to look in the men's dressing room for any clue about Renee, especially in Howard's things.

The men's dressing room was a pig sty. The cupboards were full of masks, props, smelly clothes left over the years, tools, and spare yardage. Above the cupboards was no different. However, I did notice there were no rat cakes. I stopped at Howard's dressing table and went meticulously through his things. Nothing.

When I heard Graham announce a five-thirty call time tomorrow, I knew notes were over. I took a last look at the dressing tables and then started for the crossover.

As I rounded the corner, I saw Howard sitting on the ottoman near Renee's fatal ladder fall. He was weeping. I approached quietly.

"Howard," I said. "Are you all right?"

"Sure," Howard said looking up at me embarrassed with eyes still moist.

"I . . ." I hesitated going for the jugular to save my neck because I was overwhelmed with this lonely man's sadness. "I wondered if . . ."

Graham's voice bellowed from the stage.

"I'm locking up. Is everyone out?"

"No," I called.

"We'd better go." Howard stood and left without another word.

I went to grab my bag from the women's dressing room and headed through the wings. I heard Graham saying good night to Howard.

Tomorrow I would show no quarter to Howard. I would ask the hard questions and get answers.

⌘

CHAPTER 32

"There is no darkness but ignorance."
-Shakespeare, *Twelfth Night*, Act 4, Scene 2

On Tuesday morning, I woke at six with no old movie channel to turn off. I had crawled into bed and forgotten to turn it on.

In my study, I sipped my pumpkin chai tea, caffeinated this time. I didn't need to delve into fictional crimes or characters because I had a real mystery to solve and my own skin to save. I needed to find out who knew what and then piece it all together

Tonight, I planned to question Howard and Bryce first. Howard was the most viable suspect to me, and Bryce the best witness. He had his bird's eye view of everything; that is, if he wasn't busy getting high.

After a tea I was still lagging. Finally, I resorted to the ultimate caffeine boost, coffee. It got me going in full gear.

I studied my script, internalizing my character's blocking, business on stage, physical actions, cues, and emotional arc. My performance was so far high school quality, but not irretrievably so. Acting is a muscle and a skill that has to be exercised. I hadn't done that in a while.

At ten-thirty, I tried ringing Bryce but I was interrupted by an incoming call from Graham.

"Veronica, I'm glad I got you. Are you going to need that ear piece to cue you on your lines opening night?"

"Am I that bad?"

"Not to worry, I am just going in that direction to get your altered costumes."

"It would be too distracting. I'll be ready."

"O.K.," Graham acquiesced. "And I need you at the theatre an hour early to rehearse your big scene with Kevin."

"I'll be there."

I was more than glad to work one on one with Kevin, anytime.

"Bring your updated headshot, too."

"I don't have one."

"That's one way to stay young," Graham laughed, enjoying his own humor. "I have the old one."

"Good. Save some time to talk to me about strategy, too."

"Strategy?"

"Investigating Renee's death," I snapped, irritated that Graham was so obtuse when it came to saving my neck.

"Oh? That. Look, I haven't heard from the detectives. I think they've moved on," Graham said dismissively. " But more importantly will you order pizza for our dinner break to boost morale. I'll pay for it."

"Hold on. Do you really think they've moved on?"

"Who?"

"The detectives!"

Graham's preoccupation before an opening night was usually charming to me, but this time it was not. I was a murder suspect. And I am sorry but pizza does not trump murder.

"We haven't heard a peep. And seriously, who would really murder Renee? Mel? Well, I guess maybe," Graham chuckled. "See you at the theatre. And order the pizza."

"Sure." I hung up in disgust.

Graham was no help. He was either in denial or correct that the detectives had moved on. I felt under pressure from all directions. I chose to buy into Graham's denial and spent the rest of the time emotionalizing on my character.

At three, I ordered the pizzas. I knew I'd be footing the pizza bill that night.

Then I returned as many friends' texts and emails as I could with a quick word or two, some misspelled.

I threw on jeans, a white blouse, and boots. I grabbed my brown leather jacket, my bag, and left for the theatre.

* * *

On the way, I was excited about being on stage again. I wanted to take the audience with me on every moment of my character's emotional roller coaster. Contrary to our real daily lives, for acting the failure or embarrassment is to hide, or worse, not to have real emotion.

I was an actor again and I decided to take a short detour and drive to the theatre via Sunset Boulevard and my memory lane.

The trip was worth the dense late afternoon traffic. I drove past the old Grauman's Chinese Theatre, now called the Mann Chinese Theatre. I had gone there with my parents for my tenth birthday, bedazzled by the neon up and down the Sunset Strip.

I passed the Samuel French Bookshop. I recalled the plays I bought every week to prepare for my sadly unfruitful auditions right after college, before I got married.

I was glad Graham was still my friend and grateful for every time he called me no matter how small the part. I was excited to be part of the

Hollywood theatre scene again without having to suffer the audition and rejection process.

I was happy, notwithstanding the reality that I, and everyone, had to visually and mentally filter out the encroaching population of skinny, dirty homeless runaways and teenage prostitutes. They were arriving in droves. They were attracted by the media to the "glamorous life," but almost always met with disappointment and no way to make a living.

* * *

Nearing the Valentine, I saw the small Checca Café where a group of us college seniors, including Graham, did a dinner theatre production of selections from Edgar Lee Masters' *Spoon River Anthology.* A rogue associate professor, now tenured, broke the university rules and secretly produced an off-campus project during semester break in January. She was a pistol. We all felt radical and empowered and like "real actors."

Our little band of players prepped in the cold, dark alley outside the café's kitchen door. Then we muscled past dishwashers and cooks in the filthy kitchen to get on the tiny theatre in the round. It was just a clearing in the sunken dining room encircled by small round tables. During performances the tables were sparsely inhabited by college friends who could barely afford the price of desert and coffee. We did costume changes in a narrow hallway shared with servers running past us balancing plates of hamburgers and chili-cheese fries. I chuckled remembering one costume change when my arm hit a platter of chili-cheese fries. I finished the second act with a chili and cheese stained sleeve, emotionalizing on the fact that it fit my character.

My character was Margaret Fuller Slack who at the turn of the 20th Century "had the old, old problem: should it be celibacy, matrimony, or unchasity?" She wanted to be a writer and "would have been as great as George Elliot, but for an untoward fate." The "untoward fate" was marriage to the rich John Slack, eight kids, and then dying ironically of lockjaw from a pin piercing while washing baby things. I loved her then and love her more now. For now, I feel I might also have been George Elliot, instead of some mystery writer, but for my "untoward fate" of marriage.

A couple of years ago Graham and I went back to the café. There was no dinner theatre, the small stage was populated with dining tables, and its specialty was its blue cheese and bacon burgers served with sweet potato fries. They were good, but not as good as our little troupe.

At a red light, I Googled the Drama Department. On a lark I called the professor who had led our rebel Checca Café troupe.

"Of course, I remember you," she gushed. "I'll never forget that crazy semester break? How are you?"

She was genuinely happy to hear from me after all these years. When she asked me what I was doing, I of course told her I was an author. Then, I heard myself say I was also "writing" a play and on my way to a meet with the "director." I didn't mention it was "just" Graham. Nor did I clarify that I was merely editing the play. How could I?

She had to cut the conversation short because evidently she had married also and needed to beat the rush hour home to her kids. Ironic.

The call ended. I was pleased with my well honed exaggerations to the professor. In point of fact, I knew I would never have to "clarify" anything with her because her mommy track didn't include populating theatre performances of old students.

* * *

When I arrived at the theatre, I was glad to see Bryce alone on the steps smoking a cigarette. I hadn't been friendly since he manipulated the lighting the night Renee fell. I needed to repair that. After all, Bryce would be lighting me. No lights, no me. And, although I was clinging to Graham's hope the detectives were gone for good, I needed to find out exactly what Bryce saw that night.

"Bryce," I called. "Where have you been hiding?"

"In my balcony." Bryce took a long drag of his cigarette. "How have you been?"

"You see everything from your little eagle's nest, so you tell me . . . how have I been?"

I renewed our long-standing joke that he should critique the actors' performances because he sees everything from his balcony.

"You've been great actually." Bryce formed his closed-mouth smile. "Your mother's a more interesting character than Renee's. And you have three days left to make it your own. You'll be fine."

"Thank you, Bryce," I said with a little curtsey.

Bryce had been watching performances for eons and knew more than most directors when he was not high.

"Are you ready for my big scene up the staircase?" I asked casually.

"Not you too? I'm sick of being harassed. I won't do the blue light again. Why can't everyone just let that drop?" Bryce ranted in his deep base voice. "I told the cops I shot the blue light across because Renee and I always joked about ghosts. That's all."

"I wasn't talking about the blue light," I said, startled at the intensity of Bryce's reaction.

"I'm sorry. I thought you were."

"No."

I knew now how guilty Bryce felt.

"You understand then. It was all in good fun. Renee was such a believer," Bryce said settling down. "And everyone talked about the publicity to bring in full houses."

"Of course."

I lied. In my view, playing with danger on stage was never in good fun and Bryce deserved his well-earned guilt feelings. But I kept that to myself. After all, I was going up the Victorian steps in the storm next and I wanted him to like me.

"I have to go and do a scene with Kevin," I said, thinking he should look elsewhere for his absolution.

I went into the lobby. Bryce followed and headed up into his balcony.

Then it hit me. Bryce had used the word "everyone."

I turned to ask him who he meant by everyone, but he was gone and I was late reporting in.

⌘

CHAPTER 33

"For the rain it raineth every day."
-Shakespeare, *The Taming of the Shrew*, Act 5, Scene 1

As I entered the theatre proper, I saw Kevin already on stage adjusting the set furniture with Graham, Scott, and Alistair.

Going down the center aisle, I was not happy to see Mel and Nicole in the front row. I didn't need them as critics at my rehearsal with Kevin. I hurried up the stage access steps and onto the stage.

"Hi," Kevin greeted me with his ever-beaming smile. "Let's nail this thing."

"Okay. Let me drop my bag in the dressing room. I'll be right back."

"Did you order the pizza?" Graham whispered as I walked by him.

"Yes, $77.30, not including tip."

I didn't expect him to pay, but I hoped.

"I'll get it to you. Take a look at your costumes when you go back there."

* * *

In the dressing room, I put my bag down on the table. I saw my three costumes hanging in plastic bags on the wardrobe rack. I took them out of the thin plastic bags. They looked small, especially around the bust. I inspected the inside bodice seams. They had been let out to the max using up all the extra material. I hoped I could squeeze into them.

I stood for a minute and gathered my thoughts for the run-through with Kevin. I pushed the detectives and Renee's death to the back of my mind and focused on my first lines in Kevin's scene. If I remembered the first lines, I usually recalled the rest. I hoped my work all day internalizing the mother's emotional arc would pay off. I wanted her to be natural and have refined emotional subtleties. An actor had to let go and trust the preparation. I did.

Both Kevin and I took our positions in the wings opposite each other. I waved ready to Graham. Kevin was across with his head down. This was our big scene; a scene between me, the distressed wife, and the doctor who has loved her throughout their lifetimes from afar.

"Places," Alastair called.

Bryce took the stage lights down. I walked out to my mark and I heard Kevin walk to his. I was ready. The lights came up. I felt the heat on my neck and stepped backward to catch more light on my face. I turned to give my first line.

"Look. Look," Nicole yelled laughing. "They look like twins."

I broke character and, as Veronica not the mother, checked out what Kevin was wearing.

Nicole was right. We had identical outfits---jeans, a white shirt, boots and a leather jacket. Kevin stayed in character and didn't miss a beat. I pushed myself back into character again. I pleaded desperately with the doctor, handsome Kevin, to help me. It wasn't hard.

Nicole's sabotage had failed. Kevin and I lived through the scene together and in character. I cried and he consoled. He exploded in anger and I gently placated him. Not one dropped line. No cue missed. The real emotions we experienced carried us through the scene on a wonderful roller coaster ride. I felt it and so did Kevin.

The scene ended with Kevin holding me as we looked into each other's eyes. We were both emotionally spent. I thought it was a shame the scene ended in a blackout before our characters kissed. In the blackout, though, we continued to hold each other in the dark. I believed it was a prolonged moment. And, I believed Kevin intentionally prolonged it.

The embrace, however, was interrupted by loud clapping from the back lobby of the theatre.

The lights came up and Kevin released me, or I released him, and we stepped back. I held my hand to my forehead to block the stage lights and see who was clapping in the house.

My heart sank. The two detectives had returned. They were standing up in the center aisle.

This was the last thing I needed. They had just observed my success at doing Renee's role and I had yet to even have a clue as to who the real murderer was.

My emotional high from the scene plummeted. How would they ever believe I didn't aspire to an acting career? How could they know that I only aspired to Kevin?

"Gentlemen," Graham said as he struggled from his seat. "Can we do something for you?"

"We're here to get fingerprints and do some follow-up," the older detective declared.

"We're rehearsing now," Graham protested, upset the detectives having abandoned their investigation.

"Let's get it started. Here is fine," the older detective ordered his partner.

Alastair walked up the aisle to the detectives to diffuse the situation and take command. "Wouldn't the lobby be better? There'll be more light. I'll send everyone out and I can get you both a cappuccino.

"Fine," the older detective agreed.

"I could use one, too" the young detective said.

"Bryce, come down for the detectives," Alastair shouted. "And Scott, get out to the lobby and get these men a cappuccino. Let's cooperate, people."

"Miss Kennicott," The older detective called to me. "You're coming out for fingerprints?"

"Yes, of course," I replied, wishing I had narrowed my list of suspects.

"She has notes now," Graham interceded more politely, taking his cue from Alastair. "But she'll be right out."

The detectives went to the lobby.

Graham then turned to Kevin and me still sitting on stage. He gazed at us for a long moment and then he threw his pad of paper down on his seat.

"Good job. What else is there to say? Don't lose it."

Graham turned and went up the center aisle to the lobby muttering.

"Fingerprints and cappuccinos. What's next?"

⌘

CHAPTER 34

"When sorrows come, they come not single spies, but in battalions."
-Shakespeare, *Hamlet*, Act 4, Scene 5

Fingerprinting the entire troupe put a pall on our rehearsal for act one, not to mention their pointed questioning during the process. Anything that could go wrong did. The pace was slow, cues were missed, lines forgotten, and Nicole took advantage of every mistake and ad-libbed both lines and business to make her role bigger.

The detectives left after the disaster that was act one.

Then the pizza delivery man came and interrupted Graham's act one notes.

"Take care of that, Veronica," Graham bellowed. "What next?"

"I'll help." Tim followed me out to the lobby.

"We'll finish the notes later with act two's," Graham announced. "I got us all pizza for our dinner break. Enjoy. Thirty minutes. It's 7:15. Get back here at

7:45 on the dot. No one can be late for any reason. Opening night is upon us."

* * *

While Graham was being thanked, I paid and tipped the delivery man. Tim helped me set up the pizzas along the concession glass case. I knew his motivation was being the first to dive in.

"Great. Two pepperoni's," Tim said, grabbing a piece.

The troupe trickled into the lobby. Anna and Joel took vegetarian pieces. Alastair picked up a napkin and read the pizza chain name printed in yellow and blue across it.

"Who would eat anything from this place?" Alastair waived the napkin for emphasis. "Graham is so cheap."

Alastair left the theatre and turned right up the sidewalk for the French restaurant and bar where he often enjoyed a glass of wine to get through the night with an even keel. Mel and Nicole walked by the pizzas without a glance and followed him.

Geoff, Scott, and Bryce took a whole pepperoni pizza outside to eat with their nicotine fix. Graham and Scott ate the everything pizza. Kevin took a vegetarian piece and joined Anna and Joel.

"Good job today," Howard said, as he walked up to me with a slice of plain cheese pizza.

"Thanks." With the detectives' investigation clearly continuing, I renewed mine with Howard. "I'm sorry about your falling out before Renee died."

"It wouldn't have lasted anyway."

"Why do you say that? You looked so happy."

I was direct and probing for information. The detectives had turned up the heat with the fingerprinting and I turned up mine.

"I think she was just a good actress." Howard looked at me and then down at his pizza, giving me a view of his bald head matted with the long sparse hair. "I knew all she really wanted was free publicity spots from me."

"What do you mean?"

"I told her at dinner the night you showed up that I had used all my contacts but no one wanted to interview her about this play or anything else." Howard took a deep breath. "She was mad. She was through with me before I fell on the stage."

Looking at him, I realized that their match was more than unlikely, it was a fraud and Renee had been a user. I felt sorry for Howard.

"I'm sure she would have gotten over it."

"No. But that doesn't change the way I felt about her."

"You felt deeply for her didn't you?"

Howard didn't answer the obvious.

I thought back at Renee's look across the room at me at the cookie party. She thought we were both cut from the same cloth. We weren't. She was a user. She hurt people. Howard found that out the hard way.

Even though Howard was vulnerable, I had to push him for information now. My freedom was at stake.

"Howard, did you see anything up there on the steps that could have tripped Renee."

Howard looked down at the ground and took a deep breath.

"I have to be honest. I don't see much in the dark backstage. I have astigmatism. But I know something tripped her."

"How?"

"I heard her gasp before she screamed, like she was surprised. At first, I thought it was the blue light, but the timing was off. It had to be something else. The detectives thought so too."

"The detectives? You told them?"

"Yes."

"What else did you tell them?" I asked exercising patience that was really beyond my ability at that moment.

"Nothing."

I saw he was overwhelmed and I was under-whelmed. Howard had confirmed this was no accident, but he gave me nothing else to go on.

"I've got to get some air."

I watched Howard's penguin-like waddle toward the front doors. His waddle was born of him carrying his weight on his heels to counter the weight of his ever- growing pot belly.

Anna approached me drinking her cranberry herbal tea and carrying her half eaten piece of vegetarian pizza.

"Poor Howard." Anna watched him walk out the front doors.

"Yes."

"Hey, I saw your scene with Kevin. It was terrific," Anna beamed." You two have chemistry."

"Thanks." I basked in the compliment and noted that she had observed our chemistry. "When does Joel's shoot with Stephie Sevas start?"

"Don't know." Anna finished the last drop of her tea.

"I was wondering something," I said, taking this opportunity to ask her about Renee's fatal night. "Did you . . ."

"Oh . . ," Anna moaned and held her stomach. "Sorry, my tummy hurts. I must have eaten too too fast. I'm going to go get another tea."

"Sure." I speculated that she was avoiding the subject.

Anna left for the dressing room.

* * *

At 7:40 Mel and Nicole burst through the front doors laughing arm in arm and well-imbibed. Alastair followed. He marshaled Geoff, Scott, and Bryce from the front steps carrying their empty pizza box.

"Scott, clean this up. Everyone take the extra pizza back to the dressing rooms," Alastair said, obviously over-animated and relaxed from his wine break. "Come on people. Time for acts two and three if you ever want to get home. We start in five. Let's go now. Second act, first scene actors get up on stage. Places, everyone."

I grabbed the half full vegetarian box to take to the women's dressing room. I knew Anna liked it and so did I. Scott was left grumbling about cleaning up minimal mess and empty boxes.

"Good job tonight." Geoff caught up to me and walking with me into the theatre. "Different from Renee's interpretation. I like it."

"Thanks." I saw a chance to ask Geoff about Renee's fall rather milking further compliments from this seasoned thespian. "But I wish Renee was still here. It was a terrible way to go."

"Yes. We had a lot of fun together with the ghost thing. Too much maybe. Do you think she took it too seriously? She was older. She might have . . ."

"No, she enjoyed it all." I reassured him with a white lie because down deep I did believe he and Bryce had gone too far.

"Good." Geoff flashed an uneasy smile.

As we walked down the center aisle of the theatre, I wished everyone would stop looking to me for absolution. I needed to hear their confessions manifested by a modicum of guilt, but I wasn't marketing forgiveness. Indeed, I was looking for information to point the finger at one of them, including Bryce or Geoff and their practical jokes, even if I didn't find the real murderer.

I had learned from plotting mysteries that any murderer worth his or her salt always pointed a finger at viable other suspects. It was a good counter move in a police investigation.

* * *

When I got back to the dressing room, I found Anna sitting bent over at her dressing table. I set the pizza down.

"Still hurts?" I asked.

"Yes, more." Anna kooks up. "It's got to be the flu, but Joel and I had our flu shots at the pharmacy. I thought we couldn't get it after that."

"I think you can . . . some strains." I grabbed my flashlight and script to leave because the last thing I needed was to get the flu. "Can you rehearse?"

"Yeah," Anna said, getting up and taking a long drink of her tea.

* * *

The first half of the second act went even better than the first. Then, near the end, Anna distracted me and everyone else. She was changing her blocking to lean on tables and chairs. Even though this was supposed to be a run-through without interruptions, she engendered quick censures by Graham.

Something was terribly wrong with Anna.

But Graham didn't care. He just cracked the whip.

⌘

CHAPTER 35

"Frailty, thy name is woman."
-Shakespeare, *Hamlet*, Act 1, Scene 2

At the end of the second act, Graham announced a ten-minute break and ordered us all to review our blocking for the technical run-through tomorrow night.

The tech run just before the final dress rehearsal allowed Graham, Bryce, and Scott to coordinate the lighting, sound effects, and set changes. The actors stood in their blocked places and gave the first or last few words in their speeches as cues for the technical changes.

"Notes now?" Alastair stepped out from the wings holding his script.

"No. After the third." Graham headed for the men's dressing room where most of the leftover pizza was. "And get everyone back here in ten if they want out of here tonight at a decent hour."

Alastair called out, "Ten minutes . . . that's all. Get back here on time."

* * *

I headed out the wings to the dressing room. I tossed my script on my dressing table and went through the other door to the hall restroom.

As I approached, I saw Nicole standing banging on the door.

"Hey, we only have ten minutes," Nicole yelled through the door. "Anna, hurry up."

"Anna's in there?"

"Yeah, She's never coming out. I'm going to the lobby heads."

Nicole marched down the hall in her tight washed blue jeans topped by a bulky, down, white ski jacket.

"Anna," I called through the door and knocked gently. "Nicole went up to the lobby. How do you feel? Can I help you?"

"One minute." Anna opened the door a crack. "Nicole's gone?"

"Yes." Anna's face was white and her nose had a small amount of blood dripping from it. "You have a nose bleed?"

"Oops. Just a drop." Anna was embarrassed and dabbed it. "I think something was wrong with the veggie pizza."

"No one else is sick."

Anna sat down on the toilet lid and looked up at me. I shut the bathroom door and locked it so Nicole wouldn't barge in and make a scene.

"What's wrong with me?" Anna murmured, resting on her elbows on her knees and holding her head face down in her hands.

"Maybe it's the 24 hour flu?" I touched her forehead to see if she had a fever. "No fever."

"Can you make it through the third act?"

"Sure. At least I think I can. I'll call in sick tomorrow at work and rest. All I have is a lunch shift."

"Anna?" Joel called from the other side of the door.

"We're in here." I opened the door for Joel and then closed and locked it.

"There you are. How are you feeling now?" Joel knelt next to Anna.

"Bad."

"Don't worry. It's probably the 24 hour flu," Anna said reassuringly.

Joel looked relieved and began stroking Anna's head.

"Do you want a water?" Joel asked.

"No. I have my tea."

"No more tea. You need water," Joel said taking her tea and tossing it into the trash can near the door. "Here's my water."

I left the two together and went back to the dressing room.

* * *

In the dressing room the vegetarian pizza was on Anna's dressing room table. To be super cautious, I folded the flimsy box of pizza in half and stuffed it in the trash can.

"How's Anna?" Nicole asked, coming into the dressing room from the hall.

"I think she has a touch of the flu."

"Tough break," she remarked, matter-of-factly, paused, and then added "Is she staying for the third act?"

"Of course."

Nicole trounced out to the stage without saying a word.

I knew she didn't care about Anna. She wanted to step in and read Anna's part to show her stuff since Mel was not going to help her.

Anna barely made it through the third act leaning on the chairs and the stair rail.

Nicole watched Anna the way a vulture circles and watches for the smell of death.

⌘

CHAPTER 36

"Wisely, and slow. They stumble that run fast."
-Shakespeare, *Romeo and Juliet*, Act 2, Scene 3

That night I slept hard. In fact, I slept with my old movie channel on, but it did not keep me company because I was out like a log.

I was startled to wake in full daylight the next morning. I was more startled when I saw my electronic clock showed 10:08 am The clock was probably as confused as I was at not waking up before dawn.

I enjoyed my tea and made myself a big breakfast of eggs, fried potatoes, and two pieces of buttered whole wheat toast with mounds of my exquisite Scottish orange marmalade. I was hungry. Renee's unfortunate, but timely, death had given me what I needed; a new lease on life at the theatre.

It was a positive morning for me. More positive than any morning in a long time. I was occupied and optimistic, even with the murder investigation looming, because I had faith in my sleuthing skills, justified or not.

After breakfast, surprisingly, I was in the mood to write. My muse had returned.

I looked at the first and only chapter of my fourth mystery book and made the command decision to abandon it. I deleted the document, which had been my nemesis for seven months.

I opened a new document. At the top, I put Theatre Murder and today's date.

A new book had swirled into my mind with a young protagonist who was an actress. She told me in detail about her life. I typed furiously as she recounted her uphill battle in Hollywood and described the people she met on the way.

I drafted three hours without stopping about a disguised Valentine Theatre and all the wonderfully distinct and quirky people I had met there, including Renee, me, Graham and Kevin, but with altered names of course.

When I came to the necessary murder for my mystery, my progress and my fingers skidded to a stop.

Who would I murder? Then, after some thought, I had the answer. The simple and obvious answer was my fictional, but recognizable Renee. And who would murder her?

I stopped writing. I realized I didn't like where the book was going. The clearest choice for the murderer in my new book was the fictional but recognizable me.

The fictional me who would kill for a part in Hollywood.

My morning optimism floundered. I knew as the great mystery writer Agatha Christie once wrote that "Nothing turns out quite in the way that you thought it would when you are sketching out notes for the first chapter, or walking about muttering to yourself and seeing a story unroll." But did it have to lead to me as the murderer?

I sat thinking. I studied the bright afternoon sun sparkling in the blue water in my pool. The autumn brown leaves floated clockwise with the flow of the circulating pump.

I had made "the me" in the book an ambitious professional actress. I also made the Valentine Theatre a large Equity house with influence on the national theatre scene. Even with the differences, however, I was overwhelmed with the logic that "the me" in my book was the only one with a sufficient motive to kill "the Renee."

I was scared. I saw now why the detectives were focusing on me, even if the real Valentine Theatre was only 99-seats and the real me had no aspirations to an acting career. They suspected me because it was easy and sexy and made good news; "Actor Kills for a Part in Hollywood."

I decided the sleuth in me had to take over. I had to get to the theatre. I had to look for clues and question everyone. Most importantly, I had to question Graham because he should have seen something. After all, he is the director and should have control over everyone. He should know where they are at all times.

* * *

I packed my theatre bag. With my fictional friends back, I hadn't had time to review my blocking and lines for the tech run. I knew I would make mistakes. The truth was that I just hadn't had enough rehearsal time to blend my lines, blocking, and business. I'd have to focus intensely while waiting backstage.

With no time to eat, I grabbed an opened but almost full box of chocolate chip oatmeal granola bars for energy at the run.

Then, I remembered my query letter still sitting in my study. I needed to graduate quickly to real author status to negate the motive the detectives had for me to kill Renee. I stuffed the query letter in an envelope. I addressed it by hand and I did the same with a self-addressed envelope. I stamped both.

My phone rang several times, but I screened the calls and let them go to message.

The only call I would take time for was Kevin's with my dinner invitation. It didn't come, but I decided I would still fight for him the way women do. I took a few minutes to touch up my make-up because those minutes would not make or break a good crime solver and there probably wouldn't be anyone to question at this hour anyway.

I looked quickly for an outfit to motivate Kevin; one that wasn't a Nicole and Anna neon invitation to sex, but, instead, was an understated inducement to dinner, and then sex. I pulled on my expensive white cashmere, which was not tight or low-cut, but enticing, and straightened it over my basic black wool pants.

If I had any of Nicole's and Anna's flashy capability left, I would have used it, but I didn't.

I looked at myself quickly in the mirror and hoped it would be enough. I needed to go.

I put my purse in the trunk and threw my theatre bag and the query letter on the backseat.

I was going to find a plausible candidate as the suspect for Renee's murder, real or not. But I still did not see any connection between Renee's and Charlie's deaths or the Fresnel incident.

⌘

CHAPTER 37

"I have no other but a woman's reason."
-Shakespeare, *The Two Gentlemen of Verona*,
Act 1, Scene 2

At the Valentine on Wednesday evening, I parked curbside and Graham pulled up behind me almost simultaneously. When I grabbed my bag from the back seat, I saw I had forgotten to mail my query letter. I glanced up and down the street, but there were no mail boxes. It stayed where it was and I pursued Graham.

"Hi. I wanted to catch you," I called as Graham opened his door.

"I'll get you the pizza money later." Graham struggled from behind his steering wheel with his large stomach. "I couldn't get to the bank. I had to replace the lace napkin Anna used. Young actors don't care about props. In my day, we would have used our shirtsleeves to catch the blood."

Graham had tech run nerves. I had catered to them many times, but didn't cater to them today.

"Forget the pizza money. I got the two for one special anyway. I need to talk about Renee."

"What?" Graham opened his trunk, set a bag of props on the pavement, and then handed me a stack of discount boxes of candy bars for the concession stand and a bag of props to cart in.

"Here carry these. I'll get sodas."

"I need some answers, Graham." I was irritated that Graham was ignoring me. "I need to know what everyone was doing in the theatre before Renee fell."

"Oh," Graham locked his car as he juggled the boxes of sodas and then grabbed the bag of props and walked to the double theatre doors. "I have no idea."

I was angry at Graham's cavalier response, but kept my cool.

"You were sitting in the theatre directing."

"Veronica." Graham struggled to unlock the theatre doors. "I don't have x-ray vision. I can't see backstage."

* * *

In the lobby, we set everything on the glass concession case. Graham began storing the sodas and candy underneath.

"Graham, think. Please. You know the detectives have zeroed in on me."

"I know. Sorry. Who would have guessed they were so . . ."

"Stupid?"

"Yeah." Graham paused from storing his goodies. "Well, I heard Alastair jingling his coins backstage. Nicole threw that hissy fit about going to pee, but that's nothing new. And no one missed their cues to come on stage. You know, you should ask Alastair. He's the people pusher."

"Fine."

I didn't like Graham's unconcerned attitude and gave him a personalized reality check.

"You do know I am fighting for your opening night too, Graham. Can't you remember anything else?"

As I calculated, Graham responded to the threat facing his opening night. He paused and looked at me for the first time since I had arrived.

"No. But Howard was really off the charts in that fight scene with Renee. I don't know if that helps. It was actually good acting for once."

"Or, not acting at all?" I thought of the free publicity Renee wanted from.

"Come on. Howard wouldn't hurt a flea." Graham finished storing the fresh candy and sodas under the concession counter. "Damn, the mint patties are completely gone. Someone's stealing candy. I'm going to have to lock this."

"Renee wasn't a flea," I refocused him.

I didn't care who stole a few candy bars. At this point, I was just looking for reasonable doubt and pointing the finger at anyone, including Howard.

"Did you know Renee was trying to get free publicity from Howard?" I asked.

"Everyone knew that. If Howard didn't know why she was nice to him, then he's nuttier than I thought."

"You knew?"

"Of course, honey, I've been around the block more than once," Graham smirked. "And so have you."

I told Graham about Howard confessing to me that he had jerked Renee's arm and Scott's table being moved by someone else, possibly so that Scott would not be back there.

"In other words you have nothing." Graham paused. "Bryce was in the lighting booth. Ask him."

"I will."

I was angry Graham hadn't shared with me about Renee's quest for publicity initially. I walked away.

"Veronica," Graham called me back.

Graham reached out and took me by the shoulders with his big hands.

"Those detectives will be back with the forensics. You've got to throw suspicion on Howard. I can take over his part easier than I can take over yours. We are not going to be shut down."

Graham was more ruthlessly single-minded than I had realized. He evidently believed in that silly saying he was always quoting, "the show must go on." It was scary.

At least, I thought, now he wanted to throw Howard under the bus and not me—even if it was simply because he could perform Howard's part more easily and not have to dress in drag or use a falsetto feminine voice.

* * *

I went to drop off my bag in the women's dressing room before I talked to Bryce.

I opened the door but the black curtain had been pulled across the opening. The black curtain was used during performances in small theatres because it was quieter than the door. Amateurs often got too excited and slammed the dressing room doors during performances.

When I pulled back the curtain, I saw Nicole standing at Anna's dressing table holding a bottle of Anna's cranberry tea. Nicole slammed it down and faced me.

"What are you doing here? It's early."

"Meeting with Graham." I looked at the cranberry tea she set down.

"Anna told me I could have a tea," Nicole announced.

"Oh." I assumed Nicole was lying and I had caught her stealing a tea.

"I'm going to get a coffee instead." Nicole left abruptly.

I deposited my bag down on my dressing table and noticed crumbs of the green rat poison on mine and Anna's dressing tables. I brushed the poison off to the floor again. I was annoyed the rats were being lured by the green cakes onto our dressing tables for the kill.

As I turned to leave, Tim burst through the black curtain and came in.

"Hi," he said excitedly plopping into a chair. "I just nailed an audition for a graduate film. Where's everyone?"

"Everyone?" I knew full well he meant the delectables, Anna or Nicole.

I stopped needling him, which was apparently going over his head anyway, and asked about the audition. I wasn't interested, but viewed it as a *quid pro quo* to interrogate him about Renee's death after.

I listened about his audition for the role of a corporate New York executive. I knew he had no appreciation of the fact that not too long ago he would have been cast only as an ethnic Asian, instead of being considered for mainstream roles.

"That's wonderful," I said with the rah-rah enthusiastic approval requisite in this industry. "Listen. Since you're here, I need to ask you about something else."

"Sure." Tim was pumped up by his audition and the fact he thought he had impressed me with his rendition of it.

"The night Renee fell you were one of the first people to get backstage. I passed by you with Graham. Remember?"

"Right. I was right there. That's what I told the cops."

"Oh, what else did you tell them?"

"Graham ordered us not to move in the black out. I didn't. But then I knew someone had to do something. So, since I was closest to the wings, I inched my way over. Then, I started backstage and ran into Nicole and we both went back to help."

Tim beamed with pride.

"Ran into Nicole?"

"Backstage. She beat me there."

"Was she coming out or going your way?"

"I don't know." Tim said impatiently.

His attention span on anything other tan himself was short.

"But when you . . ."

"Hi." Anna popped in through the black curtain.

"Anna!" Tim greeted. "Did you get my news?"

"Yes," Anna smiled and gave him a big full-body hug. "I got your text. So the audition went well?"

"Great." Tim started recounting again the blow-by-blow euphoric rendition he had given me.

Anna seemed recovered from yesterday. She laughed in the places Tim expected her to, as I had. She picked up her tea and took a sip. I started toward the door. The positive energy that both these baby actors were volleying back and forth was off-putting.

As I reached the door to the stage, Scott shoved by me. He also full-body hugged the plump young Anna, and joined in the exuberance.

I escaped out the black curtain.

Tim's new piece of the puzzle could be the key, but key to what?

Nicole would have tripped Anna, but why Renee?

⌘

CHAPTER 38

"And thus I clothe my naked villainy."
-Shakespeare, *Richard III*, Act 1, Scene 3

I started for the balcony to talk to Bryce, as Graham had suggested, but too late. Alastair called places for the tech run.

I took my place for my first entrance in the wings. From the opposite side of the stage, Kevin smiled. I smiled back.

Alastair turned to me and said with a wink, "Behave yourself."

I was embarrassed. And then I thought, why should I be embarrassed? I was single. I could flirt with any man I wanted, especially one who had made overtures. I considered not waiting for Kevin's call any longer and decided I would make the dinner date if he didn't.

Scott came and stood next to me, waiting for his sound cues and set changes.

"Why'd you leave? Tim had a great audition story.

"Yes, I had already heard it," I said, knowing he had no clue how maturity changes one's perspective. "I had to get my lines in my head."

"Right," Scott agreed, but both he and I knew that with his photographic memory he never had to run his lines in the wings.

"Scott?" I said, seeing an opportunity to glean more information. "When Renee fell where were you exactly?"

"Where do you think I was?" Scott smirked sarcastically. "Sound effects. Remember?"

"Of course," I said with equanimity, wondering why he was always a smart mouth. "I just thought you might have seen something out of place or unusual."

"Doing the sound effects? Hardly," Scott said and then lowered his voice to a whisper. "Look, Veronica, like I said, my money's on Howard. Add it up. We both know he's weird. I mean, he lives with his mom. Renee pissed him off. Put two and two together together. Psycho . . . Weirdo."

"Scott, get that table out here." Alastair yelled. "It's your cue. This is a tech run. Stop fooling around."

"Shit." Scott ran off.

I turned my attention to the run and my cue for my entrance.

* * *

In the wings, I watched the ensemble scene on stage. Kevin and Geoff were professionals. They gave their brief word cues and quietly moved to each place on stage.

For the younger actors, on the other hand, it was playtime. Nicole poked Joel with her finger, tickling him. Anna, from across the stage, watched jealously. Tim, meanwhile, tried to get Anna's attention with jokes. It was a circus.

Graham finally shouted, "People, pay attention or we'll never get out of here. Bryce can't hear my instructions over you. Nicole, I want you to enter again from stage left now and hit your mark."

"Okay," Nicole said, sauntering slowly into the wings next to me.

"Kevin, you give Nicole her cue to enter. Bryce, that same cue is for you to bring up the spot on Anna. Get it right this time and keep that spot on Anna. She is the focus of this scene, not Nicole. I don't want the light to hit Nicole," Graham ordered.

"She'll just find it again," Bryce protested from the balcony.

Nicole laughed as she stood in front of me waiting for her entrance.

"Or I'll just reset the light later," Nicole muttered under her breath.

"What?" I asked, realizing that Nicole had been resetting the lights to hit herself on stage.

"Oh," Nicole said glancing back surprised to see me behind her. "I said I didn't take Anna's spotlight."

Before I could ask anything, Nicole got her cue from Kevin and entered stage right. She kept out of Anna's spotlight this time.

I continued to watch Nicole, even when I was on stage. I watched her watch Anna. Nicole did not take her eyes off Anna the rest of the act. She was studying every movement Anna made.

* * *

There in the dark of the wings, as any good criminalist would, I put the information I had gleaned together.

Graham had changed rehearsal from the first to the third act the night Renee fell. That change made Renee and not Anna the first person who exited from the Victorian staircase.

If Anna had fallen, she would have been injured and Mel would have handed the lead to Nicole. But because Renee fell she died. She was just too old and fragile to withstand a fall from that height. I imagine she also couldn't move quickly enough to grab onto anything to break the fall as Anna probably would have.

As I observed Nicole I was more and more convinced that Nicole was after the lead and would get it by any means necessary. She was the one who put something across the ladder to trip Anna and tripped

Renee instead. She didn't care about anyone. She probably used wire from the scene dock that caused the marks on the wood ladder. Nicole was the first one backstage when Renee fell to get the wire off the stairs.

Everything made sense now.

Renee's death was a mistake, a terrible and fatal mistake. It was the classic murder by mistake that I had used in my third mystery book. The murder in my book defied rational thought and had no motive, no reason, and no logic just as Renee's. That is why neither I, nor the detectives, focused on Nicole for Renee's murder.

Now my investigatory mind concentrated on Charlie's death. It had to be connected, but how?

I looked across the stage at the brightly lit Nicole, again stealing Anna's spotlight. She was a desperate, evil, calculating monster. The detectives were right about Hollywood actors killing for a part, but I was the wrong suspect.

Nicole had eliminated the wrong actress by mistake. But how could I prove it?

Nicole had already ingeniously set me up to take the fall.

And, unfortunately, I had set up Howard.

⌘

CHAPTER 39

"It smells to heaven."
-Shakespeare, *Hamlet*, Act 3, Scene 3

At the end of the first act, Graham announced a thirty-minute dinner break.

"I need forty-five. I'm meeting Mel," Nicole called out to Graham.

"Fine. Forty-five. But be on time and be ready to work. No more fooling around."

It was clear Graham had given up fighting with Nicole. He had to agree because he knew she would do what she wanted anyway with Mel's rubber stamp of approval.

Everyone scattered for dinner, but I went back to the women's dressing room to look through Nicole's things while she was gone. I needed proof.

Nicole's black bag with the wide red stripe along the zipper was on her dressing table.

I put the black curtain down and shut the door for double protection. I hoped to find the smoking gun, the wire that tripped Renee, or the old paint brush. Something. Anything.

I didn't need to unzip Nicole's bag because the zipper was broken.

When I pulled it open I was disgusted. It was stuffed with lipstick covered tissues, make-up soiled wipes, unopened mail, cheap drugstore makeup, smelly gym clothes, ratty tennis shoes, wrinkled and ripped glamour magazines, and a roll of the same toilet paper stored in the theatre restroom. I didn't want to reach in, but I was hopeful a pack rat like this would have kept something incriminating.

As I rummaged, I found two unpaid electrical bills and at the bottom of the morass the stolen candy bars from the concession stand. To my surprise I also found two of my chocolate chip oatmeal granola bars and one bottle of Anna's tea.

There was no evidence. I was upset and deflated. Then I thought if I were writing this plot, I would not have the protagonist have such an easy time of it anyway. I needed to search elsewhere.

Then, to my shock, when I took my hands out and pushed the broken zippered top back together, I saw that I had left green powder prints on the red stripe.

I looked at my hands. They were covered with crumbled and powdered green rat poison from inside the bag. I dug again and found an unsealed baggie of broken pieces of green rat cakes.

I was disgusted. If Nicole was this filthy, I understood why she needed rat poison at home too. I stuffed the baggie back in the bag. I went to the restroom and washed my hands and then wiped the green powder along the zipper off. Nicole wouldn't notice. How could she?

Since I missed dinner, I went to get a granola bar in my bag. There were only two left in the box. I opened my small change purse. Most of the bills were gone too.

I ate one granola bar.

Alastair called for the rehearsal to begin. I went back to the stage disappointed.

I had found no proof Nicole was the murderer. She was a petty thief, a toilet paper thief, but not a murderer.

* * *

The forty-five minute dinner break had helped the baby actors blow off their steam and settle down. Nicole came back, not too late, a few glasses of wine to the better. As she walked in, her body was suctioned to Mel's. Mel apparently didn't care about her thievery and filthiness. It was inconceivable he didn't know about both.

Nicole came up the stage steps to the wings and stood in front of me waiting for her entrance. I stared at the back of her head desperately wondering how I could prove what I knew she had done to Renee.

"Veronica, it's your cue," Graham boomed. "Pay attention."

The second act was arduous and distracting, both because I hadn't reviewed my lines and because I was focused on Nicole.

By the third act, I was drained. The theatre was cold and Bryce picked up his lighting cues like a snail, a snail high on marijuana.

I got nervous as my fight scene with Howard and my stairway exit to the crossover approached. I had to be careful. I didn't know what Nicole had planned for me.

I began to imagine Renee's last seconds of life as she plummeted and lay unable to move. I suspected her thoughts were of Howard jerking her arm and Bryce playing with the lighting, the two betrayals that, in my mind, tipped the scales to guarantee her plummet as she was tripped.

* * *

I got my cue in the fight scene to head up the stairs. I did. Nicole stood on stage at the bottom and Howard followed me. The lightning flickered and the rain sounded. Then came the glass breaking and the wind.

Everything went like clockwork. Howard didn't jerk my arm. There was no black out or blue ghost streaking across the stage. I exited out the velours. I didn't go down the backstage ladder though. I hovered on the crossover platform because Scott had not put the reflector tape on the steps. I waited to use the Victorian stairs on stage when the tech cues were done.

I had astigmatism, like Howard, and had trouble seeing depths, especially black on black, which was everything backstage in the theatre. I needed the white reflector tape on the steps. I also needed to practice on the stairs in my long costume. A long rehearsal skirt would have sufficed but in my rush I didn't think of it.

A basic black long rehearsal skirt was standard when doing a period piece and helped master the movement in the dress of the period.

At the end of the scene, I came back out of the velours to the stage. When I started down the Victorian staircase, I saw Howard looking up at me. He had tears in his eyes.

"Here," he said putting out his hand. "Let me help you."

I took it. He was seeking redemption.

When I was safely back on the stage, the tension drained from my body. But then nearby I saw that Joel had his arm around Anna's waist. She was sick again. Anna sipped her tea and Joel touched her forehead.

"Okay, people," Graham bellowed. "Let's focus. Last two scenes and then we'll set the curtain call. Anna and Joel pay attention."

Joel called out, "Anna's sick. She needs to rest."

"She can rest when we are done." Graham barked in his true insensitive director form and then caught himself. "Anna, can you get through the last scene?"

"Sure."

Anna stepped forward to her mark alone. She got dizzy and started to lose her balance. Joel caught her.

"She can't. I'm taking her home," Joel said, supporting Anna with his arm around her waist.

"Fine," Graham said seeing he had no choice but to let them go. "Scott you get in here for Joel. Bring your script. I'll read Anna's lines."

"No, I can do it," Nicole blurted out and ran forward.

Everyone looked at Nicole in surprise, even Joel who was helping Anna down the stage stairs. Anna was oblivious to the predator who was vying for her role.

Joel led Anna up the center aisle and out.

"Fine, Nicole," Graham said. "Get your script."

"Wait," Nicole said starting off stage. "I have to find it."

"We don't want to be here until dawn, Nicole" Alastair said. "Do you even know where it is?"

Nicole swiveled her head around on her neck. She zeroed in on Alastair who was standing in front of me. Her eyes narrowed into evil lasers.

"Shut up, Alastair," Nicole said with a lizard-like hiss.

Alastair stood, nonplused at the venom. But he acted for the good of the order and shoved his script into her hands.

"Use mine."

"Sure." Nicole pasted on a smile as she turned back to the rest of the cast. "Ready."

"Places," Graham called.

Nicole did tech cues for both scenes without a mistake, without hesitation, and even with stage-worthy and very interesting emotional fullness.

I noticed that she glanced at the script at all the right moments. But I studied her and knew she was not relying on the script. I realized she knew the blocking, the business, and the cues perfectly. To do this she had to know Anna's part cold, every line and every movement. I looked around. It appeared that no one else noticed Nicole's mastery of Anna's part.

I, however, now had found a transparent motive; her total preparation of, and not mere desire for Anna's role.

Transparent at this point, that is, if she chose to make it so to more than just me.

⌘

CHAPTER 40

"Our remedies oft in ourselves do lie."
-Shakespeare, *All's Well That Ends Well*, Act 1,
Scene 1

At the end of the act, Mel applauded from his seat in the theatre, and shouted, "Great job."

Nicole found the hottest spotlight center stage and curtseyed, accepting Mel's accolades as hers alone, as we all knew they were intended to be.

"Stop. Stop. Let's get out of here. It's late, people. Everyone is released."

Graham cut off Mel's applause and Nicole's basking in the spotlight center stage.

"We'll set the curtain call tomorrow at final dress. Call time is five-thirty. Have your make-up and costumes on and be ready to go at six-thirty sharp. A run-through with no stopping. Final dress. Go."

"Okay," Alastair repeated authoritatively. "You're released. Call time five-thirty tomorrow. Dress rehearsal. Bring everything. Full make-up. Don't be late. Five-thirty for a six-thirty start time."

I got my things out of the dressing room and left quickly. I was tired and I had to figure out how to get real evidence against Nicole. I went to my car parked on the street and pushed unlock on my key.

"Veronica," Kevin called.

I was pleasantly surprised to hear Kevin's voice.

"Hi." I turned to him in the late night, un-trafficked street.

"I'm glad I caught you." Kevin looked down at me with his warm green eyes and drenched me in his winning smile.

"Good tech run." I could not suppress my smile or think of anything else to say.

"Yes, it was. But poor Anna. It was nice of Nicole to step in like that though."

"It was."

I simply agreed because because it was clear to me he had not seen the truth yet.

"Sorry I haven't called for dinner sooner. I knew you were swamped with the lines and, since Graham gave me this part, it has jump-started my career."

"Really?"

"My agent is keeping me busy."

"That's wonderful. Congratulations."

I stood just enjoying this handsome man's attention and his very acceptable rehabilitative excuses for not having dinner with me.

"So dinner tomorrow?" Kevin asked reaching for driver's door and opening it. "We can catch up."

I threw my bag and purse across to the passenger's seat.

"Sure."

I slipped past him to get in my car, luxuriating in the smell of his musty aftershave on the way. Now, I was glad that I hadn't called him for our dinner date.

"Tomorrow then." Kevin closed the door, crossed in front of my car, and stood on the sidewalk.

As I pulled away, Kevin stood and watched me near the curb. I glanced at him through the shot gun window with the street light washing over his leather jacket and washed blue jeans. I was momentarily running on "happy", with my adrenaline pumping. I wanted tomorrow's dinner to be right now.

* * *

On my drive home Kevin's image gave way to Nicole's vicious glare at Alastair and her automaton smile which followed. I knew she had been scrutinizing Anna all night so closely, not only because she was memorizing Anna's new post-edit blocking, but because she was planning how to get Anna out of the play.

As I turned into my driveway, I decided the Fresnel falling on Anna's chair my first night had to be Nicole's doing too, but I had no proof.

I sat in the dark driveway thinking. Everything started to fit together.

I remembered Nicole in the hall when Charlie died. She had thought the body was a woman's. Anna's? Had Nicole tampered with the vent? Was she responsible for two deaths? I couldn't fathom the evil, the lack of conscience and remorse. Was everyone who touched her life a mere functionary? A means to be used for her ends?

I laughed at the irony Anna's flu presented now. Nicole might have gotten Anna's part without two murders.

I called Graham. He had to know about Nicole. He didn't answer. I left a message to call me.

I went into the house. I was exhausted from being on my feet for hours, giving the tech cues, and, needless to say, the stress of sharing the floorboards with a murderer on the prowl. I needed to consider what to do about my discoveries in the morning. In point of fact, I was not a real criminologist, nor was I a real crime solver, although I admit I seemed to be good at it. I was merely a person looking for meaning in an otherwise dull life and, now, trying to stay out of prison in the process.

I threw myself in bed without my classic movie companions. When my head hit the pillow, my thoughts were only of Kevin and fantasizing about our dinner. I recalled his smell and smile and his image under the street light as I drove away.

I slept deeply and soundly.

* * *

Thursday morning I awoke with far less surprise that it was already daylight. I had slept long and hard and through the wee hours of the morning that were usually mine. Even with the late rising I still didn't feel rested. I also missed the tranquility of the sunrise over my pool in the pre-dawn hours.

I made a cup of very strong caffeinated tea and sat in front of my computer. I looked at my script and couldn't bring myself to open it, let alone study Renee's role.

As I sat there, the protagonist in my new theatre mystery book compelled me to write. I suddenly grasped that I was analyzing and solving the Valentine murders, Nicole's murders, through my new mystery. The characters came onto the page through my fingers with such speed that I couldn't keep up.

Before I knew it, and three cups of high-octane tea later, it was noon. My muse was back and my protagonist screamed the words at me in capital letters. The evil young actress in my book was on the verge of getting arrested for murder because the police found the missing piece. They discovered her fingerprints on the paint can used to cover up the evidence showing where the murdered older actress had been tripped.

I stretched in my chair and looked at the wind pushing the leaves around in my pool against the tide of the pool pump.

I shook my head. Too bad Nicole hadn't made that mistake. I knew she had disposed of the old paint can and brush she used. It was Scott's last brush and he had to purchase more. I thought of possible fingerprints on the Fresnel that fell, but that would be explained away because Nicole had helped set up the lights for Bryce. She was smart. I knew any evidence in Charlie's office was long ago contaminated. Besides, mixing in Charlie's death, still deemed accidental even though quite coincidental, would give the detectives more of an excuse to close down the show allowing the Crenshaw Troupe to step in with their money.

I was startled from my crime solving by my cell phone ringing. It was a friend, but I let it go to message. The call reminded me to call Graham to get his support to nail Nicole. He had to help, even if he needed Nicole because Anna had the flu and even if Graham preferred to throw Howard under the bus until the play opened. Nicole was too dangerous.

Graham did not pick up his phone. I left another message to call.

I took a minute to quickly return emails to get my audience to the theatre. My writing teacher Mavis was coming on opening night with some classmates. The senior citizen homes were organizing a bus trip for a Sunday afternoon matinee and dinner. They wondered if I was going to have a book signing at the theatre. Too bad I didn't have a book to sign. I didn't respond.

I called Graham again to no avail and left a third message.

I ate and did stretching exercises while I waited for Graham to return my call. I always stretched to get in touch with my body for smooth and coordinated stage movement.

An actor's body is his instrument. It has to be not only emotionally available but also physically and vocally capable of living through and demonstrating the character's moments on stage or film. The more refined and capable the instrument the more deep and interesting the acting. It's as simple and complex as that.

I tried Graham once more. He didn't answer yet again so I decided to get down to the theatre early to see if he was there.

I packed my bag with the usual, including an emergency peanut butter and honey sandwich in case we went too late, and this time included all my stage makeup to age myself for my character and an old hair piece.

When I threw my bag in my car, I saw my query letter still sitting on the back seat. Of course, I didn't need to mail it now because I had the murderer, thanks in part to my new protagonist and my new theatre mystery. It had great potential, I thought.

As I drove, I used the time to hone my persuasive arguments for Graham and do my vocal exercises to get a good vocal range, volume, and diction. I wouldn't have time once I got there.

One driver stopped with me at a red light, gave me a strange look, and sped away quickly from me and my odd facial contortions when the green light popped on. I didn't care. The exercises were necessary to relax my vocal cords, limber my tongue and lips, and help my diaphragm breathing. Being a stage actor was being a vocal athlete.

Vocal coaching helped, but then it was expensive and repetitive. I'd had enough. I felt that way about acting coaches too. They all said the same thing using different vocabulary. They all taught actors to live through the moment, but also, of course, not to forget technique or sink into mere emotional masturbation.

I got to the theatre vocally prepared for the dress rehearsal, but more importantly armed with the identity of a serial murder; albeit an accidental serial murderer, but a serial murderer all the same.

I was proud of my sleuthing, but frightened of

Nicole. I had to get Graham on board. I had to get real evidence for the detectives.

⌘

CHAPTER 41

"Something wicked this way comes."
-Shakespeare, *Macbeth,* Act 4, Scene 1

Inside the Valentine lobby, I saw Joel talking to Tim, Scott, and Anna. Listening nearby were some young and wide-eyed acting students from the Valentine's upstairs afternoon classes. They were observing Joel with the reverence a "real," "working" actor should get.

"Did you hear?" Anna bounced over to me and said, bursting with pride. "Joel's agent finally had him sign the contract for Stephie Sevas's movie."

"That's wonderful."

I was genuinely happy for them both and noted the acting students whisper amongst themselves when they heard the name Stephie Sevas.

"But, how are you feeling, Anna?"

"Fine. And thanks for all the help." Anna walked back to the group with me. "Listen. Joel's telling about the first film he ever made. You'll love this story."

Overnight, Joel had become a respected authority on how to make it in the biz. He was in the limelight and Anna was hanging on his every word, even though I was sure she had heard the stories many times.

It appeared Anna was over the flu.

I joined the group and the young acting students inched closer.

". . . and there I was . . . an extra in this wild west rock music video," Joel said, dramatically building the suspense. "We were shooting on a mountain top in the dead of winter. Shooting an Indian fight against the cavalry. I was freezing in this loin cloth get-up with war paint all over me leading an Indian raiding party."

"And that was the first thing on your film resume?" Tim asked.

"Yeah. A rock music video. And I was glad to get it. No credits but I was glad to get anything for my reel."

"Tell them the funny part, Joel," Anna said looking at Joel with adoring eyes. "You guys will love this."

"Love what?" Nicole called out as she strutted into the lobby from the theatre, glaring at Anna.

Nicole was already dressed in her costume, a black Victorian maid's uniform. However. She had left the front buttons open showing her ever-bouncing cleavage.

"Joel's story about his first shoot." Anna smiled at Nicole and then looked back at Joel.

"Everybody has one of those. Just because you landed that Sevas film doesn't make yours the best."

Nicole went behind the concession counter and leaned on it so all eyes couldn't avoid at least a glance at her bulging cleavage precariously mounding over.

When Joel continued his story everyone's attention, including the acting students, went back on Joel, everyone's except Scott's. He kept his eyes on Nicole's breasts.

"Listen, Nicole. You'll love this." Joel glanced again at her projectile cleavage and then back to his audience.

Nicole was in my line of sight behind Joel and I was held spellbound by her transparent jealousy of Joel and Anna. She was ruthless, cold and ambitious. I ignored her obvious beauty and watched her pale predatory blue eyes zero in on Anna as Joel spoke.

Joel continued his story with a flourish.

"The fight started on the mountain top and all us Indians were being killed by the soldiers. When all my warriors were killed, I screamed an Indian battle cry and charged. Then I got shot and broke my blood packet on my stomach. I staggered toward the camera dying for about 25 feet. But I never heard the director say cut . . . so I stayed in character and fell to my knees and kept going toward the camera. Then I started crawling and finally died right in front of the camera. I mean, I couldn't go any further. I laid there dead on the ground and all of a sudden applause came from everyone, the director, the actors, and the crew."

"Wow," Tim said.

"Wait. Listen." Anna held up her hand. "This is so funny."

"The director had called 'cut' way back when I first got shot," Joel said laughing. "I didn't hear him."

"He was really in-the-moment." Anna laughed like it was the first time she heard the story. "Imagine that as your first paying shoot and doing a scene like that by accident."

I laughed with everyone else. It was funny. And, of course, now that Joel was on his way to the top of the biz in Stephie Sevas's film, people would always laugh at his stories, funny or not. He had been rubber-stamped by a hot leading lady.

"I've done a lot since, but you always remember your first." Joel enjoyed the moment.

"That was great. I would kill to have that on my reel," Tim exclaimed.

I looked over at Tim and smiled. If he only knew he would not be throwing around that word.

I thought of my very short and very ancient reel stored in my attic. I sent it around for a year to agents decades ago to no avail. It had nonspeaking student film clips and one speaking graduate film clip. Most student films had no audible dialogue, just music and action, like silent films. I didn't stay in the biz long enough to get an independent film.

"So. Then . . ." Nicole leaned into the group silently demanding attention with her unbuttoned costume. "What you mean is you goofed at your first shoot."

"Come on, Nicole, that's a great story," Tim said, still laughing and then turned and asked Joel. "Did the director use it?"

"No, but he loved it," Joel bragged, looking at the acting students and generously including them in his audience. "He gave me a copy and it's the first thing on my reel."

"My first shoot was a grad film and between my scenes I ran the dolly," Scott said, vying for the lobby audience. "It was wild. I got one scene for my reel the rest went on the editing room floor. I was pissed. I . . ."

Joel interrupted, taking his position as the alpha actor.

"Stephie Sevas told me her first studio film role ended up on the editing room floor, too," Joel said, name dropping with abandon and speaking with authority loud enough to include the wide-eyed acting students. "It happens."

"Big deal. It ended up there because it belonged there," Nicole shouted out still leaning over. "My first shoot was a porno flick."

There was silence. Everyone looked at her. The men with the carnivorous eyes that were always aroused when a woman announced her blatant availability whether tactile or imaginary. I looked at her not with surprise, but instead with calculating eyes, because nothing Nicole said surprised me anymore.

Anna looked at Nicole, startled. I was worried about Anna. It appeared that she had no idea Nicole was after her. Nicole wanted out of that maid's costume and into Anna's bright yellow leading lady costume at any cost, but how could I prove it? Nicole was a force to be reckoned with.

"Gotcha," Nicole laughed, walking to the oak theatre door, swinging it open, and stepping though. "In your dreams."

As I watched Nicole leave, I realized the chink in her armor, her weakness. She liked all the attention all the time and had a point of no return in trying to get it. Once that switch flipped, she would sacrifice anything to be in the spotlight, to be better than everyone, and to be smarter or simply show-off. I would find that point and flip that switch with witnesses.

"Did she really do that to get a reel?" Anna said sincerely looking up at Joel. "Could she use that for a feature film reel?"

Scott watched after Nicole as the theatre door swung shut. "She's kidding, fooling around. Besides, if she were in a porno I would know."

"Yeah," Tim laughed. "And so would I. We had porno night every Wednesday at my fraternity."

"I love Nicole. Never a dull moment." Scott walked toward the theatre door. "I have to set up."

"Congratulations on signing the contract and sealing the deal." I gave Joel his due which I knew he would get from now on, deserved or not.

"Thanks."

"And that was one of the best first filming story I've heard,." I added.

"I bet you have some good stories too."

"Nothing like that. I better get dressed."

I admired Joel's skill at including everyone, even the young acting students who were still taking in everything he said. I knew he was destined to be a star-- barring booze, pills, women, vanity, a big head, and offending anyone in his whole professional life. But he did seem to have the politics of the acting world down at this point. And that is what acting is in the end, a very political animal.

"We'd all better," Joel said starting into the theatre. "See you on stage."

"Yes," Anna agreed, jumping up.

Tim caught up with Joel and put his hand on Joel's shoulder as they walked out. The students watched them leave and started whispering to each other.

The pecking order was defined. The sucking up had begun in full.

Even Nicole was sucking up in her own way. Her mounding breasts were an offering at Joel's new altar.

I knew it and so did Joel. Anna did not or pretended not to.

⌘

CHAPTER 42

"I am a kind of burr; I shall stick."
-Shakespeare, *Measure for Measure*, Act 4,
Scene 3

After they left, I decided to catch Bryce in private before I talked to Graham. Perhaps I could get more ammunition. I headed to the balcony to find out what he meant before when he referred to "everyone" planning the blue ghost light.

As I ascended into the dark, I understood why Bryce was nutty. Who wouldn't be, stashed up here with Graham always bellowing at you?

"Bryce," I called at the top of the stairs.

"Veronica?"

I stepped into Bryce's dark balcony world and, as my eyes adjusted, I saw the scattered fallow lighting equipment and stray abandoned props. The organ and the organist who had played during the funerals were long gone, but I felt the shadows of their presence. I watched for rats and cockroaches as I made my way toward Bryce through boxes, piled Fresnels, spots, and stored set lamps.

My hands touched rat droppings on a box as I made my way forward.

"Rats!"

"Of course," Bryce said matter-of-factly. "Nicole gave me some rat cakes, though."

"Oh? That's nice."

I lied and wondered what quid pro quo she had elicited in exchange. I noted the deceit I engage in for my authorial life had prepared me well for my newly revisited acting activities. I knew there was nothing nice about Nicole. She was a calculating machine and a thief. She took what she wanted, including Bryce's spotlights meant for other actors on stage. I now suspected that Nicole courted Bryce, in part, because he might have seen something damaging to her and, after all, how many people could she kill in one small theatre.

"Yeah, she's okay."

Bryce's eyes sparkled at the mention of Nicole. He was oblivious to the reality that Nicole would throw him to the wolves in a minute.

"I told her you would never hurt Renee and she agreed."

"Thanks," I said disingenuously, realizing Nicole had done her undermining up here too.

"Of course," Bryce replied, ignorant of Nicole's true motives. "Hey, I'm sorry I got so upset about the blue light stuff before. I mean Renee loved that stuff. She thought it would bring in bigger audiences if we had the ghosts return full force."

"She planned it?"

"Sort of," Bryce hesitated. "Geoff and me planned mainly, but she gave us the idea."

"Don't worry. I don't think the lighting that night made any difference." I consciously gave Bryce his absolution, but only because I needed information from him.

"The detectives didn't think so either," Bryce said.

"Really? Why? Did you tell the detectives about anything unusual you might have seen from up here?"

"No. Graham was running around like a chicken with his head cut off, yelling like always. Scott checked the set with Nicole following him around blabbering about something. Alastair was going . . ."

"Wait. Back up. Nicole was checking the set with Scott? Why? Did she always do that?"

"Lately. When she's here early, she helps out. Lights, paint, Sets. Anything. Why?"

"Paint?"

"Yeah. Why?"

"No reason."

I had to play my cards close to the vest.

"I know you're worried, but don't be. Nicole says the detectives will just go away." Bryce was dismissive of my my impending probable arrest as he was with most everything in life. "And I promise no more blue lights streaking across."

"Thanks, Bryce."

I was disappointed in Bryce for so many reasons, but among them his vulnerability to Nicole's lies.

Nicole had positioned herself as a helper and put her fingerprints everywhere. Forensics was a dead avenue for any hope of proving my innocence. I needed more skill than I had gotten combined from Sherlock Holms, Agatha Christie, or being a mysterian over the last several years. I needed to inhabit a more devious criminal brain.

"I'll light you good down there. No more ghosts," Bryce called as I started down the steps. "Break a leg tonight."

The hair stood up on the back of my neck at those words.

⌘

CHAPTER 43

"Have more than thou showest, Speak less than thou knowest."
-Shakespeare, *King Lear*, Act 1, Scene 4

I slipped down the dingy balcony steps discouraged because, as the detectives in my books often observed, "hard evidence was hard to come by." But then, in all fairness, given my detectives' characterizations in my mysteries, "brains" were hard to come by too. But I would not give up trying to sic the detectives onto the true murderer, Nicole, and get Graham past opening night.

I dropped my bag off in the dressing room and looked for Graham. He was nowhere around so I headed for Scott's scene dock at the back of the theatre. Scott did his building there and it was the only place I hadn't looked for something that might help me.

At the scene dock, I flipped the bright work lights on and shut the door. I was dwarfed by the massive raisers, platforms, flats, and set pieces surrounding me. Graham's carefully designed collapsible rolling platforms were stacked up to the ceiling along the back wall along with rectangular, round, and square matte black portable stage risers used to create areas or rooms on stage. There were stacks of tall, unpainted plywood panels resting precariously on the platforms and along the walls. A large plastic trash can was empty.

I stepped through sawdust, screws and nails, small pieces of rope, wire, wood painted the colors of our set, and rat droppings. I worked my way over to a tall metal cabinet. In it I found everything needed to build sets: hammers, circular saws, hand saws, Phillips and flathead screw drivers, spools of wire, spools of rope, levels, and sanders. The bottom shelves were crammed with quart and gallon used-paint cans with colors dripping down their sides. There were two new cans of black matte paint at the end, but no old ones that might have had fingerprints as in my new mystery.

Next to the cans I saw the two new paint brushes Scott bought with Graham's money, but no old ones. That merely confirmed what I knew. Nicole had disposed of the cans and brushes she used to cover up the marks from the wire she had used to trip Renee.

I looked at the unorganized spools of copper, steel, and colored electrical wire. There were no smaller pieces that could have been used to trip Renee. I rummaged through the box of Phillips and flathead screwdrivers of all sizes that Nicole could have used one to loosen the straps on Charlie's heater vent. But I knew Nicole's fingerprints alone were useless. Even fingerprints on the three wooden ladders up against the far wall would mean nothing, because Nicole had made herself so helpful and omnipresent. Her fingerprints were legitimately everywhere.

I slammed the metal cabinet door shut.

I screamed when a large gray rat reacted and ran from under it across the room into the stored sets.

I turned to leave.

"What's going on?" Scott burst through the door.

"Nothing. A rat . . . I saw a rat. How can you work with rats running around? You should get some rat poison."

"That's what Nicole says, but that stuff is bad news. So what do you want?" Scott was territorial about the scene dock where he worked his magic building the sets.

"Nothing." I was through sharing any of my plans or suspicions with Scott. "I was looking for . . ."

I couldn't finish the sentence. I was out of creative excuses, but I did think the old paint can and brush would be useful in the end if they were still around. I decided to ask Scott for them whether he megaphone mouthed it or not.

"I want to know what you did with that last dried out brush and old can of paint?"

"Why?"

"I won't say just yet." I hoped Scott's very bright, but judgment-devoid, mind would just let this go.

"Tell me." Scott imped a smile and sat on a nearby saw horse. "I know you're trying to get the cops off your back. Fill me in."

"I'll share later. I'm in a hurry . . . dress rehearsal." Scott was playing a cat-and-mouse game with me and he knew he held all the cards.

"You know who killed Renee, don't you?"

"Maybe or maybe not." I deflected Scott's digging. "Can you help me out here?"

"Yeah," I can because I know who you're after."

"Who?"

"We both know." Scott paused grinning mischievously. "Howard. And he's always been my first pick."

"Right." I didn't care what he thought.

"But why the paint brush and can?" Scott stopped grinning and studied me intensely. "Because you're lying? It's not Howard."

At that point, I knew he didn't have a clue who I suspected, but I could see his very sharp, undisciplined mind working. I was sorry I had asked him.

"I have to go get ready for dress." I stood to leave. "I'll catch you later."

I had called Scott's bluff. He was unhappy. He treated all conversations as games of one-upsmanship and he had lost. He was smart enough, in a sea of not-so-bright actors, that he usually got his way. The irony was that I had already jeopardized my investigation. Scott now knew the paint brushes and paint cans were important to me. He had gotten something and I gotten nothing.

As I left, I turned back to Scott to rehabilitate myself because he was a loose cannon.

"See you later," I said cheerfully.

I pretended, and I thought effectively, that the outcome of our standoff was of no consequence to me.

Scott smiled, but didn't answer.

I didn't like that.

⌘

CHAPTER 44 ˋ

"O true apothecary!"
-Shakespeare, *Romeo and Juliet*, Act 5, Scene 3

I hurried back to the dressing room to get my costume and make-up on. My practiced, knowledgeable, and evidentially supported revelation to Graham would have to wait.

In the dressing room, my admittedly mature eyes were met with the effrontery of the young and beautiful or "Y and B" as they say in the business.

Nicole's tight bare ass was front and center, covered only with a black butt-floss thong. She leaned over her dressing table to the mirror to put her eye makeup on close to the mirror. Her long lean pale body was otherwise naked, except for her heels, a string of a push up bra, and, of course, her skull and crossbones tattoo.

Tim sat in a carefully placed chair salivating at her rounded ass, every inch of it. Nicole shifted her weight on her heels sending a chain reaction up her long legs. It tenderly jiggled the prize Tim wanted.

"I'm starving," Nicole announced.

She adjusted her thong provocatively. Her beautifully presented ass screamed doggy style.

Nicole was imprinting herself on every man in the theatre.

In the corner behind the white rice paper changing screen, I saw Anna reflected in the jigsaw of mirrors quietly changing. Tim glanced in the mirror at Anna taking off her sweater behind the changing screen. Then he caught my eye.

"Hi, Veronica," Tim said, taking his eyes boldly back to Nicole's firm body, as if this show was his due.

I had caught him at the nudie show and he was immune. He was neither son, nor husband, nor a male under my thumb. He knew it.

I sat at my dressing table and got out my make-up. Reflected in my mirror, I saw Nicole lean nearer to her mirror to finish her mascara. She glanced at Tim to make sure he responded to her new position.

Tim did. He zeroed in on the butt floss and followed it down and down to the dark tunnel under her rounded buttocks.

* * *

I hated these hormonally drenched dressing room nudie shows. This voyeuristic subculture, however, came with the territory.

Ambitious actresses used everything they had to manipulate any and every male. And I had found there were literally no men that did not enjoy watching the dressing room shows. Some, like Tim, unabashedly camped out when the pre-show show began. Others only poked their heads in dressing rooms without knocking to get a snapshot when they knew the costumes were going on or off.

Interestingly, in men's dressing rooms the dynamic was different. Men stripped when they needed to, matter-of-factly, whether women were around or not. Over the years, I had unfortunately seen it all, but by happenstance not choice. Amongst the abundant lean young hard bodies there were bare hairy beer bellies, boxers with holes, saggy briefs, stick legs, and pimply backs. I always vacated post haste.

What did I want with other women's testosterone "treasures"? And I use the term loosely. Looking at the men my age was like a jolt of the grotesque and seeing the younger Adonises was akin to post-pubescent baby-sitting. To me, however, Kevin was the exception. Of course, he was the exception to everything for me. I was looking forward to dinner tonight.

I eyed Nicole and then decided to put an end to her nudie show, or semi-nudie show, and her prattle about her hunger and dinner plans. I'd had enough from this woman who was throwing me to the wolves so skillfully that I could not effectively react defensively to her chess-like moves.

"Tim," I said with the authority of the dressing room elder. "You had better go get your costume on."

Nicole gave me a dirty look because she was enjoying showing Tim what he could never have. Tim obeyed because he knew that men were not allowed here unless invited and I had uninvited him and his drool.

"Later, Tim." Nicole waived cutely in the mirror just above the firm mounds of white flesh displayed by her push-up bra.

I shut the door after Tim and now theatre etiquette required males to knock before entering. Although some men knocked and opened the door simultaneously for a peek, most adhered to the rule.

With Tim gone, Anna popped from behind the accordioned changing screen. "Can you do me up, Nicole?"

"Ask Veronica."

Because the Tim-show was over, Nicole slid her maid's costume over everything that was Mel's to touch, obviously, just for now.

"Here, let me help you," I said, buttoning the back of Anna's yellow silk dress with lace and ruffles. "You look fantastic in this with your dark hair up like that."

"Thanks." Anna sipped her cranberry tea from a bottle on her dressing table. "Want a tea? Either of you?"

"No," Nicole answered. "But thanks anyway. I have water. Veronica, take one of my water bottles."

I was surprised at Nicole's offer and wondered at her sudden act of camaraderie. But participated in, and acknowledged, the suspiciously friendly moment. Keep your enemies close, I thought.

"Thanks. I brought my own. I brought nuts too. I'll leave them out if you guys want some."

I finished Anna's last button.

"Great." Anna looked in the mirror for the last time. "I'm ready. See you out there."

"You forgot your tea." Nicole grabbed Anna's tea and handed it to her.

"Oh, thanks." Anna took her script and headed to the stage. "If Alastair misses me, tell him I'm in the wings."

While Nicole put on her make-up, I dressed behind the screen in my act one navy blue silk taffeta dress trimmed with white lace on the throat and cuffs. I was right. The bodice was tight, but not too tight to wear. As I noted before, the seamstress had let out as much as she could and I would have to make do. The shoulders were fine so I could move well. I would watch what I ate for the next few months. I hoped months if we did well enough opening night.

I thought of poor Renee because this costume was ordered to fit her.

* * *

When I came out from behind the screen and hung up my street clothes, I was shocked at Nicole's make-up. It was out of character for a Victorian maid: sapphire blue eye shadow, thick black eye liner, heavy mascara, and apple red lipstick and lip liner smeared on outside her lip line making her lips pop out like red balloons. Graham would give her a note on it, which she would undoubtedly ignore with Mel's support.

As I put on my stockings and Victorian heels, Nicole complained.

"I could use a coffee. It's so cold in here."

"It's not that bad." My mind snarled—she wouldn't be cold at all, but for her naked display for Tim.

Sharing dressing rooms with baby actresses taught me they were consumed with, and endlessly kept everyone alerted to, their bodily functions and comfort level. Their discourse began and ended with up-to-the-minute reports on whether they were either cold or hot, hungry or full, tired or rested, thirsty or in need of going pee. I had learned to endure this with neutral grunts. Only sometimes, out of polite necessity, I elevated my responses with the appropriate levels of sympathy or elation, pretending their physical comfort or discomfort was of any interest at all to me.

"Your dress fits well." Nicole looked at me with a bright red lip-sticked smile that was meant to disarm and please. "Do you want me to button you?"

"Sure." I fenced with her disingenuous syrupy sweetness.

I didn't know what her new agenda was but I engaged because it suited mine. I needed to nail her for Renee's death and, possibly Charlie's, any way I could.

"A little snug," Nicole said as she buttoned me. "But it will work. And navy is a good color on you,"

Nicole's compliment and upbeat attitude were out of character and rang with a transparently false note. I didn't like it, but at this moment I would not look a gift horse in the mouth. I shot a question at Nicole ever so casually.

"So, Scott said you helped him with the set work and in the scene dock."

"What do you mean by that?" Nicole barked, finished the last button, and buried nice. "What has Scott told you?"

"Nothing."

Nicole powdered her clown face in silence. That overreaction was out of line and meant something, but what?

I tied the velvet navy blue cumber bun tightly around my loose waist, sat down quietly, and started my make-up.

Nicole put on her white apron and button-like white hat with a black ribbon and lace fringe. She smoothed the skirt and straightened the hat. Then she glowered in her mirror at me.

Without a word, Nicole went stomping out and slamming the door behind her.

* * *

I eyed the mirror—the empty space Nicole had occupied. To me it was not vacant. Her presence was lingering and potent, her inhuman presence. She was evil, instinctive, single-minded, and fearless.

I turned back to my reflection in my mirror. Time was short now.

I quickly put my hair up in a Victorian style with hair spray, large hairpins, and my old brown hairpiece I had packed to add volume.

As I began the process of aging myself twenty-five years, I pushed Nicole and my investigation out of my mind. I had to focus on my performance.

I had done aging make-up before and knew in a small theatre like the Valentine I had to be subtle because the audience was close. Since I was alone, I ran my lines out loud. I categorically never invaded another actor's ear space like other actors frequently did. To me this was intentional sabotage.

Sabotage was not uncommon in the industry and theatre. I remembered when I went in a limousine with five fellow actors going to a location shoot. The driver blared heavy metal music and refused to turn it off or at least turn the back speakers off. Our performances and the film suffered. Usually, skilled actors can isolate themselves from anything, but this was too hard for me. No one can take care of your performance or your instrument but you.

I ran a dark brown pencil lightly through all my exposed creases and lines: forehead, eyes, lips, nose, neck and hands. Then I highlighted along each brown line with white powder and blended these low lights and high lights together until they looked natural. I applied very little eye liner and sparse mascara, unlike Nicole. I added pink blush on my cheek bones and hollowed my face by putting a dark brick color beneath.

Lastly, I patted baby powder into my Victorian styled dark hair. Baby powder was the best way to age hair because it brushed out after the performance and took hair oils with it. As long as you didn't mind dull hair, you didn't have to wash it out every night.

I finished. I was unhappily happy with my reflection in the mirror. I looked Renee's age. She had not needed any make-up to play this role. Thankfully, I did.

I took my script and my flashlight, turned off the bright dressing table lights, and turned on the low ceiling lights that would not beam out to the wings. I left the door open and dropped the black curtain down as I went to do dress rehearsal.

* * *

I took my place in the wings for my entrance behind Geoff who was queued behind Nicole. I ran my lines in my head and prepared for my first entrance.

"Ten minutes." Alastair hurried by and whispered to me. "Is everyone out of there?"

"Yes," I answered.

Geoff glanced over his shoulder at me. "Break a leg, dear."

"Thanks," I whispered. "Have a good show."

Nicole then turned and smeared a smiled at me with her bright red lips.

"Yeah, Veronica, break a leg."

My heart sank.

⌘

CHAPTER 45

"I have no other but a woman's reason."
-Shakespeare, *The Two Gentlemen of Verona*,
Act 1, Scene 2

The stage lights were on, the house lights were down, and dress rehearsal began. The actors in the first scene took their places on stage. I waited in the wings for my entrance.

It was just a little after our six-thirty start time.

"Curtain," Graham called from his seat out front.

Scott pulled the rope for the front red grand drape from the wings across stage, steadily and smoothly hand-over-hand with the thin rope pulleys.

Curtain pulling was a learned skill like everything else in the theatre. I remembered my first time. I jerked the grand drape open haltingly in front of the audience, making them dance and sway at the bottom, very amateurish. Worse, however, that night I also pulled the curtains open at the wrong time. I exposed two actors on stage while the scene continued which was supposed to be in front of the closed curtains proscenium on the apron. The erroneously exposed actors thought fast, froze, and created a human tableau. But, from then on, each time I tested the direction of the curtain with a little tug on the rope.

While I waited for my entrance, I went and looked out the peep hole in the red grand drape out into the audience. It was unnoticeable to the audience in the large curtain. Graham and Mel were together seated in the front row. I was also surprised to see two people barely visible further back. My concentration was shattered, just like the limousine incident. It had to be the detectives back again, I assumed.

I leaned back against the walls in the dark. I shut my eyes and took a deep breath to gather my thoughts.

When I opened my eyes I shook my skirt and screeched, "Ah!"

The cockroach fell and I watched it run towards the dressing room.

Alastair turned, walked toward me from the wings. "What the hell was that?"

"Nothing," I said, shrugging my shoulders. "A cockroach."

"This is our final dress. Get a grip."

"I know. I know. Won't happen again," I whispered.

"Good. I don't have time for this. These people don't know their lines and I have to prompt the little buggers."

Alastair went back into the wings. He took his job very seriously and he was well-trained from his Broadway years.

My entrance was coming up. I had to refocus because I was on a train that didn't stop: detectives or not, cockroaches or not, rats or not, Nicole or not.

I stood in the dark with stage light streaming by me in between the black velour legs, overwhelmed.

All of a sudden, I wanted to be home, go to bed early, rise before the dawn, and be amongst my fictional characters. Indeed, I had overcome my writer's block with a new theatre mystery. I didn't feel its character deserting me, yet. And I liked my niche as the local mystery writer and crime solver. What had I done taking Renee's role?

I had abandoned my comfortable life and, in the process, become a murder suspect. I now spent my nights with cockroaches and rats. Rats of more than one type I thought as I watched Nicole on stage. She bathed in the hot spot light like a cold-blooded snake warming in the sun.

My spirits picked up when Kevin walked on stage from the other side. I was looking forward to our dinner tonight, even if I had to change into street clothes and remove some make-up.

My entrance was near. I pressed on my Adam's Apple to relax my vocal cords, a technique learned from an opera singer. I shut my eyes and isolated myself amidst all the distractions and got into character. I was ready. I opened my eyes and listened for my cue, but it didn't come. Howard went up on his lines and Nicole added two lines to her speech. Between these two incompetents, they skipped my cue and the reason for my entrance.

"Those idiots," Alastair whispered as he walked up to me. "You've got to get out there."

"How?"

"Go. Go, I don't care how. Just get out there . . . ad lib and go on," Alastair said waiving the script at me.

I created a line conforming to Kevin's next speech and stepped out under the bright stage lights and into the Victorian world Graham had created.

Unfortunately, Kevin simultaneously changed his line to take the play back to my proper entrance. It was chaos. Kevin and I, two seasoned actors, had corrected Nicole and Howard's mistakes in two different ways. I was floundering on stage when I should have been the hero, much like Howard when the Fresnel fell.

My fellow actors on stage eyed me as if I had made the mistake. They rejected my accommodation— my entrance—as too early, and Kevin's accommodation as heroic and smart. Howard and Nicole's mistakes which caused this were forgotten. Now, the ensemble adjusted their lines to compensate for my "early" entrance.

Early entrances, dropped lines, and missed cues made live performances interesting to me, but not when they were mine.

Amazingly, audiences rarely noticed mistakes when skillful actors covered them easily, especially in first run plays like Mel's. With the classics, especially Shakespeare, it's not the same, because the exact lines are well known. Some audience members, like me, have even performed the roles.

I personally was jarred at a *Macbeth* performance once when the actress changed a line in her "out damned spot" speech. As was true with many other actors, I even knew the differences in Lady M's speeches from Shakespeare's First Folio and later versions.

Act one ran fast. Tim sped it up more by erroneously skipping forward a quarter of a scene to his monologue.

Despite his jumping forward, his monologue was remarkably riveting. No one bothered to bring the play back to its proper place, including me. I was already labeled as a mistake-maker, instead of a scene-saver.

* * *

After Tim's monologue, Kevin and I exited. I was through for the first act. I went to the crossover to practice on the ladder behind the Victorian staircase with my costume on. Kevin followed for his entrance on the other side. I stopped at the ladder.

"What's up?" Kevin asked from behind.

I turned and looked at the silhouette of his broad shoulders.

"I have to test the ladder." I leaned forward and whispered because the play was in progress.

"I'm sorry I didn't hear. What?" Kevin bent over and whispering so close to my ear.

I felt his warm breath on my neck and his hair sweep against mine.

"Practice on the ladder," I said getting on my tiptoes and putting my lips near his ear.

Kevin's smell was fresh and spicy and intoxicating. The darkness and the moment were un-inhibiting. I resisted an urge to lower my lips from his ear to his neck and place a quick, soft compelling kiss on it. I wondered if he was having the same thoughts.

"Okay," Kevin said, standing straight, smiling in the darkness, and then leaning in again face-to-face. "Need help?"

"No. No," I said embarrassed by my thoughts. "Your entrance is coming up. Go."

I watched him fade into the darkness through the crossover's stacked clutter.

Then Nicole's face and her automaton smile flashed in my mind. I shuddered involuntarily. I looked for anything on the steps that might trip me. Scott had not put the white reflector tape on the edges yet. It was petty revenge for not sharing with him in the scene dock. I set my script and flashlight under the steps, picked up the front of my long full dress, and started up the steps.

When I reached the platform, I turned and I looked down. Against Scott's earlier recommendation, I decided to go down face front because I could see everything better. I lifted my full taffeta skirt, put it over my left arm, held on to the rail with my right hand, and started down.

I felt the preceding step with the back of my ankle to make sure I was on the step--an old trick I learned in modeling classes in my youth.

I stopped after two steps. Descending face front, like Renee had, gave me no control and I noted that I couldn't see anything because of my full skirt.

I turned around, tucked the skirt into my cumber bun, held onto both rails, and backed down carefully. It worked.

I was not going to end up like Renee.

⌘

CHAPTER 46

"Is this a dagger which I see before me?"
-Shakespeare, *Macbeth*, Act 2, Scene 1

Halfway down the stairs, I heard furniture rattle down in the crossover. I turned and saw Anna in her bright yellow dress below. She staggered into a table stacked with props and boxes making another louder noise.

"Quiet backstage," Alastair whispered loudly from the end of the crossover.

Anna sat on the ottoman at the foot of the steps hunched over with her head in her hands. I continued down. Anna had her head down and didn't notice me.

"Anna?" I went to her. "What's wrong?"

Anna looked up at me through the dark startled.

"Veronica. Thank heavens it's you. I feel sick again."

"You're done until the second act. Let's go to the dressing room."

Anna got up slowly and held onto the stove near the ottoman.

"I'm dizzy."

"Let me help you."

* * *

We got to the dressing room without knocking into anything in the narrow pathway to elicit Alastair's ire again.

I shut the dressing room door and turned on the bright lights to look at Anna. She was pale and didn't look well. She picked up her cranberry tea and drank some.

"Do you want some water?" I asked.

"No, I just want to lie down until act two."

I looked around and saw a stack of remnant fabrics, old tablecloths, and curtains piled on near the changing screen. I got a few, shook them, and laid them out on the floor near Anna's dressing table. I helped Anna lay down.

When I grabbed a larger velvet remnant for her head, a coiled piece of wire dropped onto Anna's yellow skirt.

"What's that," Anna shrieked, sitting up and brushing it frantically off her lap. "A rat?"

"It's just some wire." I grabbed the wire off her dress.

Anna was embarrassed. "There are so many creepy crawly things here."

"Don't worry. Lay back down. Nothing will come out with these bright lights on. Besides, the rats have been eating those green cakes. Maybe they are gone. See?"

I pointed to the rat cake I had thrown under Nicole's dressing table with my hand holding the wire. The cake was almost gone but not from chewing. It had been broken off. I wondered if Scott took some, but only for a split second. Suddenly, I focused on the wire in my hand. Could it be the piece of wire that that tripped Renee?

"I'll be back. Just rest. I have to get my script and flashlight from the crossover."

While I needed my script and flashlight, I really wanted to check the piece of wire. I hoped Nicole had made the mistake of hiding it in the remnants.

"All right," Anna said, finishing her bottle of cranberry tea and then laying back. "Don't be too long."

"I won't."

As I walked out, I examined the wire for black paint or blood. I didn't see anything, but that didn't mean it wasn't the "smoking gun."

* * *

I hurried backstage and through the narrow crossover with the wire. I went halfway up the stairs, held the wire between the posts at the top, and it was long enough to fit amply across the step and around the posts. I applauded my sleuthing and adept eye. I reveled in the possibilities of this being the hard evidence I needed to support my theory and motive. I felt more like a professional than an amateur.

Now, I really had something for Graham. I had to confer with him, but not Mel. Mel was our Achilles heel as it turned out. He had kept Nicole one step ahead of us.

Then, through the dark from behind I heard a voice.

"What are you doing?" Nicole snapped.

I jumped, turned on the steps, and lost my balance.

"Careful." Nicole reached up and grabbed my arm. "You'll fall."

I pulled on my arm, but Nicole held it like a vice. In the dim light, I saw Nicole's blue eyes hone in on the wire I held. She then glared at me.

"Let me help you down."

"No thanks."

Nicole wouldn't let go of my arm. It hurt.

"I'm looking for my script and flashlight." I jerked my arm away and hid the wire in the folds of my dress.

"They are there under the stairs."

Nicole's ice blue eyes eyes cut through the dark and burrowed into mine.

"Thanks." I fumbled with the wire and tried to get to the bottom of the steps.

Nicole stood her ground and blocked my path for what seemed to me to be an eternity. She was looking at me and thinking. Then, she turned and went down the steps.

"Dinner break," Nicole called out, as she trounced back toward our dressing room.

I stood frozen on the steps. I had to find Graham, now. We would have to warn Anna about Nicole, proof or not. I had to get the wire to the detectives.

Grabbing my arm was Nicole's declaration of open warfare.

I hurried back to Anna.

⌘

CHAPTER 47

"This thing of darkness."
-Shakespeare, *The Tempest*, Act 5, Scene 1

Back in the dressing room, I found Joel kneeling over Anna. Nicole stood over them both shaking, one of Anna's teas. I slid the wire into my bag and turned my attention to Anna.

"Just drink more to keep from getting dehydrated," Nicole said, handing the tea to Anna.

Joel held Anna's head up to drink.

As Anna drank, Joel looked up at me, and asked, "Isn't that the right thing to do--drink a lot with the flu?"

"Yes," I said. "But it looked like she was feeling better today in the lobby, on stage?"

"She was until now," Joel said.

"You always feel worse at night." Nicole took off her costume, threw it over the rice paper screen, and stood in her black push up bra and thong.

Joel took a long look.

"Nicole's right. I think I get run-down by night."

Joel laid Anna's head back down.

"That's right," Nicole said, pulling on her black jeans and green low-cut sweater to go to dinner.

"Did you go to work?" I asked Anna.

Before she could answer, Graham burst through the door.

Graham gestured excitedly and boomed, "That was terrific guys. A few mistakes, Veronica, but good job. Joel I have news!"

"Yeah? What?"

Joel stood and Graham saw Anna lying there.

"Anna!" Graham cried out. "What's wrong?"

"It's just the flu," Anna said, sitting up again and trying to look energetic.

"I just need to rest a minute.

"That's just about what you have, a minute," Graham said dismissively and then turned his attention to Joel. "Joel, Stephie Sevas is out front with her manager talking to Mel. She wants to see you."

"Stephie Sevas and her manager," Nicole squealed.

"Shh, Nicole," Graham said, turning back to Joel. "She loved you in the first act, Joel. She loves the play and she wants to help us out with the opening tomorrow night. Floodlights, publicity, and people. Industry people. Big reviewers."

"Reviewers. That's amazing, Joel, that's amazing," Nicole jumped up and down and hugged Joel with her breasts bouncing on his chest.

Joel hugged Nicole back and jumped with her and her mounds of pale cleavage popping over the green sweater.

"I can't believe it." Joel instinctively grabbed the bouncing Nicole tighter.

"Get out there, Joel," Graham said, "She wants to see you."

"I'll be back, Anna," Joel said quickly, running out and not looking back.

Nicole's icy blue eyes glanced at me, direct and defiant. She followed Joel. Graham followed both of them.

The stakes had just gone up. Nicole would do anything to take Anna's role on opening night.

* * *

Anna and I were left alone. There were tears in her eyes, but she was smiling.

"Anna, what's wrong?" I kneeled next to her.

"I'm just so happy for him." She replied, looking up at me and then lying back down. "I've got to rest for the second act."

Graham stuck his head back into the dressing room.

"Come on, Veronica. Come with me in case Ms. Sevas has any ideas about the play. You're still the resident editor. We'll rewrite anything for her."

Graham left.

I looked at Anna. "Rest."

I didn't want to leave her alone, but I had to help Graham. More than that I needed to talk to him about Nicole.

I zipped my bag with the wire in it and followed Graham out of the dressing room.

Not only had Nicole declared open warfare, but Stephie Sevas' gala opening with press coverage had upped the stakes.

Opening night was now more than murder-worthy.

⌘

CHAPTER 48

"Hob nob."
-Shakespeare, *Twelfth Night*, Act 3, Scene 4

I paused in the wings and peered out into the theatre. I didn't care about Stephie Sevas. I needed to get Graham's ear.

I saw Stephie sitting on the edge of the stage soliloquizing dramatically to a small group standing before her: Mel, Joel, Nicole, and Stephie Sevas's manager. Bryce focused a follow spot on Stephie from up in the balcony. She bathed in its warmth and she instinctively and skillfully angled her face to catch the maximum light.

Graham rejoined the small group. He immediately transitioned to an animated audience member with an ear-to-ear smile in his best suck-up mode. Nicole hung on Joel's arm trying to attach herself to his rising star. Mel was smiling but I knew him and knew his brain was calculating how to ingratiate Stephie's obvious assets into his television pilot and his film projects.

Stephie's manager stood patiently. He was understandably not interested in Stephie's story which he would have heard endless times.

My gaze finally rested on Graham. He was so excited at the prospect of a grand opening night he was clapping and laughing at anything and even nothing.

The Valentine Theatre needed life breathed into it and Stephie Sevas was that breath.

* * *

I slipped unnoticed down the stage stairs to join the esteemed group. I beheld Stephie, the biggest female box office draw in the business, being progressively energized by her small audience.

Stephie was diminutive. She wore torn washed jeans with a beige ruffled low-cut blouse that displayed a boney, cleavage-less chest. Although she was in her mid-thirties, I understood how she played much younger roles with that energy, small body, oversized gray eyes, and mass of short blonde hair.

I had seen every one of her movies. She was and is a great actress. She has done it all with no plastic surgery and no enlarged boobs. She has a reputation of being very astute and very bright. It was her raw energy, brains, and exceptional social IQ that helped her become the Hollywood royalty she is today.

I joined the small group at the foot of the stage. I noted Geoff, Alastair, Scott, Tim, and Howard watching Stephie from the wings, too. They were all slowly inching forward, all but Howard. I observed that Kevin, who I chose to believe was above being "star struck," was not there.

Stephie was telling a high school theatre story about her lead in *My Fair Lady*. I tried to wedge into the assembly of suck-ups but was shouldered out by Graham and his enthusiastic gestures. The select gathering of the chosen few laughed simultaneously at all the right times and at just the right volume. Once or twice, in awkward enthusiasm, the less experienced suck-ups chortled out of sync in anticipation of a punch line delayed. The others in the little group brought them back into the synchronized group appreciation section with darting glares.

"And there I was walking on stage for my biggest song as Eliza Doolittle telling Professor Higgins that he could go to 'Hartford, Hereford, or Hampshire' and . . ."

Stephie pronounced the English cities with a perfect Cockney accent and then held up her hand commanding silence during a dramatic pause, suppressing the less skilled suck-up's from their premature awkward pre-punch-line laughter.

"And I opened my mouth and . . . nothing came out."

Stephie then brought her hand down; gesturing emphatically to cue the novice suck-ups that, that was the punch line.

Everyone laughed on cue. And so did I.

Was it funny? Was it even marginally funny? I didn't think so, but I burst into laughter anyway. If this was a cocktail party, and I was drinking, then the laughter would have seemed natural. But it wasn't a cocktail party, I wasn't drinking, and the laughter was forced. I was a whore along with everyone else.

Graham made the error of howling just a little too long this time. The group looked at him. He cut it off in mid-laugh.

"All right, Alastair," Graham barked up to the stage covering his embarrassment with authority over his minions. "Get those people to their dinner break . . . thirty minutes."

Graham turned back to Stephie and smiled, satisfied his embarrassment at his prolonged laughter was covered by his assertion of authority. He surreptitiously waved away the group on the stage that had been inching forward.

His dinner command had to be followed without further action to be truly reflective of his directorial power.

Stephie went on with her story. The disappointed group on stage left quietly for dinner up the side aisle, turning back and gawking.

* * *

Without genuflecting, I stepped back into the shadows away from the little assembly to disengage in the worship.

Stephie's manager looked over, caught my eye, and stepped away with me. He introduced himself.

"Hello, Bernie Abramoff," he introduced himself with a deep, soft, base voice extending his hand to me. "Wonderful job up there."

Bernie was only slightly taller than me. He was that kind of completely bald that screamed I shave every morning and don't want to comb my hair over my bare crown. He was trim under his dark brown suit that hung expensively and perfectly tailored over his soft coral shirt open at the collar. His expressive ebony eyes complemented his tanned face and large Roman nose, which was symmetrical and fit his face. He looked fifty and had no skin unnaturally stretched by plastic surgery, unlike Mel.

"Thank you."

I was happy that someone had acknowledged my talents. I was not above susceptibility to flattery, true or not.

Of course, this compliment I believed to be completely true. Why not? I knew, without a doubt, I had created a complex, interesting character for this role, even in this short time. To me my enhanced improved acting talent over recent years came from authorial life. As an author I created characters daily, characters who had to be real, quirky, interesting, full, and unique.

I owned the compliment with a smile.

"I'm Veronica Kennicott."

"Why is that name familiar?" Bernie said, not letting go of my hand nor his big smile with white but imperfect teeth that were uncharacteristically not veneered or capped.

"I don't think we've met."

I hoped my undeserved reputation as a writer had not gone before me. I didn't want to do the dance of the unpublished imposter tonight with him. Frankly, I doubted he would buy it anyway. Either that or he would have just the right agent to recommend.

"Right. I'm thinking of a Verna Alcott. But I see now she's much older than you." Bernie let go of my hand and looked carefully at my stage make-up. "And I see your part is much older than you are, too."

"Not that much."

"Yes, that much. You are very good at make-up and the physicality of being older on stage. I'm impressed again. I take back the word 'wonderful.' You were great."

"Thank you."

I was charmed with the compliment, but knew it was overstated. He was either a man who pursued generic popularity or actually wanted to please me. Either way, I now had graduated to uncomfortable and changed the focus.

"Isn't it wonderful that Joel got the part in Stephie's new movie?"

"Yes, I think she has taken a real shine to him. She's going to take him under her wing, so to speak." Bernie smiled and looked at Stephie still spinning her yarn and bathing in the attention and stage lights.

Kevin walked in from the wings onto the stage. He had changed into his street clothes.

"Ready, Stephie?" Kevin said leaning over and helping her up.

"Sure." She stood in the bright lights down center stage, gave Kevin a full-body hug, and then kissed him on the lips more than casually. "Let's go."

Kevin jumped down from the stage and helped Stephie, holding her by the waist. She giggled like a teenage girl.

"Joel, you coming?" Kevin said, not even noticing me.

Joel pried his arm loose from Nicole and followed Kevin and Stephie up the center aisle like a little puppy. Nicole whispered to Mel and then ran up the stage to the dressing room.

"Bernie," Stephie called without turning around.

"Excuse me. The boss calls." Bernie took his leave.

* * *

I was left standing in the dim theatre. Alone. Kevin, although I was sure he saw me, hadn't even acknowledged my presence. More than that, he hadn't bothered to break our dinner plans.

I was unhappy. No. I was deflated, miserable, and angry. I decided I would publish all my books and sell the movie rights and then finance one as a play. Then Kevin would "Stephie Sevas" at me.

I thought I should check on poor Anna since no one else was. I'd give her part of my undoubtedly smashed peanut butter and honey "just-in-case" sandwich, if she thought she could keep it down.

I stood in stasis, rationalizing, according to the well-known rules of rejected women, that not having dinner with Kevin was for the best. After all, now I didn't have to change into street clothes and redo my make-up.

Nicole rushed back onto the stage from the dressing room in her street clothes with her purse. She jumped off the stage near Mel and suctioned her body into his.

"I'm ready," Nicole took his arm and rubbed anything female she could against him--just as she had done to Joel during the 'Stephie Show.'"

"Sure, babe," Mel said. "Come on. We'll join them. I'll pick up the tab."

Graham saw me and came over.

* * *

"I guess we're chopped liver." Graham was more angry than I was, and justifiably so, because he was the director.

"Minced liver."

I didn't try to make Graham feel better because I was not up to telling him even one little white lie. We were left standing alone. I thought at least Graham should have been included.

"Minced? Not funny." Graham mumbled. "But true."

"I have some granola bars. Want one?"

I reserved the sandwich for Anna and me.

"Sure."

Graham made no attempt even to feign animated enthusiasm. He was visibly deflated by his exclusion from the dinner.

"Good. I need to talk to you."

"Fine, but I don't want you messing up my opening for anything. Not with Stephie and the reviewers here."

Graham followed me up the stage stairs to the dressing room.

"I'm not messing up anything, but we need to talk."

"Fine, but get my granola bar first or I'll be eating concession candy."

Graham was loud and irritated and lashed out at me like a wounded animal not allowed to feed with the pack.

⌘

CHAPTER 49

"There is special providence in the fall of a sparrow."
-Shakespeare, *Hamlet*, Act 5, Scene 2

When Graham and I got back into the dressing room, we found Anna still on the floor and throwing up under the dressing table.

The smell of vomit hit my nose.

Anna turned her pale face and watery eyes slowly to us. She tried to sit up but was too weak.

"What next?" Graham muttered. "We open tomorrow."

"Stay down." I grabbed a few tissues, knelt near Anna, and threw the tissues on the vomit for now.

"I'm sorry about the floor. I couldn't get to the trash can."

"It's all right, Anna."

"I am really sick. I need a drink."

"Here."

I took her cranberry tea from beside her, lifted her head, and gave her a drink. "You need to get home and in bed."

"No," Graham snapped.

"What?" I turned to Graham, angry at his lack of compassion but not surprised by it. "She can't finish tonight. She needs to open tomorrow."

"But Stephie Sevas is here."

"It doesn't matter. She's sick."

Graham turned on his charm. "Anna, dear, I'll send Alastair to the drug store for Ipecac. It'll make you stop throwing up."

"Sure," Anna said doubling up more and groaning. "Anything."

"Let's talk outside, Graham." I grabbed the granola bar from my bag and took Graham out the dressing room door.

* * *

I shut the dressing room door and stood with Graham backstage in the dim work lights. Graham was agitated and his eyes were popped open wider than I had ever seen them in his oversized face.

"Veronica, stop interfering."

Graham's forehead was dripping with sweat and his jowls dropping over his shirt were glistening with moisture too. I understood Graham was desperate, but he needed a reality check.

"But . . ."

"You have to stay out of this," Graham cut me off, shaking his head so that his jowls flapped drops of sweat down onto my face. "Stephie Sevas and her manager will put us and the Valentine Theatre in the spotlight again. We need to keep her on board tonight with a good dress rehearsal."

"Then what about opening tomorrow? What if Anna can't do it?"

I kept my voice down unlike Graham.

"I don't know?" Graham said even louder.

"Shh," I said. "Anna will hear you."

"Okay. Okay. Okay," Graham said walking away and turning his back for a minute. "You're right. Tomorrow is more important. Maybe Ms. Sevas will leave."

"Yes, then Alastair can read Anna's lines and we will get the run-through done.

I was worried about my part and lack of rehearsal, too.

"You're right. Look, we'll stall. We'll fake technical difficulties. She'll get bored and leave. Then we'll finish the run-through with Alastair reading Anna's lines."

"It'll work. It has to."

"I'll get Bryce to have a lighting board issue," Graham said. "You get Anna home in a cab. I don't want that damn Joel walking out of here too."

"Fine."

I knew it was a viable plan, but I still hadn't had a chance to tell Graham about Nicole.

And I still had to do that. Had to. Graham raced off to talk to Bryce in the balcony and set up technical "difficulties" to get Stephie out of here.

I turned, took a deep breath and collected my thoughts as I looked at the dressing room door. I unwrapped the granola bar and took a bite.

I thought of Graham's worn out phrase "the show must go on." It was hackneyed, but true.

Through my few years in film and theatre I had seen costumes cover broken legs in casts and burns and cuts in bandages, as well as make-up cover bruises, scabs from measles, and bags under the eyes from illness, hangovers, or just plain fatigue. The audience never knows. The show goes on despite an actor's mother dying or the actor himself foregoing critical heart surgery until the film wraps.

In view of the fact that an actor's trade is feeling emotion, it does seem incongruous. Ignoring their own problems and emotions, however, is ingrained in actors who train and live theatre and film. It is particularly prevalent in film where there is big money at stake and coworkers' jobs.

* * *

When I opened the dressing room door, I saw Anna sitting at her dressing table. She was touching up her make-up. She had picked up the materials off the floor and cleaned the vomit. She looked at me with hollow, deep set desperate eyes.

"I can make it."

"No." I threw the rest of the granola bar in the trash and sat next to her. "You can't. The only thing important is you making it to opening night."

"No, there's you. You need the rehearsal."

"I don't."

The lie came easily out of my mouth for Anna's sake.

"Look, I've opened before without even having a complete run-through. Go home. Get well."

Anna leaned over and hugged me. I held my breath and accepted the hug with the trepidation of someone being exposed to typhoid.

I helped her get her costume off and threw it over the screen. With a joint effort we got her street clothes on.

"I'll never forget this."

"Let's get you home in a cab."

"I don't have that kind of money. What about Joel? He can run me home." Anna picked up her bag.

"The production will pick it up."

I knew I'd be picking it up, but we needed Joel here and the dinner group was already overdue.

"I'll wait for Joel." Anna started to put her bag back down. "I . . ."

"I know you're worried about him with Stephie," I said bluntly, looking at Anna's anxious sunken sick eyes with tears welling. "Don't worry. He loves you. And we have to get you home. Now."

This was the way it had to be for the good of the production. I felt like a mini-Graham manipulating Anna for the sake of opening night.

"You just concentrate on being well enough for tomorrow's opening."

I guided her out of the dressing room and down the hall back to the lobby. I waited for the cab with Anna in the cold night air under a street light in front of the theatre. I had to support her at her waist because she was dizzy, nauseated, and weak. I helped her get down into the cab when it came.

As I shut the door, Stephie, Joel, and Kevin came out of the French restaurant up the block laughing and talking, with Mel and Nicole arm and in trying to catch up. They walked toward me on the sidewalk and Anna in the cab.

Joel was laughing with Stephie as they approached and didn't notice Anna in the cab pulling away. I saw Anna looking at Joel and Stephie as the cab blended with the Hollywood traffic.

Joel didn't notice Anna.

Kevin didn't notice me either.

I went back into the theatre. At least tonight, I wouldn't have to worry about Nicole doing anything to Anna. Anna was gone and I could take care of myself.

I started down the center aisle to the dressing room to lick my wounds and eat my sandwich. As I walked toward the stage stairs, I heard Graham and Bryce up in the balcony planning the lighting board mishap to halt rehearsal until Stephie left.

"Graham, quiet," I turned and shouted up to the balcony. "They're on their way back."

⌘

CHAPTER 50

"Give me my robe, put on my crown."
-Shakespeare, *Antony and Cleopatra*, Act 5,
Scene 2

In the dressing room, I dug through my bag for the piece of wire that could ensure my freedom. I couldn't find it. I rummaged to the bottom of my bag. It was gone.

* * *

I was interrupted by Nicole bursting in from the dinner break, tipsy.

"What stinks?" Nicole shrieked, glancing at me with my hands in my bag.

"Anna threw up."

I knew where the wire was. Nicole had taken it when she changed before dinner.

"That's foul." Nicole smiled at me with defiance and satisfaction as I took my hands out of my bag. "She should clean it up. Where is she? In the bathroom?"

Nicole sprayed the fabric renewer used to refresh costumes on the vomit stain. It helped immediately. She sat down at her dressing table, slathered on her lipstick, and threw a handful of breath mints in her mouth.

"She went home," I replied, angry at myself for leaving the wire there.

"Home?" Nicole said not surprised.

"Yes."

"Good. She won't get me sick. I'll do her lines."

"Alastair's the stage manager. He'll read her lines."

"No. I'll do it." Nicole jumped up.

"You have a role to do and we open tomorrow."

"I only have a few lines. Alastair can read those." Nicole flipped through the costume rack and knocked my change of costume for the second act on the floor. "Where's Anna's damn yellow dress?"

"Nicole, settle down."

I picked up my second act costume and hung it up again.

"There it is." Nicole dragged Anna's yellow dress from over the changing screen.

"Careful with that dress. Anna will need it tomorrow."

"Like hell," Nicole muttered as took off her jeans and green sweater and put on the yellow dress trimmed with lace. "She's history."

"What?"

"Nothing. I'm talking to Graham." Nicole grabbed her script and rushed out of the dressing room in the yellow dress with the back unbuttoned.

I followed.

Nicole stopped in the wings and turned around to me.

"Do me up," she ordered.

Nicole expected the courtesy every actor gives another when dressing, but never extended herself unless it suited her agenda. I hesitated, but the communal theatre courtesies between actors were too ingrained, especially for actors in shoe-string productions.

"Please." Nicole whined.

"Stand still," I ordered, hoping that buttoning her costume might unbutton her big mouth. "So, Scott says you help out in scene dock a lot."

Nicole was silent. She was smart.

While buttoning Nicole's dress, out the corner of my eye, I saw Stephie laughing with Joel and Kevin at the back of the theatre. Her manager chatted with Graham and Mel down the center aisle and exchanged cards with Mel.

Stephie laid a full-body hug first Kevin and then Joel, threw on her jean jacket, and walked with them out into the lobby. The manager shook hands with Graham and Mel and followed Stephie out.

Graham had succeeded in getting Stephie and her manager to leave.

I had succeeded only in losing my one piece of hard evidence and helping Nicole take over Anna's part by buttoning her costume.

As the lobby door, I finished buttoning Anna's dress for Nicole.

It fit perfectly.

* * *

Costumed and ready, Nicole immediately raced down the stage steps and up the center aisle with the yellow costume flying.

The minute Graham saw Nicole running towards him in the yellow dress, his smile turned into a scowl. Mel's mouth dropped open. Nicole fell into Mel's arms and stroked him like a big dog, whispering in his ear. Mel smiled and chuckled.

I knew the deed was done. Nicole would be Anna for tonight.

Nicole red-lipstick kissed Mel and ran back up the stage stairs. She shoved past me with her script in hand. She stood in the wings, her head down, getting into character for Anna's role.

I personally was looking forward to her making a fool of her self. Her doing Anna's role during the tech run was one thing, but a full-blown dress rehearsal was another.

Joel and Kevin came back into the theatre from the lobby. Graham caught them coming down the center aisle and talked to them quietly.

"She's sicker?" Joel exclaimed, starting up the center aisle to leave.

"Joel, get back here," Graham bellowed. "Please."

Graham looked at Kevin in desperation.

"Joel," Kevin ran after him. "We need you."

Kevin caught Joel at the lobby door. They talked. Joel returned back down the aisle with Kevin.

Kevin had obviously convinced Joel not to desert the dress rehearsal.

* * *

We began the top of the second act. Nicole held her script and hit every mark Anna would have.

Joel hit none of his marks nor any of his emotional moments. His mind was clearly on Anna, and every time he looked at Nicole in Anna's costume and saying Anna's lines, his concentration was broken.

As the second act progressed, I watched Nicole carefully. She was glancing at her script, but only pretending to read it. She was planning to go on tomorrow night and this was her one and only dress rehearsal.

As the detective in my third book aptly put it, "Motive, once discovered, tells all." Nicole was too vain not to "tell all" by essentially, to any knowledgeable eye like mine, disregarding the script. She used it as a mere prop, displaying her preparation for Anna's role.

But would motive suffice without more?

⌘

CHAPTER 51

"Vaulting ambition."
-Shakespeare, *Macbeth*, Act 1, Scene 7

By mid-act Nicole began to hit her stride. Still holding the script as a mere prop, she was doing a marvelous job. To my surprise she did have talent.

Nicole, however, did not go public and put down the script for everyone to see. To the untrained and unobservant eye, she still appeared to be relying on it.

In true Nicole form, though, she did maliciously "upstage" her fellow actors on her lines by walking upstage and forcing them to turn to her with their backs to the audience. Nicole thereby became the focus of every scene. Naturally, it didn't work on Geoff, Kevin, or me. We veterans countermanded Nicole's upstaging by ignoring her walk upstage. We delivered our lines skillfully facing out to the audience beyond the fourth wall. This is known in the theatre as "cheating out."

Novices, like Tim and Joel, were upstaged because they feared facing out to the fourth and imaginary wall between the stage and the audience. For that matter, amateurs usually also feared facing toward the camera lens. It was the magnetic window that caught their soul on film. If their soul was empty they had nothing to be caught, so they averted their eyes from the view of the camera, often looking down.

Newby actors either didn't have the emotions to show or were embarrassed by them. I always remembered what I read in *Creating a Role* by Constantin Stanislavski, "In the language of an actor, to know is synonymous with to feel."

Veteran actors crave revealing their raw emotions, facing the audience or the camera lens with their eyes welled with tears or flashing with rage. But no matter what, veterans don't "break" the fourth wall by looking directly at the audience or at the camera lens, often only a few inches away.

* * *

As the second act progressed, I learned the concept of ensemble acting and the spirit of generosity on stage were literally unknown and completely foreign to Nicole.

Unlike Anna who brought out the best in Howard on stage, Nicole transformed Howard into her prop. She moved down stage center, facing the audience, and left Howard in the background. She found the heat of Bryce's spotlight, glanced at her script only infrequently, and with her face to the audience lived through every emotion her character required and cried real tears.

She was masterful. It was a full, practiced, and planned performance. She had done this all on her own.

* * *

When the second act was finished, Bryce brought up general lighting on the stage and the house lights. Mel applauded loudly and didn't stop.

"Bravo," Mel shouted with wine induced inhibition. "Brilliant."

Tim, Geoff, and Scott joined the applause from the wings across the way. Howard got up quietly and walked off stage left to the men's dressing room. Kevin and Joel, who were standing adjacent to me in the wings, did not clap. Nor did I.

"Very nice, Nicole," Graham said sincerely.

The relief in Graham's eyes let me know he viewed Nicole as his savior if Anna didn't return.

"Take twenty," Alastair shouted. "We start the third act on time. No exceptions, Nicole."

"Yes, sir." Nicole saluted Alastair and walked offstage for the dressing room.

Joel ran off stage taking his cell phone out of his pocket to call Anna.

Kevin caught me by my arm as I turned to go to my dressing room for my costume change.

"Sorry about dinner," Kevin said apologetically, with his green eyes sparkling in the filtered general stage lighting.

Even his light touch on my arm disarmed my anger at being jilted for dinner.

"Don't worry about it."

I smiled up at him because I couldn't help it and because I was too proud to do otherwise.

"Stephie and I go way back. I didn't know she would be here," Kevin said, feeling more comfortable. "We caught up."

"Good. Old friends are important."

I covered my disappointment and started for the dressing room. My priority was to rattle Nicole's cage while she was fresh from her triumph and perhaps unguarded.

"Another time?" Kevin said as I walked away.

"Sure," I called back.

I hurried away, knowing I had displayed neutrality and casualness, the hiding place for all vulnerable women who suspect their affections are not returned.

* * *

In the dressing room, I found Nicole fixing her make-up and reciting Anna's longest monologue from memory.

"You know all of Anna's lines?" I took my sandwich out of my bag.

"I just picked some of them up. Why wouldn't I?"

"I wouldn't. In fact, I couldn't," I said, taking a bite of my sandwich despite the residual smell of Anna's vomit.

"Well, your brain is addled."

I did not respond. Age is the bullet women take in this society and I had been wounded too many times to react.

Nicole finished powdering her face, stood up, and looked at herself in the mirror. She smoothed the pleats in the yellow dress at the hips and turned to leave. I saw my chance to up the ante.

"You forgot your script," I said pleasantly, putting a shot over Nicole's bow. "You should at least pretend you need it."

Nicole stopped, picked up the script, and then turned to me with an automaton smile.

"Thanks. Oh, and, by the way, do you know what happened to the carbon monoxide detector?"

I turned and looked at the socket where I had plugged in the carbon monoxide detector. It was gone. A chill went up my back to my neck. My shoulders shivered momentarily and involuntarily.

Nicole trounced out in victory.

I wondered what Nicole would have done tonight if Anna hadn't gotten the flu. I regretted my open challenge to Nicole.

I jumped up and hurried to check the heater vent in Charlie's office. It was in place. It was that vent displacement that had caused the carbon monoxide buildup in both the dressing room and Charlie's office. Then I went backstage to check the ladder in the crossover again for the third act coming up. Renee's death scene, now mine.

I saw Scott still had not put reflector tape on the steps and hurried to the scene shop to find the reflector tape or Scott. I threw open the scene dock door.

The bright lights and the smell of marijuana hit me.

I stood shocked at what I saw.

* * *

There was Nicole's tattooed round ass bent over the work bench, being fucked by Scott with his black pants at his ankles and his white hairy legs thrusting a climax.

"I thought you locked the door!" Nicole looked at me and shrieked. "Get off me."

Scott couldn't react immediately for the obvious reasons and then did. He threw a work rag over himself as he withdrew, bent ass bare, and picked up his pants. Nicole stood and dropped her yellow dress into place.

Scott wiped the lipstick off his lips with the back of his hands, picked up a joint from a clear glass ashtray, and took a short drag.

"I . . ." I started to apologize, but I stopped mid-speech as Nicole charged toward me.

Nicole shoved her face in mine and spit venomously, "Mel won't believe anything you say to him so don't bother. If you do, I'll bury you. Now, get the hell out of my way."

Nicole shoved me aside into the door jamb and left. A pain shot from my shoulder down my arm.

Scott smiled. "She's hot, isn't she?"

I stood looking at Scott, a man ruled by his ego and hormones.

"Don't mind Nicole. She's like that." Scott said, revealing that this was more than a brief encounter. "What can I do for you?"

"The reflector tape. Can you put it on now before my exit in the storm?" I stuttered, rubbing my shoulder.

"Sure," Scott said grabbing the tape and twirling it in a circle on his index finger. "I have it right here."

"Thanks," I said, wondering how the man with the biggest mouth in the troupe had kept this secret.

"You aren't going to make trouble are you?" Scott said, juggling the reflector tape in his hand and ignoring my obvious shoulder pain. "We've kept this under the radar."

"No, Scott. You're adults."

I looked at Scott twirling the tape. I understood my silence was a quid pro quo for Scott placing the reflector tape. More than that, I realized Scott and Nicole were allies, but I didn't know how far their allegiance went.

To murder?

I left the scene dock knowing Scott was the wild card, possibly a witness, and unquestionably a rat.

I was convinced that was why Scott preferred his fellow rats rather than poison in his scene dock.

⌘

CHAPTER 52

"It smells to heaven."
-Shakespeare, *Hamlet*, Act 3, Scene 3

The third act began roughly, not because of Nicole, but because of Howard dropping lines. Howard was usually dependable by final dress rehearsal, not brilliant, but dependable. Tonight Alastair had to prompt Howard repeatedly from the wings. Howard was distracted by Nicole.

Unlike Anna, Nicole performed the role with speed and a riveting intensity.

Nicole was still holding her script, but began openly and demonstratively to ignore it as she got into the part. Everyone on stage observed her in amazement. She played the role with an organic, heightened emotional life, from elation to abject sadness.

* * *

When Nicole finished her first big scene with Tim and Howard flawlessly, never once looking at her script,

Kevin broke character on stage with me. He gave me an inquisitive look and a nudge.

Kevin whispered, "She's word perfect. I didn't know she was an understudy."

"She isn't."

Nicole lowered the script and held it at her side closed. She put aside all pretense of needing the script and performed with fully nuanced emotional depth.

Across the stage, I observed Geoff watching Nicole intently, not as his character would have, but as Geoff, amazed at Nicole's riveting performance. I glanced at Tim, who was spellbound.

Nicole's vanity had just caused her to make the critical error. She revealed too soon in front of many witnesses that she had fully prepared Anna's role. This preparation, of course, had to have been done before Anna even got sick.

Nicole was now on an equal footing with me as a suspect as far as motive went. I needed an ally or witness to push her further.

In the middle of the act, Nicole finally threw her script on a Victorian chair. She was ready to do her cathartic father-daughter scene with Howard without it.

From the wings Geoff, Kevin, and I watched and waited for our entrances in the ensemble scene right after. Scott stood near to remove a chair from the stage in the blackout.

* * *

During the emotional father-daughter scene poor Howard couldn't look at Nicole. Every time he did he broke character. To him it was clear he was not with his "daughter." Nicole was too dynamic, too emotionally full. Howard's lack of eye contact ruined the father-daughter intimacy required for the scene.

* * *

"What the hell is wrong with Howard?" Scott whispered to Kevin behind Geoff and me.

"He's just thrown because Nicole is so different than Anna in the part," Kevin said matter-of-factly. "It threw me for a minute too. He'll get over it."

"He'd better. Tomorrow's opening night," Scott retorted. "I told Graham he shouldn't give Howard such a big part. He can't handle anything. Never could."

"He'll sort it out," Geoff British'ed to me.

"I think so." I looked straight at Geoff in the stream of stage lights that traversed his face and lied. Howard didn't have enough time left before opening night to adjust.

"Well, I think Nicole's doing a damn good job," Scott whispered, leaning in behind Geoff and me. "I personally don't want Anna back to open. Nicole has my vote."

I glared at Scott, but my glare was lost to him. His attention was on Nicole under the spotlight on stage. And I knew why.

They had covered their relationship superbly with their fighting and arguing, but I knew his agenda now. I speculated that the fighting may have brought them together to begin with, like elementary school playground romances.

"Nicole could do it," Kevin said to Scott thoughtfully. "She has the part down and she's good."

Geoff looked over at me said under his breath, "She's mastered Anna's part all right . . . it must have taken hours and . . ."

Geoff stopped in the middle of his sentence and stepped back into the shadows.

I turned and looked at him with surprise and hope. I thought I had an ally and maybe the witness I needed. I stepped over to him and whispered.

"You know, don't you?"

"No. I don't." Geoff looked down at me intently. "I only suspect. After 60 years under the lights, I've seen it all. And I've seen this before too."

"This?"

"Sabotage. Sabotage gone wrong, accidents, mistakes, you name it."

"Did you tell the detectives?"

"No," Geoff whispered. "And I won't. Been there, done that. In London a long time ago."

I looked at Geoff surprised.

"What do you mean?"

"It didn't go as far as murder." Geoff looked back at Nicole on stage and then whispered to me almost inaudibly, "I tried to be the hero in London for a young ingénue being sabotaged by her official understudy. No one believed me. Not even the ingénue. I became *persona non grata*. Why do you think I'm rattling around in this theatre wasteland in America? Why do you think I resorted to Hollywood? Why do you think I'm here at the Valentine?"

"Will you help me?" I looked at him with hope.

"How? With speculation? I didn't see anything or I would have told you. Privately of course," Graham added. "No. I couldn't prove anything against that official understudy in London. So what could I do against this unofficial understudy? Besides, Hollywood theatre is as low as I go."

"But you planned the ghost business that night."

I regretted the veiled threat as soon as it came out of my mouth.

"That was all Bryce . . . Bryce and Nicole . . . not me. Excuse me. That's my cue."

Geoff turned stepped and forward onto the stage. He immediately turned into his character and focused on the scene being played on stage. I watched him acting with Nicole. He looked right at her and matched her intensity and cadence. He was playing off her and she off him. They were a magnetic duo under the lights.

As I watched Geoff's professional performance, I took him at his word. He was not getting involved. He was not making the same mistake he had made years ago.

I had no ally, not even Graham yet. I had to have my Agatha Christie moment with him tonight.

* * *

I studied Nicole on stage in her glory, performing masterfully with no script. She was lizard-like on the stage, finding the heat of each of Bryce's spotlights. She soaked in the illumination and attention.

When Joel entered from the other side, she kept him from the hot light and skillfully upstaged him again. Geoff, Kevin, and I were the only matches for her on the stage and played the three-dimensional chess game well. Thank God I did not have to compete with Nicole in the third act. In this act I remained seated, until my big scene; or more accurately, Renee's death scene with Howard in the storm as they went up the Victorian staircase.

Before my entrance, Scott leaned over in the darkness of the wings and said, "Hey, Veronica. What did Geoff tell the detectives?"

"Nothing."

Scott had been eavesdropping, or at least trying to. I knew everything he did hear would go straight back to Nicole. This shouldn't have been a surprise to me. A real mysterian would have known about Scott and Nicole. I had to sharpen my skills of observation. There were probably a hundred moments showing that Nicole had two confidants who fed her information, Mel and Scott, and neither knew about the other. I had missed them all. Very un-Sherlockian of me.

Unfocused and not in character, I took my entrance on cue and my place on stage in my Victorian chair. All I could do was berate myself as I watched Nicole perform. She continued to change her blocking just enough to upstage Howard and Joel. Every time she did, Howard became more flustered and dropped more lines. Joel became distracted, but did not drop his lines like Howard. Instead, he dropped his character and emotional depth.

Finally, the ensemble cast exited into the wings.

It was now time for Joel's and Nicole's romantic parting. Nicole threw herself into Joel's arms and into the scene. Their parting kiss lasted too long and was changed by Nicole from a Victorian proper parting into a non-Victorian full-body wrestling match with a sloppy full-on tongue-to-tonsil fencing game.

"Hey," Joel objected.

Joel ended the throat kiss. He pushed Nicole by the waist and forced her away from him.

Nicole didn't care. She didn't break character and walked downstage for her dramatic weeping goodbye speech. She faced the fourth wall, ignoring her love Joel standing in shock upstage with her lipstick smeared across his face.

"Was that a joke?" Alastair whispered to me in the wings jiggling his pocket coins nervously. "It looked like the beginning of a porno scene."

"Yes, porn, public, and Nicole style."

But I didn't care. I was about to do Renee's death scene.

I didn't want it to be mine too.

* * *

It was the end of the third act and Howard and I did our fight scene with the lights flashing and the storm special effects loud and threatening. Howard forgot his lines three times and looked at me with a blank stare. Each time I fed him his lines quietly under my breath.

At the end of the fight, I ran up the stairs and Howard followed me. He grabbed my arm very gently to stop me. I pulled my arm away easily unlike Renee that fatal night.

I opened the black velour upstage traveler and made it out to the platform in the dark crossover just like Renee had.

"Oh, no." I gasped.

In the dark even the double row of reflector tape Scott put down to buy my silence barely showed.

I had to get down tonight, opening night and every night we ran. I inched forward and felt the first step. My heart was beating and I wished I wasn't alone. I turned to go down facing backwards, lifted my skirt hem with my left hand, and held on firmly to the right rail. I took each step slowly feeling carefully for any obstruction. There was none.

At the foot of the stairs, where Renee had lain, I stood looking back up at the ladder.

My heart sank as my eyes were adjusting to the dark. It was actually easy coming down. Too easy for anyone to fall without help in the plummeting. The detectives knew it.

At that moment, I confirmed that my only salvation from prosecution would be nailing Nicole.

When Anna returned tomorrow for Friday's opening night, which I believed she would, I had one last chance to catch Nicole.

Nicole would not let Anna get on that stage, at any cost.

⌘

CHAPTER 53

"Hell is empty and all the devils are here."
-Shakespeare, *The Tempest*, Act 1, Scene 2

When dress rehearsal ended, Graham quickly set the curtain call. Nicole reveled in spreading Anna's full yellow dress out and taking a prolonged deep curtsey.

Then she grabbed a seat front and center under Graham's nose for notes. She was poised for his praises to wash over her. Scott and Tim book-ended Nicole. The rest of us distanced ourselves from the Nicole-show by populating the second and third rows behind.

"Wonderful job, Nicole. Wonderful. If we have a problem tomorrow, you step in."

Graham smiled at Nicole and then got very serious.

"People, you adjusted well to Nicole in Anna's role. I saw some problems, but the audience won't. It played well. We had a new intensity. But, Nicole, if you go on tomorrow, lay off the kiss. A young Victorian woman would not tongue anyone."

"I disagree. Victorians weren't any different than us," Nicole rejoined smugly. "But fine."

"And powder your lipstick so it doesn't smear on Joel," Graham added.

"Yeah," Joel muttered next to me and wiped his lips with his hand.

"Howard," Graham continued. "Go over your lines and be prepared to do this with Nicole if Anna can't come back."

"She'll be here," Joel blurted out and then stood. "I have to go."

"Hold on. One minute for good news," Graham said. "Bernie called and told me that Stephie Sevas is treating the audience, and all of us, to an opening night party right after the show. Thanks, of course, to our Joel. Wine and food. I expect you all to stay and promote the show. Not that any actor would refuse free food and drink. Bring nice clothes to change into. Bernie is going to get reviewers here and try for some industry suits. So we'll have press and we may get some paparazzi action with Stephie here."

"Great," Scott blurted out, clapping.

"Wow," Tim called out. "It's like a showcase for our acting. An audition!"

Everyone down to a person applauded, including me. The publicity and contacts afforded that night meant something different to everyone. To me, it meant I would get my "man," specifically Nicole. The stakes were higher and Nicole would play her hand against Anna who Joel said would return.

Nicole glanced over at Scott and smiled the only warm, happy smile I had ever seen on her face. Did she love him? Or, at least, genuinely like him?

"Stop . . . let me finish," Graham said. "Tim is correct. It is like a private audition for any one of you who aspire to film. So do your very best. Let's get this production on the map."

Graham was not above seizing any opportunity to manipulate anyone's dreams.

There was another smattering of applause from the ambitious and hopeful, evidently including Kevin who joined in.

"People. People," Graham seized control of the meeting again. "Some house keeping. If you have any friends using your comp tickets, have them pick up those comps twenty minutes ahead of curtain or the seats will be released. No latecomers. Tell your friends that."

"It's Friday night rush hour. What if they're late?" Tim asked.

"It's not like traffic is a surprise here in L.A. Twenty minutes ahead or their comps are gone. We're selling them," Graham said. "Moving on, Alastair, get those coins out of your pocket. I can hear you backstage playing with them."

"Yeah," Scott badgered Alastair like a child seeking negative reinforcement and attention from his grade school teacher.

"Scott, shut-up," Graham barked with an uncharacteristic inelegant word choice. "People, it's late. I'll catch you individually with your notes. Joel, you're released. You all are, except Scott and Bryce and Alastair. You three see me about some changes. And, Veronica, after you get into your street clothes, see me too."

"Sure," I called, knowing I had to speak to Graham too.

* * *

Back in the dressing room, Nicole was still flying high as we got out of our costumes and makeup.

Nicole sang an awful rap song about sex as she took off her make-up. She kept peeking obliquely at me in the mirror. She wanted adoration and acknowledgment. She wasn't getting it from me. Nicole stripped down to her underwear and sang louder. Apparently, she was going to get it from me, her way.

I took my street clothes and changed behind the screen. I watched Nicole's prismed reflection in the mirrors.

She hung the yellow costume with great, and uncharacteristic, care. Then she meticulously wiped the dust from the stage off the hem.

Nicole behaved like the costume and the role were hers. She somehow knew that she was doing Anna's opening night. Why? Joel had said Ana was coming back.

Nicole threw on her street clothes, took her long blonde hair down from the Victorian bun, and started brushing it. She was ready to leave. I decided to ask the question I needed to. I would see her reaction in the mirror without her knowing.

I called over Nicole's singing from behind the screen watching for her reaction.

"How long have you known you'd be opening in Anna's part?"

Nicole didn't answer, She continued singing and staring at herself in the mirror, but stopped brushing her hair. After a moment, she slowly started again, but she did not answer.

"We both know you put a lot of work into it." I probed more, still watching Nicole's reflection.

Abruptly, Nicole stopped singing. Her ice blue eyes looked up with a cold glare directly into my mirrored eyes.

Nicole still said nothing. She knew I had been observing her the entire time. I couldn't look away. I was frightened. Still staring at me, Nicole's lips turned up ever so slightly and she lifted her chin.

"Be careful, Veronica," Nicole warned.

She stood, picked up her bag, threw her hairbrush in it, and left without another word.

* * *

I remained behind the screen unable to move. The wind was knocked out of me. I shuttered. I needed to get out of this place and home to my sanctuary. I grabbed my things, turned off the lights, and went out to the stage.

As I stepped down the stage stairs into the theatre, Nicole and Mel were leaving up the center aisle. Mel had his hand on her ass and they both laughed as they walked out through the lobby door.

Only Graham and Alastair remained down near the stage, Alastair on his cell.

"Veronica, come here. Alastair is calling Anna," Graham commanded.

"No answer," Alastair said.

"Try Joel," I said as I joined them.

"Worth a try." Alastair punched in Joel's number.

"I got your messages," Graham said to me. "Whatever it is, it has to wait until after we open?"

"No. It can't."

"Joel doesn't answer either," Alastair interrupted. "I'm out of here."

"Check the dressing room lights first," Graham ordered, gathering his things to leave.

"Women's are off," I volunteered.

"Thanks," Alastair said.

Always the professional, Alastair headed backstage to do the director's bidding.

"Graham, we need to talk about Renee and Anna."

"What?" Graham started up the center aisle to leave.

I followed him. I knew Graham was avoiding me, and anything that would interfere with opening night. But I was desperate and worried about Anna. Both he and Mel had asked me to investigate and I obviously couldn't talk to Mel. He was a mole for Nicole. Graham was all I had left—or didn't have left because he now had his head stuck in the proverbial sand.

"Stop, Graham. This is serious. I need to know if you asked Nicole to understudy Anna's part?"

He stopped at the lobby door and looked down at me. "No. But she was stellar, wasn't she. She . . ."

"Did Mel?" I interrupted Graham's prattle.

"Did Mel what?"

"Did he ask her to understudy?"

"Not that I know of, but she was great. She . . ."

"Planned all this, Graham," I interjected. "She's going to open tomorrow no matter what. And if Anna comes back I'm afraid for her. I can't prove anything, but Nicole is after Anna."

"Veronica, I . . ." Graham stammered.

I shouted, "That's why Renee is dead. You started with the end of the third act instead of act one. Anna was supposed to get tripped. Not Renee."

"Your mystery writing has gone to your head. Nicole is planning on opening tomorrow because I told her to get ready. It's as simple as that."

"Listen to me, Graham. She was already prepared. That's the point. And if Anna comes back she'll be hit by a Fresnel or topple down those stairs or be gassed or something worse."

"For Christ's sake, Veronica," Graham yelled. "This is not one of your mystery books and you're not a detective. This is my opening night. My premier. It is happening no matter who plays the part."

Graham's face was red and his eyes fighting mad. He was cornered and I knew behind those frantic eyes he was calculating whether Nicole or I were more necessary to his opening. At this point, I only cared about keeping myself and Anna safe.

"She threatened me in the dressing room just now."

"Who threatened who?" Alastair chuckled, coming back through the wings from the men's dressing room. "Cat fight? I love dirt. Come on give it to me."

"Forget it, Alastair. Go check the parking lot door before we leave." Graham waited until Alastair was out of earshot. "Veronica, I have enough trouble now. You're making more trouble with your little investigation."

"Our investigation." I corrected Graham.

"Fine, but look. We are having our premier with all the bells and whistles, a big one thanks to Stephie Sevas and I don't want you going after Nicole now. We may need her."

"I don't like this. I don't like the detectives putting me at the top of the list or Nicole threatening me."

I did not mention Scott and Nicole's relationship because Graham was clearly on overload.

"We'll deal with this after tomorrow. We are where we are. We are opening on schedule with no interference from you or anyone else. The . . ."

"You're not going to say 'the show must go on,' are you?"

"Yes. It has to. Please, Veronica, for me. Forget it for now. There's nothing more Nicole can do to anyone. She wants this show to open as much as we do. Anna's very sick. She won't be back. Nicole has the part. Come on?"

I looked at my friend begging with me to wait just twenty-four hours. I didn't have a choice really because, in the final analysis, I had no proof against Nicole, anyway.

"Okay, we'll get the show up first."

"Thank you. I won't forget this."

He lied. He would. In fact, he already had.

"Back door's secure." Alastair came back.

"Let's go," Graham said.

As we three left the theatre, the crisp fall air washed over our faces and into our lungs.

"Brisk night," I said.

Alastair agreed and Graham ignored me.

The men watched me get in my car safely. The gesture seemed ironic in view of what I had told Graham.

I started home.

I was glad to be leaving the theatre. I thought of not coming back.

⌘

CHAPTER 54

"Why then tonight let us assay our plot."
-Shakespeare, *All's Well That Ends Well,* Act 3,
Scene 7

At home, I slipped into bed with a decaf ginger peach tea. I turned on my old movie channel and tried to distract myself. The two 1930's stars singing and dancing and falling in love nauseated my sensibilities. More of life's delusions.

I decided I needed something stronger than tea and 1930's drivel to get Nicole out of my mind. I got a generous tumbler of my coffee flavored aperitif.

As I finished it, my thoughts pleasantly turned to Kevin and then to Bernie's lingering handshake, which tickled my mind.

I dozed off.

* * *

I woke late on Friday, which was becoming a habit, and I was still tired, which apparently was becoming a habit too.

I took a warm shower and then turned the valve to super cold. It was a trick I had learned at a spa to snap into running mode. I donned my usual jeans and my beige cashmere sweater.

In my study, I charged myself with caffeinated tea, which was becoming a habit too. I watched the fall leaves drop in my pool until the gears in my mind started churning again. They did and happily so did my muse.

Finally alert, I turned to my computer and opened my theatre mystery book. My wonderful protagonist made my fingers fly for hours, but then it happened. I came to an impasse. If this book continued as it must, then it meant I, or rather the actress based on me, would be arrested for murder.

I stopped writing again. I knew I would never get Nicole if Anna didn't come back as bait. I called Anna and then Joel to get Anna's status, but there were no answers. I left messages.

As I waited for one of them to call back, I scanned through my emails. Mavis, my writing teacher, and a few fellow students were coming to opening night. Some friends bought tickets for other nights because the opening was sold out tonight. It was remarkable, a full house, a sell-out at the Valentine on a Friday with Los Angeles traffic.

I ate lunch and then laid down on the couch to review my lines and my objectives in each scene. I wanted my emotional lines crystal clear, as well as my relationship with each character. I took the time to put each character in Meisner categories like parent or child. I had learned at my Meisner classes that clear objectives and relationships made scenes more alive. I also emotionalized more on Howard as my husband so that I would react organically in our scenes.

I shut my eyes to rest for a minute and fell asleep.

* * *

I was jarred awake by my cell phone. I was irritated because I was still cumulatively fatigued by the tension at the theatre. When I looked at the time on the cell screen, I realized I had been asleep for two hours. It was a good thing the cell woke me.

"Hello," I answered.

"Veronica, it's Joel. I got your message."

"Joel." I sat up instantly alert. "How's Anna?"

"Better. She's asleep. Thanks for taking care of her last night. I shouldn't have gone to dinner with her so sick."

"You didn't know. Besides you had to." I blatantly told him what he wanted to hear. "How could you have known she would get worse?"

"You're right. But thanks anyway. We'll never forget it."

I knew they not only would forget it, but they would also forget me. I had lived too many years and learned, in the process, exactly what the median line of human nature was. And these people were of that ilk, the median if not below. I viewed them as neither exceptional nor deficient.

"I'm glad she's better."

I wondered how much better. I thought selfishly of my own predicament and the opportunity to use Anna as bait for Nicole.

"If I hadn't taken her to the hospital when I got home, she wouldn't be though."

"Hospital? What do you mean?"

"She had a nose bleed and we couldn't stop it. So we went in. They gave her a Vitamin K drip thing for about four hours."

"Why?"

"It stopped the bleeding and made her stomach okay. She's fine now. She's resting. She has some pills to take four times a day."

"Wait. Vitamin K. Why Vitamin K? For the flu?"

"She didn't have the flu. She had rat poison in her system."

"Rat poison." I thought immediately of the green rat poison cakes at the theatre and in Nicole's bag. "How?"

"Well, remember my nose bleed?"

"Yes."

"The doctor said that was probably rat poisoning too. So he tested the cranberry tea Anna had in her purse because we both drank it."

"The tea?" I remembered Nicole near Anna's teas in the dressing room and her accusing Anna of taking rat poison for attention. "But wouldn't you taste it in the tea?"

"I guess not. The hospital is reporting the tea company to the Feds."

"That's horrible," I said.

I knew the Feds would find nothing wrong at the tea bottlers because I knew Nicole poisoned Anna. But again I had no proof.

"We threw away all the tea."

"Oh, all of it?" I asked looking for another avenue to prove up Nicole's criminal acts. "Even the bottles in the dressing room."

"Ah, I don't know if there are any. We'll check tonight."

"So Anna's coming? She's well enough for the premier tonight?" I asked, moving on to my own self-interest much as Graham would have.

"Sure. She ate lunch. No pain. No hurling."

"I'm so glad." Of course, Joel had no idea how truly glad I was, or that I was going to use his girlfriend as bait to clear myself. "Did you tell Graham?"

"Not yet."

"I'll let him know."

"That's great. I gotta rest too."

"Of course. I'll see you at the Valentine later."

I hung up.

* * *

I wasn't going to tell Graham or anyone and neither would Joel for now. I didn't want Graham or Mel to know because it would get back to Nicole. She was just where I wanted her, overconfident.

When Anna showed up tonight it would be a surprise. Nicole would be desperate and shocked. She would do anything to have the lead on opening night for the reviewers and Stephie Sevas's industry friends. Surprised and desperate were a bad combination, even for Nicole. She would make her move and I would be there.

I wished my husband had not passed away because I could use a confidant on my side, another head to bounce ideas off of. This was a fight for my freedom and Anna's life. And Graham was useless.

I just hoped the detectives' forensic results would be delayed or, if they did show up, they had nothing but a bluff which I would call. I knew that in Hollywood, an actor on actor murder would be too sexy for them not to try to make an arrest, whether they had the real murderer or not. It could make their careers.

I skipped my usual pre-performance stretches to get to the theatre before Anna. I didn't bother to change, but did remember to grab my black silk pants and gold beaded sweater for the opening night party. And maybe, if I weren't in the clink, I would be using them at a late supper with Kevin.

I packed my theatre bag with a peanut butter and honey sandwich, three bottled waters, and a bag of semi-sweet chocolate chips for energy. I took a split second to grab two boxes of sourdough pretzels from my pantry for the dressing rooms. Bringing nibbles for the dressing rooms during performances was traditional. Then I grabbed a third for Bryce. I felt badly that Nicole had manipulated that defenseless, guileless old hippie.

I left for the Valentine within minutes of Joel's call.

I had to catch Nicole startled, frantic, and at her most vulnerable. And I needed to confiscate any opened and contaminated bottles of the cranberry tea.

⌘

CHAPTER 55

"My words fly up, my thoughts remain below."
-Shakespeare, *Hamlet*, Act 3, Scene 3

On the way to the Valentine, I tried to focus on my vocal exercises in the car as usual, but my mind was on Nicole.

* * *

When I arrived at the theatre, two men were setting up four huge round white floodlights on wheels at the curb in front. They would shoot up into the sky. It was not quite dark and they hadn't been turned on yet, but I felt the excitement of a publicized and celebratory opening night. The closest parking place was up the block near the French restaurant and bar.

I opened the back door of my car and grabbed my bag and the pretzels. My query letter dropped out onto the asphalt.

"Damn it," I muttered when I realized I had forgotten to mail it, yet again.

I picked it up and threw it back onto the seat. I had other priorities now.

I grabbed my things and headed for the theatre.

In the lobby, I saw that Graham had been working hard decorating for his premier and the after party.

A big bunch of plain gold and silver Mylar balloons filled the corner near the cappuccino machine and also covered the walls on each side of the large oak door into the theatre. The concession case was arranged with the usual array of candies and chips under the glass, but on the glass were two flower arrangements with brochures and bowls of free mints. I took a mint. Behind the counter were several cases of wine, a huge plastic bag of plastic wine glasses, and platters of cheese and crackers with notes taped on them saying "after-party".

I walked over to the headshots on the wall. My headshot had replaced Renee's. It was from when Graham and I first reunited and he asked me to do a small part over our late supper. Even though it was old, and therefore younger than it should be, I didn't do enough acting to warrant the price of a new one. I was unrecognizably aged in this performance, so it didn't matter anyway.

I glanced at the baby actors' heavily made-up glamour shots, which actually hurt their casting chances. Those glamour shots were wishful delusions. Veteran actors' headshots were natural and actually looked like themselves. They knew if they walked into an audition and didn't look like their picture, they might as well turn around and walk out. The first cut for any role is the headshot and then, if you fit the look at the audition, you were taken seriously.

Nicole's picture had replaced Anna's. I was reassured that no one else knew Anna was coming back tonight, least of all Nicole.

I set my things down and ran down the side hall to see if there were any contaminated cranberry teas left on Anna's dressing table. I was desperate for any hard evidence I could find.

Desperation did not make evidence materialize. There were two full bottles, but I tested the caps. They were sealed. I was out of luck.

* * *

I walked back up the side hall to the lobby to get my things. I was discouraged.

I grabbed one barrel of pretzels and took it up to Bryce's lighting booth in the balcony. After all, without him I had no spot light on me

"Hey, Veronica," Bryce said when I reached the top of the stairs. "What's up?"

"You're here early?"

On the other side of the balcony, I saw Bryce's thin silhouette backlit by his lighting booth with its assorted colored lit switches and soft over lighting. He grabbed two bottles of wine next to him and quickly secreted them down into the shadows at his feet.

I didn't really care that he pilfered Stephie Sevas's wine because I didn't care for Stephie Sevas. More power to him. I just hoped he didn't open them until after the performance for Graham's sake.

"I brought you a barrel of pretzels to munch."

"Thanks." Bryce got up and came over to get the pretzels.

" Gotta run."

"Hey, that Nicole is a little competition for you."

"What?" I stopped and looked up at Bryce.

"She is really good at finding that light on stage . . . like you, I mean."

"Oh," I said, not caring about lighting at the moment and turning to go down again. "Well, keep it on me. And don't fool around with your blue ghost light on my exit backstage."

"I won't. It's over." Bryce assured me. "Nicole says we don't need the publicity anyway."

"What do you mean?" I stopped and turned back to Bryce.

"She said we don't need the ghost stuff for publicity."

"We? Who? Was Nicole in on the blue light gag with you and Geoff?"

Bryce looked at me sheepishly.

"Yes, but she didn't want the credit. Don't say anything to her."

"I won't. Did you tell the police?"

"No." Bryce avoided my eyes. "I'm sorry, Veronica. Nicole said they'd blame her."

"But they're blaming me, Bryce!"

"Nicole says . . ."

"Says what, Bryce?" I snapped.

I was agitated. This flower child, with half his synapses fried by booze and drugs, was playing with my life and a puppet for Nicole.

"She said you didn't do anything and the cops will go away. She's on your side."

"Right." I backed off, knowing I had just learned another piece of the puzzle.

I looked at this stupid, frightened, sad man for a moment. He was a crispy-critter with a wretched life. I didn't say anything more. The damage was done and I realized nothing I said could change any of his actions or omissions.

I covered my anger because we needed a great performance and I needed my lighting. "Have a good show."

"You too. And I'll keep the spot on you."

"Thanks."

I hurried down the narrow stairs putting the pieces together. Nicole was not above doing anything and used her wares with any man, even Bryce.

I had to get ready for the performance and stick with Anna like glue when she got here.

Where Anna went, Nicole would follow.

⌘

CHAPTER 56

"Knock, knock! Who's there?"
-Shakespeare, *Macbeth*, Act 2, Scene 3

I grabbed my things from the lobby and went into the theatre. Graham was on stage arguing with Scott.

"Get the black paint and touch the stage up so it will dry before everyone gets here."

"Okay, but it looks fine to me." Scott stomped off to get the paint.

I walked down the center aisle. The stage looked fine to me too. Graham was clearly up tight and needed to be treated with kid gloves. He had more than his usual opening night nerves and rightfully so. Stephie Sevas had made this an opportunity of a lifetime for him and his acting troupe.

"Graham, the lobby looks fantastic," I gushed, walking up the stage stairs. "You out did yourself."

"Oh, my dear, you don't know the half of it. I've been running around all day. Balloons, flowers, everything. I'm so glad you're here early." Graham gave me a big bear hug. "Did you see the premier floodlights outside? Four."

"Who could miss them?" I flattered Graham and stroked his ego.

"And did you see the wine Stephie sent over to ply the audience with and the goodies for the after party?"

"Yes, thanks to Joel you hit the big time tonight."

"Who would have thought," Graham laughed nervously. "Stephie's people said the wine is free. I wish we could charge for it. But we'll get money from our candy and chips at a dollar a pop."

"Good," I acknowledged, thinking Graham was really being penny wise and pound foolish and it would look cheap.

"Or perhaps that's bad thinking," Graham mused, obviously aware of the incongruity. "But we need the money."

"Do we have reviewers coming?" I asked that to avoid any conversation about Anna.

"Yes. I have all the press packets ready and the VIP rows cordoned off. Stephie even got the *Examiner*."

"You shouldn't have told me about the *Examiner*. That's big time. Now I am nervous."

"You shouldn't have asked."

We both laughed. For just a moment I forgot about the danger Anna and I were in.

"I can't believe we have a full house and a wait list." Graham was delighted and oblivious to the threat to his opening when Nicole saw Anna return.

"Amazing," I added, with the weight of the night coming back to me.

"Stephie did a local TV news spot announcing Joel as her new co-star and our opening tonight and she bought a big block of tickets for her friends. We're not going to have to resort to any of Bryce's ghost tricks for publicity."

I was happy Joel's career was skyrocketing in just one week and the Valentine along with it, but I was more interested that Graham seemed to know about Bryce's ghost plans.

"You knew about that?"

"Knew about what?"

"Bryce's plan."

"What plan? Bryce has been trying to make me pull a Mrs. Valentine for years."

"Did you know about Bryce's ghost effects for Renee's scene?" I asked him pointedly, thinking it was obvious Graham had tacitly approved the publicity plan.

"Who cares? We're going to have great publicity without ghosts," Graham chuckled.

I backed off. What difference did it make now?

"You deserve it." I was genuinely happy for Graham's success, but unhappy that he had played hide-the-ball with me. "I bet Mel's pleased."

"Mel and Nicole. She's already here and getting dressed. I told her I hadn't heard from Anna.

"She's here?" I concluded she came while I was talking to Bryce.

"Yes, what's in the bag?"

"Barrels of pretzels for everyone."

It was evident to me that no one knew that Anna was returning or about the poisoning. No one would hear it from me.

"You're such a dear." Graham hugged me again.

"Thanks," I mumbled, buried in Graham's huge arms.

"The whole production has such a positive aura with you around," Graham paused and then chuckled. "That is, forgetting that you murdered Renee!"

"Not funny."

"Just a little black humor. Relax," Graham added, running on high with the excitement of his gala opening night. "I don't mean to speak ill of the dead, but Renee was so negative. I should have cast you in the first place."

"Next time."

I was glad I didn't tell Graham about Anna's recovery or the poisoning. His priority was the opening of his premier play and mine was Anna's safety and clearing my name.

"Did you get the dedication to Renee in the program?" I asked.

"No time."

"Too bad," I said, adding as I left. "Speaking of Renee, have you heard from the detectives?"

"No. And we better not tonight." Graham hurried away into the wings and I heard him bellow. "Scott, get that paint out here."

* * *

I headed to the men's dressing room to deposit the pretzels before they all arrived and I could be subjected to naked chests and boxer shorts.

I knocked and Howard called, "Come in."

I was too late.

There was Howard—shirtless and bare-chested. I wished he had just said wait. I didn't want to see his white belly hanging over his striped Victorian pants. I averted my eyes, which was hard to do in a room walled with mirrors.

"You're early too," Howard remarked, mercifully pulling on his t-shirt and sitting down at his dressing table chair. "Did you see the floodlights on the street and the wine and everything? It's exciting isn't it?"

"Yes. And some big reviewers are coming."

"That's star power. I could never get them here, even with all my contacts."

"You've done well by Graham."

"In small ways," Howard sighed, taking a deep breath. "Renee would have loved tonight. She always told me about her Broadway openings."

"Yes, she would have. Speaking of Renee, have you heard anything from the detectives," I probed, wondering if they had resurfaced without Graham knowing.

"No," Howard replied turning around and tucking tissues around neck to start his make-up. "What does it matter? Nothing will bring her back anyway."

"I'm sorry, Howard," I said, thinking it mattered a lot to me and turned to leave. "I've got to get dressed."

"Break a leg." Howard started to apply his foundation that gave his white skin some color on stage.

"Good show," I said, unable to use the traditional good luck phrase and surprised that Howard could.

I went through the crossover to get to the women's dressing room. I didn't stop to check the platform and stairs then because I knew Nicole believed she would be using them in the first act doing Anna's role.

* * *

In the women's dressing room, I saw Nicole had arrived. But there was a new red bag on Nicole's table instead of her usual bag.

I scanned the room for the old one with the incriminating crumbled rat cakes in it. It was no where. Did she know someone had been through it? In all that mess how could she have? I stood, unnerved, at Nicole's dressing table looking down at the new red bag. I was defeated yet again.

"What are you doing," Nicole yelled bursting through the door.

I jumped. "Nothing. Great new bag."

Nicole eyed her red bag and me. Then she walked over and grabbed Anna's yellow costume. She let the hanger fall to the floor and held the dress up to her shoulders. She admired herself in the mirror.

Nicole grinned at me. "It should have been blue for my eyes."

* * *

With perfect timing, Anna came through the dressing room door carrying her make-up case and bag. The color was back in her face. She looked healthy and rested.

"Good evening, all," Anna chirped, setting her things down on her table. "Can you believe the floodlights out front?"

Anna walked directly over and hugged me.

"Thanks for the help last night. I'll never forget it."

"You're welcome." I returned the hug and grinned at Nicole who was staring at us speechless with her mouth open. "Glad you're well."

Anna turned to Nicole, who had not moved a muscle since Anna's entrance. Anna walked over to Nicole. Anna gave Nicole a hug with the yellow costume sandwiched between them.

"And thanks for helping at the rehearsal last night. It was so kind of you to step in. Joel said you were great."

Anna did not acknowledge Nicole's obvious attempt to supplant her last night. Nor did she comment on Nicole holding the yellow dress.

Nicole was stiff, unresponsive, and silent in Anna's arms. As she looked over Anna's shoulder, she glared at me in the reflection of the mirror. Her eyes bulleted through me as if they were ripping apart my insides.

The dressing room became a vacuum of evil.

⌘

CHAPTER 57

"Fortune brings in some boats that are not steer'd."
-Shakespeare, *Cymbeline*, Act 4, Scene 3

Anna cheerily turned to unpacking her make-up and water bottles. She shoved the two remaining cranberry drinks aside. She was either oblivious to Nicole's quiet coldness or didn't care because she was in the power position again.

Nicole slowly let the yellow dress sink to the floor, still grasping it tightly.

"Oops." Anna smiled taking the dress from Nicole and draping it over the back of her chair.

Nicole went back to her dressing table seething. She glared at Anna's back reflected in her mirror.

"What are you doing back? What if we all get sick?"

"I'm well." Anna busied herself with her make-up. "Turns out I didn't have the flu. It was rat poisoning."

"How do you know that?" Nicole stood like a deer caught in the headlights and poised for impact.

I sat at my dressing table. I unpacked my make-up keeping one eye on Nicole's reflection angled in the mirrors. I waited for Nicole to slip up.

"The hospital found out." Anna began putting a liquid base on her face. "Funny, huh?"

"Rat poison? No big deal." Nicole regained her composure. "I knew some girls who took it in middle school to get attention."

I suspected Nicole's middle school rat poison story was really her story. That's how she knew its effects were akin to the flu.

"I wouldn't do that." Anna looked at Nicole in the mirror. "It was in the tea."

"The t-tea?" Nicole stammered, sitting in her chair slowly, her eyes on the two teas Anna had shoved aside. "Did . . . Does . . ."

Nicole was at a loss for words for the first time since I had known her. Anna went back to her make-up.

"Don't worry. I threw them away and I'm going to dump these. I'm drinking water from now on."

"I'll dump those for you," I said thinking I might have evidence of Nicole's poisoning.

I grabbed the bottles. When Nicole didn't make a move, I knew she had not contaminated the teas since I checked them earlier. Why should she? She had no idea Anna would be back. I surreptitiously checked the caps. They were still tight and the seals not broken. I was out of luck. I tossed them in the trash can.

"And they reported it," Anna continued her story and her make-up process with blush and then eyeliner.

"Who?" Nicole asked.

"The hospital."

"To the police?"

Nicole was rattled again and dug around in her make-up bag, her hands trembling.

"The police? No. The FDA. A federal thing to get the bottling company," Anna said, oblivious to Nicole's reactions.

"Oh," Nicole said with too much relief in her voice.

I observed the tension leave Nicole's face.

"So you're totally better?"

"They gave me Vitamin K and I am almost as good as new."

Nicole saw me scrutinizing her and, without a word, got up and walked abruptly out the dressing room door.

* * *

With Nicole gone, Anna said, "I didn't take rat poison to get attention. That's a nasty thing to say. You don't believe it do you?"

"No I don't. Not for a minute."

I assumed Nicole had gone to cover up the poisoning by spreading the rumor that Anna did it to herself for attention. Then, I was sure she was going to find a way, any way, to stop Anna from getting on that stage tonight.

"Nicole's disappointed. I understand that," Anna added. "But there is a limit."

"Evidently not," I answered. "I'll dump these bottles."

I turned to leave, not to dump the useless tea non-evidence, but instead to follow Nicole. She was desperate and angry, not disappointed. This was the surprise moment I was waiting for and had skillfully set up.

"Can I tell you something?" Anna paused from applying her make-up.

"Sure."

"When I showed up, I think Graham was disappointed too. Did he want Nicole to do the part? I mean he put her headshot up already."

"Don't be silly." I engaged in untruths quite naturally for the good of the order and to get out of there. "It's opening night. Graham's overwhelmed. And I'm sure Nicole put up her own headshot."

I felt like a mini-Graham, protecting the premier at all costs. Anna was oblivious to Nicole's true evil and now was not the time to enlighten her just before she stepped on stage. I decided if I had to talk to anyone I would talk to Joel about Nicole, not Anna.

"But I put my headshot back up." Anna smiled proudly.

"That's as it should be."

I began to think this woman had more fiber than she let on. She might be a match for Stephie Sevas, who was after her man, but she was still no match for Nicole.

"I'll be back," I told her, as I left to follow Nicole's trail of evil.

* * *

To find Nicole I did as any good mysterian would, I anticipated what diabolical act Nicole had left in her repertoire to usurp Anna's rightful place tonight.

I checked the crossover, the scene dock, the men's dressing room, the halls, the lobby, and the restrooms. Nicole was nowhere to be found and no one knew where she was.

I returned to the dressing room to get ready for opening night and stay near Anna.

Over an hour later Nicole had still not returned. That was fine with me. If Nicole never came back I was confident we could work around her absence on stage. Anna and I were dressed and ready to go on. I always relaxed once my costume and make-up were on. I figured I could get out on stage at a moment's notice.

Anna and I ran our scenes. I told her how the curtain call was set up.

Alastair knocked on the dressing room door. "Are you decent?"

"Yes," Anna called.

Alastair entered, dressed elegantly for opening night in his plum velvet jacket with a pink shirt. His moss green striped tie and handkerchief in his breast pocket looked very coordinated and smart. I admired him. He lived his life with pride despite his slide down the theatre food chain.

"You look dashing," I said.

He beamed.

"Welcome back, Anna," Alastair said. "Heard you went to urgent care at the hospital."

"There was rat poison in the cranberry tea I drink. The hospital reported it to the FDA."

"Yeah, that's what Joel told us. That's horrible. But you seem fine."

It looked like Joel had unwittingly preempted Nicole's malicious story about Anna and rat poison. Good for him I thought. But, suddenly, I became more worried that Nicole had been thwarted both in spreading the rumor and in not getting rid of Anna.

"I am."

"Good. Cast meeting in five minutes in the theatre before I open the house."

Alastair looked at the costume rack, walked over to it, and then grabbed Nicole's maid costume. He held it high in one hand and put his other hand on his hip in exasperation.

"Where's Nicole?"

"She was here," I said.

"Why isn't she dressed?" Alastair threw Nicole's costume over the back of her chair. "Graham is going to have a fit."

Alastair jingled the coins in his pocket and stood there a second thinking.

"That girl is going to be the death of me."

My immediate thought was that poor Alastair did not know how real that statement might be if he became her target.

"Help me find her, Veronica." Alastair headed for the back dressing room door that led to hall, the restroom, and the parking lot door. "Help me comb the theatre. You go the other way. I'll tell Graham we're looking for her."

"Sure. Happy to be of assistance." I didn't mind checking again to be careful, but I believed she wasn't here. "But maybe you should check Coffee and Conversation or better yet the bar at the French restaurant."

"The bar? God, could she be drinking?" Alastair disappeared out the door.

"Should I help?" Anna asked.

"No, you stay here. I'll be right back." I didn't want Anna alone and vulnerable around the theatre.

I left Anna and went back to the scene dock to see if I had missed Nicole and she was drowning her sorrows with Scott.

* * *

At the scene dock I knocked. No answer. When I cracked the door and turned on the lights, I only saw one rat, the four-legged kind, running behind the plywood sheets against the walls. I shut the door and checked the crossover again. I took a last look up the ladder to make sure there were no wires across. Then, I went to the men's dressing room door and knocked.

"Are you decent?"

"None of us are decent," Scott bellowed and laughed. "But we're dressed."

I was in no mood for Scott's juvenile wit. I opened the door to an array of Victorian clothed actors ready to begin our play. Scott was in the traditional stage-hand garb—all black clothing. It helped him blend with the black backstage and also hide him from the audience when he exchanged props or set furniture during blackouts with an open curtain.

"Hey, Veronica, thanks for the pretzels," Scott called out, hyped up for opening night. "But where's the beer?" Scott laughed again loudly by himself.

"Yeah, thanks for the pretzels," Tim chimed in. "That's great of you. My dinner!"

"Alastair sent me in search of Nicole. Anyone seen her?"

There were a couple of "no's" and head shakes. I started to leave when Kevin ran up in his in full period dress.

"Wait, Veronica."

Kevin's green costume brought out his green eyes and displayed his tall lean body. I was still in love, dinner or no dinner. Kevin took my arm and led me out of the dressing room door. As I followed, I thought to myself that I would go anywhere with him.

Outside the door in the dark passage he whispered, "I didn't want the others to know, but after I got coffee I walked by the French restaurant. Nicole was there with Mel and martinis at the bar. They were arguing. I popped my head in to wave, but it was just too intense. I left before they saw me."

I was happy Nicole was not in the theatre near Anna and equally happy to be near Kevin with his hand still holding my arm. But, I needed to leave instead of indulging my lust.

"Thank you. I've got to go and tell Alastair."

"Wait," Kevin said still holding onto my arm. "When I got here and found out Anna was back, I knew what Nicole and Mel were arguing about. The lead. I think Nicole's mad Anna's back."

"You think?" I couldn't hold back the sarcasm.

"Well," Kevin said. oblivious to the sarcasm or ignoring it. "I thought of something that would placate her and get her back here."

"What?" I reigned in my cynicism.

I knew please-everyone Kevin had no idea about the depth of Nicole's vicious designs and that nothing short of Anna giving up the lead would ultimately placate her. But I listened, and enjoyed Kevin's beautiful musty smells.

"Graham could give her one or two performances in Anna's part? On a Saturday night maybe."

"I see. Thanks. I'll pass it on." I made the comment as sincerely as I could, knowing that even if Graham extended the offer Nicole would not settle for it.

"Knock 'em dead tonight." Kevin let go of my arm and gave me a quick hug.

"You too."

I prolonged the hug. Why not? He initiated it and it felt good, even if his choice of traditional opening night wishes jangled me. Under the circumstances, I felt death was not to be bantered about lightly, but evidently no one else was sensitive to my concerns. Perhaps because they were not suspects or targets.

I hurried out to the theatre to let Graham know where Nicole was and pass on Kevin's plan to appease her, as I had promised. I was confident Alastair would find Nicole at the French restaurant.

Graham was not backstage or in the theatre.

I went up the center aisle and opened the lobby door.

"Oops!"

I jumped back and shut the door.

⌘

CHAPTER 58

"Lord, what fools these mortals be!"
-Shakespeare, *A Midsummer Night's Dream*,
Act 3, Scene 2

The lobby was already strewn with audience members. I was in full costume and makeup and could not be seen before the performance. I re-opened the door a small crack. No one had noticed me.

I saw the four floodlights through glass entry doors shooting up into the dark winter sky. Victorian era harpsichord music was playing over the chatter in the lobby.

Lobby music was an old theatre trick to set the mood for the play. I remembered Graham once had to use light comedic songs to signal to the audience his production was intended to be funny. It was a poor tribute to the actors, but the technique worked. The audience laughed at that performance and every one after.

In the lobby, I also saw my teacher Mavis with three of my regular classmates, Agnes, Jody, and

Herbert, picking up the comps I left for them. An older friend of Graham's, who always helped check the audiences in, was fumbling in his efforts to get their programs. For small theatres like this one the program acted as the tickets, because it saved ticket printing expenses. The house was open seating.

Mavis and my classmates worked their way through the crowd and got glasses of wine. Then they studied the headshots, particularly mine, until they heard Stephie Sevas's resounding laugh from across the lobby. When they turned and saw her, their eyes lit up. They realized who she was and turned their attention to star watching.

Stephie Sevas's little group, including Graham and Bernie, were at the far end near the coffee machine and balloons. Stephie was holding court, again. She was so small but such a heavy presence, a magnet. She ran her fingers through her short blonde hair and smiled electrically. They sipped wine from their plastic glasses. I knew Graham was pretending to sip because he never drank. Next to Bernie, I recognized the director of Stephie's new film from the pictures in the grocery store checkout tabloids.

This opening night had become tantamount to a private showcase for Joel and an audition for my fellow troupers with the larger parts. Nicole was not amongst them, as she well knew. Her maid's role, essentially a walk-on, made her an almost invisible presence in this career building milieu.

Joel had brought star power here and he hadn't even made the movie yet.

I hoped Anna could weather Stephie's obvious and carnal plans for Joel, but I was pleased for all the actors and Graham and for myself too. I knew my writing world coinage had gone up in value when my teacher and classmates saw Stephie here. It was a good last hurrah because I had decided this would be my final foray into acting. This production had been too traumatizing for me. I felt out of control. At least in my books, I knew that I would not be arrested and real people would not die.

I tried to catch Graham's attention through the crack in the door. A woman looked over and I shut it. I waited for another chance.

* * *

Finally, I cracked the door again, but the lobby had become denser. Dense was good when it came to pre-performance theatre lobbies, but not for catching Graham's eye. Graham did look in my direction several times, but never saw me.

When I threw caution to the wind in desperation and opened the door wider, I saw my Armageddon. My heart dropped.

The detectives, silhouetted by the spotlight beams out in the street, strolled into the lobby from the cold night.

"Oh, my God," I whispered to myself.

I shut the door and leaned against it catching my breath. I wished I had Nicole's bag with the rat poison in it or the wire with Renee's DNA or a cranberry bottle with residual rat poison and Nicole's prints—but I had nothing. I had no corroborating physical evidence as they say in detective-speak.

I turned and peered through the door again. The detectives had bee-lined over to Stephie. They had uncharacteristic silly grins smeared on their faces. The young one was looking down Stephie's low-cut black top. At what? I didn't know because she had nothing there.

Graham was visibly trying to usher them away from her. It didn't work until after Graham got Stephie to sign programs for both of them. They then followed Graham away from Stephie and her entourage.

I hoped against hope that they had just come by the Valentine to rub elbows with a star. As cops investigating a possible homicide, their badges extended them privileges, valid or not.

Graham was bringing the detectives towards the oak lobby door where I was. They were the last people I wanted to see. I shut the door and quickly stepped down the center aisle lifting my long skirt so that I wouldn't trip. I got up the stage steps to the wings just as I heard them come into the house and the door shut. I went behind the red grand drape to the peep hole in the velour stage right. I watched them.

Graham and the detectives stood in the center aisle arguing. The older detective's face started turning red. His veins in his temple popped. Graham waved his hands in the air as he always did in a crisis.

Suddenly, they stopped. They stood silently at an impasse, but were poised to begin again

I knew then the detectives had not come to star gaze. Something bad was about to happen.

It was clear that Graham was fighting for his opening night. I hoped he did not throw me to the wolves in the process.

Just then their intense, silent stand off was interrupted. Alastair opened the lobby door slamming it into the older detective's back, who caught himself from toppling down the center aisle steps. More than a few heated words followed, but they were turned on Alastair's battery of the detective.

The older detective was interrupted by a call and Alastair and Graham took the opportunity to retreat from the battle. They escaped, scurrying towards the stage whispering.

At the stage steps, Alastair and Graham whispered frantically beyond my hearing. Graham started waving his hand in the air, again.

Graham finally blurted, "Get everyone else out here now. I don't care if they are dressed or not. And don't tell Veronica."

My heart sank. Tell me what?

⌘

CHAPTER 59

"The miserable have no other medicine, but only hope."
-Shakespeare, *Measure for Measure*, Act 3,
Scene 1

Alastair started up the stage steps. He was playing with his coins in his pocket and did not look happy. He turned back to Graham.

"You know Nicole isn't here," Alastair informed Graham.

"Oh, for Christ's sake. Where is she?"

"I went up the street to check. She's at the bar in the French place with Mel downing martinis. Getting plotzed."

"Is she coming back?"

"Probably."

"What's next?" Graham muttered.

Alastair continued up the stage steps with his right hand in his pocket jingling coins nervously.

"Get those coins out of your pocket before curtain." Graham shouted.

Graham then turned and leaned on the stage shaking his head, undulating his double chin.

I couldn't take my eyes off Graham. He was completely defeated. I had never seen him like that before.

The detectives took seats at the back of the house. They were arguing between themselves now. I presumed about the call.

I thought of the hard evidence I had tried to collect and failed. Then I did a mental checklist of what I actually knew. It was a lot, but unfortunately all unsupported conjecture. I knew it was not enough to save me, at least from an *ad hoc*, expeditious arrest by two detectives who were as pro forma and superficial as the detectives I created in my mysteries. Perhaps this was my comeuppance?

I needed a *deus ex machina,* a technique used in old Greek and Roman plays where a machine lowered an actor onto the stage and that actor played a god who solved the protagonist's problem or resolved the plot. Of course overtime, it has taken on a broader meaning. Today, *deus ex machina* is essentially a plot rescue device for characters in impossible situations. I used it in my second book when my protagonist was completely thwarted in her search for evidence. Very simply, in that book, I created a package that came in the mail with evidence in it that led to the arrest of the murderer. Needless to say, I needed something like that now.

But first, I needed to know what Alastair was not supposed to tell me. Was I was being taken in for questioning for murder or worse yet, arrested, booked, and charged tonight?

When Alastair marched across the stage to wrangle the troupe backstage, I waved from the wings.

"Psst," I whispered. "Alastair. Here."

* * *

I got Alastair's attention without being seen by the detectives or Graham whose back was turned.

Alastair hesitated and then came over and stood behind the velour side leg with me.

"What are the detectives doing here?" I whispered.

"So far checking out women. Getting autographs."

"I'm serious. What are you not supposed to tell me?"

"You heard?"

"Yes, I heard."

"They said some forensics are back and they asked for you. That's all I know," Alastair said, fiddling with his coins again. "Graham didn't want to upset you."

"He didn't want to upset his opening night you mean."

"I'm sorry. Graham said there's nothing we can do anyway. They're playing hide the ball."

"Some ball."

I wasn't angry. That was the nature of the beast called theatre. Always—always—the curtain will go up on time and the show will be performed. I wondered who I would call to bail me out or even if they would set bail for a murderer. I hadn't researched that for any of my books and didn't know.

"Are we still opening?"

"So far."

"That's a good sign for me, isn't it?"

"Yeah, I just hope I don't have to play your part. Navy blue is not my color," Alastair whispered with an impish laugh.

"That is not funny."

It wasn't funny because it was true. They could open without me. Stranger replacements had happened in the theatre to get through performances than Alastair in drag.

"Comic relief, dear," Alastair said taking his hand out of his pocket and giving me a little hug. "Relax."

"Easy for you to say."

"Can you get everyone from your dressing room?" Alastair whispered. "Don't bother to look for

Nicole. I found her downing a bottle of wine with Mel at the French restaurant."

"I heard. Kevin saw them too."

"Well, he should have told us sooner," Alastair said. "We don't need a drunk on stage opening night. Mel ought to know better."

"No one can control Nicole. You should have seen her when Anna showed up."

"No, I shouldn't have. I'm not into cat fights."

I thought if Alastair only knew how serious this was he wouldn't be joking, but I had no time to enlighten him.

"Kevin thinks we can placate her with one or two performances doing Anna's part," I added.

"In his dreams. She wants them all. But I'll talk to Graham about it."

"And tell him we can work around Nicole if he needs to send her home."

I knew both Anna and I would be safer if Nicole wasn't around.

"I'll carry the trays on stage myself," I volunteered.

Alastair looked at me for a moment, thinking.

"That would work. But haven't you forgotten one thing? Nicole is Mel's. She'll be on stage and at the party no matter what."

"We'll see."

I knew the only way to get Nicole out of here was for the detectives to drag her out in handcuffs. My mind reveled in the thought.

"Humph. The plot thickens," Alastair mused.

I didn't say a word.

"Get Anna from the dressing room. I'll get the men." Alastair had turned stage manager again.

As Alastair swaggered across the stage in his opening night jacket to get the men, he called up to the balcony.

"Bryce, get down here. Meeting."

* * *

I went to the dressing room to get Anna. As I approached the door, I stopped. I heard another fight going on in the dressing room from through the door. This time it was Joel and Anna.

"I don't like Stephie," Joel yelled. "It's opening night. Can you stop this? I love you. You know that."

"I see the way she looks at you and you like it."

"No, I don't. Stop this. Just stop it. It's business. Don't you get it?"

I listened outside the door. I felt so badly for both of them. Stephie was going to get what she wanted. According to the gossip rags, she always did. The good news was that she always moved on after her conquests. I hoped Anna and Joel could survive it.

"Just get out of here" Anna shouted.

"Anna," Joel pleaded. "Please."

"Just leave me alone."

Joel opened the door as I stepped back into the shadows. He charged out of the dressing room, not noticing me. I waited and went in. Anna was crying with her head down on the dressing table.

"What's wrong?"

I feigned ignorance.

Anna looked up with her black mascara dripping down her cheeks.

"It's that damn Stephie Sevas. She won't leave Joel alone."

"I know. I know. But Joel loves you. Look how he took care of you when you were sick."

I thought of my husband and how caring he was when he was alive.

"You're right," Anna said wiping the black from under her eyes. "But I just can't stand her all over him."

I sat next to Anna, took her by the shoulders gently, and looked directly into her hopeful ebony eyes.

"If you want Joel you will have to stand it. Just for this film. He'll get his start and never have to act with her again."

Anna thought carefully and then said decisively, "You're right. I know."

"I've seen how strong you are. You can do it."

"Sometimes I'm not sure."

"You can."

We sat in silence for a moment. I knew there was no good solution and so did Anna. Joel wanted his career as much as he wanted Anna. Who could blame him? He was already tasting the rewards of stardom. He was not going to give them up, for anything or anyone. Anna sat straight in her chair and re-touched her make-up.

"Thank you." Anna smiled at me in the mirror.

"We have a meeting in the theatre." I stood to leave.

Anna got up too. She smoothed out her yellow dress and straightened the lace at her neck.

We went out to the theatre without exchanging another word.

* * *

Anna and I walked through the wings and onto the remarkable Victorian stage set into the world Graham had created for us. Our period costumes rustled as we walked. From the opposite side, the men crossed the stage toward us in full costume.

For just an instant, I forgot all the trouble and the detectives about to arrest me. Just for a moment, I felt the thrill of opening night. There was nothing like it: the ensemble effort, the friendships, the common goal, the exhilaration. All my young memories of the stage welled up. They were, of course, filtered delicately through the rose colored synapses mercifully created by maturing minds.

There on the carefully appointed set, I reveled in recalling: the now outdated grease paint and its awful, delightful smell; the feel of pancake make-up sponged across my face; the warmth of spotlights lighting my every move; and the sound of applause—thundering applause as I recall. My chest swelled and my heart beat and I felt alive. I was happy.

Howard went first down the stage stairs. The other men waited chivalrously for us to follow. At the boot of the stairs, Howard ceremoniously extended his hand in turn, first to Anna and then me to help us down the stage stairs.

"Thank you." I smiled at Howard.

Then I was jarred back to the twenty-first century when I saw Graham still leaning on the stage, round shouldered and deflated. He avoided everyone's eyes, including mine.

As we took our seats, I saw there wasn't one person who did not notice the detectives at the back of the theatre. The Catch-22 for me was that if Nicole found out too before she made her move against Anna, she might not trap herself and clear me.

Bryce sat in the middle of the theatre because the detectives had usurped his usual spot at the back.

I took a seat in the front row on the right alone. Kevin and Anna took seats across the aisle, book ended by Scott and Geoff. Alastair sat nearby alone. Joel slid in behind Anna, not taking his hopeful eyes off her. Howard and Tim separated from the group and sat a few rows below Bryce, each on one side of the aisle.

"Where's Nicole?" Tim called out to Graham.

"She'll be here," Graham answered dismissively.

"Did Graham say Nicole could have a couple of performances?" Kevin leaned over and asked me.

"I don't know. Alastair's going to talk to him about it."

"She may not be coming back, then," Kevin whispered.

"She'll be here. Take my word for that."

"Right." Kevin smiled. "She's a trooper."

I looked squarely at Kevin in disbelief. He had no idea Nicole was not a trooper, but instead a murderer. He was so handsome and nice. Nice to everyone indiscriminately. I questioned the value of a person like that. I wondered if he really thought about what he said or if he had a mind that spurted out feel-good gratuitous niceties like an automaton to everyone.

I decided it didn't matter to me and smiled back.

⌘

CHAPTER 60

"Heat not a furnace for your foe so hot that it do singe
yourself."
-Shakespeare, *The Life of King Henry VIII*, Act 1,
Scene 1

Graham began the opening night meeting with feigned upbeat enthusiasm. After all, he was an accomplished actor himself. I, however, knew him too well and saw him glancing nervously back at the detectives.

"First, welcome back Anna," Graham said, leading the applause.

"Thank you," Anna said graciously.

"As you all have probably heard, Anna had a close call with a batch of tainted cranberry tea, but she's fine now. Please, all of you stay away from cranberry tea for the run of the show."

The theatre echoed an appropriate chuckle. It was more a release of opening night jitters than an appreciation for Graham's humor.

"Not me," Scott said. "I love the stuff."

"Can it, Scott," Alastair disciplined Scott with his stage manager hat on. "We've got a house to open."

"People, let's get serious. We have a full house. Brim full. I added chairs up the side aisles and will add a few chairs up front here if we need them. Alastair is going to cordon off the first three rows here for our VIP's, including the detectives, of course," Graham said in a friendly voice, gesturing up to them at the back of the stage. "They have questions for a few of you, but have graciously said they would wait until intermission. Hopefully, if they enjoy the play, they will wait until final curtain and join us at the after party with Stephie Sevas instead."

Graham looked up at the detectives hopefully. He had done his best to bribe them with solid Hollywood currency—celebrity.

I glanced back and saw no acknowledgement of Graham's invitation to rub elbows with Stephie Sevas and her entourage. I hoped, however, the Hollywood gold would secure a delay and give me time for my yet-to-be-discovered *deus ex machina*.

"I already caught each of you up on your most important notes from last night. Generally, just keep up the pace and energy level. It was good last night. Make it great tonight. We have the press and industry for those of you coveting a film career. So get in the 'moment' and stay there," Graham urged, convincingly positive. "Have fun and break a leg."

"Yeah, break a leg." Nicole hollered, at the top of the center aisle.

As the oak door to the noisy lobby slammed behind her, I caught a glimpse of Mel in the festive lobby laughing with Stephie, Bernie, and the director.

* * *

Nicole staggered alone and unsteadily down the aisle, oblivious to the detectives seated in the shadows.

She paused and stood tottering near the top. Her washed blue jeans shrink-wrapped her long legs and her tight, soft-blue sweater was topped with her marketable and ever-marketed cleavage.

Nicole took a faltering step and then halted again to survey the troupe gathered below.

We all stared at her—stunned. No one spoke.

Nicole grabbed the back of a seat to steady herself. Her martini'd eyes narrowed and lasered in on Anna.

"Yeah, break a leg, Anna. Break a leg just like Renee. Oops, wait . . . I mean a neck . . . don't I?" Nicole shouted, taking another unbalanced step down the aisle.

I saw a chance, one in a million, to clear myself.

I recognized that my *deus ex machina* was Nicole herself—Nicole drunk and out of control with rage— Nicole unprotected by her men. Mel lingering in the lobby to promote himself and Scott, here, but ever too selfish to tip his hand. Nicole was my package delivered just in time, as in my first book. I only had to open it. And better than anything was the fact that Nicole hadn't seen the detectives in the shadows behind her.

I grabbed my chance and stood to confront Nicole.

After all, why wouldn't I be able to Sherlock a murderer as well as Sir Arthur Canon Doyle? Why couldn't I out do Miss Marple, Agatha Christie's heroine? In point of fact, here and now I had the advantage of their collected wisdom and my own mysterian experiences combined. I was confident that, if I kept my mystery writer's wits about me, I could take full advantage of this fortuitous situation.

"Confront and corner," I said to myself.

I took a deep breath and marched into the center aisle. I faced Nicole, who was still steadying herself, near the top.

"Don't threaten Anna," I shouted, calculating my defense of Anna would further enrage her.

"Shut up, you menopausal wannabes," Nicole snarled at me.

I heard Scott snicker as I shrunk from the public humiliation.

Nicole knew how to hit below the belt. I reeled from the remarkably accurate and cutting dose of truth--

a transparent truth that had made me vulnerable to being the prime suspect. But even though I was stunned into momentary silence, I stood my ground.

With my attack interrupted, Nicole quickly zeroed in on Anna again.

"You think you're so pure. But you're a Hollywood whore like me. You're just fucking someone younger than I am."

Although my dignity had been pierced publicly, I steeled myself, not to defend Anna, but to fight again for my freedom. I got angry, angrier than I had ever been.

I took a step up the aisle to bout again.

"Why Nicole? Why do you hate Anna? Because she didn't die of the rat poison you gave her?"

"No, because everyone here knows I'm better," Nicole screamed. "Everyone . . ."

Nicole charged at me with her fists flaying. But instead of reaching her target, she tumbled down onto the dirty red carpet, landing between Howard and Tim on the aisle. She lay there laughing, unscathed like most drunks.

Howard looked at her lying spread-eagled. He didn't move to help. His chivalry was dead where she was concerned.

"Get her up, Joel. She's drunk. She doesn't know what she's saying," Graham said, sizing up the detectives from the corner of his eye.

"Yes, she does." I retorted. "She . . ."

Graham cut me off and barked orders.

"Shut-up, Veronica. We have an opening to do. Tim and Scott help Joel get Nicole back to the dressing room. Alastair, find Mel. Hurry."

Graham knew what I was doing—saving myself. But he instinctively protected his premier.

"Now's not the time, Veronica," Graham warned. "Kevin, get Veronica out of here."

"Come on, Veronica." Kevin stood, put his arm around my waist, and obeyed the director's orders.

I felt Kevin's strong arm around my waist and glanced up at his reassuring gaze. I was tempted to go with him for just an instant. But I did not. I hadn't yet elicited a confession from Nicole to assure my freedom and prove my innocence.

Kevin was Graham's functionary. All Graham cared about was his curtain going up. And all Kevin cared about was obeying the director. It was ingrained in him and in everyone else here. I had to look out for myself.

As ordered, Alastair slipped past Nicole to get Mel from the lobby. Tim and Scott ran up the aisle to help Joel with Nicole. She hit at them and Tim toppled back into a chair.

"Let go of me, you idiots," Nicole screamed,

struggling free.

She stood alone, again swaying in the aisle.

* * *

Scott and Joel posted themselves near but couldn't get at her again.

"Shut up, Nicole," Scott whispered. "Just shut up."

"Shut up yourself," Nicole spit at Scott.

Scott did.

"It's Graham's fault," Nicole screamed. "He started with the third act. I tried to . . ."

Graham interrupted her.

"Nicole, sit down," he commanded, desperately protecting his big opening night and making it yet clearer my freedom was not a priority.

"Tried what?" I shouted, breaking loose from Kevin to goad Nicole's confession and clear my name. "Tried what, Nicole?"

"Veronica?" Graham turned to me with pleading eyes.

Nicole volleyed back instantly, "To take the wire down."

There was silence. All eyes turned from me to Nicole.

The young detective stood, but the older one pulled him back down. Nicole had confessed to one crime, but the older detective shrewdly wanted it all.

Howard glared at Nicole, his face visibly white, even under the uneven make-up.

"Veronica, shut up. It's opening night," Graham ordered, and then turned to Nicole and implored. "Nicole, for God's sake be quiet. We have a show."

"Bull! We don't have a show. Anna has a show. Anna has a show in your inbred little cesspool," Nicole screamed at the top of her lungs. losing her balance again. "The Valentine sewer."

Nicole charged at Anna. Anna jumped back between the seats.

"Stop." Joel grabbed Nicole around the waist.

Nicole broke Joel's hold and leaped at Anna.

"You crazy bitch." Joel arrested Nicole mid-air.

"Get your hands off me, you male whore," Nicole shrieked fighting like a wild cat.

"Stop." Joel held her back from Anna.

"Get off me." Thwarted, Nicole twisted around and zeroed in on Graham down near the stage.

"The only reason you have a full house, you fat ass loser, is because of Joel and the horny Ms. Sevas.

Suddenly, Nicole broke lose and turned on Joel.

"Yeah. Big man. Little toy. Stephie's boy-toy. You're going to whore your way up the ladder just like your girlfriend."

"He will not," Anna yelled running into the aisle at Nicole.

"He already is, you fool," Nicole scornfully laughed.

Suddenly, Nicole stopped laughing and made a run at Anna again. This time she made it.

Nicole grabbed Anna and shook her. She grabbed the yellow costume and tore at it. She got a fistful of lace from Anna's collar and ripped it off.

Anna screamed.

"The costumes," Graham roared. "Stop."

"Cat fight," Scott called out. "Go for it, Nicole."

Joel again stopped Nicole's advance and she turned on Scott.

"Fuck you, Scott," Nicole shouted, throwing Anna's costume lace in his face. "No. Wait. Don't fuck you because you're out of weed and a bad fuck without it."

Nicole's vicious laughter resounded in the theatre. Scott sunk back into his chair. Nicole eyed Anna again but was still walled off by Joel.

Both detectives stood, but before they could get out to the center aisle, Alastair and Mel opened the lobby door blocking their approach.

* * *

I saw that the lobby was brimming with people and thankfully was as noisy as Nicole's screaming in the theatre.

Alastair shut the door and stood at guard there. Mel saw Nicole bearing down on Joel again who was protecting Anna.

"Nicole," Mel called, running down the aisle with the detectives following. "What are you doing?"

Nicole whipped around and yelled in Mel's face, "I'm not waiting one minute. I'm opening tonight. Not prissy Anna. I don't care if I have to stuff the rat poison down her throat."

"Shut-up, Nicole," Mel yelled desperately as he reached out to her.

Nicole slapped his hand away. Nicole flung her arms out fighting for her balance.

"You all know I'm better than she is."

"You poisoned Anna?" Joel exclaimed in disbelief still standing below in the aisle.

"Didn't you hear Graham? The cranberry tea did." Nicole stepped down toward Joel, slurring defiantly in his face.

Then Nicole paused and added gleefully, "With a little help."

Joel took a step toward Nicole with his fists clenched, but this time Anna leaped between them.

"No, Joel," Anna screamed. "No."

Mel reached for Nicole from behind, but couldn't protect her from her own mouth.

"Nicole, please be quiet," Mel cried visibly shaken. "You're drunk. You don't know what you're saying."

Nicole whirled back around, glared at Mel, and then leaped at him. She started flailing at his face and chest with her fists.

"You promised," Nicole cried, attacking Mel and landing blows with no mercy. "You promised me the lead, you bastard. And I'm still the goddamned maid. You killed Charlie and Renee because you're a liar."

"Honey. Sweetheart, settle down," Mel begged, grabbing at her arms to fend off her blows. "You don't mean what you're saying."

"Honey?" Nicole shrieked and then burst out laughing. "I'm not your honey. You think I like you? You make me vomit. You and your cheap facelift. I got high when we screwed. I had to. I couldn't stand it. You letch. You pig. You . . ."

Mel caught Nicole's wrists and held her at arms length. She stopped struggling. He let her arms go. She stood looking at Mel, took a step forward, and put her face near his. He stood, cowed, looking at her in disbelief.

Then in a low guttural voice she growled in his face with spit flying, "You're a joke in bed, old man."

Nicole reached for Mel again, not with her fist but with her nails, clawing Mel's surgically taut face. Joel grabbed Nicole around the waist from behind and pulled her off Mel who had blood dripping from the side of his face.

Mel retreated back behind the detectives who advanced quickly to arrest Nicole now that they had their confession. They had heard enough.

"Let me go," Nicole screamed. "I'm better than your girlfriend in the lead. And you know it. Let me go."

Joel held tight until the detectives got there.

Suddenly, Nicole looked in terror at the detectives towering over her.

"Oh, my God," Nicole stammered.

She turned around quick and cat-like, grabbed Joel's head, and pulled his face to hers.

"Don't let them take me. Please. Don't let me go," Nicole begged, kissing Joel hard on the mouth.

Joel pulled his head back. His mouth was bleeding.

Nicole tried to lock lips with Joel again.

"You loved the way I kissed you on stage. Admit it."

Joel pushed free of Nicole and threw her at Howard's feet. She burst out crying and lay on the steps with her breasts bulging and one nipple peeking from her blue sweater.

Howard stood, looking down at Nicole.

"You killed my Renee," Howard sobbed with tears running down his cheeks.

The older detective lifted Nicole from the floor, memorizing the glorious nipple that popped back under the sweater.

* * *

Nicole glared at Howard with black eyeliner smeared under her eyes and her mascara running.

"What are you looking at?" Nicole sliced Howard with a blast of contempt that forced him back down into his seat, mournful and quiet. "And she wasn't your Renee."

"You're under arrest for murder," the young detective stepped up to stop Nicole's assault on Howard.

He grabbed his cuffs from his belt. He jerked Nicole's arms back roughly and subdued her as he read her tights.

Nicole wailed in pain and stopped struggling.

"Please, stop hurting me," Nicole implored.

The young detective ignored her pleas.

Since the young detective was immune to her allures, Nicole eyed the older partner. She then played her dramatic scene to him and him alone: her ice blue eyes suddenly welled with tears.

"Please, it hurts," Nicole begged weeping.

I had never seen a better performance of victimization.

"Back off," the older detective ordered his subordinate.

It had worked. I watched the male primeval with the power to protect, actually and absurdly do so, even if she had shown no quarter to any of her victims, or me.

The older detective took out his cuffs and held them up to Nicole. Nicole looked up at him with sensuous pale blue eyes. She reached up with her fingers and tried hopelessly to wipe away her smeared black mascara. The older detective handed her his handkerchief and watched as she cleaned under her eyes and then adjusted her sweater—allowing the delicate mounds to be amply displayed.

When Nicole was ready and not a moment before, the older detective put his cuffs gently on Nicole's wrists behind her back.

"I just wanted to hurt Anna, not kill Renee. It was an accident," Nicole said to the older detective spontaneously transforming her hate into a soft erotic entreaty. "You understand?"

"Sure," the detective said. "And what about Mr. Valentine?"

Nicole stood tall again, looked at him quizzically and said, "Just a terrible accident."

She was in control again and did not make any further admissions.

"Ready?" the older detective deferred.

Nicole started up the center aisle toward the lobby full of opening night press and VIP's.

As she approached, Alastair backed away from the lobby door.

"Can you take her out the backstage door?" Graham called out.

The young detective ignored Graham and opened the lobby door wide. His senior partner straightened his shoulders and stood tall. Nicole held her head high, arched her back to trust her breasts out, and smiled as she led the detectives through the gauntlet. All three paraded slowly through the lobby.

There was an unspoken agreement amongst them. It was their moment in the limelight.

The lobby crowd was silent and the Victorian harpsichord music was all that was audible.

Nicole turned to each camera and smiled as the lights flashed. The older detective gently took hold of his prize by the arm. The young partner trailed, coat open and badge and gun displayed. He followed Nicole to his fifteen minutes of fame.

Alastair closed the oak door to the lobby.

* * *

"Enough. Enough," Graham bellowed. "People, we have a show to do. Get backstage. We're opening the house now. Ten minutes to curtain."

"Ten minutes to curtain," Alastair echoed. "Places."

"And thanks to you, Veronica, we have to cover Nicole's part." Graham added viciously. "You could have waited."

Graham was mad at me. But I was mad at him too. I believed that on balance my freedom trumped covering Nicole's small maid's role.

"We'll manage, Graham," I retorted, unapologetically.

Bryce slipped out the lobby door to get to his balcony and to start the house music. Alastair cordoned off the VIP rows and the rest of us ran up the stage stairs. I was the last one to reach the velours.

Graham shouted, "Alastair, the house is open."

The house music started. It was a recording of Mozart's String Quartet in D, the famous Hoffmeister.

I looked back and saw Alastair prop the lobby door open. A chattering crowd poured into the house with programs in hand, amped by the spectacle that was Nicole.

"The show must go on," rattled through my head.

⌘

CHAPTER 61

"Our revels now are ended."
-Shakespeare, *The Tempest*, Act I, Scene 4

Our opening night performance was mediocre. Anna was good, but ironically Nicole was right—she was better. Anna did not have Nicole's depth or intensity. To tell the truth, she was boring. I wondered if Joel viewed Anna similarly after starting the mating ritual with Stephie.

During the performance, the more seasoned actors, including myself, covered Nicole's absence well enough, but only with Alastair's help. To Alastair's great misery, he stood posted in the wings with script and flashlight giving cues. Bryce's stage lighting left some actors jumping around the floorboards searching for the light fantastic. And Scott's sound effects were mostly mistimed. Howard's and my big fight scene went well and, most importantly, I made it down the back ladder confidently. After all, Nicole had expected to use that exit before me in act one.

All in all, the entire performance was as lackluster as the play Mel had written.

As it turned out, however, it didn't matter that the play was hackneyed, we were mediocre, and the technical aspects were mixed up. Very simply, Hollywood worked its inbred magic. During the curtain call, which did not go smoothly either, Stephie Sevas stood and anointed Joel with a standing ovation when he took his bow.

Soon, the entire audience stood and cheered—that is, barring a few rational and honest people who, with their asses still wedded to their seat, defied Hollywood celebrity and the requisite herding behavior it engendered. I noted, however, that every reviewer who was in eyeshot of Stephie stood and clapped conspicuously. The reviewers were vying for favor and possible Stephie Sevas interviews. It was clear that there would be nothing bad written or said about our play, especially where it concerned Joel.

* * *

When Scott pulled the red grand drape closed smoothly and quickly, the cast celebrated on the stage behind it. Joel and Anna hugged and kissed. Howard smiled and sat in a Victorian chair exhausted. Geoff and Tim shook hands and Scott ran onto stage congratulating everyone,

one at a time. I turned to Kevin who took his curtain call next to me. He grabbed me and hugged me.

"That was wonderful," he said.

I was speechless. All I could think of was his hard body touching mine and his strong arms wrapped around my waist. It didn't matter that I hadn't sat down for him when Nicole was confessing. He obviously still liked me.

"Hey, Kev." Scott interrupted our hug. "Way to go."

Kevin let me go and, instead of shaking Scott's hand, grabbed him and hugged him the same way he hugged me—and for almost as long.

"We did it," Kevin said. "It's a hit."

I stepped back and watched Kevin go on sharing his full-body hugs indiscriminately amongst the congratulatory actors.

Graham stuck his head in through the grand drape and shouted, "Wonderful. Now get out here for the party. We have press."

I stood near the wings and surveyed the triumphant troupe. I wondered if any of these people realized the artificial Stephie-driven dynamic of the standing ovation. They had to. They had eyes. But apparently it didn't matter to them. We had a "hit" on our hands one way or another.

I decided not to look a gift horse in the mouth either. The technical aspects of the performance would inevitably improve over time. The acting—perhaps. Either way, the play would have a nice long run and I'd be excused from my writing or, more aptly put, from my writer's block which had now halted my new theatre mystery too.

As I watched Kevin congratulating each person, I also realized I would be in Kevin's company a good long while. He turned around and smiled at me from across the stage. I dismissed the fact that he gave his excessive hugs freely. After all, I had gotten the first and, I told myself, the longest. I was glad I had chosen my gold knit top for the after party. I waved at Kevin and went to the dressing room to change.

I was looking forward to the both party and perhaps after.

I guessed, in my own way, that I was a Hollywood whore too.

⌘

EPILOGUE

"For nothing can seem foul to those that win."
-Shakespeare, *Henry IV, Part 1*, Act 5, Scene 1

Six days after Charlie died the new play was an undeserving hit. The Valentine Theatre was solvent again. And Mrs. Valentine's dream of a playhouse filled with packed audiences was finally realized with no need for ghosts and apparitions.

* * *

At the end of the run, which lasted too long for me, I was done with theatre, possibly forever. I knew Graham would not be calling me soon and, likewise, for now. I did not want to hear from him. Graham was still angry that I had goaded Nicole into a confession on opening night "just" to keep myself from being arrested for murder. And I, logically, still felt betrayed because he thought I should have waited, risked my freedom, and passed by my one opportunity to clear myself.

In any event, Graham now had endless actors, better than me, clamoring to be in his productions after Stephie Sevas's "Midas touch" and Nicole's infamy.

The Valentine Theatre was on the map again. In fact, it was added to the Hollywood bus tour stops. Those tours also packed Coffee and Conversation several times a day and the chatty owner became a mini-celebrity. Now that Charlie was gone, he was the self-ordained authority on the Valentine Theatre ghosts—the very ghosts that the press publicized had possessed Nicole just as they had Mrs. Valentine so many years ago.

Even Bryce had his moment of fame, telling about the strange happenings at the theatre.

Charlie's cousin, who inherited the Valentine, put a marquis out front to capitalize on the infamous publicity. But, beyond that, she was a true absentee owner who raised the rents and, like Charlie, did nothing to improve, let alone maintain, the property. Graham was able to checkmate the Crenshaw Troupe by meeting the increase in rent with his big box office draw and also the new donors gleaned from Joel and Stephie Sevas's entourage.

At her murder trial, ghostly possession and the Hollywood star machinery became Nicole's temporary insanity defense. And as it turned out, even with her night of confession, there was only sufficient evidence to charge her with one crime—involuntary manslaughter for Renee's death. Interestingly, Nicole's hysterical opening night confession and rampage were highlighted and used by her defense counsel, not the prosecution. The two detectives, who were promoted, bolstered Nicole's temporary insanity defense. And when Nicole took the stand in her defense, she proved she was a consummate actor. She won the jury over with her testimony and abundant chameleon-like charms. And, true to Hollywood infamy, shortly after her acquittal Nicole landed her first studio film.

The entire Hollywood acting scene, however, came under a nationwide microscope and was the subject of a blog-a-thon for months. Desperate actors had their 15 minutes of fame complaining about scams and demands for sex in exchange for roles. Exposes of unscrupulous acting teachers, agents, and managers abounded on the air and rampaged through the Internet. B-list movie stars bared their "casting couch" stories to get a little buzz. The reboot worked for some who landed more film roles, although still not A-list. SAG-AFTRA and the Actor's Equity unions, however, started to fight for more regulation.

At the party, Mel was dwarfed and elbowed into the background by Stephie's industry movers and shakers, bent on anointing her new co-star.

After the trial, Mel didn't move into the big time, but did continue to pursue the Stephie Sevas connection. He still helped finance Graham's productions to be a part of the scene and have a feeding ground for young hungry actresses. I don't know if he ever wrote another play. If he did, I certainly didn't edit it.

At the party, Geoff courted a middle-aged cheery Anglophile and Tim talked to Stephie's director who later cast him in a supporting role in Joel's movie. Scott, as always, found true love for a week, Alastair got smashed, and Howard commiserated with anyone who would let him talk about his one true love Renee—who evidently never dumped him. Bryce, as usual, didn't come to the party, but I knew he was having his own up the stairs with my pretzels and the two bottles of wine he had poached.

The core of the troupe stayed together and Geoff had found a home.

* * *

Me?

I never had dinner with Kevin or heard from him again. The fragile feeling of quasi-love was shattered when I met his young Nicole-look-alike, live-in girl friend at the after party. Besides, I finally admitted to myself that he was indeed just a social whore who chronically pleased everyone indiscriminately. I tried to hit on Bernie at the party, but he was into Anna who, in turn, was into Joel, who couldn't take his eyes off

Stephie. Apparently, there was a love connection there, monetized or otherwise.

After a while I went back to Mavis's writing classes, but couldn't get back to writing. In class, I talked about my theatre mystery book as my fifth novel and shared some of the quickly written chapters, which I have to admit in my mind's eye were brilliant. They were some of my best work. But in my predawn writing time, I usually sat at my computer waiting for my muse to overcome my disillusionment. Most days, I would just wander down to my neighborhood coffee shop to talk about the Valentine, Nicole, and my heavy writing and speaking schedule. I was a celebrity there and people maneuvered to join me at my ever-expanding table of friends.

The query letter I put in my car to mail needed updating and went back in my stack of "to-do's."

Although my theatrical interlude left me with only a few chapters of the theatre murder mystery and then writer's block again, at least, it also left me with a new incomparable and glamorous cachet amongst my friends and fans. I was even more popular on the social circuit, sharing with everyone just how I determined and proved that Nicole was the Valentine Theater murderer.

* * *

I had come back full circle to my original niche and

returned to my comfortable, albeit unpublished, authorial—and now headliner—crime solving activities.

The End

*Thank you for getting to know Veronica, the Valentine Theatre, and its players. On the next page get to know the author. Her website, **DaleManolakas.com**, has excerpts of her other works, reminiscences about Ray Bradbury, free poetry, and other free reads.*

ABOUT THE AUTHOR

After a life time of writing poetry, books, non-fiction, and legal documents, it was author Ray Bradbury's friendship and encouragement that finally inspired Dale E. Manolakas to pursue writing as a career. He taught her that the characters wrote the book—she didn't. Raised just outside Los Angeles by a surgeon and a homemaker/published author, Dale E. Manolakas had always aspired to an acting career, but also had to make a living.

Dale E. Manolakas earned her B.A. from the University of California at Los Angeles, and M.A., M.S., Ph.D. and J.D. degrees from the University of Southern California. She is a member of the California Bar, had the privilege of clerking for The Honorable Arthur L. Alarcón at the United States Court of Appeals for the

Ninth Circuit, was a litigator in two major Los Angeles law firms, and a senior appellate attorney at the California Court of Appeals, as well as an Administrative Law Judge.

Before that she was a teacher, primarily at the high school, adult school, and university levels, and holds a public administrative services credential. In addition, she has pursued her acting passion, principally on the stage, but also in film and television. She is a member of both Actors' Equity and SAG-AFTRA. She has published both poetry and non-fiction. She has raised three very independent daughters and lives with her husband, a retired attorney, in an otherwise animal-free environment in Southern California.

Dale E. Manolakas, Author and Reader
DaleManolakas.com

Made in the USA
Charleston, SC
02 July 2014